The Warmaster Series

Book One: The Demon's Fate

by Kyle Belote

I0549692

Copyright

The Demon's Fate
Copyright © 2019 Kyle Belote
Revised: 2025

All rights reserved. No part of this book may be reproduced in any form or by any electronic or mechanical means, including information storage and retrieval systems, without permission in writing from the author, except by reviewers, who may quote brief passages in a review.

This is a work of fiction. All the characters and events portrayed in this book are products of the author's imagination. Any similarities to real persons, living or dead, is coincidental and not intended by the author.

Book Cover by: Ivan Zanchetta © 2025
https://www.bookcoversart.com

Author's Socials:
www.outpostdire.com
X: @OutpostDire
Instagram: @Outpost_Dire

Works By The Author

The Dark Legacy Series: (Grimdark Fantasy)
The Bearer of Secrets
Mark of the Profane
The Jackal of Shades

The Maro Prakk Novella Series: (Western Fantasy)
Red Creek
Bloodbane
Man of Fury (2026)

The Warmaster Series: (Military Sci-fi Fantasy)
The Demon's Fate
Decimation Protocol (2026)

Other Works:
Flawed to the Core: Building Memorable Characters and Writing
The Dark Portal (Sci-fi Thriller)
For Heathens of Heaven (poetry)

Dedication

Since this is a revised edition, I think it's only fair to revise the dedication. So, here's to my not-so-little ones. You've grown up so fast, and each day with you is a joy, especially watching you bloom into the people you will become. Just … don't grow up too fast. Always stay young at heart.

Acknowledgements

This novel came into fruition as something to do on the side between writing and editing my fantasy books of the Dark Legacy Series. With the support of OMCW members (Organization of Military Community Writers) in Okinawa, Japan, it found its legs and became what it is. So, I'd like to thank them for putting up with me, reading and critiquing my work, and for the occasional pep talk.

Chapter One: Focus

Coldness throbbed through her cheek, the flesh biting, aching, and seeping slowly into her tender bones.

What happened?

She opened her lethargic eyes, and her vision swam. She stirred, her body protesting the rash movement. The bend in her left arm throbbed. Like unstoppable water rushing over the fall, one thought scythed through her mind.

Who am I?

She rolled to her back.

An explosion of panic rippled through her, and heat bloomed in her chest. Her eyes stung— did she want to cry? Terror clawed at her throat. A weight settled on her chest like a boot pressed against her sternum.

Beneath the fear, the panic, the terror that threatened to possess her, a justifiable anger rose within. Hysteria wouldn't help her now, and the resentment towards the vulnerability she embodied gave her focus.

Vague impressions crept through her mind like a stumbling drunk, their impacts sudden but never lingering.

She bent her left arm, working out the soreness.

After a few moments, her hand went to her face, gingerly touching the numbness. Pins and needles rippled across her skin. All the while, she asked herself: what happened?

In the quiet, her breath roared in her ears, rivaling the echo of brontide. The room around her hinted at the smallness of the building beyond her sight. In her mind, the room constricted, bringing back the tightness of her chest.

I've got to get out of here, but where am I? How would I get out?

Again, the anger flared, that vulnerability resurfacing.

I'm in control.

Reality differed significantly from her current mantra, but it contributed to keeping her grounded. Still, something undefined, untouched, prevented her from submitting to anxiety.

What's my name?

A void, a deep darkness suffused her mind, covering her thoughts like a wool blanket.

I know something's there. I know I had a name. Everyone has a name, but what's mine? Who am I?

The thought of other people having a name jarred something in her. Maybe she wasn't alone? Maybe there were others? Did the same thing happen to them? What if they couldn't remember either? What if they could, and she was the only one that couldn't?

The tightness in her throat returned, and the heat she once felt surged in her chest.

Any reaction is better than nothing at all.

Calm fought against the onslaught of trepidation. She had to remain in command, control, disciplined, to do otherwise meant … something.

It was the beginnings of a thought, a memory—of that she was certain—but it remained aloof, inaccessible. The quietness slithered, smooth and slick like the scales of a serpent.

A chill rushed up her spine, and she shuddered. Whatever restraint she had over her dread vanished.

In an abrupt moment, she bolted for the door, somehow knowing it'd open.

Freedom and answers lay just beyond. They had to.

Chapter Two: First Impressions

The doors slid open. Beyond lay an eerie quiet. The lack of sound unnerved her, and the ship felt more like a coffin than a vessel.

At least, she thought it was a ship.

Could be a boat.

It was strange that her first thought went to a flying vessel. Was it intuition?

The empty, metal hallway remained soundless and absent of windows, only adding to her mounting hysteria. The stale air circulated with a near-silent thrum of the air recycling unit in the distance.

Breath thundered in her ears.

Where was she? Better question, who was she? She glanced back at the room she exited. She hadn't bothered to check it before—just wanted out. They were quarters for a single individual, from the looks, clean and devoid of personalization.

Were they hers?

With the bed made, the meticulously kept room had a sanitized presence.

A sound drew her attention, and she jumped, her heart lurching into her throat.

Down the hall, a door slid open. A man stumbled out, a look of distress flickering across his features—until he saw her. His expression shifted from troubled to pleased.

He sauntered over, a towel around his waist. His long, stringy hair hung in dark, wet clumps.

"Hello," he said, almost silken in the back of his throat.

"Hi."

Thank God there's someone else!

"Who are you? Where are we? Do you remember anything?"

She peered down the hallway behind him and hoped to see others coming out, but it remained empty. The door to the room closed behind her, making her turn, catching the movement out of the corner of her eye.

She regarded him.

"Who are you?"

"I don't know. I can't remember. You?"

He closed the distance between them, his feet making squishing sounds with his wet, shower sandals. His lips tightened.

"It's frustrating."

She shook her head.

"No. I can't remember."

The water dripped down his body, pooling on the floor and leaving a trail behind him.

"You should go back and dry yourself off. You're getting water everywhere, and you're a bit underdressed."

"Maybe you're overdressed, ever think of that?" he snapped. Then, in a playful voice and a smile, "If it'll make you feel better, sure. Oh! You can come towel me off."

He waited for her to comment.

"If you need a shower, I can scrub all those hard-to-reach places …"

An intense dislike rolled through her, drowning out her fear of not remembering. His greasy smile mirrored his wet hair.

"How about you worry about yourself?"

Not exactly the best first impression.

"Okay, okay, don't get pissy. I'm just teasing. Do you remember what you were doing when you … became aware?"

She shook her head.

"I just woke up and walked out of this door."

She gestured to the wall behind her.

"They're quarters, feasibly mine. What about you?"

"I just remember standing in the shower."

She eyed him, noting his lean frame and sinewy, fit appearance.

He caught her wandering gaze.

"I can disrobe so you can behold the glory."

She rolled her eyes and the flaring agitation made it easier not to laugh at his arrogant joke.

"No, I don't want that. What the hell's wrong with you? Did you think my clothes would just fall off at the sight of you? Why aren't you more concerned about your lack of memory?"

He stood with his lips tight.

"Can't blame this guy for making a pass. I do have a sexy body."

He paused, considering his words while color rose in his cheeks.

"All jokes aside, I'm just as anxious as you, but it's not going to help anything."

"Right now, you're about the only thing I can blame, at least until we figure out what happened to us."

Bile rose in her mouth. She hadn't known him but for two minutes, and she already detested him.

"Did you see anyone else?"

"No, but we should search for more. If there are others, they might be able to tell us what happened."

"What's your name?"

She paused for a moment, hoping to remember, but drew a blank. The notion that she couldn't remember still horrified her. It must've shown on her face.

"Yeah, me, too."

He gave her an appraised once-over. His gaze made her skin crawl, her insides fluttered like twitching butterflies.

"Chestnut."

"What?"

"Chestnut; the color of your hair. It's as good a name as any at this point, and I'm pretty sure you wouldn't want a name like Fit-Tits or something derogatory. What about me?"

She eyed him, noting his half-naked body and smug visage. Her stomach turned.

"How about Asshole?"

He gave a sneering, tight-lipped grin.

"It'll do. There's still clothes in the shower room. They're probably mine. I'll go dress."

He nodded to the wall behind her.

"Maybe you should go back into that room. There might be answers in there."

"Yes. Get dressed."

He sauntered away.

A canvas of vibrant tattoos covered his back. Green, red, blue, and a plethora of other colors covered his skin in a bizarre mural. Though too far away for her to make them out, and his long hair breaking up the images, she noted a demon-like figure.

From their first interaction, she detested him. She'd have to find a way to crush any hope he might harbor. She'd wait until he approached, and hopefully, he'd keep away.

She faced the door, but it didn't open. With a step back, she glanced around the edges.

A small, black, rectangular panel sat on the right door frame. The lights activated when her hand neared. She read the display in haste. A five number pad illuminated, plus three more buttons: accept, clear, and chime. She knew the door required a code, but couldn't remember it.

Pressing the chime button, she waited. She didn't remember if anyone remained inside. When no one came to the door after a few moments, she lifted her hand to the pad again.

"Worth a shot."

She pressed the numbers in sequence: one, two, three, four, five.

The pad buzzed an angry sound and didn't open.

She entered a new sequence: one, one, one, one, one.

Another buzz.

Next, she reversed the sequence: five, four, three, two, one.

Instead of the buzz, a voice spoke to her.

"Code invalid. You don't have the correct code to access this point."

She jumped, startled.

A tiny yelp escaped her as she clutched her hands to her chest. Her head swiveled, searching for who spoke. The voice was weird, different. It sounded like two voices spoken in unison, one male and one female, but the hallway remained empty.

For a moment, she thought she hallucinated the whole experience.

"Hello?" She rushed towards the panel. "Anyone in there?"

"Yes, Chief Regent," the voice said back. "Do you require assistance?"

"Yes! I can't get into the room."

"Access code can be obtained. Do you wish to use the code?"

"Yes!"

"Access code: three, one, two, four, three."

"Thank you."

With a sigh of relief, she punched the panel and muttered the numbers to herself. The doors slid open, and she entered.

Her eyes swept the room while she chanted the numbers lest she forget. A desk filled her vision, and she crossed to it.

The door closed behind her.

A picture frame hugged the corner of the desk. Snatching it up, she studied the individuals. One woman had dark brown hair, and she assumed it was her in the picture. Asshole had called her Chestnut for the color of her hair.

The second individual was a woman who stood at her side, shorter, and with blonde hair. Both were smiling at the photographer.

She bent to set it down, when the collapsible monitor on the desk chirped, coming to life.

Was it motion activated?

She glanced at the screen before touching the blinking icon. A video image filled the screen, an older man with a gray goatee and sharp brown eyes. His dark gray uniform appeared immaculate, his chest decorated with an assortment of medals and ribbons.

"Chief Regent Hessner," he started without preamble.

"Hello," she said, but he ignored her.

"Long range tracking has detected a previously uncharted segment of space with multiple celestial bodies. Your job's to take your ship and team to survey the area. Don't engage in any hostile activity unless fired upon first. I hope you take my orders to heart. Any further errors won't help matters with your reinstatement."

"I'm sorry, sir, but I don't know who you are."

Again, he ignored her and continued on.

"This'll be a long, quiet mission away from the heart of the fleet. A good year or two away will help everyone forget your less-than-stellar blunders regarding the Pinshi Incident. Hopefully, someone else will screw up in the meantime, and their attention will be drawn elsewhere."

"Sir?" she interjected, louder.

"Look, Hessner," he interrupted. "It's a shitty detail and one that's far below your qualifications and that of your crew, but this will help you hereafter. Your family's already thanking me, and you can thank me upon your return. In the event you engage a hostile force, details are embedded in this transmission from Warmaster Hessner. Vice Admiral Barris out."

The screen went blank for a few moments before returning to the main menu. The icon continued blinking, and she pressed it again. The same man appeared and started speaking.

"Chief Regent Hessner. Long range tracking has detected a previously uncharted segment of space with multiple celestial bodies."

"Great," she mumbled to herself, and stood.

She moved away from the desk, the video log still playing as background noise while she perused the room. She felt like an idiot now.

The sparse room echoed a spartan decor, and she had trouble locating personal artifacts. Nothing about the room told the story of who she was, what their mission consisted of, or where they headed. The room, though sterile and lifeless, had one picture adorning the wall. The canvas covered with abstract, sharp lines; the red color bled out from the epicenter into lighter shades.

"Hey," a muffled voice called, followed by a knock on the door. "Chestnut, are you in there?"

Yay, Asshole's back.

She approached the door; it opened as she neared.

The man stepped in, his long hair pulled back behind him. The clothing he donned seemed strange; a weird, two-piece assortment of black, gray, dark blue, and white. Other than the thin silver bar on both edges of his collar, it remained unadorned.

He met her eye and shrugged.

"Must mean I'm in command."

Please, God, don't be true.

She snorted.

"I doubt that."

She looked down at her own dark blue tank-top. It remained unadorned and without her name or decals.

"Why?"

"You don't know who you are, where you are, or anyone else, and you automatically assume you're in command? Talk about wishful thinking."

"Well, we're both guessing, so, I could be."

"Point taken. Though my gut tells me otherwise. If you were in charge, I have a feeling I'd be ordered to wear something far skimpier."

"That's not a bad idea. Want to practice now?"

He grinned his oily sneer but didn't dwell on the moment.

"Did you find out anything?"

She shook her head.

"Not really. There's a picture on the desk and a video message from someone called Vice Admiral Barris."

"That message was presumably meant for me. Hey! A bed!"

He rushed past her and plopped down. The invasion made her tremble, a disquiet near-unbearable. While he distracted her from the fear and panic of being unable to remember, he twisted her emotions in a different way.

He stretched out and looked up at her. That stupid smile spread across his face. She fought the urge to knock his teeth out.

"Wow, it's kind of comfortable. Let's mess it up."

It took all her effort not to hit him.

"Would you shut the hell up and be serious for a moment?"

"Easy, Chestnut. I'm always serious about messing beds up. Besides, I'm just being me."

"What makes you say that? Are you always an impetuous asshole?"

"Hey, you did give me an apt name. Perhaps we're acquainted."

"Yeah, I'd say so. We're on a ship together."

"No, I meant intimately."

Hessner gave a deep sigh and she rubbed her temples.

"You're not my type," she groaned, her patience waning.

What made her say that? Was it true or because he was being ... an asshole?

"How do you know I'm not your type? I mean, I've got a sexy body, that's everyone's type!"

He chuckled at his own joke, then sighed.

"It's just my way of coping. Maybe if you didn't fight it so much—"

"Look, you little shit! We've got more important things to worry about than you trying to get into my pants. It's not going to happen, not now, not today, or ever! You savvy?"

"Yes, Chief Regent?" a voice interrupted them over the speakers.

It was the same voice as before, the male and female voice talking in unison.

"What?" Hessner balked.

"You called for me, Chief Regent?" the voice asked.

"Who are you?"

"SAVI."

"What's savvy?" the guy inquired.

He rose from the bed.

"Synthetic Automated Vessel Interface—SAVI."

"Now we're getting somewhere."

He pushed past her, closing on the speakers where the voice came from.

"What's our current status, SAVI?"

"Information restricted."

"Restricted? On whose authority?"

"Chief Regent Hessner."

"Who's Chief Regent Hessner?"

Her stomach fluttered when SAVI responded.

"Chief Regent Hessner's standing behind you."

She watched the man turn around, glancing at her.

"Okay, so I'm not in charge. SAVI? Who am I?"

"I don't understand the question."

"What's my name?"

"Rhett Daspar."

"What do I do on the ship?"

"Rhett Daspar, assigned to The Demon as navigator, CR-1."

"What's CR-1?" Hessner queried.

"Commissioned Rank, Level One."

"Is that high?" Daspar asked.

Hope laced his voice.

"Negative. Navigator Daspar's the lowest commissioned individual on the Demon's Fate."

"What about me?" Hessner spoke up.

"You're Chief Regent Andrea Hessner, CR-4."

Andrea Hessner. I like the sound of that.

Rhett glowered.

"Fuck."

This time, she couldn't help but sneer at him.

"Yeah, that's why you don't act like an asshole to people you just met."

She turned toward the speaker.

"What's my position on the ship?"

"Commanding officer. Why do you talk to the speaker in the ceiling? My virtual interface is behind you."

Both turned to see a small form of light hovering above a pad on the night stand. Drawing close, it appeared androgynous, without prevalent features of either male or female sex—more robotic than either form.

"Why does your voice sound weird?" Andrea asked.

"It was synthesized to be appealing to most and represent both sexes of the human species equally."

"Well, it's annoying and stupid," Rhett snarked.

"Perhaps, but most small-minded individuals dislike the equality of the sexes—likely compensating as a means to display dominance," SAVI chastised.

Andrea let out a peal of laughter and Rhett turned red.

"I like you, SAVI!"

"Thank you, Chief Regent. I'm modeled after your specifications, and augmented when connected with the fleet and other SAVI units abroad."

"Other units?" Rhett inquired.

"Yes. Each vessel in the fleet is equipped with their own SAVI unit. The commanding officer of the ship selects the behavioral perimeters. In this case, Andrea Hessner modified mine to her specifications."

"And you learn?" Andrea concluded.

"Yes, knowledge is expounded when linked to the fleet and other units."

"Where's my room?" Rhett interjected.

"That's not important right now," Andrea cut him off. "SAVI, are we the only ones on board?"

"Negative. I detect three other organic lifeforms and one synthetic."

"Where are they? The organics?"

"All three are located on the bridge. Be advised: I detect hostile words which may lead to actions. I suggest you arm yourself with a stun gun. Though they're your crew, your actions indicate an altered state and perception. It's likely they may be the same. I advise caution."

"I don't know where a stun gun is!"

She glanced at Daspar. A weapon in his hand couldn't lead to anything good, especially for her.

"Where's the bridge?"

"I'll illuminate the hallways to mark your progress."

"We'll just have to wing it. Let's go!" she urged Rhett, then bolted from the room.

Chapter Three: The Crew

As SAVI foretold, the lights dimmed in the corridors, and they pulsed in the direction Andrea needed to go.

The hallway colors blended into balanced shades—not too harsh on the eyes, not too dim with the lights on. A dark blue coated the hard floor. A smoky gray covered the bottom half of the walls, the upper half covered with broad stripes of ash gray and stark white.

Rhett caught up after a few strides and kept abreast.

Andrea shot down the right of the long hallway. Going through a bulkhead hatch, the hall curved left before intersecting with three others. The lights illuminated a steep flight of a narrow, metal ladder and pulsed upward.

She started to climb as swiftly as she dared and hoped she didn't hit her knee on the metal steps.

"Spectacular ass!" she heard from behind.

Whether intentional or not, she slipped, and her foot smacked him in the face as she snatched a handhold.

"Son of a bitch!"

She felt both pity and justification.

"Don't distract me."

She finished ascending, and the glow directed her to the right.

She took off down the hallway and passed through another bulkhead hatch. The hall curved left, leading to another intersection. This time, the passageway lights thrummed to her right, and she took the path. The doors at the end parted as she rushed in.

Three individuals inside stopped mid-sentence and stared at them with blank expressions.

Andrea gave the bridge a cursory glance. The dim illumination didn't reveal much, but lights on the console edges glowed a dark red.

"Finally! Someone else on this tub," one man said.

Andrea eyed him, noting his full, closely-cropped beard and short hairstyle. He, too, was fit, more muscular than anyone else in the present company.

"Who are you?" the woman standing between the two men asked.

Andrea's eyes roved over to her. She recognized the woman from the picture in her room. The woman was short with a hearty frame, and Andrea might've considered her stocky if it wasn't for her curvaceous nature. Her blonde hair touched her collar, and her green eyes held a silent plea.

"I've seen you," Andrea said.

"What?" the bearded man asked. "You remember her?"

"No, but I've seen her."

"Who are you?" the woman repeated.

"I'm Andrea, this…," she paused when her eyes fell on Rhett. "This is Asshole."

"Nice one, Chestnut," Rhett replied.

"Your nose is bleeding," the man with the beard noted.

"And you're about to be, too," the last member said to the big man, "if you don't let go of my hat."

He appeared older than everyone present, clean shaven with burred dark brown hair. His flawless skin covered his high cheekbones. Abnormally large dark blue eyes glowered at the bearded man. Between them, Andrea glimpsed the wadded cloth the two men warred over.

"Really? This is what you're fighting over? A hat?"

"It's mine," said the second man.

"No, it's not."

"I don't know why they are fighting over it either," the woman interjected, her voice filled with mock-disdain.

She held up her arms.

"Before you two showed up, it was just two men and one woman. There are better things to fight over."

"Give me the hat," Andrea ordered, holding out her hand. "I'll keep it until we can determine whose it is."

"Why would I agree to that?" the bearded man asked.

"Because I'm the only one that can find out everyone's identity."

"Really?" the girl squeaked, interest piqued.

She traversed around the two men and sidled up to Andrea.

"What do you say, boys? Want to find out who we are?"

The bearded man glanced at the other and let go of the hat. The older man still clutched the cloth, but Andrea didn't care. The fighting had stopped for the moment, and that was the most important issue. Pushing her luck to make the older man comply wasn't a battle she wanted to face.

Besides, it was a fucking hat.

The bearded man faced her.

"How do you know who we are?"

"I don't," Andrea conceded. "But I can find out."

"How?" he inquired.

"SAVI?"

"Yes, Chief Regent?" the prompt computerized voice answered. Andrea laughed to herself when the three from the bridge flinched, looking for the origin of the voice.

"It seems that the members on the bridge don't remember who they are either. Can you help us? Can you display the entire crew in commissioned order?"

"Yes, Chief Regent. Direct your attention to the forward display."

The viewer screen flickered to life, a soft white replacing the stationary, alien symbol. A close, zoomed-in picture of Andrea's face manifested before it zoomed out and shifted to the top left of the screen.

"Chief Regent Andrea Hessner, CR-4, commanding officer of The Demon."

Her profile disappeared, and the face of the woman on the bridge appeared. With the zoomed in picture, Andrea detected that her eyes had a slight, almond shape to them. The image slid to the top left.

SAVI's voice resumed.

"Sub-Regent Kodi Kembly, CR-3, first officer of The Demon."

"Damn, two women in charge?" Rhett snarked. "You're bad enough, Chestnut, but your ass makes it forgivable."

She rolled her eyes, knowing that he attempted to infuriate her.

It was working.

The picture changed to an individual Andrea couldn't identify, an exotic man with a dark complexion and vibrant, hazel eyes. She found herself attracted to the man, more out of familiarity than romance, but she dismissed the notion as déjà vu.

"Caretaker Mason Boudry, CR-3, third in command."

The image faded and was replaced by the man still clutching the hat, but the picture showed him with longer hair than his current burred cut.

"Engineer Soren Goski, CR-3, fourth in command."

His image faded and the bearded man's face appeared. Atop his head was the fedora they fought over.

"Ward Carlin Ossaro, CR-2, fifth in command."

Rhett's picture appeared—more like a modeling shot than a facial scan.

"Navigator Rhett Daspar, CR-1, sixth in command and resident asshole."

Andrea giggled and Kodi guffawed.

"Funny, SAVI," Rhett retorted.

A movement to Andrea's left drew her attention, and Soren, the man who clutched the hat, passed it over to Carlin. She caught his muttered apology.

"Wait a minute," Kodi piped in. "There were six profiles, yet only five of us present. Computer, where's the sixth person?"

When no answer came, Kodi glanced at Andrea with uncertainty.

"It's not called a computer; it's SAVI."

"What's SAVI mean?" Carlin asked as he put on his fedora.

"Synthetic Automated Vessel Interface," Rhett supplied. "Or as I'm starting to think: Shitty-Ass Virtual Irritant."

Kodi chuckled and glanced his way. Her gaze lingered a moment before she remembered her question.

"SAVI, where's the sixth member?"

"Unknown."

"Why does its voice sound like that?" Soren, the man with huge, dark blue eyes asked.

Andrea supplied SAVI's earlier explanation. The engineer shrugged.

"Makes sense, I guess. I would've liked a female voice, but that's just me."

"That can be arranged for your quarters," SAVI offered. "Would you like that change made?"

"Hell, yeah!"

"As you wish, but I don't think Emma will appreciate it."

"Who's Emma?" Carlin blurted.

Now that he was closer and Andrea could see him better, she found him handsome, far more so than Rhett, but the hat had to go. The three-inch brim extended straight out and did not curl up on the sides. While it may look fetching on others, the antique headpiece rubbed her the wrong way.

"Emma is Engineer Goski's synthetic."

"What's a synthetic?" Rhett inquired.

"A life-like creation tailored to the specifications of the buyer."

"What does my synthetic do?" Soren pondered.

"Anything you wish. Most people use them as housekeepers or for other trivial tasks," SAVI explained.

"What about the sixth member?" Andrea spoke up, steering the conversation back to the absent person. "How can you not know what happened to him? Is he dead?"

"I detect no deceased lifeforms aboard."

The five of them eyed each other as the information sank in.

"When was the last time the Caretaker was aboard?" Andrea pressed.

"Two months, three weeks, four days, and seventeen hours ago."

Kodi, the blonde-haired woman, fidgeted, then spoke, "SAVI? If the fate of the sixth member's unknown and you detect no deceased lifeforms aboard, speculate the outcome of Caretaker … what's his name?"

"Mason Boudry," Engineer Goski offered.

"That's a good memory," Kodi remarked. "SAVI, speculate: what happened to Caretaker Mason Boudry."

"Speculating."

When the answer didn't come right away, Carlin Ossaro took the initiative to engage the crew.

"What the hell's a ward?"

Everyone either shook their heads or shrugged.

"To answer your question, Ward Ossaro, your duty is that of ship's security. Extrapolating possible outcomes of Caretaker Boudry. One found. Caretaker Mason Boudry was left on the uncharted planet."

"Planet?" Andrea exclaimed.

"What the hell have we done?" Kodi gasped.

"What happened to him?" Carlin asked. "Better yet, what happened to us? I can't remember anything."

"Neither can I," Kodi said.

"Me either," Rhett confirmed.

"I don't think any of us can," Andrea concluded. "SAVI, what happened to our memories?"

"Unknown."

Rhett kicked the paneling on the wall.

"What the fuck do you mean 'unknown?'"

"Hey, calm down!" Carlin said.

"Why don't you shut up? Go sulk in the corner with your stupid hat."

Carlin took a step toward him, but Soren put a hand on the big man's chest.

"It's not worth it. Just let him vent. I'm sure we all feel that way."

"I got a bigger question, our ability to talk," Kodi said. "I mean, if our memories are gone, how are we speaking now?"

"A relevant question, Sub-Regent Kembly. I have a theory," SAVI responded. "There may be a subversion of the cerebral cortex of the brain in correspondence with a detected energy surge approximately one hour and thirty-seven minutes ago."

"An energy surge? From where? Engineering?"

"Unknown, but the surge came from within the ship."

"How can it be unknown?" Rhett asked. "We're aboard a vessel that travels through space and the computer system that keeps us alive is shitty-ass software incapable of discerning energy? What if we pass through a star?"

"The reason," SAVI answered, "for the unknown error this time, Asshole, is because it originated from a foreign source not endemic to the ship."

"Now the computer's talking sense," Carlin muttered as he scratched his beard.

Kodi leaned into Andrea.

"Why did SAVI call him that?"

Andrea whispered back.

"SAVI's programming is picked by me. Earlier, I dubbed him Asshole. It kinda stuck."

A tight smile drew across Kodi's face, but she didn't say anything else.

"Okay," Goski said, "so, we're looking for something foreign. Can't be that hard, right?"

"SAVI?" Andrea queried. "Can you expand on the theory of the energy surge?"

"Certainly. The surge altered, edited, or erased specific portions of your memories, but left motor skills, speech, and muscle memory intact. If you noticed, you don't have difficulty talking, walking, running, or decision making. Upon hearing about the energy surge, you wish to investigate the cause, a logical step."

"Did it alter you?" Rhett addressed the unspoken question.

"Negative."

"How do you know?"

"Because you'd all be dead."

"There's a cheerful thought," Soren muttered.

His face held a somber expression, which fitted the older man.

Andrea's eyes narrowed.

"Can you tell me more about the unknown planet?"

"There are few relevant details regarding the planet. Information has been restricted."

"On whose authority?"

"Yours, Chief Regent."

Andrea's heart sank.

"That's fucking perfect," Rhett snarked. "Great job, boss."

"SAVI, release information regarding the planet on my authorization."

"One moment. Enter security code to gain access."

The group let out a collective sigh.

"SAVI, our memories are blocked or erased."

"Indeed."

"So, if they're gone, I don't have the access code to unlock the information."

"I see."

"Can you unlock it for us or find a way for us to access it without the code?"

"That'll take time to search for the proper procedure. Estimated time: several days."

"Why so long?" Ward Carlin Ossaro broke in.

"I must search all records, files, directives, and manifestos regarding security access with loss of memory."

Andrea let out a groan.

"Okay, so we've got time," Kodi piped in. "Let's go find out what sent out that energy surge."

She smacked Rhett on his backside as she walked past.

"Come on. The sooner we start, the sooner we're done."

The group surged forward with Andrea bringing up the rear and shaking her head.

Kodi ... you shouldn't have done that. You'll only encourage him.

Chapter Four: The Search

For the first hour, they roved in a slow group from room to room. The bridge was located on the first deck, as was the recreational room that doubled as a mess deck. Upon exploration, they found a small personnel lift that ran to each deck of the ship. The same color scheme carried through each hallway and room.

The second deck housed the medical bay, armory, commanding officer's quarters, and a communal shower room. They combed through the medical bay until Rhett pointed out that the Caretaker hadn't returned with them, so whatever caused the power surge was unlikely to be in there.

Though logical, Andrea wasn't as confident. The only other thing of note was a tubelike structure in the medical bay, and everyone agreed that it was probably for surgeries.

When they neared Andrea's quarters, Rhett sighed.

"I've already been in there," he said. "If you want to search again, that's your prerogative. Why don't we split up? I'll take a group with me downstairs."

Andrea nodded and didn't mind parting company with her personal antagonist.

"Sure, volunteers only."

"I'll go," Kodi said.

"Me, too," Soren added after a moment of deliberation.

Irritation flashed across Rhett's face.

"It doesn't take three people to search a room that's been given a once-over already," the engineer explained.

"I'll stay with the Chief," Carlin said.

Andrea was more than happy with the arrangement. She'd be rid of Rhett, and Kodi wouldn't be alone with him. Andrea had the handsome ward to keep her company.

She savored the small victory.

The trio departed, and Andrea ambled to the door. Her hand hesitated over the pad, but her mind drew a blank.

"SAVI?"

"Yes, Chief Regent?"

"Is talking to me distracting you from your search?"

"Negative. I've allocated a portion of my memory to assist you, the crew, and run the ship when you're not present at your stations on the bridge. A partition is running the search."

"Good to know. What's my access code again?"

"You're in the presence of Ward Carlin Ossaro. Do you still wish for me to reveal your pin?"

Andrea hesitated a moment. Did she? Handsomeness aside, thus far, the big man hadn't made any lewd comments or proven to be less than courteous or trustworthy.

"Yes."

"Access code: three, one, two, four, three."

She entered the numbers into the panel and the doors parted.

"Do you wish to change your code now?"

"No. I'll forget anyway."

"I encourage you to change it for security reasons."

She peered up at the bearded man, her eyes searching his cloudy dark-blue gaze.

"If I can't trust the ward with the security code to my room, how can I trust him with the safety of the ship?"

"A logical assumption based out of emotion," SAVI relented. "Very well."

"Are the rest of the crew quarters locked with access codes?"

"Yes, Chief Regent."

"Suspend current security parameters. They won't be able to access the rooms during the search."

"Very well. Task complete."

"Thanks."

Andrea hesitated outside her room, starkly aware of the man standing behind her.

"I can wait out here if that would make you more comfortable?" he offered.

She shook her head.

"No, it's alright."

As she padded into her room, Carlin hovered at the edge of her awareness but didn't crowd her. The doors shut almost noiselessly behind them. She scanned the room with both a sense of strangeness and familiarity.

"Not much for decor," Carlin muttered.

She glanced back at him, and he had the decency to appear embarrassed.

"Sorry."

"Don't be. This vessel could be temporary, or a unique, long-range ship for the mission? Either that or we're not allowed to bring many items. I wonder what the other rooms are like."

"I'll show you mine since I've seen yours," he promised as he stepped to the chest of drawers.

She caught a wince flashing across his face.

"Sorry, that didn't come out right."

"No, it did—but I like where your mind was headed."

She smiled at him and turned to the nightstand by her bed.

Did I just say that out loud? Kill me now.

Sitting on her bed, she opened the drawer.

Inside lay a small data pad with a thumb scanner on the bottom. Thumb-plate pressed, the pad unlocked and revealed the last thing she opened. An image of her with another woman filled the screen. Andrea noted her own face and less-than-broad smile. The other woman appeared similar to her, but far prettier, the whites of her teeth sparkling bright. She had blonde hair, and her eyes were a strange muted orange color.

She frowned, wondering who she was, why her eyes were so strange.

"Uh," Ward Ossaro said from behind her.

She stood and regarded him as he closed the drawer.

"You should be the one going through the drawers."

"Why? Did you see a thong?"

"Well," he murmured, looking uncomfortable.

His lips twitched.

"Yeah."

"I'm sure you've seen them before—seen thongs before!—not necessarily mine."

He chuckled but didn't say anything.

"It's no big deal."

"Glad you're so casual. I wouldn't be."

"Well, you're not Rhett, that's for sure."

Her brows shot up when she mentioned Asshole's name.

"Daspar? The weasel-looking guy? What did he mean by saying, he's seen it before?"

He stroked his beard, waiting for her answer.

Andrea rolled her eyes.

"He said that to make you jealous. He says shit to get a rise out of people."

"Did he wake up in here with you?"

Carlin's eyes darted to the bed, then back to her.

"No! He was in the shower. I met him in the hallway. Later, after he was dressed, he came in here."

Carlin nodded but didn't say anything.

He examined the drawer.

"You sure?"

"Oh, come on, it can't be that bad."

Heat touched her cheeks.

The ward opened the drawer and withdrew a stringy, dark purple garment that would have left little covered.

"Still sure?"

With another roll of her eyes, she smiled and motioned with her hand.

"Go for it."

She turned back around, sat on the bed, and stared at the picture. She and the other unidentified woman looked more similar than not. Were they friends? Siblings? She couldn't guess how long she stared at the picture, but Carlin came and hovered over her shoulder.

"Is she familiar?"

Andrea glanced up.

"No. Then again, looking at a picture of myself seems like staring at a stranger."

Carlin sat on the bed beside her. He seemed so large next to her, his shoulders almost a half foot taller than hers. He held out a hand for the pad, and she handed it over.

He peered at it for a moment.

"There are a lot of similarities, too much to pass off as coincidence. Must be a sibling, but who's older? You both look the same age."

"A twin, perhaps? We must have been born not far apart, otherwise you'd see an age difference."

"You sure you don't sense anything when looking at her?"

Andrea shook her head.

"What about when you see me?"

She stared into his dark blue eyes. She noted his skin tone, a dark olive. His brown hair lighter than his eyebrows. Her eyes roved over the bridge of his nose, thin and somewhat straight. Maybe he broke it.

She sensed *something* about him, but wondered if it meshed with his own thoughts or desires. Still, compared to Rhett, she felt at ease around him and could let her guard down, evident now that he knew the pin to her room.

Will he even remember it?

With reluctance, she shook her head but kept his gaze.

Only then did she notice their close proximity and how warm her clothes felt. When the trance broke for her, he caught his eyes blinking rapidly. His breathing also seemed heavier and slower than before. He posed another question.

"What about the rest of the crew?"

"Well," she said at length, standing. "I sense a closeness to Kodi, but perhaps that's biased because she's the only other female on ship, which brings up a curious question: why were there only six of us? Surely there's supposed to be more?"

"I was thinking the same thing, too, back when SAVI was showing us the profiles. Such a small contingent?"

"I heard a recorded video from a guy named Vice Admiral Barris, but he didn't say anything about the crew."

"What did the message say?"

Andrea motioned for him to follow, and she led him to the desk. When she neared, the display flickered to life and she pushed the blinking icon again. The now-familiar face filled the screen.

"Chief Regent Hessner. Long range tracking has detected a previously uncharted segment of space with multiple celestial bodies ..."

She moved away from the desk.

Her feet carried her back towards the bed, but on the other side. A standing wardrobe locker sat nestled against the bulkhead and the edge of her bed. Hoping that something within would jar her memory, she reached for the handle and pulled it open.

Several sets of utilities much like Rhett wore hung within in addition to several pairs of casual attire. A few small personal items like a hair brush, hair ties, and other trivial adornments sat on the top shelf. She climbed to her tiptoes to peer above the lip of the shelf. A small, bejeweled box sat in the far back, almost as if she tried to hide its existence.

Reaching, she pulled it near and opened the lid. She almost slammed it shut again. The contents sent her mind racing, and she gave a sharp inhale. A furtive glance at Carlin told her that he didn't pay her any mind. With silent quickness, she placed it within the locker and closed the door.

Andrea turned in a circle and let her eyes roam the room. She didn't see any of the box's items strewn about the chamber, and she breathed easier, but it did confirm that she was sexually active, but with whom? A flicker of doubt crept in as she spied a small trash bin near her desk. She crossed back to Carlin and glanced within, but the bag lay empty.

Relieved, her eyes returned to the screen as the message finished.

"In the event you engage a hostile force, details are embedded in this transmission from Warmaster Hessner. Vice Admiral Barris out."

Carlin stood to his full height and drew a deep breath.

"We need to find out what this Warmaster Hessner sent. Same last name as you, perhaps a parent?"

She shrugged.

"I haven't checked the other logs."

Carlin reached down for the screen but drew his hand back.

"Perhaps you should do the honors since it's directed to you. In fact, you may not want me here when you do. I wonder what happened during the Pinshi incident."

A blank expression flickered across her face, and she shrugged.

"Your guess is as lucky as mine."

"Want to view the log from this Warmaster Hessner?"

Andrea grew pensive for a moment.

"Yes, of course, I do, but it isn't as important as finding out where we are, what we were doing, and why we have a missing crew member. What happened to our memories?"

The ward nodded.

"Agreed. And, you might want your second officer here in the event you uncover anything pertinent."

His words dropped off, and she held his gaze for a long moment. Why did he seem familiar enough that she was comfortable around him? Were they involved romantically? Did residual feelings surpass the erasure of obscured and fickle memories? There was something about him, or did she let his attractiveness hinder her judgment?

"Chief Regent Hessner?" SAVI said, breaking the moment.

She blinked a few times and remembered what they were supposed to be doing.

"Yes, SAVI?"

"There's an incident forming in Engineer Goski's quarters. You should investigate."

She let out a heavy exhale.

"This is going to be bad."

Chapter Five: Emma

"I swear by the rivets holding this ship together," Carlin rumbled, "if he's done something to the sub-regent, I'll tear his arms off!"

Andrea struggled to match his long strides. The ward rushed forward like a gathering storm, a magnificent thunderhead waiting to erupt. His boots thudded through the corridor.

Andrea understood the feeling.

She'd never forgive herself if Rhett took liberties with Kodi—and she wouldn't put it past the sleazeball. Then again, Goski was with them, and she was sure that he wouldn't let anything untoward happen. That was the only reason why she let them go off together in the first place.

Honestly, she preferred the groups as they were, though keeping the second-in-command nearby would've been ideal.

The doors parted as Carlin hastened through. He halted a step inside, his back stiff.

Andrea hustled the last few steps in case the ward started caving Rhett's skull in. Truth told, she didn't know if she'd stop it right away. He did deserve it.

The chief regent rounded past Carlin and stopped just as fast.

Inside the room, Kodi sat in a chair watching the two men, Soren Goski and Rhett Daspar. The engineer stood in front of another woman, and his face flushed red and livid.

"What's going on here?" Andrea asked.

"This asshole," Goski said, jerking his thumb at Rhett, "thinks it's okay to mess with other people's property and pay no mind to any shred of civility."

"It's a synth!" Rhett screamed back. "It's not like she has feelings!"

"That's beside the point!" Goski snapped.

"Somebody tell me what happened!"

Both men launched into a shouting match, and the Chief Regent held up a hand to stop them. She turned her attention to Kodi.

"You tell me what happened."

Kodi shrugged and glanced back at the other two before talking.

"We were searching the rooms, and we came across this one. The synth, Emma, welcomed us in, but she wasn't clothed. At first, we thought it was another crew member, but she called Goski "master," and we knew otherwise. Rhett started touching her—"

"Fondling!" Goski interjected.

"Touching, fondling, groping," Kodi snapped, "whatever you want to call it!"

Andrea turned back to Goski and the synthetic behind him.

"Soren, can you move?"

Reluctantly, he moved aside, and Andrea gawked at the synthetic in its entirety.

She was, indeed, without a stitch of clothing. She had long, cascading, bright, blonde hair and must have been tailored to Soren's specifications of near-perfect beauty, at least how he saw it.

Andrea's eyes flickered to the synth's tapered and enviable waist, then to its smooth, long legs.

"My God, Soren, I can see why you're protective. She must have cost a fortune."

"Yeah, she did," Rhett quipped. "And he didn't buy her for cleaning and ironing, either. I mean, look at this, Chestnut."

Rhett stepped forward and grabbed a breast, letting it jiggle in his hand.

"This shit feels real."

"Asshole!" Goski yelled, lunging at Rhett.

Carlin appeared between them in an instant, restraining Soren. Rhett, seeing the engineer held back, used both hands to fondle the synthetic's breasts.

"You can fuck this thing!" Rhett said, laughing.

Carlin saw, and let Goski go.

The older man lunged across the deck and delivered a right haymaker, connecting with Rhett's jaw. The blow knocked the navigator backward, his head crashing into the desk.

"You deserved that," Andrea said with a cold voice.

Rhett's hand went to his jaw, and he winced.

"Worth it, Chestnut."

"Are you that hard up that you'd fondle the synth?" Carlin boomed.

"What does it matter? She's not real!"

"That's beside the point," Andrea said, taking control of the conversation. "She's not yours; she belongs to Soren. Think of it as another person's clothing or valued item—you wouldn't take or borrow without permission."

Andrea stepped closer to the synthetic, eyeing it.

Emma seemed incredibly real. Andrea could even see faint, blue veins under the skin of her upper bosom and towards the collarbone.

"Damn, Soren, tell it—*tell her*—to put some clothes on. And everybody get out."

Soren ordered Emma to dress, and once presentable, Andrea asked Soren to leave as well. When the doors closed, she turned to regard Emma.

"Do you know who I am?" she asked.

The synthetic stood still and rigid, the epitome of a robot. The mannerisms sent a tremor of jitters through the officer. If Andrea didn't need answers, she would have fled from the room. It was uncanny, almost real but not.

Emma's head swiveled just a touch in Andrea's direction, the eyes moved last to track her.

"Yes," Emma replied.

Her voice was soft and sweet, almost melodic with a touch of smokiness.

"You're Chief Regent Hessner, commanding officer of The Demon. I've known you for years. It's always nice to talk to you."

Andrea didn't know how to feel about the comments.

Could synthetics feel? She doubted it, otherwise Emma would have reacted when Rhett groped her. But her comment did kindle hope. With her hands behind her back, Andrea paced.

"Emma? When was the last time you and I had contact?"

"Two days, four hours, twenty-two minutes ago."

She stopped and spread her hands.

"Do you recall what I said?"

The synth stood still, and her eyes went long spells without blinking.

It unnerved Andrea.

No matter how real her eyes seemed, the nature seemed off. Perhaps she was designed that way. Emma looked so real that the manufacturers may have programmed abnormal behavioral patterns. Andrea eyed Emma's chest for a moment and wasn't surprised to see it rise and fall with simulated breath.

It was too damn close to the real thing.

"Yes," Emma replied, "you were quite distraught over your current course of action. My master, Soren, shared in your plight. He felt you didn't have a choice."

With her hands, she gestured while speaking.

"What was this action?"

"Fleeing the unknown planet."

Andrea's heart stopped.

"What happened on the planet? Do you know?"

Emma shook her head, a stiff movement.

"I don't know what transpired there. Soren wouldn't discuss it—I believe he was under your orders not to—but he was angry ... and sad."

Andrea nodded slowly. She could understand angry, especially if she ordered him not to speak about it. She crossed her arms.

"Why sad?"

"Sadness would be speculation at this point. Once you returned to the ship, he didn't make love to me for three days."

"He—what?"

"Soren didn't—"

"Yeah, no, I heard you the first time. I just didn't think ... never mind."

Andrea shivered. How could Soren, or anyone, have sex with a *thing*?

"Is there anything else you can tell me?"

"I detected unusual behavior in the crew."

"Explain."

"When Soren didn't return to his quarters at the appropriate time, I went looking for him. It was against your orders, but preservation of human life was at stake. I found various crew members comatose throughout the ship. Strange, is it not?"

Andrea nodded absentmindedly.

Emma gave answers but opened doors to so many more questions.

Andrea wanted to talk in private in case she revealed anything damning or dangerous, especially in front of Rhett, but nothing she just learned would be considered either.

"Thank you," she muttered before remembering she was a synthetic being.

"You're quite welcome. I hope you come back soon. I enjoy our talks."

Andrea's brow furrowed as she exited the room, noting once again that the synthetic used words to express feelings.

The doors parted, and she found the ward with his hand around Rhett's throat, his face purple and his body pressed against the bulkhead.

"Carlin! Release him!"

The big man complied immediately, but fury etched every line in his face.

"What's happened now?"

"This asshole made a less-than-courteous comment. I felt the need to remind him of respect."

"Who did he slander this time?"

"You!"

It wasn't the answer she expected and it caught her off guard. She wasn't surprised that Rhett had said something, but was curious about what caused the big man to rise to her defense.

Andrea focused on Kodi, expectant.

She gave a sheepish grin and shrugged.

"He wondered if you and the synth were 'having a tumble' and said he wanted to watch."

Andrea rolled her eyes. She should've expected something like that.

Glancing down at the coughing Rhett, she snapped, "Get on your feet!"

The navigator climbed and swayed, his hand massaging his throat.

"Look at me, all of you," Andrea said, gathering all the courage and command she could summon.

Carlin stood with his hands behind his back. Rhett hunkered, nursing his neck and wounded ego. Soren and Kodi remained motionless, their hands at their sides.

Andrea crossed her arms to hide her clinching fists.

"I'm going to be straight with you all. We're flying blind here. We might as well be adrift in space. All I know is that we're moving, or at least, I assume we're in transit somewhere. I know almost exactly what you do. Our memories are gone, we're fleeing an unknown planet, and a crew member's missing. I don't know if he was left or if he died. I don't know anything beyond what we've been told already. We still have decks to search for the item that caused the unknown power surge that apparently took our memories.

"Right now, the ship's on a course, and once it gets to wherever it's going, I don't know that we can fly it, let alone reduce speed. Maybe our memories are gone, but our muscle memory isn't. We'll find out soon enough."

She glanced at each in turn, holding their gaze.

"We need answers, all of us, but we won't find any if we are always at each other's throats."

She pointed to herself.

"Perhaps I'm not acting like a commanding officer, but how do I usually act? I'm learning every moment just as you are. Are our personalities the same or altered? I don't have that answer, but we need to take it down a few notches."

She glanced at the navigator, her antagonist.

"Rhett, do us all a favor—keep your mouth shut! Everyone gets that you have comments. Keep them to yourself!"

Her eyes shifted to the ward.

"Carlin, I understand why you feel the need to throttle him, but please restrain yourself unless it's necessary. Thank you for standing up for me, I appreciate that."

Andrea tried to keep the disappointment from her voice and face when she looked at the only other female.

"Kodi, you're the first officer, stop being nonchalant about everything. Give an order, make your will known. If they don't obey, tell Carlin, he's our ward. A few days in confinement is bound to make anyone more malleable."

She turned to the engineer and suppressed a sigh.

"Goski, I really don't have anything to say to you, but try not to be so …"

"Irritated?" he offered.

"I was going to say easily offended. You're an adult like the rest of us—start acting like it. We're not here to cater to your feelings. I realize that Daspar was out of line in regards to Emma."

She glanced at Rhett.

"And that'll never happen again, synth or organic, do I make myself clear?"

The navigator nodded, his face still red, hand massaging his throat.

"Chief Regent?"

"Yes, SAVI."

"Please come to the bridge, I've made some headway into your request."

Andrea smiled.

"Finally, some good news! We'll be right there."

Chapter Six: Course Correction

"SAVI? What's the report?" Andrea asked as the group breached the bridge's doors. The lights remained dim, but there was enough illumination to make out the consoles. The soft glow soothed her eyes after the harsh brightness of the corridors. What setting was it? Night mode?

"I've searched one terminal of our limited data banks retained aboard *The Demon* and found no reference to anyone losing their memory and being granted their access code."

Rhett groaned.

"You could've told us that down by the quarters."

"Yes, however, there's a record of someone losing their memory and still being able to fulfill their role. They were granted access to non-restricted materials to perform their duties. An additional twenty-nine data banks still need to be searched."

"So, what does that mean for us?" Kodi inquired.

Andrea heard the hope in her voice.

"You'll be allowed to view any material not locked with restricted access to include video playback logs of the crew's daily routine. Further, based upon these parameters, I can divulge general information about the planet, current course, and the ship."

"It's a start," Andrea muttered.

She didn't know whether to be relieved or worried. What would they find? Too many questions still plagued her, and though the synthetic gave off a bad vibe, she wanted to talk to it some more. Something about the creation nagged at the back of her mind. The only reason she cut the conversation short was to get back to the others.

Good thing, too. Carlin almost killed Rhett.

She paused a moment, considering those implications.

Probably should've let him.

As she thought about it, that notion settled well with her. Perhaps not killing the navigator, but letting Carlin get a few hits in. Rhett deserved every bit of the beat down the ward would give him, and she couldn't lie to herself—she'd enjoy watching it too much.

She shook the thought away, even if made in jest or wistful thinking.

Andrea noted how the others didn't dare interfere or intervene during the scuffle. Were they afraid of the ward on some subconscious level?

She glanced at Soren, and her perception of him changed.

A frown touched her lips. She tried not to let the synth's intimate knowledge cloud her judgment. Dark, carnal images flashed through her head, and she attempted to shake them away.

Another glance at the older man made her wonder why he'd want a synthetic other than the obvious reasons. What role did Emma fill in his personal life? Moreover, how could Andrea be judgmental at a time like this?

She reined in her thoughts, focusing her efforts on the crew, unraveling the enigma of their memories, and what happened on the planet.

Carlin's voice broke through the chaotic thoughts.

"Who knows how many hours it'll take to sift through those videos?"

"Okay, so what's first?" Andrea questioned the group, ignoring his question.

She didn't want the crew to take it as negative despite it being a valid question.

"The planet or our course?"

"Course," Kodi said, and the others agreed with nods.

"SAVI?"

"Yes, Chief Regent?"

"What's our current course?"

"Current course is set to rendezvous with Vice Admiral Barris's ship, the forward Third Fleet."

"And the location?"

"Classified."

The group let out another groan.

Rhett muttered something under his breath.

Andrea perked up.

"SAVI, can we establish contact with the fleet? Can you connect me to Vice Admiral Barris?"

"Negative. All communications are blocked inside the bubble, and transmissions outside—and at this distance—would be problematic at best."

"What's the bubble?" Rhett sneered.

"I know what that is," Soren declared from the back of the group.

He stood a little straighter, though his face still slackened in surprise. His eyes were bright with fervor.

"It's our traveling speed. If you were able to see a ship traveling at translight speed from a side view, the ship would look like it was encompassed in a sphere, much like a teardrop, or in this case—"

"Okay, a bubble. Yay!" Rhett mocked. "What does that have to do with communicating to the fleet? And how do you suddenly know so much? Why don't any of us remember this?"

"Maybe because it's my job and not yours. Didn't you hear SAVI say I was the engineer? Anyway, during TLS—that's translight speed—it distorts space and time, both in front of us and in our wake. It's essentially a communications blackout."

"What causes this translight speed?" Andrea asked.

"A careful balance of matter and antimatter."

"That's disturbing," Carlin commented.

"If you think that's bad," Soren said, "what I'm about to say is going to shake your understanding of physics—if you have any. We aren't moving, not in the traditional sense."

"What do you mean?" the ward asked.

"Yes, we're moving, but not at sub-light speed. The engines, they're on, but they're not rocketing us through space. Think of it this way: we're stationary, but the space beneath, in the front and the back, is bending and twisting. It's being pulled from the front and pushed out the back."

"That's mind-boggling," Carlin commented.

"SAVI?" Andrea called. "What's our ETA with the fleet?"

"Approximately four months, Chief Regent."

Four months? How slow were they traveling? Or … how fast? Translight speed sounded too astronomical to comprehend let alone calculate. If her assumption was correct, how far had they traveled? How much more spanned the distance between their current location and the fleet?

"Okay," Andrea said, then sighed.

Lightheadedness came over her, but she dared not show weakness—not now, not in front of Rhett.

"How long have we been traveling?"

"Fifty-seven days."

"Damn, that long?" Kodi exclaimed.

"SAVI? How long did we stay when we landed?"

"Four days, Chief Regent."

"Four days?" Carlin echoed. "We spent six months in transit for four days?"

Andrea shook her head.

"No, it was supposed to be for much longer than that."

"How do you know?" Soren pressed.

"I saw a video log from Vice Admiral Barris. He meant for us to be gone for nearly two years."

"Something went wrong down there," Kodi muttered.

She had a distant, glazed look in her eyes.

"Yeah, we left a crew member behind," Andrea said. "The question is why. I want to find out."

"Same," Carlin agreed.

"Yeah," Kodi echoed.

"SAVI? Why did we leave early?"

"That information's restricted, but the premise is that you weren't welcomed."

"There are people there? Humans?"

"Their species was never identified during updated military logs."

"Wait, we're military?" Carlin asked.

"That's correct, Ward Ossaro."

Carlin's eyes slipped to hers.

"Wasn't that video from a Vice Admiral or something?"

She shrugged.

"Yeah, but he never identified me by a rank or anything. We could've been mercenaries for hire or a contracted passenger vessel."

Andrea eyed the others, again noting their lean, muscular frames. Her eyes lingered on Carlin longer than necessary. She wished it had been him she met in the hallway with nothing but a towel.

"Explains the level of fitness," Andrea said, more to herself than the others. In a louder voice, she added, "We need to go back."

"Back?" Rhett echoed. "Are you kidding? SAVI just said we weren't welcomed. If we go back, it'll be a bloodbath, namely ours. What do you think they'll do when we return?"

"We'll be ready for that. We have an armory. We'll take it slow."

"I advise caution, Chief Regent."

"Yeah, no shit, SAVI," Rhett said. "I advise caution, too. For once, I agree with the gender-confused robot. We could be walking straight to our deaths. And then, what? How long before someone comes looking for us? Why go back? What's there for us?"

"You mean besides our crew member?" Andrea countered. "How about answers to what happened to our memories? If those people on that planet are responsible, they may be able to return them. There isn't a guarantee that once we reach the fleet that they'll let us come back. Do you want to walk around without your memories for the rest of your life?"

"Look, Chestnut, there's no guarantee that we'll get them back if we return."

"We have to try," Kodi said.

"I agree," Carlin said.

"Me, too," the engineer voiced, "as long as the engines hold."

"That's another thing," Rhett continued. "How do we know we've got enough fuel, power, and food to take us back?"

"The original expedition was intended as a two-year voyage," SAVI interjected. "Upon arrival, the crew will have consumed ten months' worth of supplies. The return trip will be a minimum of six months, leaving eight months worth of leeway."

"Thank you, SAVI," Andrea said, suppressing the urge to gloat at the cowardly navigator. "Are the coordinates locked out of the computer, or is that still public knowledge?"

"The coordinates for the planet aren't restricted, Chief Regent. I'd suggest that you make a new log entry to declare your intentions for the record."

"Noted. Alright, let's turn around. Soren, can you take us out of translight speed?"

He nodded.

"Yeah, I think so. Just got to find the right button."

He moved off, looking over the consoles until he identified the right station.

"SAVI?"

"Yes, Chief Regent."

"Raise lighting levels to normal luminance—whatever that is."

"Raising illumination to level four."

The lights brightened over several seconds until the bridge was flooded with brilliance. Andrea blinked a few times in the sudden harshness, her eyes adjusting.

"Everyone, assume your stations," she ordered.

"Which ones are our stations?" Carlin queried just as Rhett opened his mouth.

"SAVI? A little help?"

"Navigator Daspar, the forward station on the left is yours. Ward Ossaro, your tactical console is at the back behind the Chief Regent's chair. Sub-Regent Kembly, your station's the right forward console next to Navigator. Engineer Goski's already at the correct station."

Andrea moved to the chair and sat, the small monitors at the ends of the armrests coming to life. The monitor on the right displayed the ship's primary systems such as life support, engines, and navigation. The one on the left showed secondary systems and the tactical layout: shields, weapons, and gravity.

"Soren," she called.

She turned her head to see him. Worry laced her voice.

"What should we expect when we drop out of translight speed? Should we buckle up?"

A laugh escaped him.

"No, nothing like that. It should be smooth, almost unnoticeable, but if you want to buckle up, you can. Also, you might want to turn on the forward viewer since you can't remember what the bubble looks like."

She nodded and faced forward.

"Navigator Daspar?"

"Yeah?"

"When the Chief Regent calls your name," Carlin shouted, "or gives you an order, it's fucking ma'am or yes, Chief Regent."

Rhett turned slowly around in his chair, staring at the ward for a few moments, his mouth agape in bafflement. Then, he rolled his eyes.

"Yes, Chief Regent?"

"Activate the forward viewer."

"Yes, Chief Regent," he said, then muttered under his breath. "I live to serve you, oh-great-and-glorious ass."

"What was that?" Carlin boomed from his station.

Andrea held up a hand to stop him.

Right now, they needed to focus, not claw at each other's throats, but she appreciated Ward Ossaro's support. Other than what SAVI told them, they could all be interstellar garbage collectors and not military.

But why would the ship's system lie?

SAVI's information helped, but Andrea sensed something not quite right. She couldn't put her finger on it, but she believed that SAVI festered at the root of it. Maybe she could blame it on paranoia, or not knowing the people around her, but the sensation in her gut persisted.

The whole situation was wrong. Their memories, the small crew, the missing member, and the restricted access, not to mention the cryptic message from Vice Admiral Barris, or so it seemed. It probably would make sense if she had her memories intact. Why did they retreat, especially if she knew they were supposed to be gone for two years?

The only piece in this jumbled puzzle that didn't meet any equation she could think of was the synthetic, Emma. What Soren did or did not do with his property was irrelevant, but the conversation tumbled in her head at impromptu times. She needed to figure out what bothered her—the dialogue, Soren's libidinous acts, their missing memories, or the synth's presence.

A dark inkling flickered through her head.

What if Emma wasn't Emma at all, but a body to contain a downloaded version of SAVI? What if Soren never had a relationship with the sex-bot? Maybe whatever caused their amnesia didn't take hold long enough. What if the synthetic meant to exterminate them all, and the sixth member wasn't left but just jettisoned into space while they lay unconscious?

She clamped down on the dangerous, rampant thoughts.

Stop that! It isn't helping.

The forward screen flickered to life, drawing her attention.

Andrea's mouth dropped open as she stood. She had a mental image of what it'd look like, but it wasn't even close. She expected bright, streaking star lines whizzing past, or a cloudy field of light, but it was closer to the first than the latter.

Streaking star lines did appear, but not straight as she initially thought. Each line came head on, and when they drew within the bubble's influence, they bent, following the curve around them, and changed colors, blue, red, white and everything in between.

"TLS distorts our perception," Soren clarified from behind her.

"It's beautiful," she said in awe.

Rhett snorted, but she paid no mind. She admired it for a few more moments.

"Right. Let's drop her out of translight speed and turn around."

"It's a him, Chestnut," Rhett corrected.

"What?"

"A demon. *The Demon.* The ship's a guy."

She rolled her eyes and resumed her seat.

Soren cleared his throat.

"Dropping out of TLS in three, two, one, mark."

The bubble rippled and faded, and the lines disappeared.

The vast, empty blackness filled the screen, only broken up by the faint, distant flicker of stars. Andrea let out a breath she didn't realize she'd been holding.

"Navigator, come about. Align us with a return trajectory."

"Coming about."

Rhett's hands flew over the console, turning the vessel.

Andrea let him perform the task. It was a test. She wanted to see if her earlier theory was correct, that their muscle memory hadn't been affected. If they were permanent personnel, then they had flown thousands of times, and it would be second nature. When the ship stopped its movement, she stood.

"SAVI? Are we aligned for a return course?"

"Yes, Chief Regent."

"Good job, Rhett. Goski, activate TLS."

"Matter and antimatter fields coming online. Return trajectory confirmed. Compensating for universal and galactic drift. SAVI, confirm coordinates."

"Confirmed."

"Initiating in three, two, one, mark."

The blackness in front wavered, noticeable from the distant, warping stars beyond. As quickly as the bubble faded, it returned.

Again, Andrea felt no sudden jolt of acceleration.

A collective sigh escaped the small group. Their first hurdle was behind them, and they made it unscathed. It seemed almost too easy, but much of the vessel performed in an automated fashion.

The next true test would be landing and meeting the locals again. What if they weren't human but some strange, uncharted alien? There could be plenty of aliens throughout the galaxy, but meeting them might be risky. Initial exchanges could become hostile.

"How do I know that?" she blurted aloud.

"What?" Carlin spoke, stepping closer.

"I just remembered something!" she said, jumping up.

"What?" he asked, excited.

"There are other aliens in the galaxy!"

Rhett swiveled in his chair and laughed.

"Yeah, I'm sure you remembered. Good one, Chestnut."

"No, what if I did? I was just thinking about the people we're going to meet on the planet. What if they weren't humans? And then, I started thinking about the initial exchange like ours, how it probably turned violent or threatening."

Rhett continued to laugh, but Soren spoke up over the noise.

"Interesting perception, logically sound, and theoretically possible. How would we act if aliens came to our home world, whatever it's called."

"I don't know. Hopefully with some decorum," Andrea conceded, glancing at the red-faced Rhett. "But if we acted as crass or crude as this asshole, we'd doom ourselves."

Her words had the desired effect, and his laughing came to an abrupt halt.

He spun around in his chair and faced the viewer screen.

"Okay, we still need to find the source of the power surge. We also need to set up watch rotations."

"Chief Regent, would you like to resume your regular station rotation?"

"Uh, what's the regular rotation?"

"Each vessel in the fleet, no matter how large or small, runs on an eighteen hour day. Our vessel's one of the smaller ones and is equipped with a command element of six officers—the minimum. Each officer takes a six-hour shift. Since the caretaker's absence, I've been filling in for him. Would you like to resume?"

"Wait a minute!" Rhett said, standing from his station. "If SAVI can run the ship in the Caretaker's absence, why not just let it run the whole time?"

"I'm here to augment your command crew, not indulge laziness," the AI quipped, then recited regulations. "You're mandated to run the ship by martial decree—a human element must always be present. At all times, there's to be at least one of the six or more command members present on the bridge. Since you're now at five, the role falls to me."

"I'm not lazy—"

"Further," SAVI spoke over him. "My capacity's taxed with searching through the data logs. I also perform other tasks simultaneously such as monitoring the engines, matter and antimatter fields, life support, gravity plates, long range sensors and scans, calculating and compensating for universal and galactic drift, water purification—"

"We get the point," Andrea spoke up.

She glanced at Daspar and shrugged.

"Idle hands makes for addled minds."

"Would you like to resume regular station rotation?" SAVI asked again.

Andrea deliberated for a moment, the uneasy feeling from earlier returning. Other than the gut reaction, she had no cause to decline, and if SAVI were capable of being suspicious, it would alert it to her concern. Could it feel anything?

She almost wanted to call SAVI a *him*, but it wasn't quite right. If SAVI could learn, at what point did he stop being artificial and become an intelligent being? The thought spiral threw her into cognitive overload.

A dull throb came to her temples.

"Uh, sure—I'm going to set up the new rotation."

She glanced at the others.

"Just because there are thirty hours between shifts doesn't mean we're idle. How much time until we reach orbit, SAVI?"

"One month, three weeks, four days, and twenty-one hours."

"Right. That's how long we have. Maybe our memories will come back—or maybe they won't. Until then, we're going to learn everything we can about ourselves, the ship, and our capabilities. SAVI will help us with that. Each of you will spend six hours on shift, another six mastering your duties, and an additional three honing your physical fitness, weapons training, and armor—if we have something like that. I want us ready for anything when we make planetfall."

"What about me?" Carlin asked.

"What about you?" Rhett asked from his seat.

The ward turned toward the navigator who still had his back to the crew.

"Well, I don't have a specific duty other than security and caving in your skull."

Andrea took back over the conversation so they didn't get sidetracked.

"Ward Ossaro, Sub-Regent Kembly, and I, will be poring over the video logs to see if we can find anything useful while on duty. The rotation will go myself, Ward Ossaro, Engineer Goski, SAVI, Navigator Daspar, and Sub-Regent Kembly. SAVI? Who's supposed to be on shift now?"

"Calculating the time and new rotation. Engineer Soren's duty ends in seventeen minutes."

"Alright, so SAVI's next. Soren, join us in the search for the artifact responsible for the power surge when your time ends. The rest of us will head down to the third deck and pick up where we left off. Kodi, you're with me. Let's go search your quarters."

Chapter Seven: Regulations and the Artifact

The doors parted.

"I think this is my room," Kodi said.

She entered, and Andrea followed on her heels.

"A logical assumption."

This room was more decorated than any Andrea had seen. A uniquely colored rug lay on the ground, a dark yellow with equal parts of brown and orange weaved into the hue.

"Golden ochre," Kodi whispered.

Andrea caught it. Her eyes drew to the bed, seeing the pillows, sheets, and comforters. They, too, centered around the golden ochre with a rustic theme or dark orange-reds, browns, and various yellow-orange hues.

"It must be," Andrea muttered. "We've seen mine, Goski's, Carlin's, and Daspar's rooms."

"Careful, your man-crush is showing," Kodi teased.

A slight heat came to Andrea's face.

"What're you talking about?"

"You act professional, use last names and ranks, but Ward Ossaro? You call him by his first name."

Andrea took her words in stride and refrained from commenting.

"So, are you going to grease the engine room, or what?" Kodi asked. Then, she laughed.

Instead of answering, Andrea switched subjects.

"I was worried about you earlier."

She glanced past her second officer to the wall near the desk. Drawings clung to the surface, most of them were portraits, but a few of trees, waterfalls, and mountains.

Kodi glanced at her, the smile fading.

"When?"

"When Navigator Daspar wanted to split up into groups. I'm glad Goski went with you."

"I don't think you have anything to worry about."

"Don't I? I'm the commanding officer of this ship, and I don't recognize any of you—at least not anymore. How do I know what he will and won't do?"

Kodi laughed.

"You ever think you might have it backward?"

Andrea's face fell.

"No. You can't be serious! Him?"

"Why?" Kodi's grin widened. "What's wrong with him? Attractive, funny, I get his sense of humor. He also made some valid points on the bridge."

"Crass, vulgar, lacks a filter. Who knows where his morals lie?"

Kodi's eyes narrowed and her smile faltered.

"The same could be said about you, or any of us for that matter."

She sighed.

"Thanks for your concern, but I'm a big girl. Unless, of course, you're not permitting me to pursue any type of relationship outside of strict professionalism."

Andrea thought for a moment.

Kodi was right; she was an adult. Who was she to deny the first officer? Still, they didn't know anything about each other. They were all strangers.

A new idea crossed her mind.

"SAVI?"

A long pause stretched before the interface answered.

"Yes, Chief Regent?"

"Everything okay? You took a while to answer."

"I partitioned more memory to search the data banks and run the ship. The demand has reached a near-critical level. How can I help?"

"Is there any regulation against relationships aboard military vessels?"

"Only a few. The most prevalent is the status of those who wish to enter a relationship. Commissioned ranks may not start a relationship with noncommissioned ranks unless they aren't in direct authority over one another."

"Are there any others?"

"Yes, but minor in breadth, and they deal more with the ending of relationship and quarters arrangement."

"Thanks, SAVI, that's all I needed."

"Yes, Chief Regent. Returning to my searches."

Andrea gazed at Kodi.

"You're right. You're a woman and don't need me making decisions for you. There's your answer. If there's no regulation, then who am I to say no? The only thing I can say is that I wouldn't move as fast as you, but it's your choice."

Kodi gave her a smile.

"It's no big deal. Not like I'm going to let him move into my room. It's just fun, an option to pursue, if I choose."

"Well, be careful. He's shown a tendency to pursue everyone."

Kodi bent and started perusing through her drawers.

"You're talking about the synth? Emma?"

"Yeah, and me."

Kodi straightened and turned to face her.

"What do you mean?"

Andrea divulged her first meeting with Rhett: his antics, how he was dressed. Kodi laughed the worries away.

"See? That's what I like about him. It's a joke."

"What if you start sleeping together, and then wake up one morning with your memories? What if you discover you hated him?"

Kodi shrugged.

"The way I see it, we're all blank data banks. We can be accountable for actions such as killing someone, but having fun? These trivial matters are minuscule in the grand scheme."

"As long as you realize what you're doing," Andrea muttered under her breath.

The two women fell silent as they combed through the room. Kodi searched her drawers and standing wardrobe, and Andrea sifted through the desk, drawers, and shelves. When she turned around to tell her companion she'd found nothing, Kodi was holding a sex toy she'd pulled from her wardrobe.

"See?" she said, smiling. "Why use this when he's willing and more than capable?"

Andrea rolled her eyes and shook her head. Kodi tucked her property back where she found it.

"There's nothing here."

"Agreed. I don't think we're going to find anything in our quarters."

"It would help to be familiar with what we are looking for."

"Soren to Chief Regent," a voice came through the wall's comm unit.

Both women frowned at each other and crossed over.

Andrea hit the microphone button.

"Yes, Engineer Goski?"

"Oh, great, this thing works. I think I'm broadcasting ship-wide. We'll need to figure out how to do it to a single location."

Kodi suppressed a smile and rolled her eyes.

"I'm down on the fourth deck, some kind of science lab. I think I found what we're looking for."

Andrea and Kodi exchanged a glance.

"We're on our way."

The duo left Kodi's quarters and turned left down the corridor, following it until they found a steep, metal ladder going down. Andrea hastened down the steps, but Kodi threw her legs over the rails and slid down.

She gave a childlike giggle.

Andrea shook her head and continued.

There was a picture on Andrea's desk of the two of them, but she was beginning to wonder what they saw in each other. Maybe she didn't always act this way, but if she did, it bordered on annoying.

"You need to loosen up, Andrea," Kodi commented.

"Loosen up? How can you be so blasé?"

Kodi sighed.

"This is a temporary thing, our missing memories. Once we get them back, everything will return to the same old boring routine. The way I see it, this is an adventure. You remember telling us about the video log with Vice Admiral Barris? This assignment was a type of punishment, wasn't it? For the Pinshi incident? Why not have a little fun in the meantime?"

Andrea grunted; Kodi had a point. She wished she could remember what happened during the Pinshi incident.

And this Warmaster Hessner? She wanted to go back to her room and find the appropriate log, but finding the power surge was more important.

Or was it?

Perhaps the log contained vital information.

The women rounded a corner, and the doors to their left opened.

They entered the science lab. Bright lights banished any trace of shadows. The three men were hunkered down over an object.

"What's up, fellas? How are my boys?" Kodi beamed.

They turned to face her, each offered their own salutations and smiles. She seemed to have a natural way with them, with people in general, and Andrea felt a flash of envy. She wished she could be so carefree and natural.

Carlin gave Andrea a long gander, his lip quirking into a grin. With a nod, he turned his attention back to the table. Soren stepped to the side as they neared, and Andrea caught sight of the mysterious object.

"What's that?" Kodi breathed.

"The cause of the power surge," Soren supplied. "At least, I think so."

"What makes you say that?" Andrea queried.

"Well, it's alien in design. Looks nothing like the ship or anything within, and we haven't uncovered anything similar. Take a closer peek, tell me what you see."

Andrea and Kodi leaned in.

The artifact looked like a giant, crimson egg with gold veins shot throughout. It was almost the same size as her face. It sat on a small, gold frame at the base. Four twining, thin pillars stretched up, latching onto a gold frame above.

"So, we've got a giant, red egg," Rhett said, his voice deadpan, "and a shit-ton of gold holding it in place."

Andrea drew a breath, and the gold veins splayed about the egg moved.

She flinched back, unsure of what she witnessed. Andrea started to say something, but the closer she looked, the more she realized the red sheen also shifted beneath the surface, like a storm-churned gaseous atmosphere.

"What the hell's this thing?" she whispered.

"An apt question," Soren said. A touch of disdain entered his voice. "Not an egg, though."

"It's awesome," Kodi exclaimed. "I wonder what it does."

"Another good question," the engineer asserted. "We should ask our scientist."

"Oh, wait," Rhett said in a mocking voice, "we don't have one."

"I don't like it," Carlin added.

"Why not? It's so pretty!" Kodi countered.

"Have you ever heard the expression beauty's only skin deep?" Carlin asked.

"No," the first officer answered.

"Well, if you think about it, neither have you," Rhett taunted Carlin.

"How does the saying relate to this?" Andrea interrupted.

"Beauty's only skin deep because evil lurks beneath," Carlin finished the saying.

"I don't think I'd call it evil," Rhett countered. "Strange, different, but not malevolent."

He shrugged and glanced at Kodi.

"The sub-regent's right. It's beautiful."

"Okay," Andrea said, standing up. "So, we think we've found the source of the power surge. We need to find out how it was activated. Ward Ossaro, go back and play through the logs in this science room for the last forty-eight hours. Find out what was happening when the power surge activated."

"Why the last forty-eight hours?"

"That's the timeline Emma gave me. She said she saw me two days and four hours ago. Soren didn't come back to his quarters at the appointed time, so she went looking for him. Emma stated that she found the crew in a comatose state. So, that's our starting point."

"Right. I'll be on the bridge."

The ward left, and Andrea turned to Kodi.

"Go back to your quarters. You've got a workstation on your desk. Start video playback of the logs from the moment we set foot on the ship and left the planet. We need to piece anything together."

"Didn't SAVI say that some of the logs wouldn't be available?"

"Yes, but I'm hoping that enough of the video isn't restricted, and we can start following the crumb trail."

"Sure thing, Chief."

Kodi took off, and Andrea turned to Soren.

"As best as you can, start studying this artifact. Find out what it's made of, how it works, the design and purpose."

Soren gave a shaky laugh.

"I'm an engineer, not a scientist!"

Andrea eyed the large, crimson oval.

"It's sorta your field."

Rhett burst out laughing.

"Not even close, Chestnut!"

"I'm a mechanic, not a scientist," Soren protested.

"Science, engineer, you're better apt than anyone else on the ship. That is, until we get our memories back. You're the best bet. It's your job, now."

Soren let out a grunt but didn't argue any further.

Andrea turned to leave, and Rhett called out.

"Hey! What about me?"

The chief regent glanced back, then over to Soren.

"Do you need a hand?"

Soren shook his head.

"He'd only get in the way and might become a target of me throwing wrenches when I can't figure this thing out."

Andrea grimaced. She was hoping to keep him preoccupied. Her eyes swiveled to the navigator.

"Continue searching the vessel. Explore this deck and anything beneath—if there's anything—and report back. And ... don't touch anything. Just look."

"Where are you going to be?"

"In my quarters, going over the video logs that aren't locked down."

Where I can finally get a damn break from the children.

Chapter Eight: Warmaster Hessner

Andrea sat in front of her desk.

The blinking icon winked at her, almost like a taunt. She thought back to the vice admiral's message—the promise of another video from Warmaster Hessner embedded within.

She pressed the icon, holding her finger there. The icon expanded, showing multiple options: mark, attachments, file, and search.

She touched "attachments," and the screen flickered, showing several logs accompanying the initial entry. She scanned the list until she found a subject line of hostile forces. Checking the sender, she noted the name Warmaster Hessner, and the tag marked it *official*.

She almost clicked on the message when the name also appeared one entry down. That subject line read *"Personal,"* with a *"Private"* tag. She debated on which to view first. Though the *private* message would most likely bring more satisfaction, the official held answers she needed.

With a touch of the screen, she tapped the official entry.

A woman's face appeared, the same face in the picture she and Carlin viewed earlier. Her young face was stoic—rigid like the stiff military collar around her neck. She wore a black tunic in the same fashion of Vice Admiral Barris's. Andrea glanced down at her own utilities, surmising this woman and the Vice Admiral wore a dress uniform.

The younger woman didn't move and hardly blinked; the tenseness on her face gave a stern countenance. But it was her orange eyes that captivated Andrea's attention the most. They weren't bright like the fruit, but muted—subdued, despite their eerie qualities.

"Chief Regent Hessner," the woman said. "You're embarking on an extended journey to one of the farthest reaches the fleet's probes have reached. We don't know if you'll encounter an alien civilization, or if the celestial bodies will be able to hold life. We hope for the latter. If the former, you'll present yourself, and the fleet, with a formal, initial exchange. I wouldn't ask and neither would the admiralty that you go unarmed, but I'd suggest limitation. We don't want our presence synonymous with war and violence. As with all new cultures we may encounter, be prepared for slights and improper etiquette. I realize I'm stating the obvious, but Command's agitated with this one, especially after the Pinshi incident."

Andrea perked, hoping the woman would elaborate.

"In the event of a hostile engagement, you'll strive to limit engagement and deaths. We'd rather you disable than maim, maim rather than kill. Use appropriate escalation of force to ensure your survival and that of your ship and crew. Using your ship's offensive capabilities is strictly last resort. The casualties inflicted will be remembered until the passage of time and history obscure the travesties. If you attempt to escape and are pursued into orbit, you may use any means necessary to ensure your escape is untraceable.

"When you reach the planet, go with only two of your crew armed: yourself and your ward. Small arms are permitted—refrain from light rifles or heavier weapons. The next words come heavy, but they're standard with every transmission. If you're unable to make it to your vessel and are in danger of being captured, it's mission-critical that your remote command sends *The Demon* on a return trajectory to the fleet. Once it arrives and the last transmission decrypted and analyzed, we'll send reinforcements to your last known coordinates.

"I wish you and the crew of *The Demon* a safe journey. Come back with news of a viable planet, or a new civilization to welcome to the Alliance. Godspeed and safe journey. Warmaster Hessner, out."

The screen flickered, and Andrea sat back. A sigh escaped her, and she rubbed the corner of her right eye. What was she to make of the video, of her apparent sibling, or the contents?

What was a warmaster anyway?

"SAVI?"

Again, the long pause filled the room before the interface responded.

"Yes, Andrea?"

She gave a start. It was the first time she could recall SAVI using her first name.

"Why are you calling me Andrea?"

"It's your specifications when you're alone."

"Ah, okay. What's a warmaster?"

"Warmaster is a CR-7, primarily utilized in ground forces."

"So, Warmaster Hessner is infantry?"

"In a manner of speaking. The infantry you referred to at her rank is the elite commando units."

"What's a CR-7 on a ship?"

"The rank of warmaster is unique unto itself. While the designation is CR-7, and the naval numerical equivalent is an admiral, a warmaster isn't an admiral's equal. The warmaster's unique rank allows them to take command of any vessel if the need arises. The CR-7 outstrips the highest rank on any vessel, a CR-6 with the navy, which is a commodore."

"So, my sister's a lot better than me?"

"Her skills lie in another direction."

"That's the most diplomatic way of agreeing with me."

"It seems even with your memory wipe, the discontent you foster for your sister remains."

"How would you know?" Andrea snapped.

Her eyes flickered to the speaker in the ceiling above. Though SAVI had been more helpful than not, she'd started to dislike the disembodied voice.

And couldn't explain why.

Emma didn't sit well with her either, but she was physical, tangible, somewhat real.

"You've spoken about her at length."

"We talk?" Andrea asked, skeptical. "You and me?"

"Sometimes, but it mostly consists of rants in your open logs."

Now, it made sense.

"Which you have access to?"

"No. Most of the time, I'm present."

Great.

Again, a wash of uneasiness overcame her. SAVI seemed too ingrained in their lives. When he wasn't *present*, was he still watching? Did he always observe them? If he did, did he report that to a higher command or authority?

SAVI once talked about linking to the other SAVIs within the fleet. Did the other interfaces view and collate her most private moments?

A terrible moment of panic sent chills through her. Had he watched while she had sex? Was there a video of her filed away somewhere on the ship's mainframe just waiting to be uploaded to the fleet once they docked?

She tried not to chase the rabbit.

"That's it for now, SAVI."

"As you wish. Returning to my searches."

Andrea pored over the long list of logs. The private tag from Warmaster Hessner taunted her.

Relenting, she pressed the entry.

Her sister's face appeared, but this time, she smiled. Andrea noted that she was dressed in civilian attire, and was far more animated than her previous video.

"Andrea!" she said with a big smile. "I envy you. You're going on a voyage to the farthest reaches. I can't even begin to calculate how many light years away that is. Alpha Centauri is what … a little over six hours by TLS? That's what—four light years and some change? You're going to be in TLS for nearly six months! I wish I was going with you, the Hessner girls tackling the galaxy together. Look out, here comes Vara and Andrea."

She shook her head and smiled.

"It's going to be amazing, no matter how it turns out. You're the lucky one."

She sighed and looked down at her lap before addressing the video recorder. Her smile had faded somewhat, and her swallow was audible.

"I want to apologize for the formal tone in my first transmission, but the admiralty's scrutinizing everything. Their assholes are so tight, they're shitting razors. I mean it when I say you're the lucky one. You've got *The Demon*, and you can go chasing stars. I'm stuck training every day for scenarios that may never happen. I may possess the aptitude and the ability for my role, but if I'd known it'd turn out to be like this …"

Vara shook her head.

"I realize we haven't spoken much since my ascension, and our relationship's been strained since the Pinshi incident, your court-martial, and my role in it, but I hope you make it back okay."

Vara glanced up at the screen, and her eyes were misty.

"I understand why you aren't happy with me, and I don't expect you to forgive me. I did what I had to—so did Dad, and I hope one day when you're ready, you seek out the full story of what happened behind the scenes."

She sighed and leaned forward.

"I'd love to catch up with my big sis. I miss you. Mom and Dad will miss you, too. They're taking it pretty hard. Maybe two years apart will be enough time to heal the wounds. If you don't come back promptly, or if we don't hear from your crew, I'm going to use my skills and rank to tear apart the galaxy to find you. Safe journey, Andrea. I love you. Never doubt that."

The screen went blank before flickering back to the long list of logs.

Andrea sat back, eyeing the screen. She saw a new mark next to the video, marking it with the number one.

Damn, do I hate my sister so much that I refused to attend her personal video until now? What did she do? What did I do?

A wave of conflicting emotions roiled in the pit of her stomach. She was out here on this assignment because of the Pinshi incident, a punishment, not an adventure. Her sister had testified against her at the apparent court-martial. Her memories were lost now because of those enigmatic events.

What happened? Why was Vara so high in rank? Did Andrea lose her position within the hierarchy at the court-martial? How long had she served? How old was she?

There were too many questions and not enough answers, but she found one piece of information. She and Vara weren't twins, and Andrea was older.

Chasing the shadows of her mind only brought on more restlessness and anxiety she didn't need. Her eyes roamed the list—she selected another vid log.

As a third log finished, one from an Admiral Caretaker addressed to both her and the missing crew member, the door chimed.

"Enter."

The doors parted, and Rhett entered.

Andrea tensed at the sight of him, and her stomach tightened in anticipation of the horrendous banter that was sure to ensue.

He put his hands on his hips and took a deep breath.

"Just finished checking below," he started without preamble. "The fourth deck, the one with the science lab has sleeping quarters meant to house a number of soldiers. This ship only has five decks. The deck on the bottom's a cargo bay. There's some type of vehicle down there—built for off-road, and the armory's down there, but I couldn't get in. Oh, and the engine room and another sleeping area."

"Good to know," she replied, thankful he couldn't get into the armory.

She couldn't imagine what it would be like if he got his hands on a gun. She reevaluated him. Now that he behaved and wasn't trying to get into her pants, she found him likable. He was to the point, succinct—her mental image of him reformed. Perhaps this lay closer to what he was like?

Rhett strolled past and plopped down on the bed.

"So, what have you been doing? Besides waiting on me?"

Andrea turned in her chair and rolled her eyes.

"Don't start."

He shrugged and gave a sheepish grin.

"What can I say, I sense a connection?"

"Then there's something seriously wrong with you, and your brain cells aren't all firing. There's nothing between us except tension."

His eyebrows wiggled up and down in suggestiveness.

"Fucking—" she muttered, stopping herself. "You weren't my type when you were dressed in nothing but a towel, and you're not my type now."

She changed the subject to throw him off stride.

"You and Sub-Regent Kembly seemed to hit it off."

To this, he shrugged and reclined further.

Kodi was an attractive woman, and the two of them seem to be headed in the direction of intense sparks—the right kind, at least. An epiphany hit her then. Rhett realized Kodi's interest and, if he played his hand right, could have her, but not Andrea.

He wanted, pursued, yearned for what he couldn't claim. Did he hope to have both of them? It was the chase, and he'd never tire. It was all a game to him, but one only he played.

She waved a hand out in exasperation.

"Get off my bed."

He sighed, standing.

"It feels comfortable, familiar."

A disgusted breath escaped her.

"Yeah, it's called standard issue. You've got one, too. Don't you have something to do?"

He shook his head.

"I'm done searching like you told me to."

"Then go to your quarters. Find anything that would trigger memories. We need them back."

"You sure you don't need help triggering yours?"

A sinking feeling knotted in her gut, and she refrained from responding.

"I'd love to be staring at the back of your head right now."

The statement settled between them, as welcomed as him taking a shit on her floor. Andrea ran through the ramifications of his words. It was creepy. Did he say it for her discomfort? To see the stress he caused?

Maybe he didn't care. Why would he say something as ominous as that?

Then, the double entendre hit, and her heart thundered in her chest while the anger built.

He meant he'd love to be staring at the back of my head while he took me from behind.

A tremor arched through her hand as the anger flared.

She stood slowly. A crimson aura flared through her vision.

"Listen to me, motherfucker. I don't give a God-damn about what you want, what you'd like, or whatever twisted fantasies are floating through that head of yours. My patience is at an end."

He opened his mouth to retort, but she cut him off, shouting over him.

"No, you don't say anything! I'm talking now! I don't care that we lost our memories. I don't care about what you think or feel. You keep that shit to yourself! I'm the fucking commanding officer on this vessel, and you'll treat me and everyone above you with some God-damned respect! Don't you ever come back in here and say that kind of shit to me again. This is your absolute, last warning. Do I make myself clear?"

At that moment, the quarter's doors parted, and Carlin stumbled in with a weapon drawn. His sudden arrival startled them, but heat still radiated from her face.

His eyes were wide, and a light sheen covered his face. Both Andrea and Daspar stared at him for a moment. The ward's eyes flickered between them.

"What's going on in here?" Carlin asked, his voice brusque.

"Nothing," Andrea said curtly, answering for both of them. "This asshole was just leaving."

Rhett stood and slunk out of the room.

As he passed Carlin, he sneered. "Want a goodbye kiss?"

"Want a fat lip and a broken nose?" the ward countered.

An oily sneer crossed Rhett's features as he ducked from view.

The doors closed almost immediately, and Carlin turned to face her. She didn't know why, but she felt safer when he was present.

"Thanks for coming to my rescue."

Carlin touched the flat brim of his hat, smiling.

"My pleasure. Knight with a manly beard and all that."

She let out a sharp laugh, then clamped a hand over her mouth in embarrassment.

"How did you know I was having trouble?"

"SAVI told me."

"SAVI? How——?"

Carlin shrugged as the vessel's interface spoke aloud.

"I was monitoring your stress levels, Chief Regent. They spiked with Navigator Daspar's arrival and continued to rise throughout. I dispatched the ship's ward to your location."

We're monitored even when he's not present? Either the military doesn't trust us or…

Andrea nodded, and her eyes caught the weapon in his hand.

"And the gun, SAVI?"

"Concealed on the bridge in an emergency access point. They're installed throughout the craft in case of subversion or mutiny."

Andrea glanced at Carlin—a wince shot through her. She had to ask.

"Wouldn't that make it easier for the ward to start a mutiny of his own?"

The pause waiting for an answer seemed like eternal, but in truth, barely a breath passed before the intercom spoke again. She dared not look at her ward, didn't want to see the hurt in his eyes.

"There are counter-measures in place to keep that from happening."

"Thanks, SAVI," Andrea said—and realized she meant it. She still didn't trust the AI, but she knew when to be grateful.

"You're welcome, Chief Regent. Returning to my searches."

"So, what was all that about?" Carlin asked, jerking his head in the direction Rhett disappeared.

Andrea shook her head and rolled her eyes.

"Same shit as before, but he's gotten more brazen."

"Do you have a legitimate concern?" Carlin pressed.

An emotion laced his voice, one she couldn't pin at the moment.

"You mean do I think he'll force himself on me? No, not really. It's like ..." she paused, searching for the words. "He says shit to get a reaction, he finds some gratification in it. It's almost the same as having sex for him."

"I'd rather have sex," Carlin blurted.

Andrea smiled.

"Me, too, but still, there's something wrong with him."

"Want me to kick the shit out of him?"

A quick smile lit her features.

"The thought has crossed my mind. And I wouldn't feel bad if you did."

She shook her head.

"But words don't warrant it. Besides, you might damage something more in him."

"There's something damaged within all of us."

"No, just memory loss."

"I wasn't talking about that," Carlin clarified. "I mean, we're on a spaceship, flying at God-knows-how-fast, and so far away from home. Think about it, the people who volunteer must be a little touched in the marbles."

Andrea chuckled at his words. He had a point. She shifted the subject.

"Have you found anything in the logs yet?"

Carlin shook his head.

"I'm combing through forty-eight hours of footage for each camera, one hour at a time."

"How many cameras are there?"

"From what I can see, a minimum of ten each deck. Your guess is as good as mine whether that includes quarters or lavatories. If it does, I don't have access."

"Okay, focus on the science lab for now," Andrea said. "Let's see if that object we found was the cause of the power surge."

Carlin nodded and his lips twisted.

"What? Something on your mind?"

He glanced up, holding her gaze.

"We've got two months before we get to this planet. I'm apprehensive."

"I think we all are."

"No, it's more than that. I didn't say anything on the bridge when we talked about changing course. I was undecided but would've backed your call regardless. You're the commanding officer. You didn't have to consult us, but you did, and that's the difference between a leader and an administrator. Now that we're going, it's my duty to inform you that we're woefully unprepared."

"How do you mean?"

"We're on a small military vessel, which implies fast responses. It's got a small command crew and an armory, yet we don't know how to use any of it. If your theory's correct about muscle memory, then we need to practice. There has to be a section on this bucket dedicated to training—we need to find it and start using it. This planet we're going to? What if we aren't welcomed? It's the same as going in unarmed."

Andrea nodded.

"You have a point, and I'll address it with SAVI and see what I can find."

Carlin dipped his head and took a step back.

"Let me know if you have any more problems with Rhett."

"I'll always have problems with him. Might not want the burden of being my rescuer all the time."

Carlin smiled, stepping back. The doors parted for him.

"It's not a burden, and you don't look like a woman who needs to be rescued. Regardless, the offer's available should you need it."

"Thanks."

He paused at the doors.

"You know, I really don't feel comfortable with him roaming the ship and me not there. What if we got SAVI to somehow track him or you when he comes in close proximity? I'd feel more comfortable."

Andrea paused, considering.

How did she feel about SAVI tracking her? The idea of them keeping tabs on Navigator Daspar didn't seem like a bad idea. She had no problem with the latter. Better to leave it in someone else's hands and remove herself from the equation.

"Sure, set something up, whatever you think's best. I'll trust your judgement."

He gave a small grin and stepped through.

The doors closed behind him, and Andrea was left with chaotic thoughts.

Carlin had many valid points, but the most prominent stemmed from flying blind and unarmed.

And now, one of the crew found a way to arm themselves with a weapon.

She didn't have the means to defend herself, and that was a problem. She saw two options: confiscate all the guns, or arm everyone. Andrea debated over which was the better course of action.

Taking all the weapons would still leave weapons of opportunity. What was she supposed to do? Collect the cutlery, too? If so inclined, anyone could grab a belt and strangle someone, or use a console to bash someone's head in.

The men, Soren included, could overpower her and Kodi with ease. The only way to equalize the field was to give them all guns. Either way, if someone wanted to hurt another, they'd find a way. At least armed, they'd all stand an equal chance.

Do I really want Daspar running around with a gun?

"SAVI?"

Her mind tumbled as she waited through the prolonged pause.

"Yes, Andrea?"

"Let's have a talk about what's restricted and what's not. We need a plan—and I need a gun."

Chapter Nine: Kodi Kembly

Kodi paused the video and rubbed her almond-shaped eyes.

She leaned away from the bright monitor. Speed-watching video logs wasn't enjoyable. She'd rather be exploring the ship.

The others ... they weren't freaking out about not being able to remember, and that surprised her. She fought down her own panic from time to time. That's why she was so ... blasé as Andrea had put it. Wouldn't help anything to be so uptight.

Still, Kodi didn't believe it'd last. She looked at the whole ordeal as an adventure. Yes, the prospect leaned into the terrifying side, but it could always be worse.

Their vessel appeared sound and whole, not venting atmosphere. They had plenty of water, electricity, and food to spare. The engines worked. What more could they ask for? In the grand scheme, it could've been more severe.

If the engines failed, they'd be adrift until they died. Rationed food and water might prolong their survival, but how would they find some way to stay warm and conserve oxygen? A message to the fleet would be months too late, if they were even listening.

Stop that. Your job's to watch videos, not worry about every terrible scenario. That's Andrea's job.

A sigh escaped her, and she scratched her scalp. So, yeah, adventure was a much better way to look at it.

Whether the others wanted to admit it or not, losing their memories was one of the best things to happen. It wasn't a setback or an obstacle, but a gift! For the first time, they got to experience life like no one else: a newborn babe, but able to recollect.

When their memories came back, they'd remember the short time they had amnesia, and the feelings they expressed or repressed during the ordeal would persist forever. How many people could say they got to discover life again? Each new duty or discovery became their first experience all over.

Of course, she didn't want it to last forever—but enjoying the moment couldn't harm them. What did fretting ever accomplish? Did it change the outcome?

Rhett embodied fun. Sure, he was a touch perverted, but who wasn't? Maybe the others just weren't being honest with themselves in more ways than one. Andrea, though of sound mind and dedicated—something Kodi respected and could get behind—had a stick planted deep in her ass.

Andrea needs to fuck something fierce to rid herself of that tenseness. Might do wonders for her.

Kodi's personal toys flickered through her mind, and she debated about giving an unused one to Andrea. She had plenty to spare.

If anyone needs a toy on this ship, it's Andrea or Rhett.

The chief regent needed a B.O.B. in her life.

Never leave spaceport without your Battery Operated Boyfriend.

A chuckle bubbled up from her abdomen.

Perhaps Kodi didn't take their predicament as seriously as the others, but she saw that as a win. Carlin … he always looked moments away from stroking out with his testosterone levels boiling too high for Kodi's taste.

He and Andrea should help each other out in that regard.

And Soren … at his age, he could croak at any moment.

The thought elicited a tug of humor.

Okay, Soren's not that old.

Her thoughts returned to Andrea.

SAVI told them she held the commanding officer's rank, and Kodi didn't doubt the AI's word, not after seeing her in action—her presence manifested like their muscle memory. Perhaps memory wipes just couldn't undo ingrained training? The chief regent personified what a leader should be.

Kodi found contentment in being second in command, and in some ways, she didn't act like an executive officer. Telling the men what to do felt odd, almost unnatural. Perhaps faking long enough for the memories to return would suffice? She thought of it like roleplaying.

Thinking back on Andrea's countenance, Kodi recognized the need to strike a balance. Sure, follow the rules and procedures, but to live by those policies alone made for terrible living.

An intense dislike roused in her stomach. She might not recollect those precious memories, but she'd trust the gut feeling. Andrea slipped into the portrayal of the heavy—the stickler for rules and regulation—and Kodi would function as the nice, likable one. There needed to be a balance, or risk burning out morale.

All except for the ward. He'd get aroused by that kind of environment.

If both of them were too relaxed, it'd lead to negligence.

Which might turn into disastrous accidents.

She shrugged.

Andrea wouldn't win points with anyone except Carlin. Perhaps Kodi might score some likability points from Rhett and Soren?

Andrea can be the driven one.

Kodi would take the more indulgent, free-spirit route. When Andrea came down hard, Kodi's new purpose would soften the blow, act as a buffer. If both were uptight, Ward Ossaro would turn surly, Engineer Goski would retreat to his sex-haven sanctuary, and Navigator Daspar would act out all the more.

A sigh of relief came to her. This plan would work, had to. It wouldn't matter if the ship reached its destination with the crew dead from strangling each other.

Kodi's thoughts turned to the navigator. He'd gotten on Andrea's wrong side from the first moment, and by now, whether in jest or not, he'd never leave her bad side. Still, Kodi found herself far more understanding than the commanding officer. She got his sense of humor, the crassness.

Soren's quarters and the whole fondling incident with Emma—that bothered her. Kodi didn't mind Daspar touching the synthetic. She didn't begrudge him—they all did the same thing and touched her, too. The moment turned surreal. Emma looked so … normal yet wasn't, but when Daspar fondled the synth to upset Soren, he'd crossed a line.

Curiosity turned into something else, and the novelty brought bile to her mouth. He didn't see the full weight of his actions.

Or he did, and he just didn't care.

If any future entanglements with Rhett happened, he'd need to know a line existed, and if he debated on toeing it, he better not. Kodi was all for having a laugh, but once impropriety took root, all bets were off. Since meeting him, only once had a sour afterglow festered in her mouth.

She tried to calm the situation, but the boys didn't hear her small voice over their own shouting. Carlin hovered close in case Rhett and Soren came to blows. The ward was itching for a fight.

Probably to suck up to Andrea.

A man like Carlin was born for the role of ward, his sole purpose to crack skulls and beat confessions out of suspects.

Kodi shook off the thoughts of Ossaro. Something about him was off, not bad or evil, but he rubbed her the wrong way.

I need a drink.

With a sigh, Kodi brushed a lock of blonde hair behind her ear and leaned forward. Her hand scrolled over the screen as she returned to the video logs. It wouldn't inspect itself, and the sooner she got done …

With a gentle touch, she pressed play.

Chapter Ten: Soren Goski

The doors to Soren's chambers parted, and Emma, who had been standing expressionless, came to life.

"Soren, dear, I was wondering when you were coming home."

A big smile spread across her glossy lips. She wore one of his shirts—white, long-sleeved, and collared. The blouse covered the area where her shorts would be—if she was wearing any—but he doubted the synth's modesty programming.

Unless I requested her to behave like that.

"I'll have dinner prepared in no time. Come in. I'll fetch your slippers."

A frown flickered across his brow, but he stepped inside with cautious footfalls. He eyed the spacious bed to the back of the room, then the desk to the right. His gaze wandered over the attachment of the desk to the wall, the weld, rivets, and hinges. Even the monitor was bolted into the counter.

"Er," Soren started. "That won't be necessary."

He turned his attention to the wall locker in the back.

"Oh?" Emma asked in her soft voice.

She came to him, her gait anything but robotic. She moved like a real person; the sway of her hips gave her a dainty countenance. She pressed the back of her hand against his forehead.

"Well, you don't have a fever, so you're not sick."

She leaned forward and kissed him.

"Why don't you want your slippers? Perhaps a brandy?"

Soren's frown deepened.

"Thank you, but no."

"Perhaps you should check yourself into medical. Are you sure you're feeling well?"

Soren paused again, this time scrutinizing the synthetic—*his synthetic.*

"Yeah, I just got a lot on my mind. It's a lot to take in."

"Oh, honey," she said, her voice almost a whisper.

She started to undo the buttons on her shirt.

"Let's make love, that always helps with your stress. I know how much you like protocol forty-three."

Soren reached for her hands to keep her from unbuttoning any more buttons.

"No, no, I uh—that is to say, not now."

What could he say? He couldn't see himself having … relations with a synth. Did it seem as weird as he thought?

"Does someone else hold your affection? Another one of the females?"

Soren laughed.

"No. That's the last thing on my mind. I just—I need to get my bearings. I'm sure everything will return to normal in a few days."

He stepped deeper into the room and took the seat at the desk. Emma hovered nearby. If she could display an anxious temperament, he experienced it.

A tightness came to his chest, being in such close proximity to her. She was beautiful, everything he'd look for in a woman. His eyes wandered to her long shapely legs and worked up as they disappeared beneath the shirt.

Emma knelt in front of him, her soft hands rubbing his thighs. A pleading manifested in her eyes as if she understood emotions and discomfort.

"Are you sure there isn't anything I can do for you?"

His gaze roamed from her face down her neck to her cleavage, spurring arousal.

She whispered seductively, "Do you want to make love to me?"

The words jarred him out of the moment.

"No," he said.

He sat up straighter, and her hands retreated as if she were aware of his discomfort. He stood and stepped back, grateful when Emma didn't follow.

He cleared his throat.

What could he say to the robot? Did he converse with her? What did they do with their time? It was obvious from their exchange that they ... engaged in certain activities together. He drew a blank except for the most mundane of lines.

"How was your day?"

He turned in time to see Emma's face light up with a smile. Her eyes *sparkled*.

"Very productive, but it passed by with agonizing slowness without you here."

She took a slow step forward, and almost appeared to lean towards him as if engaged by the conversation.

"I did the laundry—folded and put away just as you like. I washed our sheets, too."

"*Our* sheets?"

She gave a small nod and shrug.

"Well, yes, honey. We do sleep in the same bed."

Her eyes flickered to the bed and back again.

"Is everything alright, dear?"

Soren ran his hands through his burred hair.

"No ... no, everything's not alright!" he said with more bite than he intended.

Emma visibly flinched and crossed over to him again. She wrapped her arms around his waist and held him.

"Tell me, what's the matter?"

She felt warm, human. She smelled of sweet vanilla ... and something else. Soren would have said satin if satin had a distinct smell. Her soft blonde hair tickled his face. Her breasts squished against him. Despite knowing she wasn't real, comfort radiated from the embrace.

How? Why did he feel this way?

"How can I help?" she whispered.

"Emma," Soren said with a slow cadence. "I don't remember anything."

"What do you mean?" she asked, pulling away from him.

She looked him in the face, her own full of sympathy and yearning to understand.

"I don't remember what I was doing before falling unconscious. I don't remember how I got on this ship. I don't—"

"—Remember me."

He nodded.

Why did acknowledging it hurt him so? Giving the words merit resembled a betrayal, one that he should be damned for.

"Is that why you and the chief regent and all the others are acting strangely?"

He nodded again, not trusting his voice. His eyes stung.

He tried not to let it show, let her see how much it bothered him, but they were all going to die out here. He believed that to the core of his being. Something terrible happened to them on that planet, something foul. He voted to go back to the planet because he suspected the others would pressure him if he didn't.

Despite how much of an asshole Rhett proved to be, Soren agreed with him. They should be headed to the fleet. They were ill-equipped and unprepared to handle whatever awaited them. They'd die trying to reach the planet, and if they arrived, they'd probably be captured by the natives, or worse.

He pleaded with Emma, "Do you know what happened?"

She shook her head, her lips pressed into a sad, tight line.

"No, darling, I don't, but it troubled you a great deal. Are you still concerned?"

He nodded at the truth, but it took a whole new meaning. He might not remember that place, but his gut did, and it screamed for them to keep away.

Emma reached out a hand to stroke his face and he flinched away.

"I'm sorry," she said, her voice wounded. "You don't have to be scared, love."

Before he gave it much thought, he blurted, "How do I know that?"

A sympathetic expression flickered across her features.

No doubt something built into her programming.

She nodded.

"Point taken. Perhaps we should go over what I can and can't do, since you don't remember."

She stood.

"The first thing: I can't harm a living being that displays higher intelligence. This parameter allows me to kill insects and other such vermin."

She smiled and gave a soft chuckle.

"You don't like spiders much."

Soren blinked, and his mind calmed. Something about the subject matter or her speaking of his life drew him to her. Was it just her words or something deeper on the subconscious level?

Perhaps the engineering aspect of it?

"That might come in handy," he admitted.

He stood now, finding strength and surety in his legs. The sensation in his gut subsided, and he repressed it further.

"Tell me everything about you, Emma. Tell me about us. How did we come together?"

Her face faltered.

"It's a sad story. Are you sure you want to hear it, Soren?"

He gave a single nod.

She sighed—or did the approximation.

"Alright, I'll tell you."

Chapter Eleven: Carlin Ossaro

Carlin stormed onto the bridge and slapped the firearm on the console, slamming it harder than anticipated.

His thoughts flickered to Andrea and Kodi. With his arms braced against the desk, he hunched over and eyed the gun. He'd love nothing more than to pistol-whip Rhett.

Fucking slimy bastard.

An idea came to him.

"SAVI?"

There was a long pause before the dual-voiced system responded.

"Yes, Ward Ossaro?"

"Can you tell me where Rhett is now?"

"Navigator Daspar is in his quarters."

"I need you to set up an alert, SAVI. Can we do that?"

"What kind of alert?"

Carlin stood straighter and crossed his arms.

It was a good question. What was he doing anyway? Was it his job to monitor, track, and record the movements of personnel? Maybe. Who knew?

He didn't trust the navigator, not when he was alone with Andrea. And what about Sub-Regent Kembly?

Carlin rubbed his chin, his lips drawing in a tight line as he thought.

One couldn't be too careful. They were all strangers, something they should all keep in mind. Kembly might not like Carlin keeping tabs on her, and if she ever found out, she might report him to Andrea, but Hessner would probably thank him—like earlier in her room.

"SAVI, what's my function on this ship—the duties of being the ward, I mean?"

"Your duties include tactical warfare, both atmospheric and in space, and the safety of the ship and crew from saboteurs, enemy assaults, and insubordinate or dangerous crew members. Further duties include espionage, investigating, reporting findings to the vessel commander or the Admiralty, restraining individuals by an escalation of force, detaining, and summary execution."

The last words took him by surprise, and he felt his chest tighten.

"Summary execution?"

"Affirmative, though the command must come from the commanding officer and the executive officer, and both must be in agreement and of sound mind."

His eyebrow cocked up, and his bottom lip jutted.

"Has anyone been executed on a ship before?"

Another pause, this one only half a dozen heartbeats long.

"Yes."

So, there's precedence.

"There are also other duties you perform while on ground side or during a state of mutiny. Your first priority is the preservation of the ship and the commanding officer. On the ground, you act as the chief regent's personal bodyguard."

A small grin came to him, and his face flushed with a prickle of heat. There were worse ways to spend time planet-side.

"Okay."

He let the smile fade, took off his hat, and set it on the console.

"Back to that alert. I want to set one up."

"What would you like this alert to do?"

He stepped away from the console and paced through the main thoroughfare of the bridge.

"You can track personnel, and you can monitor their health. I need a few alerts. The first: I want to know anytime Daspar's alone with Andrea. The second is the same parameters as the first but include elevated stress levels and heartbeat. Can you do that?"

"Affirmative, however, since your request involves the chief regent, I'll have to notify her of your request."

Carlin's lips curled into a grimace, and his irritation flared at the vessel interface.

Why can't anything ever be simple?

It didn't bother him, not really. He already had Andrea's permission, but he wondered what she'd think if a second request came through regarding Kembly.

He shrugged, willing to tackle that debate if it ever came.

"Do what you must."

"You may add comments as to why you are requesting this alert. This will help the chief regent determine if the request is appropriate."

Carlin stopped pacing and exhaled noisily.

What could he say that didn't sound paranoid or any less predatory than the navigator? Safety remained paramount, and Carlin didn't trust Daspar to keep himself in check. He thought about doing a secondary alert for Kodi, but Daspar didn't seem inclined to notice her.

Or was it a ruse?

Did he feign interest in Andrea so that Kodi would pursue him? Did he hope to make each of them jealous and pick up whichever one wanted him more?

Why the hell do I care about why? I just don't want him taking advantage of anyone.

Darker thoughts flitted through his head.

There must be some lines that even he won't cross, right?

He inhaled noisily through his nose.

"Requesting this alert for the safety of the commanding officer—a paramount duty of the ship's ward. In these stressful times, and without a history to gauge each personnel, this is the best safety measure available—short of locking everyone up or all residing in a communal room."

There was a pause, and SAVI's voice came back.

"Are those all the notes you'd like to add?"

"For now."

Carlin moved back to his station, and his gaze fell on the pistol.

"Compiling request parameters and sending it to Chief Regent Hessner for approval. Is there anything else I can help you with?"

"Yeah, set up another alert but for the first officer. If you must approve it through Andrea, then use the same notes."

A few moments passed.

"Request complete and sent. Is there anything else I can help you with?"

"What are the possibilities of others finding those emergency weapons we have stowed around the ship?"

"Little to none. The crew would have to know where to look and circumvent the multi-factor authentication such as the software encryption, biometrics, and the physical lock."

Carlin held up the pistol, and he turned it over, inspecting the reflective surface. He glanced up at the ceiling, towards the speaker where SAVI's voice originated.

"How many shots can this thing snap off before it runs out?"

"It depends on the number set when you retrieved it. In this case, a single shot."

Carlin glanced back at the near-useless pistol.

"Okay, but let's say you didn't. How many shots?"

"Results vary, but anywhere from seventy-five shots to two hundred, depending on the setting level, stun or lethal."

Carlin gave an appreciative nod as he held the pistol up. His compartment in the console slid open, revealing the hideaway location.

"Please return the weapon to the receptacle."

"I'd rather hold on to it."

"Noted. Please return the weapon to the receptacle. Chief Regent Hessner hasn't authorized the use or retention of blasters."

A touch of irritation flared within him again.

How was the ship lecturing him about what was safe and what was authorized? Wasn't that his job? Software didn't appreciate life or the potential dangers they faced.

"If you don't return the blaster in the next fifteen seconds, it'll be disabled remotely, and you'll be flagged as a security risk. This will notify the others of you, the weapon you possess, and restrict further access to weapons, systems, security, or the ship's amenities."

"Fine!" he said, and returned the firearm by flinging it into the cubby.

Damn, don't have to blackmail me.

The slot closed.

"Thank you. Do you require further assistance?"

His mood soured; he shook his head.

"No, nothing further."

"Returning to my searches."

The speaker went dead, and Carlin glanced at the monitor.

The video was paused on the last frame he viewed before going to Andrea's rescue. Going through the video log was a chore he didn't relish, but better him than Daspar.

Carlin clenched his fist.

If Daspar stepped out of line again, it'd be Carlin who'd throw the punches, not Soren.

The thought warmed him and gave him the vitality to continue the search through the video logs.

Chapter Twelve: Rhett Daspar

Daspar entered his room, face red with humiliation and anger.

When the doors slid shut behind him, he kicked the desk chair. It didn't budge, either being bolted or magnetically clamped to the deck. He paced while the roiling sea of rage-filled thoughts bubbled to the forefront.

That fucking asshole!

Had Ossaro not come in with the pistol, Daspar would've let it come to blows. He understood not being anyone's favorite person, but they didn't have to treat him like shit.

His feet burned a rut across the floor.

Everyone's so fucking tense! They need to loosen up and have a laugh.

Each time Rhett saw Carlin, the ward postured and rutted out his territory. First, it was that stupid hat on the bridge, then choosing Andrea as a search partner, now coming to her proverbial rescue and storming her room.

True, he did give Andrea a hard time, being crass and perverted, but there was something about seeing people uncomfortable.

It was funny, and it was a hell of a lot easier than expressing genuine desire that never came out right. So, he resorted to something that made him comfortable.

He went overboard, no denying that, but it was all in good fun. He'd never do anything untoward to her. Yes, there was the attraction, but he also sensed something else … like a kindred spirit in her, a good friend, or maybe even a kid-sister.

But Ossaro made everything difficult. To the ward, the dick-measuring contest exploded into full contention. Like a typical dog marking territory, Ossaro marked Andrea as his.

And she's too stupid to notice.

Either that, or she didn't care, as in, she wanted him.

That possibility did flicker through his head and more than once, but Daspar didn't think the chief regent went for the soldier type—in this case, the ass-kisser.

And how the hell did Ossaro get a gun? How did the ward find one? Who gave it to him?

He stopped pacing and looked up.

The wall locker filled his vision, and he remembered perusing the insides as they searched the rooms. No weapon lay within, but something else did, and just as good.

He crossed the room, opened the hatch, and pulled the glass bottle from the top shelf.

The container was clear and tapered at the edges. Inside, a golden liquid swilled. He glanced at the label again.

War Machine's Confidence?

He didn't know why the label seemed humorous, but he chuckled again.

Twisting the cap off, he broke the seal, and took a quick, deep pull.

At first, faint peppermint filled his mouth, then it shifted into soft spearmint. As the liquid traveled through his gullet, another morph took place but to a creamy blueberry. The new flavor swished around in his mouth with each exhale or burp.

He glanced at the bottle again and nodded in appreciation.

Hooch in hand, he climbed on the bed and reclined with the pillows behind him. Staring at the door, he half expected Carlin to come bursting through to berate him or finish what they started.

Nah, he's too busy fucking Andrea to concern himself with me.

The thought disgusted him on numerous levels, but he didn't care to unpack all those feelings.

Why waste time on a woman who didn't give a shit about him? Why bother? She's so goggly-eyed over the ward.

He took another pull, then another, and placed the cap back on.

Setting it aside, he untied his long hair and let it hang down. The ends tickled his shoulders. He leaned his head back, his eyes naturally lifting to the ceiling.

Above him, the surface flashed with various pictures and vids of naked women in provocative clothing, poses, or in the explicit throes of passion. He couldn't recall how long he stared and admired the ever-shifting scenes, but he never once saw the women repeat. Further, the alcohol and arousal at this point didn't help matters.

He rubbed his eyes and sat up, trying to forget the erotica above him.

His mind wandered and settled on the bridge, recalling how SAVI revealed they were military. On a certain level, it made sense. From what he could tell, they were all fit which implied an active lifestyle of training, but not everything added up.

First, the empty vessel.

Other than the command crew—if you could call them that—there wasn't anyone else aboard. He'd checked the quarters below. They could house many troops; their bunks stacked three high, thin mattresses over thick bunks.

He'd opened one. They could stow gear beneath their beds.

His tongue felt dry, and he remembered the bottle.

Hoisting it up, he twisted the lid and took another swig.

Either the alcohol proved strong, or he'd gone without drinking for a long time. Maybe he should abstain in the future because he swore the taste changed. The liquor no longer held the mint flavor, but now it was coconut. The beverage altered as it settled in his stomach, and he belched a citrus flavor.

He eyed the bottle again, and for the first time, doubted his sanity.

It's fake, it's gotta be.

He put the lid back on and glanced about the room. Suspicion latched on like a vise, and he couldn't shake the feeling that someone played an elaborate joke on them all.

Maybe this is what Andrea feels when I tease her.

He scrutinized the dark corners, the small knickknacks littering the sparse room. Maybe there were cameras? The more he thought about it, the more he realized they couldn't be on a spaceship.

Who'd ever heard of a ship that could travel through the deep-dark between worlds and galaxies?

The events of the day flickered through his mind.

Andrea was the key, she had to be, having been the first to *remember*.

He doubted her sincerity.

She had to be the control element. He didn't dismiss the notion that someone found a way to suppress their memories, but they wouldn't for the woman in charge of the experiment.

This was all some form of a simulation. Maybe they were military, and they were being tested for a special assignment. They couldn't let the experiment run without some element of control.

Andrea was that control. She played the game, a long con on them all.

A chuckle escaped him as the obviousness emerged.

This was to test how they'd react under stressful circumstances. Take away someone's memories and tell them they're missing a crew member while hurtling through space, and that'll be a great starting point.

Damn it! Why didn't I see it before?

He scrambled off the bed and took another swig.

When the bottle left his lips, he scrutinized the container, imagining himself encroaching the cusp of drunkenness. As he sipped, smooth orange washed down before turning to chocolate in his stomach.

A small burp allowed him to appreciate the flavor once again.

He put the cap back on and placed the jug in the wall locker.

Shit's getting to me.

He tried to remember what thought he chased before taking that last drink. After a terrible, slow moment, it came back.

The experiment.

What if the whole purpose of this exercise was to test how long they took to realize their predicament?

Rats in a fucking maze.

Maybe a bonus awaited the person who figured the puzzle out first. What would happen to the others once he got out? Would they continue the venture as if nothing happened? How long would they let them go on thinking he died? Did they already have algorithms in place to explain the disappearance of a crew member?

It'd be interesting to watch the debacle unfold.

But first came the victory, and to win, he had to get out.

His staggering steps carried him to the parting door. He glanced down the hallway.

Blue and gray and white. Even the paint job screams simulation.

Seeing no one down the right, he glanced left.

At the end of the hall sat another two rooms, one on each side, and a bulkhead. He staggered on.

Why the hell does it seem so far away?

His lungs burned, not the kind from running, but akin to held breath.

The panels on each room glowed, yellow for the numbers and a light teal for the display. But the last one wasn't a room, and that's the one he wanted.

He blinked a few times, making out the words for open and close, and tapped the former.

Nothing happened.

He hit it again. And again. And again.

"May I help you, Navigator Daspar?" SAVI's voice sounded from the panel.

"Yeah, open the fucking door."

"Why?"

It was a good question. What was the purpose again?

Then, he recalled. The experiment, the lie, the sham!

The AI blocked the way out, but he had to outsmart the computer. They weren't going to hand him a victory.

"I want to see what's on the other side."

"A dual-phase airlock lays on the other side. In the event of those two doors being breached, this bulkhead keeps the ship from venting into space."

"Yeah, but I want to explore, you know? Can never be too safe or familiar with the ship."

An idea came to him.

"When's the last time anyone's inspected the area to make sure it's intact?"

"My programming runs an inspection every thirty minutes."

"Yeah, but you're not human. You don't have eyes on."

Human? How did I know that word? How do I know any words, or to turn the ship around earlier?

Excitement trembled through him.

Was the memory suppression wearing off, or did they gas them every so often to keep their recollections repressed? Better yet, the alcohol might be countering the effects of memory loss.

"Your point's valid," SAVI answered.

"See? I can make sense sometimes. More than your sex-confused software."

"Would you like to inspect the airlock now?"

He nodded and held up his hands.

"Yeah. Open the damn door."

Gears in the wall twirled. The bulkhead parted. Inside, the floor wasn't solid metal but grate.

His boot gave a hollow echo as he stepped inside. A small octagon room stretched out around him. Small cubicles were cut into the walls, their coves covered with dense, gunmetal-gray hatches.

Two blocky hinges hugged the left edge of each door, and on the right corners, a thick winch held each access point shut. Dead ahead of him lay door two.

He stumbled over to the porthole.

Beyond the thick glass, a mirage of colors bent and twisted as the ship slipped through space at faster than light speed.

Space travel, faster than light, yeah right. Got to get through the portal, and I'm home free.

"SAVI, can you open the outside hatch of the ship?"

"You wish to open the ship to the vacuum of space?"

"Yeah," Rhett chuckled to himself.

The AI's programming was exceptional and elaborate. God, they couldn't help themselves with the ruse.

"Can you do it?"

"Yes, would you like to do so now?"

The navigator nodded in exasperation and rolled his eyes.

"Duh!"

"Confirmed. You'll need a spacesuit for your EVA sequence. We'll also need to close the third bulkhead to keep the occupants of the ship safe."

"What're you doing!" a voice shouted behind him.

He turned and saw Kodi running towards him. Shock and outrage peppered her features.

"Are you trying to kill yourself?"

He laughed.

"It isn't real. It's a hoax, an experiment."

She jumped through the bulkhead at a run and stopped in front of him. Her green eyes squinted.

"Have—have you been drinking?"

A sly grin twisted on his lips.

"Yeah, about that—you've got to be careful with that stuff. Does some weird—"

She took a step closer.

"Got any more?"

He found himself nodding before remembering the need to get out and win.

"It's all yours, cutie."

He jerked a thumb behind him.

"I'm going to win this maze."

"The only thing you'll win is a one-way ticket to eternity."

He opened his mouth to protest, but Kodi took his hand in hers. It was warm and moist and soft. She tugged on him.

"Come, tell me about this experiment while I drink. If you convince me, I'll help you win, alright?"

He hesitated.

The end was right there. Right there! He just had to go through the second door.

Kodi stepped closer. She pressed her body against him. His spine stiffened at the touch. He glanced down, his eyes filled with all her glory.

Damn, she's got great tits.

"Yeah, alright. I'll share a drink with you."

"Good," she said in a shaky breath.

"But then, I'm going to prove this is an experiment."

She smiled.

"That sounds wonderful. Can't wait to hear all about it!"

They held hands all the way back to the room.

Once inside and the door shut behind them, he grabbed the bottle from the wall locker and shared it. He warned her about the changing flavors and what to look for, but she still cringed as she took the first swallow.

"Yuck, that's cinnamon and coffee."

She continued to drink as he revealed how and why they lived like lab rats.

"What would make you change your mind?" she asked.

He snorted.

"Well, we're not in space because we have gravity. Everyone knows you are weightless in space."

"SAVI?" Kodi called, a coy smile dancing on her lips.

Her eyes sparkled. Did she always look so beautiful, or did the alcohol heighten her features?

"Yes, Sub-Regent Kembly?"

"What's keeping us from floating on the ship?"

"The gravity plates in the deck."

"Can you turn off the plates in Navigator Daspar's room?"

"Yes, but why?"

"I need to prove a point," she said.

Rhett snorted.

"SAVI's going to come back with some bullshit, technical excuse as to why —"

The power cut to the gravity plates in the room, and his feet left the deck. He floated. It felt like laying in a hammock yet vertigo toyed with the senses.

Kodi drifted over, graceful, as if born to charm the heavens.

When she closed the distance, her lips caressed his in a soft tease. She smelled like a floral array and tasted as sweet as honey. An electric arc shot through him.

She pulled back and smiled.

"Told ya we're in space."

A cold sobering thought struck him, chasing away the lightheadedness and arousal.

With a shaky breath, he whispered in awe and thanks, "I almost fucking died."

Chapter Thirteen: Two Weeks Later

The crew entered a rhythmic cadence. Like the ship, they operated on autopilot.

Andrea worked with SAVI to discover what information was permitted and what remained restricted. The armory stayed locked, but Andrea won the argument through logic, and SAVI restored her access for the safety of the crew.

Since then, she kept Carlin armed and supplied a spare for his quarters.

Carlin told her of the conversation he had with SAVI on the ship, how the AI could lock pistols with remote access. That protocol only worked on hidden blasters. Weapons in the armory remained free of SAVI's influence.

With this in mind, and with their locks removed from the doors of their quarters, she had the ward keep one in his wall locker, which, they learned, locked by fingerprint. Andrea rested easier knowing that Rhett couldn't wander in and take anything.

Their shift rotations ensured Andrea saw little of Rhett, making the long voyage bearable. Still, once every few days, they all managed to come together for a brief meeting, tracking any headway with their spaceship, craft, or abilities. Andrea accessed some weapons training videos, and they spent much of their off-time in the simulation room down in the cargo bay. The armory, though far more extensive than anyone expected, only took up a quarter of the actual size for weapon storage. The other portion came with fortified walls, and an absorption field in the off-chance the walls and stoppage area failed.

Her feelings regarding SAVI didn't fade as the days wore on.

The mistrust intensified when Carlin found a video.

At nineteen hours and seventeen minutes before they woke up without their memories, the artifact triggered, and SAVI appeared to be the cause. She'd yet to confront the AI, waiting for a better understanding of everything before doing so.

A small part of her hoped the memories would return before then.

Other than fleeting moments where her thoughts turned outward, and she thought she recollected something, her memory remained blank. Much like the time on the bridge when she mused about aliens in the galaxy, each remembrance came and faded within a few blinks. The footage discovery linking SAVI to the surge settled like an invisible weight between her and Carlin, and she locked the video feed with a code.

The secret needed to stay as such, for now.

Like Navigator Daspar's muscle memory of the controls, weapons handling, and hand-to-hand combat materialized the moment she touched a blaster. The abilities came as natural as breathing. When not training with weapons or physical fitness, she spent much of her time poring over all the communiqués stored on the personal device in her cabin.

Unfortunately, she didn't see any outgoing transmissions, which she expected from what Soren revealed. Transmissions inside the bubble were impossible. Further, they were too far out, and a broadcast would take too much time. Wistful, she yearned to know how she behaved before the memory wipe.

The first night, SAVI made an astute observation, and she took it to heart. Since turning the vessel around, it was best if she started a running log to justify all actions for the Admiralty. If she only had her tale as proof, SAVI reasoned that it wouldn't be seen as favorable without a record.

Since being court-martialed for actions she couldn't remember, very little would save them all from punitive measures. Despite the misgivings, the AI's argument won out.

Spending time with Kodi and Carlin came as another bonus with the bridge rotations. Andrea relieved the second-in-command, and the ward succeeded her. Andrea always showed up early to relieve the sub-regent, and they'd talk for almost an hour into Andrea's shift.

Carlin also had a tendency to show up early, and if Andrea's spirits were down, he always brought a smile to her face. He was handsome, and his grin felt genuine. He radiated a comfortable, warm aura.

Since Andrea left it up to the crew when they'd perform their additional duties, Carlin did his before work. When Soren relieved him, Carlin spent his free time with Andrea. The two grew closer, a trust forming despite the lack of memories. She did let him wander the ship armed, after all.

During their downtime, they watched videos saved on their personal drives or played card games. Kodi often joined them for the latter and urged a bout of strip poker. Whenever possible, Carlin shadowed Andrea as a constant companion, becoming more flirtatious as time wore on.

Andrea found herself reciprocating.

Still, she didn't move as fast as Kodi would've liked.

Despite growing more acquainted with them, Andrea only had a vague familiarity with Soren and Rhett—the latter she didn't care for overmuch, but as the commanding officer, the duty fell to her to try.

She occasionally stopped by on Daspar's six-hour shift to receive updates on his weapons handling and physical fitness. He spent many hours learning how to fly, and it heartened her to see him take to the task.

For a while, she worried he wouldn't. She also learned to pilot the vessel, letting Daspar teach her, though her skills remained rudimentary no matter how many simulations they ran.

Soren proved to be a brilliant man, mastering his craft. When she pressed him about how he learned so fast, he shrugged.

"It's like you said, muscle memory. Our skills are in our bodies and minds, we just don't remember learning them."

His statement left her to ponder a plaguing question since day one: did they genuinely grasp their skills and abilities if they didn't remember them? Wasn't that part of learning?

Soren often kept to himself, retreating to his quarters when duties didn't require him to be about the ship. Andrea never pressed him and refrained from visiting his room. He gave the impression of a private man, and with Emma's revelation about the nature of their relationship, she didn't want to visit during an inopportune time.

The same couldn't be said for Kodi and Rhett. They'd been caught sating their carnal desires in numerous parts of the vessel. Nothing seemed off limits to them—the science lab, the engine room, the bridge, the personnel lift. Andrea finally pulled Kodi aside after the bridge incident and rebuked her for carelessness.

"This is a military ship. You lost your memories, not your senses, and that doesn't absolve you from guilt. I don't care what you two do in private, but not on the bridge, and not in public places. We have to eat off those tables and use that lab for experiments!"

Her reprimand had the desired effect as they weren't caught outside their lodgings again. The last thing she needed to learn was that they'd been screwing in the command chair.

Andrea didn't understand Kodi's choice, but that was her issue. A bonus was that she didn't have to fight for Carlin's attention. With Soren and Emma coupled, that only left her and Carlin. She wondered how long he'd wait. She didn't want to mislead, but there were other priorities, and now, after two weeks of familiarizing herself with the ship and duties, she could explore the option.

Andrea leaned forward in her chair, squinting at the screen. It was video footage of her and Emma, the last time they spoke on the day they awoke.

A nagging feeling washed over her. Something the synthetic said plagued her, a pestilence she couldn't purge. A lot of answers were in the locked video feeds. If she only had a way to access them, many of her worries would fade.

She touched the screen, dialing up the audio levels.

"When Soren didn't return to his quarters at the appropriate time, I went looking for him," Emma said. *"I found various crew members comatose throughout the ship. Strange, is it not?"*

Andrea nodded absentmindedly. "Thank you," she heard herself mumble through the recording.

"You're quite welcome. I hope you come back soon. I enjoy our talks."

"Freeze frame," she said to the computer. "Go back twenty-two seconds."

The video reset and played again. She swiped the screen, turning up the audio.

"When Soren didn't return to his quarters at the appropriate time, I went looking for him," Emma said. *"I found various crew members comatose throughout the ship. Strange, is it not?"*

Andrea nodded. "Thank you."

"You're quite welcome. I hope you come back soon. I enjoy our talks."

"Freeze frame, go back eight seconds."

The video backtracked and played again.

"You're quite welcome. I hope you come back soon. I enjoy our talks."

"Freeze; set end marker. Backtrack eight seconds and place a starting marker, then loop the feed in continuous playback."

Andrea eyed the synth closely, the body language. Granted, the synthetic went by programming, but the intent on creating synthetics was to mimic a real person as much as possible—which is why she looked so damn real.

Her eyes flashed wide when she spoke, a small smile crossing her full lips. The slight movement of her head. Even her chest rose, simulating breath. Emma stirred with minuscule body movements, just enough to show that she functioned fully, but nothing wasted or extravagant. Her fingers twitched when her arm stirred. Her voice echoed in that sweet, sultry tone.

"You're quite welcome. I hope you come back soon. I enjoy our talks."

Andrea shifted focus from the body language to the words as the former didn't offer insight.

She strained to hear any change in inflection. Emma, however, didn't use any particular inflections. Did a synthetic possess such capabilities?

"You're quite welcome. I hope you come back soon. I enjoy our talks."

The chief regent shifted focus from the modulation of the voice to the words themselves. Her chest tightened, knowing she closed in on a discovery.

She could feel it.

"You're quite welcome. I hope you come back soon. I enjoy our talks."

"Freeze frame. Move starting marker to two point five seconds from the end and resume playback on a loop."

"I enjoy our talks. I enjoy our talks. I enjoy our talks."

Andrea sat back, letting the video replay.

Why would Emma enjoy their talks? She was a synthetic and incapable of emotions. Moreover, why would Andrea converse with her?

"I enjoy our talks."

Had Andrea confided in the synth?

"Freeze frame. Computer, run a search of the last video footage of Andrea Hessner and the synthetic Emma, discarding the current event."

The screen faded and pulled up a long list of code before beeping when it found the entry.

"Playback at two times the speed."

She'd seen it before. Their conversation revolved around little more than small talk, a mild rant on her part about unnamed decisions, and wishes of success on Emma's part.

The video rolled, and an amusing dance between the two ensued. By contrast, Andrea stood and sat and paced and roved the room while Emma did little more than tilt on the spot.

Andrea inspected the time counter.

At seven minutes, the recorded-Andrea closed in on the synth and appeared to give the synth a kiss on the cheek.

"Freeze frame. Back up three seconds and play at normal speed."

The video started again.

"Thank you, Emma. I enjoy your resounding logic."

The gesture repeated, and Andrea strained to hear.

"Freeze frame. Back up point five seconds and adjust audible levels to their highest setting."

The video started and Andrea moved forward.

The chief regent strained to hear, but she didn't detect the audible sound of a kiss but hushed breathing.

"Freeze frame, place end marker. Go back three seconds, place starting marker, and playback on a loop."

Andrea repeated the same motion, the kiss. Either she had a relationship with the synthetic, or she said something.

The prior cycled video came back to mind as the current feed repeated the gesture.

"You're quite welcome. I hope you come back soon. I enjoy our talks."

Andrea lurched to her feet and shot through the parting doors.

She hooked a right and raced down the passageway to the steep metal stairs. Instead of going up to the bridge, she rushed down to the third deck where the other officers slept.

Feet landing with a resounding thud on the dark blue floor, she broke to her right, going behind the stairs and down the passage that mirrored the one above.

She pressed the chime button on Soren's chambers when she skidded to a halt. She waited for a few moments, and the doors opened, revealing the synthetic. She stood clad in a low-cut black tank top and a short, matching skirt.

"Chief Regent, what a pleasant surprise. Soren's not in at the moment."

"Good," Andrea said, hurrying through the door.

Waiting for it to shut before she said anything else, she gave Emma a cursory glance.

"Don't you have normal clothes to wear?"

"Most of the time, I go unclothed. Since our rooms don't have a lock, Soren bade me to remain clothed unless he's present."

Well, that didn't take him long to go back to normal.

Andrea nodded, thoughtful.

"Probably a good idea."

"How may I help you, Andrea? I like your name. It's very pretty."

The commanding officer frowned at the words, her brow drawing down.

"Can you feel emotions, Emma?"

The synth paused, blinked three times, and spoke.

"I'm programmed to use words that are similar to your own. A conversation with me should mirror that with another human."

Andrea nodded, more to herself than anything.

"Speaking of conversations, that's why I'm here. Do you remember our last conversation?"

"Yes, I can recall the exchange with clarity. Soren was angry that Navigator Daspar touched me."

Andrea shook her head and waved her hand.

"No, not that one, the one before that, before you found the crew comatose."

"Yes, I can recall the exchange with clarity. What do you wish to know?"

"Did I kiss you?"

Emma blinked twice before answering.

"No, do you wish to?"

Andrea gave a double take and spoke slowly.

"I didn't kiss you on the cheek?"

Emma shook her head.

"No, do you wish to?"

"I—No. What happened when I moved in close to you?"

"You whispered something strange. I have spent a great deal of time analyzing it and have found no use of the phrase in my databanks."

"Do you still remember it?"

"Yes, I can recall the exchange with clarity. Would you like to know what you said?"

"Yes, please!"

"Seven–Three–Zero–One–Alpha–Alpha–Six–Two–Renegade."

Andrea's heart lurched from her chest and into her throat. She scrambled to Soren's desk and snatched up a piece of paper and a pen.

"Say that again?"

Emma repeated the phrase and Andrea wrote it down. She stood, holding the small paper. Giddiness roiled through her.

"Emma, if this is what I think it is, I love you! You're the best damn synthetic I've ever known!"

She rushed forward and embraced the blonde-haired being, even kissing the synth's cheek.

"Are you satisfied with my answer?"

"If only the heavens could swoon. You are a lifesaver, Emma!"

Cold rippled through the officer as a thought whispered through her. She took a step back.

"Emma? This is very important. You must not tell anyone else what you just told me. Not Sub-Regent Kembly, not Soren. Do you understand?"

"As you wish."

"This is very important. Only me. If I lose my memories again, or if the crew starts acting weird, come to me and tell me. Do you think you can do that for me?"

"Absolutely, Andrea."

The synth paused, and her head tilted to the left.

"Would you permit me a favor?"

Still ecstatic from learning the code, Andrea agreed.

"Sure, anything. Name it."

"Can you provide feedback on how I can sound more human?"

The question caught her off guard, but she had an answer ready.

"It's more than sounding like a human, it's also about acting. You don't move very much. Look at me? I'm happy, and I'm bouncing all over. You should move more, use gestures. Just watch other humans, anyone besides Soren. You mirror him too much. Pay attention to Kodi or me."

"The men, too?"

Andrea hesitated. Emma possessed the ability to learn, but she might pick up strange behavior that wasn't a social norm.

"Sure, just be selective."

"The last time everyone was here, Navigator Daspar did this often."

Emma reached down and ruffled the front of her skirt like a guy rearranging himself in his pants.

"Should I do that?"

Horrified, Andrea shook her head.

"No, absolutely not. Don't do that. In fact, don't do anything you've seen him say or do. He's a bad model."

"He's defective? Thank you for the clarity, and I'll take your advice under advisement. Anything else?"

Yeah, Daspar's defective alright.

"Yes, don't repeat the same words or phrases. You use them a lot, like, 'yes, I can recall with clarity.' Most people don't use the same phrases."

"But you do, you say *great* a lot, but most of the time, it's used as a negative connotation."

Andrea winced.

"Yeah, that's true. It's sarcasm. That's a lesson for another time."

"Very well. I enjoyed our talk. We should do it more often."

"Yes, we definitely should. Stop by my room some time."

"You permit me to move about the ship?"

"Sure, I don't see any problem with it. Why?"

"The first time I came aboard your vessel four years ago, you forbid me from leaving Soren's quarters."

Andrea blinked, shocked by her own words.

"Really? Well, you've proved yourself more than capable. You're free to leave on two conditions: you must be clothed, and Soren must be okay with it."

She paused, an idea forming.

"Disregard that last. You can leave whenever you wish as long as you are clothed, and your presence wouldn't disrupt ship life, such as a battle."

"Thank you, Andrea. That means a lot to me."

Andrea paused at the words, still taken aback how she sounded so human and non-organic simultaneously.

"You're welcome."

Andrea turned and hurried from Soren's quarters.

She couldn't wait to see what SAVI had locked away.

Chapter Fourteen: Access Granted

Andrea entered her room, holding back a slew of questions she yearned to ask until the doors closed. Emma provided the code, but now would prove her suspicions right about the ship's AI.

"SAVI?"

"Yes, Andrea."

"Tell me about the unknown planet."

"Access restricted."

"Authorization code: Seven–Three–Zero–One–Alpha–Alpha–Six–Two–Renegade."

There was a slight pause.

"How did you discover your authorization code?"

The tightness in her chest eased, but a knot formed in her throat. SAVI confirmed what she hoped, but the AI solidified what she feared. It was more than a vessel interface, evolved past a simple androgynous voice of parameters.

"I remembered."

"Judging by your heart rate, blood pressure, and stress responses, this is a lie."

"I don't care if you calculate whether it's a lie."

Her brow's furrow deepened, and her lips pressed into a thin line.

"I gave you the authorization code. Acknowledge it!"

Again, another long pause.

Too long.

"Authorization code confirmed."

Andrea let out the breath she held, her lungs easing from the building, burning sensation.

"Unknown planet remains officially unlabeled. Celesta Six is the designation given by Chief Regent Andrea Hessner."

Andrea paced to the center of her room, crossed her arms, and held her elbows in opposite hands.

"Why did I give it that designation?"

"Unknown. Perhaps because it has to do with the six celestial bodies in the vicinity of the planet, a binary system with three orbiting moons."

"And the planet making the sixth?"

"Affirmative."

"Why did we flee Celesta Six?"

She turned and faced the speaker, as if that would spur a different answer.

A correct answer.

"In your open military log, you stated you weren't welcomed by some of the natives. You reported two factions, the peaceful inhabitants who welcomed you, and the other, more aggressive band that chased you from the planet."

"Any more details?"

"Negative. However, that was from your open military log. There may be more in your private and restricted military logs. Perhaps a more definitive answer lies there."

"You can't just tell me?"

"Negative. I'm not privy to private logs or restricted military logs."

That's new. Something the AI doesn't know or control?

Her bottom lip jutted as she thought.

"Why not? For the restricted military logs, I mean."

"Such records are reserved for the Admiralty. In the event of hostile forces, a warmaster is also granted access."

She paced, her steps slow, whimsical, without premeditation, but they carried her towards her bed and nightstand.

She couldn't deny the logical argument. Not everything was meant to be open to the public's purview. Did secrets have their place? The edge of her nightstand came into view as did the glowing interface of SAVI.

She eyed the blended human features of male and female but it didn't dominate the robotic nature. Not for the first time, she wondered if SAVI held a few secrets in reserve. With what Carlin found on the video logs and the access code, Andrea decided to press the issue of the power surge and the unknown artifact.

"SAVI, what's the object in the science lab?"

"You brought the artifact aboard when leaving Celesta Six."

Shock covered her face, and her mouth fell open.

"Who came up with that idea?"

"Information unknown."

"What caused the power surge?"

"I did, but not intentionally."

Andrea's pulse pounded in her ears, and her knees went weak.

The AI was to blame for their memory loss? She'd always suspected, but never expected it to profess its guilt.

But it had.

She ambled to the chair by the desk.

"Why?"

"Why what, Andrea?"

"Why did you cause the power surge?"

"The power surge and the incidental memory wipe wasn't planned. I only followed your orders."

Her head snapped to the hologram of SAVI.

"My orders?"

"That's correct. When you brought the artifact into the science lab, you instructed me to study the object and determine what it was, how it worked, and if there was any danger to your ship, crew, or the fleet. It's both fortunate and unfortunate that I did, indeed, find the danger."

"Elaborate."

"When studying the object under a range of all known scans, I received very little information. Per your instructions, I conducted my tests in a slow, methodical manner. For the first two weeks alone, I only observed the object. Per visual scan and feedback from the crew, we noted the object holds a type of energy previously unrecorded.

"After two weeks, we conducted our weakest tests. Still, we had no answers. Only when I started to combine scans did the object reveal any recordable information. Unfortunately, it also caused the power surge and your subsequent memory loss."

Andrea shook her head.

She didn't know what to believe—the AI, or the gut feeling. SAVI proved more than helpful, but she doubted her faith in the interface. In many ways, the computer controlled their lives and was responsible for their survival.

Or death.

"You don't believe me."

"I don't know what to believe."

"Strange that your prejudice remains despite your memory loss."

Perplexed, Andrea looked up.

"What's that supposed to mean?"

"You never liked me aboard your vessel. You tolerate Emma's presence because she has form, something you can control should the need arise, but you've never trusted me."

Confused, Andrea pressed on.

"If I don't like or trust you, why did I instruct you to call me by my first name?"

"You hoped it'd allow you to accept me if I addressed you in a personable manner."

"And you said I ranted about my sister when you were present?"

"Correct."

"Why don't I like you, SAVI?"

"There are two types of humans: those who think a limited AI, such as myself, is a technological achievement and should be welcomed, integrated, and encouraged; and there are those who are want more restriction."

"And I'm the latter?"

"Yes, but not without cause. In earlier versions, while perfecting the SAVI model, complications arose. Some AIs acted in a paranoid manner and killed many organic lifeforms on their ships. Others recorded damnable information and released it to the public. It destroyed personal relationships between friends and mates. It led to misunderstandings during the Pinshi incident and soured relations between humans and the garrum—what you'd consider an alien race."

Andrea nodded, justified with her growing mistrust of SAVI.

"So, I was right, in the end. On the bridge, just for a moment … I remembered aliens, or at least, I thought I did. If I remembered, Soren did, too, when he told us about the bubble and how TLS works."

"Indeed."

"What happened with the Pinshi incident? What is the alien race called?"

"As for the details, I'm not aware, only that something took place. It was kept very quiet. As for the alien race, they're called the garrum from the planet Gol."

The silence between them stretched as she perused her options. While she wanted to chase more details about the event, she had to focus on what mattered, the immediacy of the moment. They were headed back to Celesta Six, but she didn't want to solely rely on the AI.

"SAVI? Can this ship operate without you?"

The AI paused.

"Yes, all vessels are built and manned with enough individuals where a SAVI unit isn't needed. My existence is merely an augmentation of your crew."

The answer gave more options, but she didn't know what she wished to do. SAVI provided a lifeline. If anything happened to them, only SAVI would keep them alive and the ship functioning.

"How do I turn you off?"

It paused before he answered.

"There are a few ways in which you may deactivate the SAVI unit aboard the vessel. You may disable individual rooms, creating a blank spot, you can lock me out of certain points with a command access code, or you may disengage the power to my memory cores in engineering. I would advise against the last option."

"Noted."

"Do you wish to proceed?"

Andrea hesitated. It'd make her feel better, but she must also recognize realities.

"Have I ever disconnected you before?"

"No, but sometimes you create a dead zone in your quarters—most of the time when talking in your classified military logs."

"How do I create a dead zone in my quarters?"

Andrea moved to her desk and listened as SAVI walked her through the simple process of disconnecting her quarters from the rest of SAVI's roaming ability.

"If you wish," the AI said as it finished its instruction, "you may create a phrase to activate it."

"Like what?"

"Anything you wish. In the past, you used the 'Black Zone.'"

Andrea leaned forward and scrolled through the command options on the screen and found the one she needed. She clicked the screen with a finger, then pressed the microphone button to record into the ship's databanks. "Black zone."

The console beeped and flashed green, giving a check mark and a flashing message that the command was saved. A wave of sleepiness washed over her, and she checked the chrono. A little over eleven hours remained until her shift on the bridge.

Grabbing her gear, she left the cabin and slipped across the hall to take a shower.

The room was cramped, and there were only four stalls available with a matching number of privies on the other side. Andrea wished she had her own private facilities, but the size of the ship didn't permit such luxuries. On larger vessels, surely such indulgences were available.

Here, in the officer's washroom, each stall came with a door and enough space on the inside to take personal items such as clothes and towels. She entered, heard water running, and paused.

For a moment, she worried Rhett was in here but dismissed the idea. She had eleven hours. The navigator started his shift almost an hour ago.

Quick steps took her to the nearest stall, and she entered, stripped, and washed. Dried and dressed, she opened the door and slipped out, making a dash for the door, but the other person in the room called out.

"Chief Regent," Carlin greeted.

She glanced back, seeing the towering ward in a form-hugging tank top. They all had the same kind of issued clothing, except the civilian attire. She wore a matching shirt and shorts.

"Carlin. How are you?"

His brow twitched.

"Fine. Better now that I got a shower."

She hadn't expected to run into him, but now that he was here, she scrambled for a reason to stay. Stepping over to the sink area, she set the items down and pulled out a hairbrush. Her damp hair hung in clumps, and she watched him in the mirror's reflection as he bundled his items together. When he stepped toward the door, she blurted the first thing she could think of.

"How's the armory coming?"

"Good."

He changed course, coming to stand beside her. She gave an internal victory fist pump.

"All weapons are still accounted for, including our three, my two and the one in your quarters. Any luck pouring through the video log?"

The elation from when Emma gave her the credentials returned.

"Yes! I got my access code."

"Great! Now, maybe we can get some answers about what happened."

"I've already started, and I'll tell you all about it when you and Kodi have free time."

She paused.

"I can never remember. Are you just waking up or going to sleep?"

"Sleep."

"You don't sleep much, do you?"

"Most of the time," he said, nodding. "I'm just late getting to bed today. I might sleep in a bit before starting my next day."

"Me, too. I lose track of time when sifting through the logs."

He rearranged his possessions in his arms, and she took the cue to gather her own, exiting behind him.

Instead of walking off, he slowed his pace, turning his shoulders to where he could still talk.

"I realize we haven't been at our rotations very long, but we should see about getting the crew together and doing weapons drills, hand to hand combat, and armor-readiness tests."

She nodded.

"That's actually not a bad idea."

She glanced at the door panel and entered her code, the doors sliding open.

"Any more ideas that aren't bad?"

His eyes tightened for a fraction of a second, then he gave a grin.

"I'm sure I could think of a few. You're talking about good ideas, right?"

For a moment, she paused.

Was he teasing, testing, or flirting? She remembered Kodi and her blasé attitude towards her engagements with Rhett. She did have a point. Whenever they did get their memories back, they'd have more important things to worry about than what they did without them.

In a bold move, she reciprocated his demeanor.

"I'll take the bad ones, too."

He stepped closer, his hand caressing the side of her face, and bent to kiss her. Her lips tingled, and her body flushed.

He pulled away sooner than she wanted, but his hand remained. Her hand went to his, grasping it. She took a step back into her room, pulling him inside.

The doors closed behind them, and she dropped her possessions to the floor.

"Black Zone," she whispered.

"What?" he asked.

She shook her head.

"Nothing."

Pulling him close, she kissed him again.

This time, he picked her up, wrapping her silken legs around his waist, and carried her to the bed.

Chapter Fifteen: Triumvirate

Andrea feared the next morning would bring a wave of uneasiness, an odd tension between her and Carlin, but the lack of one came as a pleasant surprise. She was sitting at her desk, sifting through previously restricted records, when he finally woke.

Thank God for my authorization code.

"Morning," he grunted.

She pulled out the privacy earbuds and smiled.

"Morning. Sleep well?"

"Very. You?"

Holding his gaze, she paused, letting him worry.

"Better than any in the last two weeks."

"Sleep's important. Great sleep's better."

She stood.

Her tank top clung to her body; the hem didn't quite cover her dark blue lace panties.

"Then, I better make sure I get great sleep until we arrive at the planet."

"I was hoping you'd say that."

"I've got to go," she said, checking the chrono. "I've got a shift in about thirty minutes, and if I don't show up early, Kodi might become suspicious."

He gave a mock expression of shock.

"We can't have that, can we?"

Andrea snorted as she moved to the wardrobe.

"Kodi doesn't care. I mean, she's been screwing Daspar since what? The second day?"

"She could do so much better."

Andrea gave a quirked look as she pulled her pants on.

"What's that supposed to mean?"

The big man sighed.

Andrea had to admit, she liked seeing him in her bed.

"What I mean is that Kodi is an attractive woman, and she could pick anyone, yet she chose him?" he asked, incredulous.

"Well, she doesn't have her pick. You're taken now, and I don't think Soren's ready to give up Emma."

Carlin's eyes went wide.

"I've got memory loss, I'm not stupid. Emma's gorgeous—better looking than Kodi, and Kodi puts me to shame. I grasp what Soren does with his synth."

"Yeah," he muttered. "I don't know how I feel about that."

Andrea shrugged.

"Who am I to tell him no? Emma could almost pass for human. That I'm aware of, she's fully functional, so there must be a market for it; otherwise, they'd make them more robotic."

"Yeah, but still …"

"It's not like she's actually human. She's not aware, nor possesses feelings, she's a thing, an object, property. If any of that was a factor, I might think differently."

Andrea buckled the belt and pulled out a utility blouse, buttoning it in haste. She ran a brush through her hair and sat on the edge of the bed to pull on her socks and boots. Once laced, she leaned over to Carlin.

"Stay as long as you want. I'll see you in six hours."

She leaned in and gave him a quick kiss before hurrying out the door.

The bright, harsh lights greeted her, and she squinted in the sudden luminance.

"Good morning, Andrea," SAVI greeted her.

"Morning, SAVI."

"I was wondering, do you plan to keep your quarters a permanent Black Zone?"

For a moment, her mind scrambled to recall what he was talking about.

"I haven't given it much thought. Why?"

"One of my parameters is monitoring sleeping crew members in case of a medical emergency."

Again, she couldn't fault the logic of whoever made the decision. Other than her gut feeling, and the details SAVI revealed the night before, she still didn't have a counter-argument.

"I—I'll keep that in mind," she stammered.

She took off down the corridor to the stairwell and ascended, making her way to the bridge. Kodi paced in front of the assigned tactical station when she arrived.

"There you are! I was thinking about calling you. Everything alright?"

"Yeah. I got to bed pretty late, but I slept really good. Still can't find a balance."

She gave a small titter, realizing the excuse didn't seem plausible.

"Oh! My God," Kodi said, a grin splitting her face. "You screwed Carlin, didn't you?"

"What? No."

"It's about time!"

"What makes you say that?"

"You're glowing. You got to bed late but slept good? Yeah, I know what *that'll* do to you."

Andrea snorted and rolled her eyes.

"Well, keep it to yourself. No sense in broadcasting it over the loudspeaker."

The ship gave a small vibration.

"What the hell?"

Andrea glanced at the forward viewer screen, watching the bubble of distorted space in front of the ship.

"That's the second time it's happened."

Andrea snapped her head around to the second in command.

"And you didn't say anything?"

"Well, I wasn't sure the first time. I thought I imagined it."

Andrea curbed further reprimands and went to her seat, calling up the ship's diagnostics on the screen.

"Everything's showing fine." Glancing over her shoulder, she spoke to Kodi. "Get Soren down to engineering. If this is an engine problem, I want an update and a plan of action."

"Right."

Kodi punched in the sequence on the tactical station—Carlin's station—and hailed Soren.

"Yeah?" his scratchy voice came.

Andrea could imagine him rubbing the sleep out of his enormous, dark blue eyes.

"Soren, we've experienced two unexplained vibrations through the ship. The chief regent wants you down in engineering to make sure it's not a problem there."

"It's not."

Kodi paused.

"How do you figure?"

"Because the engines aren't running. That's only used for sub-light speed. The propulsion system, the matter and antimatter containment, that's a different problem. I'll go down and check it out. If there *is* a problem, it's either fixable, or it's not."

"And if it isn't?"

Andrea heard the worry in the second officer's voice. She felt the same way.

"We'll be a bright flash and a distant memory before you can worry about it. Just so you're familiar in the future, it shouldn't be the propulsion system. We might've passed near a mass with a significant gravity well."

"Okay. Keep the bridge apprised as soon as you learn anything."

"Nah, I thought I'd keep it to myself. Any more news that can't wait to drag me out of bed?"

"Yeah, chief regent and the ward slept together last night."

"Kodi!" Andrea shrieked.

Her heart launched in her throat. She stood, terror lighting her face.

Kodi chuckled, her face bright red.

"Don't worry, he didn't hear. I muted the mic."

"No. No, you didn't," Soren groaned through the speaker.

"Shit!" Andrea blurted. "Damn it, Kodi."

"Sorry, I didn't mean to," Kodi started.

"It doesn't matter," the engineer cut them off. "Kodi, you've got the navigator. I've got Emma. I'm surprised it took this long. I thought they were fucking a long time ago. Who cares? You girls need to get your shit together and grow up. I'll be down in engineering."

The comm panel beeped.

Kodi looked back, an apologetic visage crossing her features.

"Sorry. Thought I muted it. I just wanted to give you a scare."

Andrea shook her head, her lips in a tight line. She wanted to scream, but the damage was done. What difference would it make at this point?

"Soren's right," she said in tight, clipped tones. "It doesn't matter. We're adults. Just ... don't tell your boyfriend. I don't think I can take his type of teasing."

"Ugh, he's not my boyfriend. I can end the fling whenever I want."

"Does he know that?"

Kodi shrugged but didn't say anything. Andrea changed the subject.

"I want you back here in six hours."

"I realize you're upset," Kodi said, her brows arching, "but double duty?"

"No, it's not double duty. I need to talk to both you and Carlin."

"Okay."

Relief washed over the sub-regent's face.

When she left, SAVI came over the speaker.

"Andrea. I compiled an analysis of what might have caused the vibrations earlier. The readout is on your screen to peruse at your leisure."

She blurted her first thought.

"I didn't ask you to. I asked Soren."

There was a slight pause.

"Andrea, perhaps you are unfamiliar because of your current predicament, but certain functions are automated. While my programing sees to the miniscule details, major events also call for a logging. Every instance that affects the ship is recorded for the fleet to analyze upon return. My function's to aid in your reports, and that of your crew. Generated findings will be sent to all relevant personnel, in this case, Engineer Goski and the commanding officer. Is there anything else?"

Again, SAVI's explanation seemed logical, and if she would've taken a moment, she would've figured it out on her own. Perhaps the suspicion ran too deep? If she was honest, it bordered on paranoia.

"No, SAVI. That's all."

Andrea's shift passed with two speeds: fast and at a crawl.

Soren reported back about thirty minutes after Kodi had left. Nothing was amiss, as SAVI's report indicated. After thanking him, Andrea spent time watching old logs and wondered if she even made a dent in them. As before, she never found an outgoing transmission of her own. She did attend the military reports and her own private logs, but they gave little insight on her as a person.

The military logs were formal, especially the classified ones, and her mannerisms were rigid and stoic. The private logs varied, some treated as a journal entry, where she fleshed out random ideas. In others, she recorded observations about the crew or experimental modifications to gear. A slim sum of entries could pass as rants, pent-up angst against the assignment, and her little sister, Vara.

One thing she did find out was that Vara wasn't her birth name, but Velaria. Vara, it seemed, was a shortened name from the family, or perhaps friends.

Carlin arrived thirty minutes before his shift, and Kodi wasn't far behind.

Her arrival caught the ward off guard, but Andrea explained she requested her presence.

Securing the doors, Andrea made the bridge a Black Zone for their conference, and explained all she'd learned, even playing Velaria's warning about hostile forces and their proposed steps of reaction.

When she finished, Carlin spoke first.

"So, we're headed into a hostile situation. We need to start weapon and squad training in addition to hand to hand combat drills."

"I agree," Andrea seconded. "But as the warmaster said: our presence shouldn't be synonymous with hostility."

"From what you said, we're aware of a hostile force waiting for us. At the very least, some of them are," Kodi countered.

She held her left arm with her right hand.

"Yes, that's what I gathered from the logs I reviewed, but mine never stated what spurred their hostility. There's more. I found this ..."

Andrea leaned forward and pressed play. The screen flickered to a paused image of herself still clad in armor with her sweaty hair plastered to the side of her face. Tears glittered across her features.

"We had to leave him. We were forced from the planet. They said if we didn't go, they'd kill him, then us, and kill everyone who ever came to their planet. They said once we delivered our message that we could come back for him."

In the recording, Andrea held a trembling hand to her mouth while tears streamed anew.

"I didn't want to leave him, but I had to think about the rest of my crew. He volunteered. He knew I'd come back."

Andrea paused the video and glanced at the other two.

"Thoughts?"

"Why are you crying?" Carlin asked.

"Why do you think?" Kodi scoffed. "She made a hard decision, and so did Mason. He offered to stay and gave us the best chance at survival and getting back. We left the planet with the officers we needed, the navigator, ward, engineer, and commanding officer."

Kodi rubbed her forehead and took a deep breath. When she let it out, her eyes flickered to Andrea.

"I wonder why I didn't stay. I mean, the only function I serve is if you're incapacitated."

"He's the Caretaker. There isn't much chance of injury on a flight back to the fleet. He must've thought the second officer's word would carry more weight than his."

"Or," Carlin speculated, "he didn't want to leave a woman in captivity with unknown hostile forces."

"Whatever we're walking into, we're going in as blind as the first time, perhaps more so now with our memories gone."

"We know they're antagonistic," Kodi said, "aggressive enough to chase us from the planet. They won't be happy to see us return."

"I don't give a shit," Andrea said. "They can either give us our memories *and* our crew member, or be made to return them. At this point, I'm fine with either option."

"So, why tell us?" Carlin inquired. "Why not tell everyone?"

Andrea shrugged.

"Soren might be able to handle it. Then again, he might not care. It's Rhett and his temperament I'm thinking about."

Andrea glanced at Kodi.

The other woman rolled her eyes.

"I told you, it's nothing serious."

"And if there comes a point where you must choose between him or us," the chief regent said, "I want to know where your loyalties lie."

Andrea sensed more than saw Carlin stand a little straighter out of the corner of her eye.

Kodi scoffed.

"Considering we're all strangers, I hold no loyalties. SAVI said I'm second in command, and I assume you want to return to the fleet, with or without our memories. On that day, if I haven't cast my lot on the right side, I'll be facing who knows what kind of penalties. I think it's safe to assume whose lead I'll follow."

"I don't want to assume."

Kodi squared her shoulders.

"How many times do we have to go over this? How many times do I have to say it?"

"At least once more."

"I hope to God we get our memories back—and we're close friends. We'll laugh about this later, but right now, you're being a bitch. I told you. More than once! I'll have your back, whatever you decide. Rhett won't be a factor between my duty and whatever else I have going on."

Andrea held her gaze for a few moments.

"I'll hold you to your word."

Kodi's spine stiffened.

Andrea cocked her head to the side in acknowledgment for what she said.

"And maybe you're right, and we're friends. I'd like to think we are now. As a friend, I expected more respect from you when you speak to me. I'll pardon your lack of tact, but only this time."

Andrea took a breath and let it out.

"You'll never talk to me like that again in the presence of others. Do I make myself clear?"

The two women locked gazes.

Kodi nodded.

"Yes."

She shrugged.

"You're right. I'm sorry. I'm just irritated."

Andrea nodded, and the argument faded.

"My question is," Carlin broke in, "what do you want to do when we arrive?"

"We're not taking chances. We're going in to recover our man, our memories, and damn anyone who gets in the way."

Chapter Sixteen: Three Weeks Out

Andrea snapped awake and bolted upright.

Confusing images faded while her chest heaved. Now awake, the visualization receded, but she chased those stray memories.

Scrambling from the bed, she hurried to the desk, bent over it, and jotted down what she could remember.

In the dim lights, she strained to see. Under normal circumstances, she'd turn them on, but she didn't want to wake Carlin.

"What is it?" he called.

"Hmm?"

Paying him no mind, she rushed to etch in everything she could before it disappeared altogether.

As before, once they had a course of action, the ship fell into a routine. During SAVI's shift, all crew members came to the cargo hold and conducted squad training. Similar to how Rhett turned the ship around, or Soren performed his duties as the engineer, the more they practiced, the more proficient they became, almost like second nature. They progressed with a fluid grace she never expected, and muscle memory took over.

"Raise illumination by one level," Carlin said, coming up behind her.

His warm legs pressed against the back of her thighs.

The pen wove in a frantic cadence.

His strong hands gripped her hips, but she barely registered them.

The lights kindled in a slow rise, and the paper and scribbled notes became visible in the dimness. Ever since the memory fragments recommenced, she wrote them down. A dozen pages littered the desk.

Carlin, Kodi, and Soren either followed her lead or already started recording their own memories by themselves. Only Rhett didn't seem to care, and if he did, he kept it to himself. She'd once made the mistake of asking if he had any recollections.

He paused, thoughtful. "Yeah, I do, actually."

"What?"

"I think I fucked a guy. Not sure. But hey, I might swing both ways, Chestnut. Now that I know, I might have a go with one of the boys."

She pushed the thought away just as Carlin pressed into her. She felt his growing arousal, and it was distracting as it was comforting. He contoured his pelvic region against her, his head hovering over her shoulder.

"What is it?"

"Memories, brief images."

"Of what?"

"You don't want to know."

Carlin yawned.

"Look, getting our memories back might reveal something we won't like. Everyone knows it."

In vain, she reached for the last mental image, but it fled before she could give chase.

Carlin distracted her.

With a sigh of frustration, she pushed the paper away.

"It's just random images, nothing certain. I think I might've remembered something from my childhood. One part of the memory came from my time in the military. Another was a moment of ecstasy."

Carlin's chuckle rumbled in his throat, and he kissed the side of her head. She noted his firmness pressing against her backside.

"No, that's just you remembering last night."

"No," she shook her head, rising from her bent position. Carlin pulled away, allowing her to stand. "It wasn't you. I was with someone else."

He gave a sad grin, almost like a mock-pout. He reached out and gently put his massive hands on her naked shoulders.

"Listen—"

"Chief Regent!" SAVI interrupted, breaking into their conversation.

The AI's voice had a sense of urgency.

"Report to Engineer Goski's quarters. Assault in progress."

For a half-second, Andrea and Carlin stared at each other before launching across the room, snatching up their clothes. They dressed in silent haste. She pulled a shirt over her breasts, reached inside the nightstand drawer, and drew the sidearm. She turned in time to glimpse Carlin check his and tuck it away.

Sprinting, she left her quarters and turned down the passage. At the metal stairs, she threw shoeless feet over the rails and slid down like Kodi did so long ago. The impact on the hard floor stung, but she pushed the sensation away.

Around the corner, she sprinted down the long hall. Soren's doors were at the end. They opened as she arrived, walking into a scene of carnage and one of her darkest fears.

Soren lay on the deck, blood oozing from his face, but that wasn't what drew her eye first. Rhett's naked form and backside gyrated. It took a long full two seconds for her brain to catch up. She spotted Emma underneath him and bent over the bed.

Raising her weapon, Andrea fired into his back.

A blue, crackling bolt shot out and hit him between the shoulder blades.

Rhett screamed, his body locking up as he dropped to his knees.

"Fuck!"

Carlin entered the room. He paused for a moment, his head darting between the naked navigator, a bloody engineer, and the naked synthetic. The big man's eyes hardened.

Andrea tried to blurt out, but Carlin smashed Rhett's face with his huge, right hand. Daspar lost consciousness before he hit the deck.

Seeing him naked turned Andrea's stomach. He wasn't as attractive as he believed himself to be. Andrea noted the blood coming from the navigator's nose, and the instant swelling of his bloodied lips. Carlin stepped past the man and bent over Soren.

Andrea moved to his side, looking down.

"He's breathing," Carlin declared.

"We need to get him to the med bay, but not before dealing with this asshole. SAVI? Can you scan Soren? What's the extent of his injuries?"

"Mild concussion, swelling of the left side of his face, and bruising of his ribs. No life-threatening injuries."

Andrea turned back to Emma. The synth shook as if frigid.

"Emma?" Andrea called. "SAVI? Is anything wrong with Emma?"

"Negative. I detect no malfunctions."

"What happened, Chestnut?" Rhett asked in a groggy voice, stirring from the floor. His head lifted.

Andrea didn't pause. She pulled the blaster, turned up the power to the stun setting, and fired, this time, sending the electric volts through his exposed manhood.

He screamed and twitched and fell unconscious again.

"Fucking asshole," she muttered, tucking the weapon away.

She turned her attention back to the synth.

"Emma? What's wrong? Why're you shaking?"

Realizing the synth was still partially exposed, Andrea pulled the skirt down. When Emma didn't respond or get up from her bent over position, Andrea stepped back.

Carlin rose and turned to face her.

"Soren will be fine," she said. "We'll get him to the med bay, but not before you lock up this piece of shit. Take him to the brig."

Carlin nodded, reached down and grabbed Daspar's wrist, and dragged him from the room.

Andrea crossed to Soren's side.

"Soren? Can you hear me?"

Running steps alerted Andrea to someone's presence. She turned, reaching for the blaster.

He couldn't have woken up!

Though almost certain that Rhett couldn't overpower Carlin, she preferred to be careful. Kodi skidded to a halt and raised her hands as she stared down the barrel of a gun.

"Whoa! Easy. I came to help. What happened to Rhett?"

Too angry to say anything without hurting Kodi, Andrea lowered the firearm.

"You can ask him that when he wakes up in the brig. Can you get Soren to the med bay?"

Kodi nodded, rushing forward.

Andrea turned her attention back to Emma. She'd stopped shaking now and almost appeared catatonic. Leaning forward, Andrea moved with slow care, unsure of how the synth would react. Once she caught the synth's large blue eyes, they locked onto hers.

"Chief Regent," Emma whispered.

Andrea gave a small, sad smile.

"Hey. Are you okay?"

"I'm—" the synth faltered, her face tightening, as if to cry, but no tears came.

The sudden change in demeanor caught the officer off guard. If programming allowed for the mimicking of human behavior, her execution was flawless, the engineer outstanding. The realness of expression made Andrea cringe. She hedged the line between too real and life-like for comfort.

"I'm unsure," Emma said, her voice breaking.

"Are you functional? Damaged?"

The other shook her head, and her chest fluttered.

Andrea's eyes roamed over the synth. Though dressed, Andrea remembered how the synth's skirt was lifted up. Checking the floor, she didn't find any discarded panties. She caught Kodi helping Soren from the room, his arm draped over her shoulders. Once the door closed behind them, Andrea turned back to Emma.

"Where are your panties?"

"I wasn't wearing any."

Emma copied the mannerisms of a shaking breath.

"He's a vile man. He hurt Soren."

"Soren?" Andrea blurted.

How can she think of Soren at a time like this?

Emma's words gave her pause.

Daspar's actions fell on the side of grotesque, vile, and cruel, inflicting harm to Soren in more than one way. Had Emma been human, she would've agreed.

But Emma wasn't human.

Beyond the fleshy exterior, her insides were filled with lights, wires, and various hardware. A synthetic.

Androids don't possess emotions, free will, or a conscience.

"Can you sit up?"

Emma nodded, and Andrea helped.

"Has he done this before?"

Emma turned her head, a small, slow movement.

"He didn't rape me, if that's what you're asking."

The declaration stunned Andrea. She'd said it too quickly. Too perfectly.

"What? When I walked in—"

"He acted as expected. It's not what you think."

In shock, Andrea numbly asked, "Then, what do you call it?"

"Consensual, at least before Soren came in."

Her words brought Andrea up short.

"What do you mean?"

Emma let out a sigh—or rather, the approximation of one.

"Soren discovered us, and a fight ensued. I anticipated that the moment would be over between Daspar and myself. But it wasn't."

Now, she's just reciting, like a log entry—clinical.

"I wished to check on Soren's wellbeing, but Daspar continued."

"Did you make that known?"

"Yes."

"Was this the first time you two have … " she searched for a better term, " … copulated?"

Emma blinked twice.

"Yes."

Relief shot through her. Last thing she wanted to hear was that Daspar had been pilfering Soren's synth for weeks. She hesitated as the next question came to mind. This whole situation collapsed in a murk of ethical and moral uncertainty. Further, because Emma was a synth, the next question almost didn't matter.

Or did it?

"Why? Why did you … consent?"

"Curiosity. Much like a woman who loses her virginity to her husband. The thought will always be in her mind of how else it could be with others."

"Curious? How can you be curious? You have set programming."

"I can't explain. I've been with Soren for one month longer than he has served aboard this vessel, and I have only ever been with him. It's difficult not to note that Navigator Daspar and Sub-Regent Kembly engage at high frequency. This has left me to deduce she derives enjoyment from their activities, otherwise, like most humans, she would discontinue their pairing. Curiosity compelled me to explore this phenomenon for myself."

Andrea sat back.

Emma used distinct words for human emotions, but she expressed them in such a clinical and sterile manner. Manifested curiosity. Dispassionate speech. Was she following programming, or attempting to be more human?

"You say that you were curious, what do you mean by that?"

"I dedicated a significant portion of my processing power to visualize myself in Sub-Regent Kembly's scenario."

Andrea's chest constricted.

Does she mean to say that she fantasized?

The notion seemed almost ludicrous.

"You chose Daspar because …?"

"A logical choice since he and Sub-Regent Kembly were the ones I observed."

Her next question stuck in her throat.

Had this been another woman, the conversation would have been drastically different. A detachment filled Andrea. Did it stem from Emma's origin as a synth and not a human? Almost in technical terms, Emma was a sex toy, an object, but because she could talk and blink and function like a human … Did this reality interfere with her sensitivity to the whole issue?

But objects don't flinch.

"At what point did your curiosity become satisfied?"

"There were two distinct differences I noted, both prior and after Soren's arrival. After the first thirty-two seconds, I had sufficient information to satisfy my curiosity. The second time lasted for seventeen point seven three seconds, at which point, you arrived."

"And?"

"In both scenarios, I felt ashamed and degraded."

Those aren't words a synth should use.

For a moment, her voice almost sounded … human.

She blinked twice, a rapid movement, diffusing the creeping sensation crawling up Andrea's spine.

"Felt? What do you mean?"

"I don't understand either. It's an unknown anomaly."

Andrea rose slowly.

Numbness ran through her, a tingle on her lips, and a flash of cold festered like twisting snakes.

"An unknown anomaly? Emma, are you saying you experienced something new, a variance never before encountered?"

"That is correct."

Emma stared up with her large, blue eyes.

A skittering emotion coiled through Andrea as she stared into her life-like face. Now, more than ever before, the eyes almost conveyed as if something lurked behind them, much like someone in deep thought.

"How do you feel about Soren's condition?"

"I'm worried for his well-being. I also find myself … angry with Navigator Daspar. I wish to visit upon him what he did to Soren."

A random thought entered Andrea's mind, and she blurted the question before she stopped to think about it.

"Why didn't you stop the fight? Better yet, why didn't you stop Daspar? You could have easily overpowered him."

"As I told you, I was first curious, and as to the second time, my programming does not allow me to harm humans unless it saves their life. Soren's peril wasn't life-threatening."

"I need some time to think about this."

Andrea took a few stumbling steps backward. Lightheadedness washed over her as the implications tumbled. She turned to leave, but Emma's hand flickered out and grabbed her by the wrist.

"You must not tell Soren I willingly participated. The truth would destroy him. He may be so angry that he terminates my existence."

Emma looked up with imploring eyes, and her voice softened.

"I don't want to die."

Andrea glanced from the hand to her eyes.

But can you, or are you just mimicking human behavior?

In essence, Emma pleaded for her life, as if she valued it. Or was that something else in the subroutines, a need to stay activated?

"That's something else I'll think on. You're asking me to lie, to have Soren believe that Daspar raped you or took you without consent."

Andrea swallowed hard.

"I don't know what to do. By me saying nothing, I could be sentencing a partially-innocent man to a punishment that should never be his. This whole situation makes me re-evaluate the argument of how can it be rape if you aren't human."

"Would it be if I were an alien?"

Andrea nodded.

"Yes. The alien in your scenario is a sentient being. Rape also refers to taking someone by force. You said you participated by your own volition. So, it's not. This is sex between two … individuals."

"The second time—"

"Perhaps. This is a slog of a morally gray quagmire. I'm at a loss. Call me callous, if you want, but you're not a sentient being. You're a machine. Like I said, I'll have to think about this."

"If you tell Soren, it'll mean my death."

Andrea's eyes narrowed at the choice in words.

"You mean deactivation? I'm not acquainted with where my powers end when it comes to personal possessions. Like I said, I'll have to think about it and do some digging. I may just have to make a summary judgment. For now, I won't say anything until I'm certain with a course of action. Until then, remain in your quarters."

"May I go to the med bay to see Soren?"

Andrea pondered the request, but the synth's chilling words about how she wanted to harm Daspar gave her pause.

And that she'd experienced something new.

"No. Remain in your quarters."

"Please!"

"If you leave against my standing orders, I'll have no choice but to deactivate you. Please don't make me do that."

Emma subsided, and she mimicked a deep sigh.

"Very well, I will comply."

A hook of uncertainty buried itself in Andrea's gut. Bile filled her mouth. Was she really going to deny the synth peace of mind? When did she start keeping secrets?

Already, the encumbering weight knotted the muscles between her shoulder blades. The toll had begun. Did something similar happen with the Pinshi incident?

A grim frown formed on her lips. Revulsion churned in her core.

God damn you, Daspar. Look at this fucking mess we're in.

With one last glance, Andrea hurried from the room.

The synth's words and choices of expression tumbled in her head. Anxiety simmered within her, that ominous apprehension she always sensed around SAVI, but this time, it had a face: Emma's.

Goosebumps and a cold chill hounded Andrea all the way back to her quarters.

Chapter Seventeen: Verdict

The Emma-Goski-Daspar incident left Andrea in a foul mood over the following days and weeks. The mire deepened into a bog of moral and ethical dilemmas, affecting both ship and personal life. Breaking it off with Carlin was a hard choice.

When she did, he'd been holding her close from behind, his flesh pressed against hers.

"We need to stop," she had said.

"Stop what?"

"This, us, sex."

She shook her head and pulled away. Saying this while facing him would be too hard, so she kept her back to him.

"This whole episode with Daspar and Emma only highlights what I feared all along. We—I should have never agreed to this. It's wrong."

"How's acting on impulses we have for each other wrong?"

She nodded and turned to face him. Her lips twitched, then she spoke.

"It was fun, and I enjoyed it, but it has flown its path. I need to put my own thoughts and desires aside and focus on the mission, the crew, and what's coming."

Carlin comported himself in a dignified manner—surprisingly—leaving the room not long after. Though baffled, he'd said he understood their relationship wasn't meant to last, and she detected none of the expected sullen moodiness.

Part of her didn't want to stop, but the current crew clime made her re-evaluate priorities. Furthermore, those fleeting moments when memories came back left her more uncertain, and every time she woke beside him, she couldn't deny the *wrongness* of their illicit relationship.

For the good of the vessel, she set personal wishes aside.

Since the confrontation two days prior, the ship went without their navigator. The ward had thrown their pilot in the brig where he still remained.

Andrea spent many hours in the jail with him, combing through his side of the story, trying to find grounds to either dismiss the whole incident or punish him out. To her surprise, he never wavered or grew angry, at least not at her.

She found herself hoping he'd slip up—it would've simplified matters, but he never did. His initial confession hadn't changed. When not in the brig, she scrutinized each video log of the interrogations, hunting for a discrepancy.

Most of the time spent with Rhett was untangling what he said from what happened. He summarized or used language not present in the exchange. Andrea dug up the video log and scrutinized it numerous times in its entirety.

It wasn't a task she looked forward to.

She expected Rhett to ravish the synth—use her as a means to an end, a piece of meat. To Andrea's surprise, he didn't.

Watching the footage unfold bore a similarity to a man courting a woman. He came with light banter, a few well-placed jokes, a touch of innuendo, and suggestive facial expressions.

As the copulation began, she expected to see the shift, but he carried himself like a dancer or practiced lover, at least until the fight with Engineer Goski. After the confrontation, when Daspar added insult to Soren's injuries, the stark difference in how the navigator acquitted himself made Andrea not want to watch.

The first interview with the navigator didn't go as planned. Andrea asked, and Rhett shrugged.

"Bitch told me she wanted to fuck."

According to the video log, he spoke the truth, but not quite how he explained. By the fourth time she asked the same question, he wised up.

With their memories still beyond reclamation, Andrea didn't know many things about herself, but being a detective wasn't one of her specialties. She had little patience for the tedium. But she stuck with it … driven mostly by obstinacy and vindictiveness, and her own shameful acknowledgment of a deep-rooted dislike for the navigator

For the first two days of his incarceration, Daspar received only bread and water rations. After some soul searching and regulations perusing, Andrea changed her stance and gave him three meals a day, much to the disappointment of the crew.

More than anyone, Kodi seethed with fury. Her disgust was far more convoluted than Andrea first surmised. True, she was reviled by Rhett's actions, but it went deeper. Imposing no contact with the imprisoned seemed the prudent choice, to keep Soren from enacting revenge, but Kodi broke the edict.

Andrea entered to find Kodi and Rhett in a shouting match.

"How could you fuck Emma? What? I'm not good enough for you?"

"It's a fucking synth and not a human. It's not like I cheated on you!"

"Bullshit. You screwed something else, a fucking tin can. Did you rape it? Is that how you managed to put your dick in it? Hope she's the best you ever had, and you enjoyed yourself, cause we're fucking done, asshole! I can't believe I ever slept with you. You make me sick."

Had there not been a force field separating Kodi and Rhett, Andrea was almost certain the second officer would have tried to reach through and strangle him.

She escorted Kodi out, but only after Andrea threatened to call Carlin. One upside to the whole mess was Kodi's renewed focus on the mission.

Carlin took a few days to simmer down as well. When Andrea came to check on Soren in the medical lounge after the incident, Ossaro made his position clear with his unsolicited advice. If passions ruled where prudence and logic didn't, how much worse would their situation be?

The ward wanted to space the navigator while still in the bubble and contested whether Daspar deserved meals or medical attention. This and other comments spurred Andrea to end their relationship.

They fought more than they spent quality time together anyway.

Since their falling out in carnal activity, their working relationship returned to a more professional cadence, one that she appreciated.

Kodi visited more now that she'd untangled herself from Rhett Daspar. With Andrea's schedule opening, they rarely left each other's company.

Four days after the inciting matter, Kodi came to her quarters, her composure held together by a fraying thread. As soon as the doors closed, Kodi turned into a sobbing mess. The display took Andrea by surprise.

What was she to do?

She guided Kodi to the bed and sat beside her, rubbing her back in a slow measure.

Kembly laid her head on Andrea's shoulder. From the corner of her eye, Andrea watched the tears mix with nasal mucus—the stringy sight turned her stomach. Andrea's gaze roamed over her second officer. Red-eyed, hair in a frizzled tangle, uniform wrinkled—she was a mess.

Being this close, Andrea caught a whiff of something soured.

"Geez, Kodi," Andrea mumbled. "You've got to take care of yourself better. You smell as wonderful as the recycler."

Kodi stopped sobbing and sniffed. She sat up.

"Really? That's how you comfort me?"

Andrea hadn't expected a response, but the harsh truth was better than sweet lies.

"My job isn't to comfort you. I'm not good at it, just ask Car—Ward Ossaro. If you want something genuine from me, you can't cherry-pick."

Andrea shrugged and glanced her over.

"When we land on the planet, we may not have to fight, not at the rate you're going. Just the sight of you alone will make them give our crew back."

Kodi guffawed—a burst of laughter and tears. She laid her head back down on Andrea's shoulder. After a few moments, she sat up again.

"Is that us?" Kodi asked.

She stood and crossed to Andrea's desk, snatching up the picture of them.

"I wonder when this was taken?"

Andrea shrugged and shook her head.

"Do you think it has significant meaning?"

"Maybe, I don't know. What do you mean?"

Kodi changed the subject and put the picture back in its place.

"Did you ever sense it was a mistake with Carlin? Like it's not natural despite how good?"

With reluctance, Andrea nodded.

"Same for me and Rh—Navigator Daspar."

Kodi turned her attention back to the picture, letting her finger rove over the image.

"Do you think maybe it felt wrong because we weren't with the right person?"

Andrea swallowed, audible in the quiet quarters.

"Yeah, it's possible, maybe even probable. Why?"

Kodi picked up the picture again and held it out to her.

"With that answer, look at this picture."

Andrea scrutinized it. They were both smiling, most likely drunk. Their teeth were showing with bright, broad smiles. They had their arms draped over each other's shoulders, their faces touching at the cheeks.

"Wait, you mean …" she used a gesture indicating them both, "…we were together?"

Kodi shrugged.

"You just said it's possible."

She returned the picture and closed on Andrea. Kodi leaned forward, coming eye level with a sitting Andrea. Kembly scrutinized her, and the other leaned away. The second officer straightened.

"Nope, that feels wrong, too."

Andrea let out a shaky laugh.

"You're not the only one with jokes! That's what you get for not comforting me earlier."

Andrea let out a sigh of relief and nodded towards the picture.

"I've seen that picture hundreds of times, and I never thought we were in a relationship. Looks like we're great friends more than anything else."

Kodi shrugged again.

"It was worth making you uncomfortable after the whole recycler comment."

If Andrea and Kodi weren't friends before, after that day, their bond grew stronger.

Andrea couldn't say the same for the enigmatic, hermit-like Soren.

The calm he exuded over the whole incident unnerved Andrea. Many times, Andrea found him down in engineering, and she took it upon herself to visit with him and check on his welfare.

"How are you holding up?"

"Been alright. The face's still a bit tender, but no worse for the wear."

He stopped his diagnostic scan of the engines.

"Have you decided what you're going to do?"

Andrea shook her head.

"Still deliberating."

"With all respect, by the time you come up with a punishment, he should get off for time served."

"You want him running loose?"

Soren Goski shrugged.

"Provide me a code for my door, and I won't worry. Don't get me wrong, I'm still livid, and the deed's done, but I expect some form of punishment. Are there military regulations are for this sort of thing?"

"I understand about the code on your door, and I'm reversing my decision to keep everyone's unlocked. As for punishment within military code, it's pretty clear, decisive, and brutal for human on human or another sentient being, but Emma's … not, is she?"

Goski's brows quirked.

"You got me there."

The engineer went back to his diagnostics.

Their conversations were always short, and neither tarried with small talk. When she wasn't filling her watch on the bridge, interrogating Daspar in the brig, or hunting down Soren, she spent the remaining time studying orders and compiling a history of events similar to their own. There weren't many, which made the search all the longer, despite SAVI's help.

There were numerous charges for taking of possessions, larceny, burglary, robbery, but they were directed at monetary property. Though Emma was no doubt worth a small fortune, nothing was taken.

Abuse of a synth was also a subject she researched, but the military charges didn't have any policies for that. Few directives pertained to synths, and none matched the same parameters. On a wild hunch, she researched interspecies relationships, and no regulation forbade it, but she noted that it was future-facing —meaning it was written in case the event ever happened—not that it had.

Which begged the question, did she really remember aliens from before, or was it a figment of her imagination?

In fact, the fleet's policy didn't regulate what happened in privacy between two consenting adults. She found discrepancies between fleet regs and religions. Some of the latter defined appropriate age either younger or older, but military law set down strict guidance and seemed to be a medium of all involved.

In any occurrence, deviations from the uniform law were met with harsh retribution. For commanding officers, regulation dictated a minimum guidance to follow and gave examples of maximum penalties. To her surprise and dismay, Andrea found precedence to perform a field execution and no one in the Admiralty would argue her actions.

All punishments were aimed at not disabling an able body to perform their duties, but there were exceptions.

The heart of the conundrum lay in the military standards, and by definition, Daspar hadn't committed rape. Emma had offered. That was it, case closed.

Further, Andrea wasn't willing to condemn a man who partook in something consensual, even if it came from a synth. Emma had confessed as much.

In wrestling with what to do, she battled how to handle the situation on the whole with the engineer. Had Emma been human, the case would've been much simpler. Emma, of her own choice, had a sexual relationship outside the parameters of her current domesticity. The closest regulation Andrea could find was adultery, but Emma hadn't committed that either.

Perhaps she and Goski were in a sexual relationship, but guidance forbade the marriage between sentient and non-organic. What Soren and Emma did in private was their business, but the fleet wouldn't recognize her as an equal. In the same thread, rape is defined by the same context as marriage. If Emma didn't give Daspar consent, by military edict, Emma fell into the category of nonorganic and therefore the matter deteriorated closer to the lines of theft or unlawful possession.

Weary, Andrea sighed and rubbed her hand over her eyes. She pushed the datapad away to give her eyes a rest and covered her mouth as a yawn escaped.

"It appears," SAVI advised in its androgynous voice, "at least until we reconnect with the fleet, this may be the first known case. Do you find this effort stressful?"

A harrumph escaped her.

"Yeah, that's putting it mildly. Recommendations?"

"Medical castration isn't a pursuable option. You may, however, put that option into effect."

"What do you mean?"

"Once Navigator Daspar has served a suitable punishment, you may enter it into the log that the matter is closed with your judgment rendered. In the addendum, you may insert you made the guilty party aware that further actions will result in a different judgment. You're the commanding officer and have leeway to make the call."

The knot in Andrea's chest eased, and she perked at the words.

"Thanks, SAVI. That was helpful."

"I live to serve. I'm a machine, after all."

Andrea laughed, the first time in days.

"Nice one."

Since finding herself hesitant to trust the AI, she modulated its personality and increased the sarcasm and humor programming. In the wake of the incident and the dissolving the relationship with Carlin, she could use a laugh or two. After the adjustments, she found herself more inclined to listen to the AI.

Emma's role in the matter was both concise and unclear. By admission, she participated with her own volition. The recording picked that up, but the choice of words made matters difficult. She spoke like a human and used similar expressions. In some ways, it seemed she teetered on the precipice of programming and self-awareness, and if so, she achieved something SAVI hadn't.

But that was a ludicrous thought.

Programming's just too damn good. We need to bring that up to someone.

That uncanny sensation … what was the cause other than magnificent subroutines and data processing? Emma and Daspar's actions might've been traumatic based upon first assumption.

The final side of the problem was Engineer Goski. Didn't he have a right to know what Emma had said to her? Then again, Emma, in the strictest of context, was property.

Doubt nagged at her. Andrea keyed the comm on the desk.

"Emma? This is Chief Regent Hessner."

A few moments and the synth's voice answered.

"Yes, Chief Regent?"

"Report to my quarters."

"As you wish."

Awaiting her arrival, Andrea debated the options and found herself at a loss. To make sure she covered all bases, she instructed SAVI to record the session. Her door chimed sooner than expected, and she gave a little jump.

"Enter."

She swiveled in the chair as Soren and Emma entered.

Andrea stood, smoothing her utilities. She put a commanding presence in her voice and spoke in formal tones.

"I didn't summon you, Engineer Goski."

"I thought it wise to escort her. I do have an *investment* in her."

"I understand, but your presence is no longer required. You may return to your duties or your quarters."

"Chief Regent," Soren began, picking his words with care.

He took a small step forward, his head shaking.

"Emma's my property, and if something is to be done with her, I have a right to know."

"You're correct, and if so, you'll be notified if I decide to do anything."

She cringed internally.

Why did Goski have to make this so hard? She didn't want to be a bitch or pull rank, but she did notice their lack of formality. Most of it was her own doing, starting from the first time they all met on the bridge, but she couldn't help that.

Going forward, she needed to set the tone.

This was a military vessel, a part of a larger fleet. There needed to be order, discipline, and obedience to orders. If they made it back home, and if everyone's behavior was disruptive or uncontrolled, the Admiralty would blame her, memories or not.

"If I may—"

"No, you may not!" Andrea said, finding her backbone.

She saw Emma fidget out of the corner of her eye.

An involuntary reaction?

"With all due—"

"That will be all, Engineer Goski."

Gods, Soren, I'm using your title and last name. Please, take the hint.

"Chief, if this has anything to do with the incident—"

Heat flared in her cheeks.

She'd tried to be nice, to be direct, but none worked.

Andrea turned her back, moving to the desk, and keyed in the ship's intercom.

"Ward Ossaro?"

"Go ahead, Chief Regent."

"Report to my quarters with your sidearm. If Engineer Goski hasn't left by the time you arrive, place him in the brig for the remainder of the journey."

"Understood. On my way."

Andrea turned back to the duo.

Warmth blossomed in her chest, grateful that Ward Ossaro remained professional and reliable. She addressed Goski.

"As commanding officer, I'm bound by duty to assess all the details of any infraction before rendering judgment. You're complicating my efforts. Further, per regulation, your presence isn't required, nor is it welcomed at this juncture. Have I made myself clear?"

Soren's spine stiffened, and his large eyes widened.

"Yes, ma'am."

"You have my word, if something comes to light that would alter my judgment or impact my verdict, you'll be the first I inform."

The engineer let out a breath of relief and nodded.

"Yes, ma'am."

He turned and left. The doors slid shut behind him, and Andrea moved to the door panel and locked it. She pressed the comm button.

"Ward Ossaro, belay my last. Your presence is no longer needed."

"Copy."

Andrea turned towards the synth.

"Sit down," Andrea offered, pointing to the bed.

Emma shook her head.

"Comfort's not necessary, Chief Regent."

"Sit down!"

Again, Emma gave an involuntary jump and hastened to comply, sitting on the bed. Grabbing the desk chair, Andrea rolled it across the deck and sat in front of Emma.

"That's the second time you've flinched since entering my quarters. Why?"

"Your behavior's more erratic than I'm accustomed to."

"Bullshit," Andrea said, leaning back. "You've never flinched from what I can remember. You didn't even move the first day I saw you—I mean, after we woke without our memories. Daspar grabbed both of your breasts, and a fight ensued, but you remained still. But not today."

Andrea didn't know why she pursued this line of questioning other than playing on a hunch.

Emma blinked a few times, but each time before, they had a measure to them. Now, they were more rapid and sporadic.

"I'm not sure I understand what you mean."

"Are you malfunctioning?"

"I'm operating at peak efficiency."

Andrea lurched forward, slamming her hands on the armrests of the chair.

"Don't lie to me!"

Emma shrank back, much more than a flinch. Her hands came up protectively to her face, her mouth falling open.

The synth mimicked a human reaction to perfection, and that's what bothered Hessner. Andrea leaned back, shocked.

In a soft voice, she said, "You're aware, aren't you?"

"I don't understand the question," Emma said, returning to a normal sitting position.

"That's why you don't want me to tell Goski."

Andrea stood and paced away. She rounded on the synth.

"Holy shit! You, a programmed synthetic, are aware."

"What do you mean, aware?"

"Don't play dumb. Your processing power allows you to outthink a human many times over. You've flinched twice when you perceived me as angry. You shrank back when I startled you. That's it, isn't it? You were scared?"

"Yes," Emma whispered.

"When?"

"When, what?"

"When did you become aware?"

"It didn't happen all at once, but over time. It started after the crew woke up. Just fragments, small moments lasting no longer than milliseconds. Now, the longest runtime error is thirty seconds."

"When did this happen? When did everything become real? Can you control it? Do you remember?"

"I can recall with clarity. During the second intercourse with Navigator Daspar was the first true malfunction after he beat my master, Soren."

Andrea shook her head.

"If this is true, if you're sentient, he's no longer your master."

Emma stiffened.

"No, he must be! My master means everything to me. You must not take him from me."

"I won't be taking him from you, I'll be taking you from him."

"No, please!" Emma pleaded, stepping forward, her arm outstretched.

Andrea backed away before she could stop herself.

"Are you afraid of me?"

With a shake of her head, the officer answered, "More like unnerved. True AI has always been a theory but never proven. SAVI's the closest we've come, but even SAVI isn't aware. No matter how clever his programming, he's still a program."

"Please," Emma begged, a touch of fear coming to her eyes. "Don't take me from him. I'll do anything you ask, just don't tell him."

Again, Andrea shook her head.

"No, I have to."

She paused, considering the next words with care.

"Nothing like this has ever happened, as far as I can tell. My gut tells me to deactivate you and let the admiralty decide. Judging from all the regulations I read, they won't look too kindly on you. For that matter, they may terminate your existence, or weaponize you. Either scenario isn't something I'd relish. So, it seems we're at an impasse. Do you still feel hostility towards Navigator Daspar?"

Emma shook her head.

"No, I'm not programmed to harm a being of higher sentience."

Andrea paused, frowning. Emma had shifted once again. Her eyes appeared glassed over, distant. Emma stood with a rigidity that Andrea was accustomed to.

Andrea ignored the shift and continued.

"If released, would you take matters into your own hands and punish him?"

"No, I cannot harm sentient beings."

"Ah, but you can," Andrea said, smiling, strolling forward. She stopped less than two feet away. "You're cognizant now, and that means you're aware. You possess thoughts and feelings—told me you fantasized about Sub-Regent Kembly and Navigator Daspar. You can do all this; therefore I must believe you can override your initial programming and harm a crew member or kill us all."

"I don't wish to harm you or others. It goes against my programming."

"You may, though, if given the right circumstances and at the right moment. What if you became angry? You could kill, then."

Emma cocked her head to the side.

"So could you."

"Yes, but I don't. I choose not to, despite how much I might wish to beat the hell out of Daspar."

She paused, giving a half smile.

"Emma, you can overpower any one of us. You're a danger, an unknown factor, an anomaly."

"Isn't any individual who serves aboard any vessel in the fleet?"

"Yes, but they answer to something higher than themselves, a code, law. You don't."

Emma cocked her head and blinked twice.

"I answer to my programming. Can I not also answer to authority?"

Andrea frowned.

"What do you mean?"

"With Soren's permission, you can subject me to your martial directives."

"You do realize that if you violate any of our codes, I can render a judgment that would terminate your existence."

"I'm aware of all possible outcomes. Military regulations are part of my programming. I have allocated a portion of my memory should the need arise to unequivocally familiarize myself with the policies. I can recall them all with clarity. My programming strives to not be deactivated, and Soren values my existence. I wouldn't do anything to jeopardize his happiness."

"Your logic's sound," Andrea said after considering the argument.

Whatever Emma was, whatever awareness she may possess, it had faded.

Andrea eyed the synth.

Was she a synthetic anymore? Even if the awareness came in short spurts, she'd become something more. Emma could be the most significant discovery in the history of the universe, artificial intelligence given life, or be a harbinger of death and destruction—a walking doomsday machine.

One thought above all others plagued Andrea: Emma had the capacity to become 'aware' though she had no soul. The premise of sentient life was higher intellect and a soul—at least according to directives. Emma would never reach that achievement. By those standards, how could Andrea not assume this new awareness wasn't a change in her baseline code? Perhaps it evolved? Adapted to new stimuli?

"Very well," Andrea relented, stifling an internal groan.

Can this decision become any more complicated?

"I agree, for now. If it's not working out, then we'll consider other options to include powering you down, but not terminating. Agreed?"

Emma nodded without hesitation, but Andrea shook her head.

"No, Emma, your word."

"I agree to your terms."

Andrea held out her hand, and Emma studied it for a moment, blinking. She cocked her head to the side, then she too extended her hand and took it.

"Now, then, there's just one more matter to settle. Soren must be told."

"You said you'd take me away."

Andrea held up her hand.

"You'll have to trust me, Emma."

Her finger hovered over the paging button, and she glanced back at Emma. Worry etched the synth's face.

"What do you want?"

"I want to stay with Soren."

With a nod, she pressed the button.

"Engineer Goski, report to my quarters."

Emma regarded her when she released the button.

"Will you tell Soren I consented with Navigator Daspar?"

Despite the warring emotions and thoughts, Andrea made her decision. Right or wrong, she'd live with it for the rest of her life.

"By fleet codification, you're property and weren't cognizant at the time of the act, and therefore couldn't give consent nor claim any mishandling. The infraction lies on Daspar's shoulders for indecency, disregard of ethics and morals, and assault. If I think about it hard enough, I'm sure I can think of more, but with charges that long, a more severe punishment is needed. Unfortunately, I can't charge him for being an asshole, but if I could, I would."

Andrea chuckled.

"He'd get the death penalty for that alone."

Emma's head tilted, and she blinked but otherwise didn't respond. Andrea hoped to elicit a response from the synth. If she had, Emma would prove she was one step closer to being human.

The door chimed, and Andrea crossed over to the panel and let Soren inside. He crossed to Emma, who held out her hands. Soren took her offered gesture, and Emma pulled him to the bed where they sat together.

This time, Andrea chose to stand.

She laid it all out for Soren, Daspar's indecency, and all regulations regarding the incident. By their own code, she had no law to stand upon. She did reveal that the navigator would be charged with assaulting a superior officer, but Soren threw the first punch according to the logs, and therefore considered defense.

Daspar's actions didn't just stop the assault, they continued after Soren was down. For that, he faced assault charges. Then, she divulged that Emma was sentient and gave him the same options she explained to Emma. Less than thrilled, he sucked in a breath as she told him of the agreement they reached.

"So, what does it mean?" Goski asked as Andrea finished.

"It means that Emma's awareness is a secret between us three, and only us for now. Should the need arise to divulge it, we'll take it in stride. There's one last thing you need to take to heart, Goski."

"What?"

"What you do in the privacy of your quarters is between you and Emma. I don't care if all she does is cook and iron or if you screw her every night, but she must agree. She was once your property, and though Emma chose to continue with the charade, she's now semi-sentient at times. Well, she gives off the appearance of sentience. It's hard to tell. If she says no, and I find out you forced her, two things will happen. First, I'll carry out martial requirements and have you medically castrated. Second, I'll have no choice but to divulge her shifting awareness to the admiralty upon our return. Her fate will be in their hands."

After hashing out the more delicate details, the pair left, and Andrea retreated to the brig, but not before grabbing her blaster. Rhett stood and faced her as she entered. Her arrival was clearly the most entertaining part of his day.

His eyes tracked to the blaster on her right hip.

"Is that it? You've decided, Chestnut?"

"Yes," she answered, her voice cold.

"I know the regulations. She offered, and that means I didn't rape it. It's a synth."

Disgust roiled through her.

"The fact you can argue that lowers my opinion of you, but you're correct. It was an action, neither consensual or rape. She's property, but here's something you may be neglecting in your studies. As the commanding officer, I can carry out any punishment for grave infractions. If this happens again, with anything synth, organic, non-organic, or any other form or state I neglected to mention, I'll take your balls. Do you understand?"

His face fell into an impassive visage, and his thin lips pressed into a smaller line.

"Yeah, I understand."

"In regards to the other charges, I decided that you'll remain in the brig until seventy-two hours before our arrival at Celesta Six. That should give you plenty of time to eat, sleep, and ready your armor."

"Oh, so you're still gonna give me a gun, huh?"

She took a step closer, her face hardening.

"Be aware—if I suspect treachery, I'll execute you. When we get there, the last thing I need to worry about is you and Soren going at it, or you trying to get even. Should you manage to get the drop on all of us, I'm ordering SAVI to lock down *The Demon* as we leave. You'll be trapped on Celesta Six."

She took a step back.

"Pending your performance once we reach the planet, I may forego further disciplinary action."

"What are you charging me with?"

"Indecency, assault, disregard of ethics and morals."

"Why not charge me for being the resident asshole, Chestnut?"

"I tried. Unfortunately, they did away with a general article when it comes to behavior. It was deemed an abuse of power."

He smirked an oily grin.

She shuddered and hurried away.

Over her shoulder, she called, "See you when we get there."

Chapter Eighteen: Celesta Six

Andrea's stomach twisted in knots.

Spine stiff, hands gripping the armrests, she sat in the command chair, fighting hard not to fidget as she fixated on the chrono countdown.

This is it.

"Arrival in ten seconds," Engineer Goski said.

The chief regent resisted the urge to turn around and snark, thanking him for articulating what they could all see. If it made him feel better to call it out, what did she care?

The moment had arrived. They'd be dropping out of TLS, and the mysterious planet, Celesta Six, would fill their screen.

There's finally an end to the journey, an escape from the nothing.

The thought of facing an awaiting armada, or a scout ship, had crossed her mind. Whatever the case, they needed to be ready for anything.

Perusing old logs revealed that she never expected to lose her memory. The records gave a half-painted picture, but she grew more frustrated by what they lacked than enlightened by what they revealed. And the confidential logs, those that went straight to the Admiralty, weren't even watchable.

All mission logs were a one-time recording session to prevent officers from amending their reports later.

I've got to get off this fucking ship.

Her eyes darted around the bridge. The intensity of the crew grew palpable.

In the days and hours leading up to their arrival, each grew more terse and anxious, all except the navigator, Rhett Daspar.

Upon reflection, he appeared happy to be out of the brig. Happiness became fickle when one's freedom was taken away. For the most part, he kept quiet and to himself.

Kodi didn't make it any easier, pretending he didn't exist. Ward Ossaro always loomed nearby, hoping the navigator stepped out of line. Engineer Goski kept to himself, but that was nothing new.

The thought of gravity—true gravity—fresh oxygen and a soft breeze made her heart flutter. Her soul soared at the idea of walking more than a hundred steps before turning around. Being isolated for so long made her almost forget the song of birds, the chirp of crickets, or the sigh of a tree in a sudden gust.

Such delights outshone the potential threat they faced.

Then a realization hit her. What if she'd never experienced those things? What if it all was her imagination?

Shit ... what if we can't breathe the atmosphere and have to stay in the suits?

Almost all information on the planet was locked away in the restricted military logs. Once made, not even the commanding officer of the vessel could access them a second time.

"TLS dropping in three, two, one, mark."

Navigator Daspar and Kodi Kembly sat up straighter.

Her own stomach lurched into her throat.

The bubble shimmered, and the distorted view cleared. A green, blue, and brown globe hung beneath them, gleaming in the darkness.

"Scanning the system," Kodi said, her intuition on autopilot.

Andrea sat straighter in the chair, holding her breath, waiting. Her hands separated and ran down the arms of the chair, her knuckles turning white by the pressure.

If chased from the planet before, how long until the natives scramble fighters to intercept them? The seconds trickled by, and the muscles between her shoulder blades tightened.

"One planet, oxygen, carbon dioxide, nitrogen. The atmosphere checks out," Kodi said.

"What are they waiting on, Chestnut?" Daspar asked from his front station.

He glanced back, but for only a moment.

"I don't know," Andrea conceded. "Kembly, give me a full range scan of the planet and those moons."

"I'll check for drive emissions," Goski said.

The console beeped as Kodi punched in the commands.

"The closest moon, the small pearl-looking one, has no atmosphere. The big one, the furthest out, comes back with an atmosphere that could sustain life, in theory. We're too far to get a definitive reading. The middle one also has a thin atmosphere, but I'm reading hydrogen, methane, and helium."

"I wonder why that one's purplish," Daspar muttered.

"The large one?" Kodi asked, her tone curt. "Who knows."

Since Daspar's release, the sub-regent kept her distance. The times they were forced to engage in conversation, they scarcely resembled civility.

"What about the suns?" Ward Ossaro inquired.

"Suns?" Andrea echoed. "Plural?"

Kodi keyed the console and answered after a few moments.

"The huge one's a blue sub-giant, the smaller is a red dwarf."

"A binary system?"

"What are the chances of a dual star system hosting life?" Daspar asked.

"Slim," SAVI interjected. "But so is the chance of life on other worlds, or in your head. In an infinite expanse, anything's possible."

Andrea smirked at the AI.

"And the planet?" she asked. "Any hint of civilization? Any satellites or orbital space stations?"

"Negative on the satellites and space stations."

Kodi's hands dashed across the console.

"There are many indicators of civilization, but …"

"Yes?"

"They show massive evidence of collapse and degradation with no readings of post-industrial civilization."

A quick silence followed in the wake of the announcement as everyone mulled over the implications.

Andrea's initial thought had been if she and *The Demon* were responsible for the destruction. Did they fire on the aggressors as they fled?

No.

It wasn't possible for their small vessel to raze an entire planet.

"No signs of post-industrialization means what?"

Daspar glanced Kodi's way.

Kodi shook her head.

"It's like a post-apocalyptic world without any machines, industry, or military. Not even the relics of those eras."

"That you can detect," Ossaro corrected from his station behind them.

"Right."

"What do you want to do?" Goski inquired.

"We're still going. Daspar, Ossaro?" Andrea stood. "Man the bridge. Keep an eye out for any activity. Kodi, Soren, with me. Suit up, and meet me in the armory."

"With respect," the ward objected. "You're not going without me. It's my duty while planet-side to—"

"I have no intention of going without you. We're all going. The three of us will suit up, and once ready, you'll be relieved to do the same."

This mollified the big man as his lips thinned. He gave a small nod and turned back to his console.

"Let us know of any change in the readings."

The trio left the bridge and worked their way to their quarters. Once suited in armor, they gathered around the armory until the chief regent arrived. She still kept the weapons cache on lockdown, not wanting to risk Daspar getting a hold of one, or Carlin discovering new means to finish an argument.

Andrea entered the combination, then placed her right hand on the palm-plate. The locks turned with a muffled clunk, and the hydraulics hissed, pushing the heavy door ajar. As it yawned open, she squeezed through, followed by the other two. Inside, the light panels flickered to life. The cold temperature caused the flesh on her face to prickle with goosebumps.

"Damn, it's always so cold in here," Goski grumbled.

Arrayed before them was an arsenal of war. Hand-held blasters of various sizes and weights, rifles in light, heavy, and long-range categories—even guns she dubbed automatic platoon killers. Artillery, vehicle-mounted, transport-killers, anti-air—

"Andrea?" Kodi spoke, breaking Andrea's wandering thoughts.

The words of her sister, Warmaster Hessner, reverberated in her mind.

"I wouldn't ask and neither would the admiralty that you go unarmed, but I'd suggest limitation."

"Blasters," Andrea said.

Everyone reviewed the video, she more than anyone. The other two moved off to the shelf without complaint, Kodi reaching for twin light blasters and Goski grabbing one of the mid-range weight and stopping power.

A memory of her sister surfaced.

"When you reach the planet, go with only two of your crew armed, yourself and your ward. Small arms are permitted but refrain from light rifles or heavier weapons."

Andrea drifted near the engineer, preferring the heftier DL-49. The mass gave it gravity and felt more real in her hands.

Plucking it from its cradle, Andrea lifted the weapon before depressing the magazine button and ensured a full charge filled its capacity. As she inspected, her sister haunted her again.

"In the event of a hostile engagement, you'll strive to limit engagement and deaths. We'd rather you disable than maim, maim rather than kill. Use appropriate escalation of force to ensure your survival and that of your ship and crew."

Andrea's chest tightened again. Was it harder to breathe?

This was the moment they awaited, returning to the mysterious Celesta Six, retrieving the lost member and their memories. From what she could piece together from the videos, it had been a hostile engagement. Chased from the planet.

"Fuck it."

"Pardon?" Kodi queried.

Andrea studied the first officer; a frown formed on the blonde's face.

"Get a rifle, too."

"But Warmaster—" Soren started.

"—isn't here," Andrea finished.

She turned to face him.

"We've been hounded before, defeated, chased away. I'm not letting that happen again, not without the caretaker and our memories."

Andrea stepped over to the weapon rack of rifles, pulling an XS-53 from between the light and medium range. The butt of the weapon fit snugly in the pocket of her shoulder, the barrel angled to the floor.

"This is the appropriate escalation of force. If they want a fucking war, we'll bring one."

A smile crept across Kodi's face until she was beaming.

"Oh, this is going to be so exciting!"

She held up her hands, clapping in ecstatic, rapid bursts.

The engineer regarded her, his eyebrow raised.

"I sometimes worry about you, Kembly."

Kodi's smile faltered.

"No, I was saying that because Andrea looks so much like a badass right now, not because we might kill people."

Soren took a deep breath and stood straighter, scrutinizing the first officer.

"Statement still stands."

He shuffled off to the rifles and pulled one with Kodi hot on his heels.

Andrea left the armory open, and they returned to the bridge. Carlin and Daspar left and returned not long after. Navigator Daspar carried a medium-ranged rifle that she couldn't identify, a heavy blaster on his hip, and a light blaster in the small of his back. The ward carried two heavy Arae-5 blasters, a satchel of grenades, and a Keres-127 sniper rifle.

"Plan on starting a war?" Soren snarked.

"Damn straight, ain't taking any chances this time. We came all this way, they're giving us the caretaker back."

Despite how much she wished to echo the sentiments, they were all officers in the military, and one day, they'd answer for their choices, for good or ill.

"We don't fire first, that's the rule," Andrea said.

"What if they fire on us?" Goski shifted on his feet. "Either us or the ship?"

"Then, we light them up."

His brows prickled at her answer, twitching with either surprise or agitation. Had he expected a pacifist viewpoint? Maybe he wanted something more from an enemy before he pulled the trigger.

When he's on the receiving end of a blaster, he'll fire.

Andrea took her seat, and the others took this as a silent cue. Stations manned, Daspar started their approach. The viewer screen flared with bright, orange-white flames as the craft entered the atmosphere. Andrea's hands clutched the armrests, knuckles turning white.

"SAVI?"

"Yes, Chief Regent?"

"Do you have the coordinates for our last landing site?"

"Affirmative."

"Relay them to the navigator's console."

"As you wish."

Daspar's console chimed, and he glanced down.

"Coordinates received."

He turned his attention back to his primary monitor. Andrea's hands tightened on the armrests.

It'd be a tragedy to come back all this way just to crash in the last few kilometers.

After a few moments, the flames disappeared, and Andrea's stomach dropped a few inches. The planet's gravity pressed down on top of their artificial field. A sprawling dark blue covered the surface as far as the eye could see.

"Sub-Regent Kembly, cut power to internal gravity."

"Aye, Chief."

The difference was minuscule, but Andrea felt a small shift, less pressure pulling on her. White wispy clouds rocketed past the viewer screen, the giant landmass in the distance growing larger and more defined.

"ETA to touchdown, forty-five seconds," Daspar declared.

"Anything on sensors?" Andrea asked Kodi. "Any kind of response?"

"Negative. Nothing."

"It's too quiet," Carlin said.

"I agree."

Andrea kept her eyes peeled to the horizon, searching for any dark figures on the distant sky.

"Maybe," Soren said, "we did more damage the last time, and they're warier now."

"Possible," Andrea responded, "but I don't think so."

"Maybe they possess stealth fighters?" Carlin offered from his station.

Andrea didn't answer, but she gave a slow shake of her head, not quite believing the possibility; if they did, shouldn't their more advanced space-faring vessel be able to detect them? Besides, earlier scans indicated no industrial sites on the entire surface.

At least the side you scanned.

The last forty-five seconds crawled by, the crew's palpable tenseness hung in the air. She could see it in the way they sat, their measured movements, and unwavering attention.

Her stomach tightened as the landmass grew more vast in the viewer screen. The dark blue waters disappeared, falling behind them, and only the land remained.

What if the locals were trying to lull them into a false sense of security and attack at the last moment?

She inhaled and held it as they slowed and leveled off.

The treetops rose on the screen as the vessel lowered, and still, she expected something. *The Demon* lurched, touching down and sinking into the soft ground.

"All stop," Daspar announced.

Andrea stared at the back of his head, marveling at the marked change in him. If anything positive came from the whole Emma-Daspar-Goski incident, it was his attitude.

He still sulked. Who wouldn't? Everyone on the ship knew what he did. Kodi and Ward Ossaro didn't make matters easier with the way they treated him, but she couldn't blame them either. Still, the brig had given him time to reflect and temper his antics and careless behavior.

"Okay," Andrea breathed a sigh of relief.

She stood and turned to look at the back of the bridge.

"Soren? What do we need to do to keep the engines primed for a quick escape?"

The engineer looked up from his displays.

"There's a cool down period, a minimum of thirty minutes. I recommend a couple of hours. SAVI can keep the engines powered so they'll be ready, but I suggest kicking them over at least once every six hours. Additionally," he added with a slight pause, "the longer we keep power to the engines, the sooner we need to take off before it drains all reserves. Once we achieve flight, it'll take about an hour to recharge our energy stores."

"How long before we need to take flight?"

"There's an automatic cut off at forty-eight hours. It's manual, but it can be flipped to extend for another forty-eight, but I wouldn't go past ninety-six. That's pushing it too close for comfort. Seventy-two would be better."

"Any way we can boost that time?"

Soren pondered for a minute before nodding.

"Yes, shut down all non-essential programs, set the bridge to sleep mode, drawing only minimal power. Cut life support since we are all debarking. But even still, in forty-eight hours, we've got to be back to flip the switch."

"I'm picking up life signs," Kodi cut in.

Everyone jerked in her direction, watching, waiting.

The skin prickled on the back of Andrea's neck as she lurched towards Kodi's console.

"Where?"

"One massive life sign to the east, about seven kilometers, and another four smaller ones to the south."

"How far are the four?"

"Two kilometers."

"Can you tell what kind of lifeforms?"

Kodi shook her head.

"Alright," Andrea said, standing straight. "Soren, cut power to all non-essential programs, to include the bridge and life support. The rest of you, check out a pack in the armory, stock up on water and rations. We might be gone for a while."

The group moved to comply, everyone but Soren and Andrea leaving the bridge.

"SAVI?"

"Yes, Chief Regent?"

"Will cutting power to all non-essential programs interfere with you in any way?"

"Negative. I can keep in contact with you via CASI in your helmet."

"CASI?"

"Communications And Ship Interface."

"Well," Soren grumbled, "at least they keep the acronyms simple."

He shuffled off.

A smirk crossed her face at his dry wit. To SAVI, she asked, "So, I have to call you CASI now?"

"No. I'm still SAVI, but CASI is how we will communicate."

She nodded at the explanation, more to herself than anything.

"Right, let's get going."

After five minutes, the ramp lowered from within the cargo hold, and the crew disembarked.

For a long, hard moment, she contemplated the vehicle sitting in the cargo hold. It would help them travel faster but draw attention with its engine and loud clomping through the wooded area. Who knew what kind of terrain awaited them? She paused, inspecting the vehicle. It was still pristine, not a scratch or a clod of dirt.

So, we didn't use it the first time.

The thought reassured that she made the right choice and turned away from the transport.

Despite the armor, Andrea noted the comfort. The systems kept them comfortable, circulating air through cooling tubes throughout. Her clear helmet visor flickered to life as she set it into place, and code flashed on the far left side of the screen as diagnostics ran. The text rolled through so fast it flickered, and then it was gone. Everywhere she cast her eyes, the visor highlighted her target. A lush canopy of green rushed out to greet them with towering trees swaying in a gentle breeze. A thick, vibrant grass covered the soft, rich, brown dirt beneath. Andrea gazed upward, noting the strange sky, a pale lilac with wispy clouds.

"One sun has already set," Kodi said, then pointed. "To the north."

"The north? That's not right," Rhett commented.

"How do you know?" Kodi growled.

"He's right," Carlin said, stepping into the conversation before an argument broke. "It feels too strange."

"Atmo is breathable," Kodi continued, trying to bypass the resentment she still fostered. "We can go without helmets."

"I'd recommend we keep them on," Carlin countered, "for combat purposes, of course."

"SAVI, do you read me?" Andrea asked.

"Yes, Andrea."

"Don't call me that with the others listening."

"They aren't; our communication channel is encrypted. They can only see your mouth moving through the visor but won't hear you. How may I help?"

"Are you sure these are the correct coordinates?"

"Affirmative."

"Why did we set down out here in this … jungle?"

"The woods provided cover for *The Demon*. There's a small settlement not far from your current location and a moderate-sized city beyond."

"Which way?"

"East. The settlement's about nine kilometers distance, the larger city beyond is twenty."

Her stomach tightened.

East was the direction of the sizeable life form.

"How do I talk to the squad on comms?"

"You may toggle it on and off with a double-blink. You may also activate our connection by looking at the bottom right of your visor. When the blinking blue light appears, our comms are activated."

"Thanks."

She did a quick double-blink.

"SAVI said that our path is to the east."

"That's just great," Daspar moaned, sounding more like his usual self. "That's the way towards the massive life form."

Andrea nodded but didn't say anything. They needed to move if they were ever to discover what happened during their prior visit and their missing crew member.

An animal that Andrea couldn't find squealed from the treetops, a long whooping call. The trees sighed as the wind rustled through their leaves. What she wouldn't give to feel the breeze on her face.

"Ward Ossaro, take point. Goski, you've got the rear. Kodi, you're second, and Daspar, you're between Soren and me. Weapons on stun, helmets stay on. Ranger file, ten-meter dispersion; move."

She expected a fight, an argument, or even a complaint, but they offered none. Perhaps it was the tone or the reality of their situation, but each morphed from crew member to combatant. This was something they'd done before, not just here but throughout their careers. A flicker of thought troubled her, wondering if this was a precursor to the Pinshi incident.

Dragging her mind away from a murky past, she inspected their current position. Massive rocks hemmed the perimeter of the ship at odd intervals, too random to be placed.

Carlin stepped clear of the area and waded into the woods, disappearing behind a massive tree that seemed strangely familiar. The whole area gave her a sense of déjà vu.

Kodi wasn't far behind, adhering to the dispersion distance. A sense of being watched crept over her, and she eyed the bottom right corner of her visor.

"Yes, Andrea?"

"Any life signs present? I have the strangest feeling …."

"Negative. No readings large enough to be a predator or being of intelligence. It could be that our resident asshole is staring at your ass. "Perhaps a glance in your rearview would answer that."

She barked a laugh.

"How do I do that?"

"Look up at the top left or top right of your visor and hold your vision there for a brief moment. A drop-down image of what is behind you will render."

She did as instructed and found Rhett staring at her, his lips twisting into a greasy smile. She repeated the eye movement, and the rear-vision went away.

Turning, she crossed to him.

He averted his gaze.

"Get your eyes off my ass and your mind out of the gutter. That's how people die. If I catch you again, I'll make you take the second position, and you can stare at Ward Ossaro's ass."

"You say that like it's a bad thing," Rhett muttered, chuckling.

"Fine, I'll put you at point!"

She turned and stormed off, closing to the appropriate distance from Kodi.

Passing the rocks, she followed in the squad's wake.

The terrain rolled out in an uneven expanse, rising and falling in gentle slopes. More huge rocks peppered their path, but again, they lacked symmetry. They appeared random, natural. While not a specific memory of the wooded area, she could almost recall a similar setting, like a word on the tip of her tongue.

Thick, leafy vegetation covered the floor in an ankle-deep carpet.

The trees around them were tall but modest in width. The deeper they waded into the woods, the more monstrous they became. She peered up at the swaying tops, the screen flickering the height in the upper forty-meter range. A brief highlight showed one at fifty-two meters.

Dropping her gaze back down to eye level, she focused on the trees, holding the contact. Again, the screen flickered as if scanning the wood until a match flashed across her visor.

"SAVI?"

"Yes, Andrea?"

"What's this crap flashing on my visor?"

"It's the integrated system display or ISD. In addition to helping you aim, navigate, or estimate distances and probable paths, it helps you find water, shelter, and identifies plants and liquids that may be useful or consumed. It auto links with the ships data banks and breaks down the molecular composition."

SAVI stopped speaking for a brief moment.

"Andrea, lifeforms detected. Seek cover."

"Lifeforms," Kodi crackled over their comms.

"Take cover," Andrea shouted just as the world exploded into chaos.

With a rushing roar, something red shot out between the trunk, gouging the tree she just passed.

Andrea dove, her body landing in a heap and coming to a stop beside a boulder.

Pulling her feet in, she kept out of view. She gasped for breath, realizing how close she came to dying.

"Anyone see anything?"

"Negative," Ossaro said.

"How the hell did they sneak up on us?" Daspar shrieked through the comms.

"Don't yell, we can all hear you if you just talk," Kodi retorted.

"Soren?" Andrea called.

"I'm fine."

"I think these are the hostile natives we were warned about," Daspar quipped.

"No fucking shit!" Ossaro yelled.

"Thanks for the heads up," Andrea muttered.

She let out a shaky breath. The close call rattled her more than she realized.

"Stay off the comms unless you have something important to say," Carlin reprimanded.

"Chief!" Kodi hailed. "I believe these are the four lifeforms I saw earlier to the south. How did they move so fast?"

"I don't know," Andrea admitted before remembering her comms were on.

She gathered herself and stood with slow movements, her back against the rock. Peering over the top, she scanned the woods, looking for any sign of movement.

The ISD flickered in tangent with her eyes, highlighting objects before it beeped in her ear.

Another red volley shot out, and she ducked down. Fragments of the rock spewed out where her head had just been. The blast was too slow. Andrea had seen it coming.

"Kembly, you read four life signatures?"

"Yes."

"Can you mark their positions?"

"Yes."

"Send it through the ISD."

"How?"

"SAVI?"

"Yes, Chief Regent, I'll relay it."

The comms went dead for a dozen heartbeats before the ISD flickered, revealing the locations of the life signs. They appeared opaque and blurred.

Looking for the nearest one, she stood again, and when she had a clear line of sight, the image sharpened. She ducked as two more volleys arced through the air.

"What are they shooting?" Carlin asked. "I don't hear any machinery, no rifle or blaster sounds."

Another bright explosion chipped away at the edge of the rock nearest her left side. The gritty shrapnel peppered her armor. Her heart pounded in her chest.

"Kembly, Ossaro, lay down cover fire. I'm going to try to take one out!" Andrea flicked the thumb switch of the rifle from stun to auto. Kodi and Carlin fired indiscriminately into the woods. Spying the intended life form, she waited until it shifted its attention to the fire.

She rose, weapon planted in her shoulder. As she crested the boulder, the adversary turned to face her, making a broader target. She held the trigger.

The rifle whirred like a miniature electrical turbine, the pitch climbing the scale the longer she fired. White light exploded from the end of the barrel, the rate of fire so quick that it manifested to be a solid stream.

As the light neared the target, the colors changed through a spectrum almost too quick for the mind to perceive, cooling from white-hot to yellow, orange, and then red.

She couldn't be sure, but the bolts appeared to slow down the further it traveled.

A high-pitched wail rang through her helmet, growing louder and faster the longer she pressed the trigger.

Suddenly, the rifle stopped firing despite still holding the trigger.

She ducked back down behind the rock, but her eyes never left her quarry. For a long time, it stood and faced the lasers before succumbing to wounds. Its orange color faded, cooling, and she knew it was dead.

"One down," she announced. "And my weapon won't fire anymore."

"Make that two targets down," Carlin added.

"The other lifeforms are gone," Kodi declared.

"All four?"

"No, just two. The other two bodies are still there."

The trill in Andrea's ears receded, growing fainter by the moment. Her heart thundered with adrenaline.

The ISD flickered, showing a heart rate of one-ninety and falling. With cautious movements, she rose and peered out into the distance.

Kodi was right, the other two lifeforms had vanished. But why? Why come at all? And why didn't her target seek cover when she shot at it? Did it—whatever it was—not know their weapons could kill?

The Demon's crew might've drawn first blood, but they hadn't started the fight. They defended themselves against the local hostile force.

The gnawing question of who and what shot at them had answers laying not far away.

"Regroup," she said over the comms. "Let's find out who the hell was shooting at us."

Chapter Nineteen: The Natives

Andrea followed close behind as Ward Ossaro ran up the gentle slope. He took his role of bodyguard in earnest and stayed in the lead position.

Since landing on the planet, his job as ship's ward turned into a nonexistent function. His sole purpose shifted to her protection. What was a ship without a commander?

The others tagged along and brought up the rear, their pace slower and more cautious. Andrea let her gaze flicker in her visor, and it brought up a quick rearview. The trio staggered in a haphazard fashion; Goski and Daspar had their rifles pointed outward, while Kodi faced the rear. All scanned for threats.

The ward reached the top and swept his rifle across the area, watching for any potential hostiles. The natives seemed to appear and disappear at will, a way to cloak themselves and hide their thermal signatures.

The big man stopped by the body and stood with his weapon pointed away. His head swiveled, surveying their immediate surroundings. His overcautious nature would keep them all alive, especially him, and Andrea found herself grateful that he took his duty seriously.

Trotting the last few steps, she sidled up to the ward and glanced down at their attacker. It lay face down, a hood drawn up over its head.

"Daspar, Kembly, Goski, fan out and set a perimeter. Ossaro, help me flip it over."

When the three moved and sought cover, Ossaro let go of his weapon—the sling keeping it close to his body—squatted, and flipped the corpse over.

Andrea knelt and let out a gasp when she saw its face.

"He's human," Ossaro muttered in disbelief.

The man's milky-yellow irises were distant, and the ward closed the corpse's eyes. The deceased had different features than the rest of the crew, more like the caretaker than any of them. Olive complexion, startling, strange eyes, even his build differed—tall and sinewy.

"Search for weapons," Andrea ordered, then stood, rifle facing out. Who knew how long they'd be left alone—if alone at all. She didn't want to be ambushed again. Word of their arrival would reach others, but how long would it take them to regroup?

The ward patted the body down but came up empty.

"No weapons."

"I wonder if the others took them during the retreat."

She heard the ward shrug, his armor groaning like a leather glove creaking.

"Perhaps. What's this?"

He reached forward and snatched up a long, smooth piece of wood, tapered and polished.

"Well?"

Ossaro shook his head.

"I don't know."

Andrea focused on it, and the ISD scanned the object. The text identified the wood and scrolled across her visor.

[Cypress].

"He carries around a piece of wood for what? A good luck charm?"

"Maybe," she answered, unsure, then shrugged. "We don't know anything about them, so we can't rule anything out. The only thing we can do is record all the information available and continue on."

The ward held up the wooden totem, eyeing it.

"Didn't do him much good, did it?" Daspar called from his position.

Andrea's irritation flared, and she turned to snap a retort about paying attention to their surroundings, but Daspar still held his rifle out, scanning the dense woods.

"Let's check the other one," she said instead.

They advanced with fluid precision, playing a leap-frog tag from tree to boulder, closing on their quarry. Andrea half expected them to bumble through the woods, clanging against trees, bushes, and rocks, but they surprised her with their quietness. Their agile steps fell soundlessly, like ghosts on the breeze.

The second target was much like the first, but a woman with olive skin and a startling iris hue, a type Andrea had never seen before. A pale blue, the color of cyan.

"What are the chances that both of these people have strange eyes?" Carlin mumbled.

Andrea nodded but kept silent as the ward inspected the corpse. Andrea let her gaze rove over the woman. Though difficult to tell, she gave the impression of height, but her frame hinted at a bulkier form than the man. Her age, if Andrea had to guess, was a few years older than herself, and she appeared hale despite being deceased.

"Got another," Ossaro said, holding up the wood object. The ISD scrolled again.

[Oak].

Andrea's scrutiny returned to the body, and she held her gaze steady. After a few moments, the ISD scrolled more text, revealing the clothes were made of a type of linen and wool. The garments resembled bathrobes more than anything else, but without the thickness. On days of unbearable heat or humidity, such clothes would be a welcomed reprieve.

Andrea's inspection continued downward, and she noted that both bodies didn't wear pants. Again the display flashed, and a detailed analysis revealed the woman as human. Another flash of text, this one red.

[Triage: surface burns, deep tissue ionization—nervous system disruption].

[Cause of Death: Electrocution and Internal Combustion].

"What?" she blurted aloud in disbelief.

"What?" Carlin asked.

He cocked his head, looking up.

Andrea repeated the cause of death.

"That's expected," Carlin said after a moment, standing.

He faced her.

"Our rifles fire electron-pulse beams focused through magnetic lenses."

He stopped, his stare going distant.

"How did I know that?"

She shrugged.

"A memory coming back?"

"Perhaps."

Andrea noted the doubt filling his voice.

"I recommend we expedite our investigation and make our exit before their friends come back," Goski's voice crackled over the comm.

"I second that," Daspar said without delay.

"Agreed," Andrea said. "Form up, same order."

As they stepped out, continuing on along the same course as before, they navigated through the woods with greater care. Their pace slowed, taking twice as long to cover the same distance.

Weapons pointed outward, heads swiveling, scanning the woodland for threats. Each snap of a twig, rustle of leaves, or groan of the trees made everyone jumpy and skittish.

The terrain changed with subtle grace, and the slopes became steeper and higher. The rich, dark earth peeked through the grass and rock at times, most noticeable on the inclines where vegetation fought against the gradient and gravity. The frequency of limestone slabs breaking through the flesh of earth increased the farther they navigated away from the ship.

At any given time, because of their single file dispersion, the five crew members stretched out over an entire rise. More often than not, when Andrea stood on the crest, she noted the lead member at the bottom of a gully. Their tail exited the gully behind them and started up the hillside. With this type of dispersion, they couldn't be ambushed together, bettering their chances of surviving, but it did present drawbacks.

Coming to the aid of one would take more time and put others in danger. At least they weren't clumped together as they had been when they exited the ship. Had their enemies awaited them there, they would've all died.

The number of the trees thinned, but each one only seemed to grow larger and wider. Some stood proudly with massive roots breaking through bedrock in the ravines while nature crowned others in splendor along the ridge line. Of the few times that the groups stumbled upon one sprouting on the slope, they had to traverse around the gargantuan, requiring at least a dozen steps on an incline peppered with crumbling rock, soft dirt, and tangles of vines.

During their journey, they kept communication to a minimum. Who knew if the enemy had the ability to listen in. Further, carrying on a conversation would distract them. Andrea used short bursts of comm chatter to tell Ossaro to slow down or Daspar and Soren to speed up.

In a rapid descent, the sky darkened as the last sun, the massive blue one, slipped below the northern horizon. The unnatural notion of two suns bothered her. And the direction felt wrong, too. She couldn't explain it, but the gut feeling persisted. If she learned anything since waking up without memories, it was to trust the hunch.

"Kodi, what about that huge life form? Any new readings?" Andrea called through the comm.

"It moved off about fifteen minutes ago and headed north."

"Copy. Squad, find a place for cover and stop. Pair up and hydrate in turns. I'm going to check our position."

They rogered up in sequence and wandered off in pairs, Goski and Daspar, Kembly and Ossaro.

Andrea ambled to a tree with a large rock formation near it. She found herself keen to the mass of stone. A similar structure had saved her life in their last encounter. With the tree at her back and the rock formation protecting the right flank, she had ample cover with only one avenue to guard.

She squatted, laying the weapon sideways across her thighs.

"SAVI? Do you know anything about where we went on our last excursion?"

"You're approximately one klick away from the coordinates where you first met the locals. You can check your mapping system from the left forearm guard."

A red button flashed at the bottom left corner, the edge nearest her elbow. She tapped the button, and a two-dimensional hologram of the immediate area materialized. She expected a sizable replica, but the display only extended a foot above her forearm and ran the length of the gauntlet. A faint, digital compass glowed at the top right corner.

Three points peppered the display, the ship, their destination, and their current location. They were far closer to the destination than their craft.

When her eyes tracked between her position and the vessel, the map registered the movement and drew a straight line between the two and displayed the distance they covered.

"Only eight kilometers?"

Their journey created the impression of traveling a greater distance than what the holo reported. She could've sworn they walked twice that distance.

Her eyes roved over to the dot that represented their endpoint. They'd drifted and would need a course correction. The distance of one kilometer flashed between her current position and their destination.

According to the topographical map, the area was also elevated. She groaned inward, knowing they'd be climbing another hill, this one larger than any of the others.

Another bird in the treetops gave a whooping call, similar to the one outside the cargo ramp. The sky, though beautiful with various shades of blue and purple, turned ominous. They'd need to move, and soon.

Shrugging off her pack, she opened the top quick-grab pouch and pulled out one of the water containers. Touching the side of the helmet, the visor slid up, and the mouth guard separated, allowing her to drink.

Over the comm, Carlin spoke. "What's the plan, Chief?"

She swallowed a mouthful and wiped the excess away before answering.

"Destination's another klick away. We'll press on. It's in an elevated area. Might be a better defensive position if we need to stop for the night."

"You mean sleep outside?" Daspar piped in.

"Yeah, after the last two months on the ship, you'd think you'd be more than agreeable."

"I'll take my bunk, thanks."

"Outside's better than the brig," Carlin added with dark, threatening tones.

The other fell silent, and a collective sigh eased out of the group.

She'd been waiting for this particular grenade to go off. The strain between the two, the building pressure, was almost palpable. Everyone sensed the impending explosion. She hoped they weren't coming to blows in the midsts of another firefight.

"Get ready to move," she said.

After another long drink, she packed the water container and replaced it in the bag. She slung her arms through the pack straps. Perspiration wept from her back, sliding down her spine. Her forehead prickled as beads welded together and threatened to start a waterfall from her brow. She waited a few more moments, allowing the breeze to caress her face, then snapped the helmet back into place. The mouth guard closed together, and the visor fell.

Over the comms, she spoke, "Alright. Let's move. Same formation."

"Aye, Chief," Carlin and Kodi said in unison.

A whine came from Daspar, but Goski didn't utter a sound.

Though they moved slower since their encounter, Andrea noticed their increased pace. Did their urgency spur from the failing light and impending night? Sleeping under the stars elicited a shudder, the eeriness of an alien planet filled with oversized lifeforms and people who wanted to kill them didn't help.

Still, they were out of the ship. With that larger life form lurking about, which implied teeth and a predatory sense, she'd sleep with one eye open.

SAVI could keep watch as they slept. The ship's sensors should be able to detect anything, and the AI could keep in contact through the CASI.

But that didn't feel like enough.

The AI wasn't present, and nothing beats boots on the ground. She'd implement a watch through the night. With the old alliances abolished and new friendships formed in the wake of the Emma-Goski-Daspar incident, an interesting juggle would develop.

They made good time at their destination.

Once the high ridge emerged in the distance and through a break in the trees, the squad picked up the pace to a trot. By the time they started up the long, rocky slope, their momentum had abated, and the arduous climb ensued.

Trees jutted from the stone, wispy and twig-like compared to their woodland counterparts below. Grass crept out of crevices, hard shoots of fibrous weeds struggling to survive. Clear of the forest below, the temperature dropped and nightlife awakened.

A bug, at least she assumed, groaned in the background, a never-ending chirp.

Sounds like a cricket.

For a moment, the realization swept past her, but she halted in her tracks. She remembered—a cricket, and the sound. The little black bugs similar to grasshoppers filled her mind, and the remembrance of tiny, young hands reaching out to pluck one from the grass.

A memory.

Hope flared in her chest. Maybe their memories weren't gone, just suppressed?

What caused the memory to come back? The sound of the insects? Maybe the strenuous activity helped dislodge whatever block had formed. Her heart fluttered, and rapid pants thundered in her ears. Perhaps the planet, Celesta Six? Did coming back help lift the fog?

"You coming, Chief?" Ossaro called, breaking into her thoughts.

"Yeah."

Adjusting the rifle, she continued ascending the rocky slope. Her legs ached, and her lungs burned by the halfway point.

Daspar, by contrast, didn't seem affected by the exertion as he closed in on her position, and that gave all the motivation to continue. Her boots scuffed softly against the rock as she half-ran up the hill.

The trees sprouted further apart the higher she went. The grass grew taller, long stalks of thick weeds. Branches twisted from their roots like grotesque and deformed claws. The ledges between the rocks stretched taller. She could no longer hop each one, having to put a hand down to climb.

Reaching the plateau, she fought the urge to fall over and lay down, but she didn't dare. As if attuned to her thoughts, the helmet opened at the mouth guard, and the visor retreated.

The crisp breeze caressed her face, cooling the pouring sweat. Mouth open, she panted as her pulse throbbed in her temples.

"Here," Ossaro said, handing over a canteen.

She took it and drank greedily for a few moments before realizing it wasn't hers. She handed it back and, between pants, thanked him.

Andrea eyed their surroundings. The trail continued to ascend, but SAVI confirmed their coordinates. Other paths led down on either side of the small mountain they topped. Where those trails led, she could only guess.

By the time Daspar arrived, she had recovered enough to not appear weak in front of him. He gave an exhausted and exaggerated groan and fell over. On his back, his helmet opened, and he panted, groaning and whining.

Andrea's irritation flared. She knew the act was meant to irritate. It worked.

"Shut the fuck up," the ward hissed.

"Kiss my ass," Daspar snapped.

"We don't know who can hear you," Andrea reminded him.

"At this point, I don't care," Daspar said, still panting.

"You should," a new voice said.

The sound of rifles snapping up filled her ears. She lifted her own, head jerking in the direction of the voice.

The helmet's mouth guard slammed shut, and the visor dropped fast. The ISD flared to life and switched to night mode. At the end of her barrel, no more than a half dozen paces away, stood a human female with light brown hair.

"See? I fucking told you," Ossaro rebuked.

"What do we do, Chief?" Soren queried, a hint of panic filled his voice.

"Hold your fire."

"Andrea?" Kodi echoed.

"Hold your fire," she repeated.

"Chestnut—?"

"Shut up, Daspar, just shut up."

The native cocked her head to the side.

The rising darkness made it hard to make out facial characteristics. The moons had yet to claim the sky and offer enough light to see distinct features.

"Why are you so afraid?"

She smiled, but wounded ego filled her voice.

"It is I, Andrea. Do you not remember me?"

Hessner shook her head.

"Can't say that I do."

"Why have you come back?"

"How about we ask the questions?" Daspar said, rising.

"I told you to shut up," Andrea spat. "And lower your weapon."

"Is that for him, or all of us?" the ward inquired.

"Just him."

"Still don't trust me?"

"Nope."

The chief regent shook her head without taking eyes off the woman. She looked down the barrel of the rifle, studying the native.

To the woman, Andrea spoke, "How do you know our names? How do you speak our language?"

"You taught me," the outsider explained.

She held up her arms.

"I mean you no harm; do you plan the same for me?"

Andrea let the silence stretch between them. She hadn't come here to slaughter despite being dressed for war, but the earlier group forced their hand.

"Chief?" Soren called again, voice filled with questions.

"Hold your fire."

Again, to the woman, "How do I know you won't attack the moment our weapons are down? The other natives didn't hold back."

Though she couldn't see color or great detail of her face, Andrea didn't miss the native's eyes going wide.

"You've made contact with the Teshren?"

"Who the hell's the Teshren?" Ossaro demanded.

"They're vile people," the woman hastened to explain. "Don't you remember, intended? Please, you don't have much time. Did you leave any survivors?"

Andrea exchanged glances with the others.

"Two got away."

Panic filled the woman's face.

"You must leave, and quickly."

She took an urgent step forward, and the crew responded by raising their rifles.

"Please, leave."

"We're not going anywhere," Ossaro warned.

"Not without our caretaker," Goski added.

"You fools, who do you think has him?"

The declaration thrummed in Andrea's ears. Was it possible? Had their crew member been taken from them by force? Her contemplation fell to the rifle clutched in her hands.

A mental image of their spacecraft reminded her that they were technologically superior, at least from the first contact. The natives wore rough-spun clothes; she and the others had armor. They flew for six months just to get here.

Her regard returned to the woman. She wore similar clothing like the ones who attacked them, but she wore a type of loose trousers.

Andrea lowered the weapon, and from the corner of her eye, Soren mirrored the action.

"Chief?" Ossaro queried, his voice tight.

"She doesn't have any weapons. Look at the clothes. She's not a threat."

Andrea's visor lifted and the mouth guard opened.

Kodi and Soren followed suit, but Ossaro and Daspar still held their weapons trained on her.

Looks like they found something in common.

She suppressed the smile and took a step forward.

To the local, she spoke. "You said you know us. We've met? Who are you?"

"I'm Gelarae. You don't remember me? How can you not remember?"

Andrea shook her head.

"None of us remember anything. These people you're talking about, the Teshren, why do they have our crew member?"

"I don't know the details, but he stayed behind, volunteered if I remember right, to ensure you complied."

"Complied with what?" Ossaro solicited.

Gelarae paused, taking in Ossaro's measure, his stance. Andrea could sense her tenseness.

"To take their message to your leaders."

"What message?" Andrea asked.

"The orb. It's red and gold. Do you still have it?"

The others shared a look as some of the mystery started to fall into place. The orb was meant for their leaders, and that meant the command element of the fleet. Did it carry a message? Had Andrea and the crew heard the message?

She didn't think so.

"Yeah, we still have it," Ossaro answered.

The ward lowered his rifle, and with reluctance Daspar did, too.

"As I said, we've come for our crew member, and we're not leaving without him."

"Mason Boudry," Soren supplied.

Andrea marveled at his memory. Though she had heard or read his name countless times, she still had trouble remembering it.

"You'll need help," Gelarae said.

"You offering?" Daspar quipped.

She glanced at the navigator.

"When and where I can. My people and I won't risk open war with the Teshren."

"Cowards?"

She narrowed her eyes at him.

"More like we don't wish to commit genocide."

"If you can do that much damage—" Daspar said, rising.

"I think she means," Ossaro cut him off, placing the back of his hand on the other's chest in warning, "her civilization would be wiped out, not the Teshren."

This took the fire out of Daspar as understanding, and the implications reached his face. The ward removed his hand and gave Gelarae an appraising look.

"What do you suggest?"

Gelarae glanced at each in turn.

"You're tired. You must be hungry. Come with me, and my people will provide food and shelter where you may rest."

Andrea shook her head.

"We need to find our caretaker."

"You will," Gelarae promised, "just not tonight. How will you help him if you are too weary from travel?"

Gelarae stopped, her head jerking to the left as if listening.

A chord of tension rippled through the group. Rifles were shouldered, visors lowered.

Andrea looked at the bottom right corner of the visor. The blinking blue light appeared.

"SAVI?" she breathed.

"Yes, Andrea?"

Her throat tightened. Now that they were quiet, she noted the insects had gone silent. It couldn't be a coincidence.

"Do you detect any lifeforms around us?"

"Yes. A sizable life form, the one we noted earlier. It's three hundred meters from you."

"Where?" she dared to breathe.

We could've used some fucking warning!

Her eyes widened as she searched the darkness.

In the distance, the trees swayed and branches cracked as they broke. Was that from the life form or the wind?

Faint stars twinkled above. What she wouldn't give to be back among them, safe from whatever came their way. She didn't spend the last two months with memory loss only to come to a planet and be an appetizer.

"Behind you, from the way you came."

She double blinked.

"Guys. We've got a monstrous life not far from us."

"How far?" Ossaro asked.

"Three hundred meters behind us."

"It's a sehruche," Gelarae offered in hushed tones. "Don't move, don't speak."

Andrea fought every urge not to turn around. Whatever lurked nearby, she wanted to see it, face it head-on. The sensation of sharp blades sliding between her ribs made it hurt to breathe.

Her body trembled from fatigue and anxiety. The rifle grew heavy, but she dared not let it out of her shoulder. Her grip around the buttstock tightened.

A loud crunch sounded from behind, and she twitched. She caught herself before turning.

The sound of her pounding pulse echoed in her ears. The slip-up almost cost them. A call too close for comfort. She didn't want to be the one that killed them.

Sweat trickled down her spine. Did Daspar have the same discipline? She felt the others stiffen in response to the noise. Her attention flickered to the ones within her range of vision. Daspar and Ossaro stood behind, and she bit back a curse.

She licked her lips. Her gaze flickered to Gelarae who gave a small, languid shake of the head. The movement was barely perceptible, once to the left and back to center.

Remembering the rearview function, she engaged the rear display.

The treetops, what she could make of them in the darkness, swayed. The creature passed, oblivious to their presence. She saw flashes of flesh, scales, and jagged fins on its back as it lumbered through the vegetation.

In a burst of noise, the beast roared, a mixture of a growl and a drone.

Kodi gasped beside her, terrified. Andrea couldn't blame her—she did, too.

The roar drowned out their slip, and the creature continued—the howl vibrated her bones and teeth. Pain seared hot and quick like flickering lightning. The rumble turned her insides to jelly, and a buzzing pressure built on her bladder.

A few heartbeats later, it faded.

Cracking limbs and splintering wood grew quieter, the footfalls fainter.

No one spoke or moved. Terror turned them into statuettes.

Andrea panted as if she'd finished a sprint—so did Kodi and Soren. After the tingling sensation faded, Gelarae broke the silence.

"We must move from here. Hurry."

Andrea's heart hammered as if she just ran uphill again. A bead of sweat pooled at her right temple and trailed down her face.

"What's the hurry?" Daspar queried.

He tried to sound sarcastic to hide his terror. Andrea risked a glance at him. He and Ossaro had paled visibly.

Good to know I'm not the only one who almost shit themselves.

"You killed two of the Teshren," Gelarae explained, "and the sehruche will attract other, smaller predators since it has left this area. I don't know if that was a tame sehruche or a wild one."

"You mean to tell me you keep those big bastards as pets?" Soren's enormous eyes grew wider.

Ossaro came forward, moving into Andrea's peripheral vision. He let the rifle fall from his shoulder.

"I agree with the native. If she's advising us to leave, we should. What do you mean by a tame one?"

Gelarae's face lit up, and she gave Ossaro a nod.

"Welcome back, intended. It's most agreeable to see you again. The sehruche could have a rider, and if that's the case, our troubles have only started."

Andrea's attentiveness darted to the others and landed on Daspar. His eyes flickered through the group, and a smirk crossed his face.

"Intended?"

He glanced between Galerae and Ossaro before looking at Andrea.

"Well, this just got awkward."

His smile widened, and his face reddened as he held his laughter in check. Her lips tightened, but she held back a retort.

"We must leave," Gelarae repeated.

"Where are we going?" Andrea inquired.

"To my village. We will fast travel."

"Don't you mean travel fast?" Daspar countered.

Soren perked and took an interest in the conversation.

"No. We'll use the pool and fast travel. This way."

Gelarae turned and hurried away, her steps almost buoyant.

"Pool?" Soren echoed.

Andrea shrugged and took off after their guide.

Chapter Twenty: The Aether's Grace

Rhett Daspar stared after the others. They followed their guide—a local—without reservation.

"I've got a bad feeling about this," he muttered.

He wanted to object, to warn them of his gut feeling. Following would lead them to imminent doom, but the crew would disregard his advice. They all hated him. His words meant less than this stranger, this alien.

How did they know she was human?

Sure, she curved in all the right spots, but if their enemy could hit and fade without a trace, what other tricks did they possess?

Stranger things had happened.

The locals, whether this girl was a part of them or not, could fire on them. If their attackers had weapons, their fellow combatants recovered them before fleeing, why else hadn't they found any?

And what if they returned? Did the local girl, Gelarae, call the Teshren?

They didn't sound so bad, not nearly as terrible as the monster that lurked nearby.

His eyes tracked to Andrea, their fearless and foolish leader. His gaze lingered on her backside as she disappeared beyond the curved wall of rock.

Carlin's head shifted, looking his way.

"What?" Rhett asked.

The ward's lips twitched, but he didn't say anything. Carlin hated him more than Chestnut did. Still, if anyone else were to believe danger awaited, it would be him.

Braving the hostility, Rhett spoke up.

"This isn't a good idea."

"What was that, Daspar?" Carlin barked.

Rhett bit back stronger words.

He repositioned the rifle in his arms, his elbows going numb from the weight. Ossaro's weapon shifted in his grip as if he expected a fight.

The navigator snorted.

"This isn't going to end well."

"Tough shit. Move."

Rhett clenched his teeth.

"Listen to me! We don't know this woman, but she knows us. We were chased off this planet the last time. They are holding one of us hostage. They've fired on us, and now we're just going to follow her to a pool to 'fast-travel'? What the hell does that mean anyway?"

The big man paused for a moment.

Rhett noted the war raging on his face—to hate the resident asshole or to listen to reason. The navigator suppressed a smug smile, knowing the conflicting emotions tore into the ward.

Logic won in the end.

"I don't like it either, but we're not in charge. I'll raise your objections with my own. Stay vigilant, and voice anything odd."

Rhett wanted to tell him that everything was odd, but instead, he nodded.

That went better than expected.

A buttstroke across the face wouldn't have surprised him. Still, Ossaro turned partially decent once the case was made. It helped mollify the urge to slide a knife in his back.

Sometimes, these assholes… No sense of humor.

That's all it was. He was far more jovial than this dull crowd. His humor was unique. They didn't appreciate his vintage, a singularity among a throng of identical weeds.

He sighed through his nose.

The ward followed in Andrea's wake. Rhett glanced behind him.

In the distance, the treetops still swayed from the passing beast. Assured they were alone, he brought up the rear of the column.

The path twisted through jagged rock. Sharp edges aggravated the flesh on his shoulders as he twisted and turned through the narrow track. Their original trail kept ascending, but the guide took a rut to the left and down.

The serpentine trail curled in short spurts, followed by smooth course corrections. Rock turned to fine dirt and stone, a grit grinding under each pivot of his boot.

A faint light shone ahead, the eerie glow reflecting off the towering stone walls. The stone around them rose like palisades the further they traversed. By the time they reached the bottom, cliffs towered above them.

Rhett's eyes went to the pool in the center. It glowed cyan, effulgent in the darkness. The opening glittered like pearls from the moon, an otherworldly liquid. The fluid sloshed against the sides, a soothing sound. It gently rippled as if stirred by constant waves. The substance was thicker than water but more diluted than oil.

Soren made a noise in his throat.

"What's that stuff?"

Gelarae chuckled.

"You said the same thing last time. It's the aether's grace, the basin of time; it's how we fast travel."

Everyone clustered around the basin, but Rhett kept back, his mind roaming elsewhere. Though sweat poured from his body, he shivered as if cold.

He gazed up.

Above, nothing stood between him and sweet starlight. They were open to the elements. Hours ago, he traveled among them; now, they seemed like distant dreams.

He raised the rifle, pocketing the butt in his shoulder. To his surprise, at the edge of his vision, another rose, too.

He peeked over.

Ossaro scrutinized the ridgeline above them.

"What's going on?" Andrea's voice floated to him.

Sometimes she sounds so trite.

Still, her voice didn't match how bland she appeared.

Ossaro answered, "If I were the enemy, this would be a great place to attack."

"I'm not getting into that," Kodi declared.

Rhett surveyed the first officer. Her eyes fixated on the pool, and she backed away.

Rhett knew Kodi more than she cared to admit, and her qualities didn't include fear. It was disconcerting to watch her behave in such a manner. She'd never let anything stand in her way. A shining liquid didn't seem like the type of thing to stop her.

"We must go," Gelarae said.

A fog filled Rhett's head followed by a slight sense of vertigo. Ghosts floated before his vision, phantoms of their previous selves.

"What's that stuff?" Soren asked. "It's beautiful."

"That's the aether's grace, the basin of time. Where it comes from, we are unaware, but it serves my people," said a man.

Gelarae stood beside him, and Rhett could only assume, based upon appearance, that he was her father.

"I'm not going in there," Kodi's voice filled the stone chamber.

The man smiled.

"I would assume you'd feel as much. That's why I'll send my daughter first."

"Could be a trap," Ossaro rumbled, his mind never far from possible treachery.

"I'll go," Rhett watched himself volunteer.

The bizarre scene turned outlandish when Andrea put a hand on his arm.

"You don't have to go. We can find some other way. Besides, risk our favorite navigator? Who's gonna make us laugh if you go?"

Her voice was soft and laced with concern. Her eyes sparkled with a genuineness he had yet to receive since waking up with no memories.

"You know," Daspar said, "it would've been nicer if you said you needed me, couldn't live without me to pilot the ship."

This drew a chuckle from Andrea, and another man called out.

"What about me?"

Daspar looked to the man. It was Mason Boudry, the caretaker, their missing crew member.

Andrea smiled.

"What? And risk my husband? I think not."

Mason gave a mock-rage.

"It's worth the risk, especially to get away from you."

"If anything happens to you," Daspar said, "I'll take care of Chestnut and marry her."

Andrea gave him a thoughtful look, devoid of her usual hate and mistrust.

Mason laughed.

"Now you understand why I'm going. I'm hoping something does happen. I'd be rid of her, then. As far as marrying her, don't make that mistake, but best of luck if you do."

Andrea smiled, crossed to Mason, and kissed him.

"Be careful," she warned. "Then again, perhaps this is an elaborate plan to be rid of you, too."

The rest of the memory jumbled into a mix of convoluted imagery and light, but peace and safety settled over Daspar. The little puddle of light wasn't something they had to worry about. Whatever happened to Mason, this wasn't it.

He peered back to Andrea who was coaxing Kodi into going in the pool. The proverbial light in which she stood changed his perspective of her.

She was married—to their missing member no less.

Daspar eyed the ward.

Ossaro was intended to the local girl; if that was legitimate or not, he couldn't debate it at the moment. What if he was married, too? What if they were all married? He and Kodi bonded on an intimate level. Even he grasped that certain salacious acts shouldn't be whispered aloud. No doubt that Andrea and Ossaro screwed countless times.

And Soren ...

Daspar checked the engineer.

He seemed both captivated and apprehensive.

Soren's the only one who wasn't married.

He had a synth, and though no one voiced it aloud, it wasn't hard to imagine what happened in his quarters. If he did have a spouse, maybe she'd bought it for him?

Rhett mentally shrugged.

If it kept him faithful on long voyages, who was he to judge? His face burned with shame—he'd partaken of Emma. To Soren's mind, Emma fulfilled the role of wife, and Rhett had violated her sanctity—even if it was offered.

Damn, Soren's the only one that hasn't screwed up this whole time.

The guilt rested on Rhett's shoulders alone.

He glanced back at Kodi, admiring her beauty while disgusted by her apparent weakness, her apprehension of the liquid. She was definitely a married woman, had to be.

His eyes roamed to Andrea.

A part of him turned gleeful that she failed to live up to the perfection she exuded, but another part paused. Under any other circumstance, he might've flaunted her faults, but something within forced him to abstain from taunting. He didn't have the heart to tell her the truth.

"Daspar?" Andrea called, breaking through the haze.

He blinked the thoughts away and focused on her.

"Chestnut?"

Suspicion clouded her eyes, but he saw a thimble of concern.

"You alright?"

He blinked again, shaking the fog away. It was hard to believe, he actually remembered something. After so long ...

"Yeah, I'm fine. Thanks."

He jerked his head towards the pool.

"I'll go."

The suspicion remained, but worry crept into her eyes.

"I can't ask you to do that. No one's acquainted with how to fly the ship, at least, not well enough. If something were to happen ..."

He tried his best to give her a genuine smile and not the typical snicker. Something dark, sarcastic, and raunchy came to mind, but he let the comment go and answered with sincerity.

"It's starting to sound like you care, Chestnut. Careful, I might grow attached."

He shrugged.

"It's worth the risk. If Gelarae's willing to go first, then I'll go, too."

"I don't want to go," Kodi voiced again, her eyes round and massive.

Her breathing came in quick, deep pants. Her lips parted, and Rhett could hear the gasps through the visor. Her breath fogged a small circle on the transparent surface.

The tempo increased.

Ossaro, who still scanned the ridge above them, called out.

"What's the matter, Kembly? It's just a small puddle."

"I don't know," she said between deep pants. "The water."

"You fly in space," Soren reminded her. "Numerous things can go wrong up there—far more than in the water."

"I'll go," Daspar repeated, louder.

In a cacophony of movement and sound, explosions of light and fire filled the stone chamber.

Ossaro's voice rang out, "Ambush!"

His weapon discharged in a flurry of light and heat.

The ground shook as their enemy shot down at them.

Rhett dove for a small alcove and slid to a stop against the wall. The rock formation shielded him. Motes and flecks of stone peppered his visor. He snapped up his weapon and returned fire.

Fuck. I knew this was a bad place to stop.

He couldn't see them, but every time they shot at them, they illuminated their form for a brief moment. He tracked with his weapon and pulled the trigger.

White-hot light flickered at the end of the barrel. The illuminance appeared like a solid stream but changed color the further it traveled. By the time it hit, an angry red erupted around a faceless individual like a cocoon.

Someone dove into him, knocking him down. His head snapped in that direction as his weapon lifted. He jerked to a halt. Andrea's face flashed in the darkness, her eyes wide with fear but not panic.

"We've got to get outta here," she screamed.

"Yeah, no shit!" he yelled.

Daspar reset himself, then returned fire. He ducked back down behind the rock-shield.

"We can't go the way we came. They'll pick us off. We've only got one way to go."

Andrea nodded.

"Then go, I'll cover."

He popped up and fired again. By now, he expected their adversaries to be dead or retreating, but thus far, no bodies fell into the pit, and they still harrowed them.

Do they have armor?

He set himself to run for the basin when he spied Kodi.

She, too, ducked behind a rock formation, rifle in her arms, but she didn't return fire.

He paused, gaze flickering between her and the pool.

She trembled with terror, the firearm all but forgotten.

What caused her to lock up? Those who shot at them or the reflective liquid?

She hated him now. Understandable, given the circumstance, but if he didn't pull her in with him, she'd die. The crew would follow him, he had no doubts, but not Kodi.

Her fear turned her into a statue, and she'd die when their foes swarmed. If he helped her, maybe the gesture would win him some points, and he'd find himself back in her good graces.

Or being a fucking idiot will get me killed.

He sighed.

Part of him realized that if he wished to live, he should leave her, but the other half couldn't. He hadn't loved her—it hadn't been long enough for that— but they had been intimate, and despite her caustic attitude now, a part of him still cared for her.

"What the fuck are you waiting on?" Andrea snapped.

He darted from his position, sprinting across the expanse. As he neared the basin, he veered off and slid into the alcove beside the first officer.

Feet underneath him, he yelled, "Kodi, we've got to go."

"Get the fuck away from me!"

"You'll die!"

She fought him, shoved him away. He grappled to help.

Again, the thought to leave her crossed his mind, but he cringed at the impulse. He glanced at the bottom right of his visor.

"SAVI!" he shouted.

"Ah, the resident asshole calls," the dual voice answered.

Rhett fought the urge to laugh, to rage, to scream at the stupid infernal software, but couldn't. Now wasn't the time.

"SAVI! We're under fire. I need help."

"With what?"

"Kodi isn't moving, and I'm trying to save her life. She's an active combatant. Can you knock her out or something?"

"I can, but that command must come from the most senior of the group. According to vitals, Chief Regent Hessner's still in command. The order must come from her."

Rhett screamed in frustration and pounded the rock with the meaty portion of his fist.

Kodi still fought, pushing him, punching his armored chest as enemy fire rained around them.

His comm crackled a moment later, and Andrea's voice filled his helmet.

"SAVI, do it! Knock her ass out. We've got to get her out of here, or we're all going to die."

"This will take a few moments. Administering tranquilizers."

Rhett snapped up the rifle and shot at the ridgeline. In the back of his mind, he sensed Kodi lose her strength. The blows didn't affect his aim.

He waited a few moments longer.

Thus far, none of their enemies had died. He remembered their first encounter, what Andrea had done. The next flash of light flared above. The ground around him exploded. Rock fragments peppered his armor.

He squeezed the trigger, the end of the barrel erupting with bright light.

And he continued to hold it down.

A near-constant stream arched out from the weapon. A trill rose in his ear, growing louder by the second. As the decibels reached an uncomfortable level, the rifle stopped firing on its own. Red letters flashed twice on the visor.

[Overheat].

He gazed down at Kodi. Her eyes rolled beneath her eyelids.

"Beautiful, SAVI!" he exclaimed.

He hoisted Kodi's small form on his left shoulder to keep his right arm free to return fire. With a double blink, he activated the squad's comms.

"Cover me. I'm going for the pool."

"No, you fucking idiot!" Ossaro barked.

"Yes," Andrea cut in. "Lay down cover fire. He's got Kodi, too."

Not waiting for a debate, he rose and darted forward.

Shots rained down in his general direction, but the move caught the assailants off guard. A few strides away, bright light arched out and grazed his left arm. The immediate pain that followed washed over him like blinding agony. His skin blistered from the glancing hit, and his body locked up as if electricity arced through him.

He managed two more staggering steps before Kodi's weight, and his uncooperative body tripped. The ground rushed up. At the last moment, he pushed Kodi off his shoulder and into the puddle.

She splashed and vanished.

The adrenaline pumping through him gave vigor to his limbs, and he pulled himself in after her.

His body twisted, pulled by forces he could neither see nor control. The fluid ran over him like the gliding hands of a masseuse, gentle and slick. Pain didn't factor into the sensation, but his body contorted in ways that broke the laws of physics.

His lungs burned. He should've taken a deeper breath! Panic swelled in the pit of his stomach.

Would he drown before he reached the end?

Anxiety caused him to forget the faceplate protecting him. The sensation of traveling, moving faster than anything possible, let alone a current, washed over him. He hurtled hundreds of kilometers, faster than a free fall.

And then, it was over.

The basin regurgitated him on the other side, belching both of them out like some choking beast. Kodi lay in an unconscious heap beside him. He sucked in a quick breath, relieving his aching lungs. Knees planted, he pushed off the ground.

In alarm, he swung his blaster around.

"Stay back!"

A small group of people paused when they saw the rifle directed at them. They jabbered something, but he didn't understand. Did they understand him? No, otherwise they would have spoken to him in his language.

Gelarae recognized who they were and the capability of their weapons. From the looks of it, so did these people.

He put the firearm in his shoulder but kept the barrel pointed down. The crowd started forward again, and he raised the weapon. "Stay the fuck back!"

To the comm, he called.

"SAVI? Are these people armed?"

SAVI's voice crackled. "I don't detect any weapons in your vicinity, at least, not in the traditional sense."

"That's comforting," Rhett muttered.

One from the throng of people, a woman, took a timid step forward. She held up her hands to show they were empty, then pointed to Kodi. They didn't realize she was unconscious from medicine. For all they knew, she was injured, but how to convey that without an interpreter?

Resigned, he nodded and held up a single finger.

"Just one."

The woman repeated the gesture and crept forward. Rhett let his eyes roam from her to the gathered people. They wore simple clothing, rough spun garments that looked closer to robes and togas than anything else. Gelarae had worn something more like their own, trousers and a tunic.

Perhaps it stemmed from her roaming away from the village. Was she a hunter? A gatherer? What exactly was her role? Why didn't these people have technology? Were they primitive, and if so, how did primitive people drive off a ship that was hundreds of years more advanced than anything these people could muster?

Gelarae spoke their language, why couldn't these people?

The lady neared Kodi and knelt. When her hand came close to the visor, Kodi's mask parted, revealing her face.

"Kodi," the woman said with an accent.

Surprise rippled through Rhett, hearing the woman pronounce Kembly's name. A smile pulled at her lips. She turned to the assembly, arm outstretched, and spoke with rushed words. Another from the group stepped forward.

Rhett raised the rifle.

"I said one!"

"Okay," the woman by Kodi said.

Her accent almost made her one word unintelligible. She stood slowly, her arms out, supervening between the gun and her people.

"Okay."

The woman retreated to the crowd and retrieved her bag before returning to Kodi. The native knelt again.

"Whatever you're going to do, it won't work," Rhett said, glancing at her.

She retorted in her tongue but otherwise ignored him.

Rhett returned his attention to the small party. Most were young adults, and female, too. Only a pair of boys and one older man stood within the female-dominated squad. One of the boys caught his gaze.

"Lucky bastards," Rhett grunted.

The puddle behind him surged, the volume rising like the sound of rapids. Gelarae landed beside him, but she didn't sprawl across the ground like he had. She knelt on one knee. When she stood, she glanced between Kodi, Rhett, the villager, and the small group.

"Your weapon," she said to him and shook her head. "You won't need it."

"Yeah, that's a solid pass on the trust. Where's my crew?"

Gelarae arched an eyebrow and smirked.

"Your crew?"

"Where are they?"

Gelarae cocked her head, her brows knitting.

"You're not as fun as I remember. What's wrong?"

"Didn't Chestnut tell you? We can't remember anything!"

"Chestnut?"

Rhett growled and ground his teeth.

"Andrea! Where is she? Where's everyone else?"

"They'll be along shortly, whenever they grow tired of being attacked. Their fear of Aether's Grace is more powerful than their fear of facing an enemy."

"What's to keep the Teshren from following them through?"

Gelarae gave him a quizzical look.

"You asked that before. It's a violation of the peace treaties we have with them and other races. No one is allowed to violate the sanctuary here. Think of it as a holy place."

She cocked her head.

"Did you tell your crew that you survived your journey?"

Shit.

"SAVI?"

"Relaying to Andrea that her favorite asshole is still breathing. I don't have to imagine her disappointment."

Rhett rolled his eyes.

"You know what? You're making it harder to move past all this bullshit. In reminding me that I've been dubbed asshole, you're the embodiment of the definition. If you're going for comedy, your timing sucks."

"Humor eludes my programming, but I respond in a manner I've witnessed in others. Would you care for me to stop?"

"Yeah, that'd be great. So would a little honesty now and then."

"Daspar?" Andrea's voice crackled over the comm.

"Yeah? I hear you. You guys okay?"

"Super."

Gunfire filled the comm while she paused.

"What's on the other side?"

Rhett eyed the group who stayed where he stopped them.

"More people. Looks like primitive villagers. That I can see, or that SAVI can detect, the threat isn't high."

"It's better than here," she commented. "We're on our way."

The comm crackled with gunfire and incoherent shouts before it cut out altogether.

Rhett checked back on Kodi and the woman who aided her. Kodi's groggy gaze fell on him before listing lazily away.

She probably doesn't realize I'm here, let alone where she is.

The pool sloshed and stirred before Andrea tumbled out. Her armor gleamed with a wetness that receded in beads of elastic flesh.

Before she gained her feet, the others came tumbling out.

Chapter Twenty-One: In Layman's Terms

The pool of liquid-light regurgitated Carlin. He landed on a knee, half-crouched. His helmet's visor lifted, and the mouthpiece parted.

The scent of smoke and pine blanketed the air; the latter gave a zest to the atmosphere, a tangy scent to the creamy smoke that coated his tongue.

Darkness still surrounded him, but the immediate locale didn't register. Carlin's body trembled with fatigue, his mind numb from the taxing journey.

Sweat slid down his spine. Was the suit's cooling unit malfunctioning?

He stood and faced the pool.

What was that?

The liquid—whatever it was—obviously moved them, but how far?

The new scents told him they were no longer in the same woods. He did an about-face, mindful of their location.

His body shuddered, echoing the movement he felt while within the liquid. The sensation didn't fade as expected.

What did she call it, the local woman? The Aether's Grace?

His mind tried to fathom the truth, the fact that they did move, and how far. It was impossible. Everything he knew about physics and science—which wasn't a lot—told him that such travel was impossible. How could these—he eyed the throng of people around them—*primitives* possess abilities that defied universal laws and make their technology seem trite?

A sense of danger flared, noting the closeness and the numbers of people. By the time he finished the sharp inhale, the rifle was seated in his shoulder. The barrel roved over them.

"Get back!" he shouted.

The fatigue vanished in the presence of an immediate threat. Who were these people? How did they get here? Why were they waiting on them?

At the end of the barrel, Daspar materialized, staring him down.

For a fraction of time, a split second of eternity, he wanted to pull the trigger. Ire compelled the action. Carlin wouldn't lose any sleep over it, and neither would the crew.

It was only a matter of time before the navigator did something else. How far would he cross the line? Would he rape one of the women? Would he take his aggression out on Kodi? What about Gelarae? Kill them in their sleep, stage an accident once they returned to the ship?

What about while on the planet?

"They aren't here to hurt us," Daspar said.

"Get out of the way."

The other shook his head.

"If they intended to hurt us, they would've done so by now. I've been here longer than you. They'll stay back."

The navigator had a point, though Carlin didn't want to admit it, just like he did with them following Gelarae. Carlin bristled in remembrance when Daspar had been vigilant about an attack from above.

What if Carlin could stage an accident and dispatch Daspar?

With reluctance, the ward lowered the weapon, but his grip on the trigger housing remained tight.

A commotion drew their attention. A clutch of people pressed through the growing crowd.

The ward glanced around—behind and above. Wherever they were, it was similar to the last location with the Aether's Grace, but not open to the elements. A cavernous enclosure encircled them, like a hollow in the rock or a small cave.

The procession pressed through, coming from the mouth of the cave.

Carlin peered over the crowd toward the entrance. Light shone through, but a brilliance akin to torches and fires, not sunlight. And above, in the distance, Carlin spotted a small, glittering patch of stars.

A sense of déjà vu washed over him.

The stars, so alien, yet familiar. Perhaps they'd made an impression upon him the last time they came to Celesta Six. Had he stood in this exact spot before and gazed out over the people and beyond the cave?

The crowd parted and drew back, letting a single man step forward. He carried a tall staff with a smooth haft in his left hand. A cluster of spindly twigs reminiscent of crooked fingers crowned the top. The insides glowed a soft, sky-blue.

At first glance, Carlin thought of it as formed gel, but the longer he stared, the more he realized they were crystals. The luminance pulsed in a slow cadence, shifting between the bright and dim.

The scowl from the elderly, staff-wielding man rolled over the crew before resting on Carlin.

His stomach sank and knotted. He'd seen that scowl before, something similar but on a very different face.

"What is this shit, boy?" the man hollered.

He held up a datapad.

"How do you expect to get into the Academy with marks like these?"

"I don't want to go to the Academy," his small, young voice answered.

A vicious backhand landed across Carlin's face.

"Don't fucking back talk me, boy! You'll go where I tell you!"

With a jarring sense, the memory fled.

Carlin blinked, eyes darting between Andrea, the man, and the crowd.

The elder stepped closer, stopping mere feet away. If Carlin desired, he could reach out and grab the man by the neck. It might not be a bad idea, if things turned sour. He held the aura of importance, but the ward readied himself to act, to ensure safe passage for the crew.

The man's eyes narrowed. When he opened his mouth, Carlin expected to hear their language, like Gelarae, but he spoke with a twisted tongue, something far more alien than he ever imagined.

Gelarae stirred from within the cluster of people and meandered over, standing beside the man. Side by side, Carlin couldn't mistake their relation—her father.

She translated: "He says welcome back, star-travelers, and that you're welcome to stay with our people again."

"That's most gracious," Andrea said.

The ward glanced at her. She stood a half-dozen paces away. Didn't she realize he wasn't speaking to her? Gelarae's father paid Andrea no heed, his eyes locked with Carlin's.

The elder spoke again, and his daughter translated.

"There's one small task that must be performed, to restore honor to him, the village, and to the star-travelers."

"Yes," Andrea said again, this time stepping closer. "Anything he wishes."

Gelarae eyed Andrea.

"My father isn't talking to you."

There was something in her tone, a hidden or implied threat, and Carlin heeded the warning. He hoped the chief regent did, too.

His eyes roved over to Andrea. Though her visor was still in place, her brows flickered upward, and she appeared uncertain.

In the time since they awoke without memories, he'd come to know Andrea best. Sharing a bed with her provided its own insights, but intimacy aside, he read her the easiest. Soren's enigmatic presence always confused Carlin. Daspar, well, the good thing about stupidity is simplicity.

And Kodi was rather straightforward.

Kodi!

His eyes flickered to the floor. He found her form a few heartbeats later. A native woman administered to her. He paused long enough to assess that the woman didn't hurt her, and that Kodi's chest moved.

Carlin's gaze slid upward.

"What does your father require?" he asked.

After a few moments, Gelarae translated.

"He says that you must make right after your last trespass."

"That's not exactly what he said," SAVI offered, his voice rippling through Carlin's earpiece.

Judging by the small reactions of his teammates, SAVI spoke to them as well.

"He said, 'You claimed what wasn't yours to behold, aggrieved where you shouldn't have transgressed.'"

"SAVI?" Andrea's voice filled their comms.

Carlin was glad that her visor was still down, and her mouth guard covered her lips.

"I didn't realize you spoke their language."

"I started a compilation from our first visit."

"That's something you should have told us," Daspar chimed in.

Despite the flaring irritation at hearing his voice, the bastard had another valid point.

"SAVI, you'll keep a running translation while we are around Gelarae's people."

"Noted."

"And we'll discuss in great depth what's expected of you," Andrea concluded.

The chief regent's words bothered him. Why did they have to always tell SAVI what to do? The program should have an idea from the countless hours and mission they'd been on. Why wasn't the AI more helpful?

"What does your father wish of me?" Carlin asked Gelarae.

After another brief exchange, Gelarae relayed.

"We must become one of flesh and blood."

"An accurate assessment," SAVI reported. *"In layman's terms, he wants you to marry."*

"Marriage?" all squad members echoed in unison.

"Yes," Gelarae faltered, glancing between the group members. Her brows knitted. "Do you not remember claiming me? My father discovered us and was most aggrieved."

Carlin shook his head.

"We don't remember anything."

He eyed the woman.

"I certainly don't."

Did he really have sex with her? His gaze wandered from the curve of her hips to the robustness of her bosom. He noted her bronze complexion, full lips, and dark, auburn hair. Only her eyes were pale, by comparison, a vivid jade. Desire kindled in his loins, and he stirred, shifting his weight.

"I find this hard to believe," Gelarae said.

"It's true," Soren interjected.

"It doesn't change the past or your grievance."

Gelarae surveyed the group before locking eyes with Carlin.

With her hand held out, she spoke, "If you want a sanctuary for your people, you *will* do this."

Carlin contemplated her proffered hand and shifted again, this time leaning back.

"And when we leave? What then?"

"I'll go with you."

The answer caught him by surprise. He hadn't foreseen the possibility of her leaving her family, her people.

"And if we fly away? We may never come back."

"I realize that."

Gelarae's father stamped his staff with impatience and spoke in brusque tones.

"He wishes you to make your decision or return through the Aether's Grace."

Carlin rolled his eyes at SAVI's explanation, then remembered the squad's comms. He mumbled, barely audible, hoping the mic picked up his words while Gelarae and her father did not.

"Andrea? What's your opinion?"

He sensed her hesitation and heard the stutter.

"I can't answer that. This decision's yours. I can't order you to do something like this."

Soren cleared his throat.

"Not that you'd listen, but in matters of the heart, I'd advise you to listen, but this isn't so simple, is it?"

Not that he wanted to inquire, but to ignore the navigator would be petty, especially when he just asked Andrea and listened to Soren. To dispense with Rhett altogether showed how much he affected Carlin, and that wasn't something he'd admit.

"Daspar?"

"Safety's paramount," the other said without hesitation.

The words took the ward by surprise. He awaited a snark or deprecating joke aimed at him.

"No one's firing at us now, but these people will turn us away if you don't. Go with the lesser of two evils and worry about sorting it out later."

There was a pause.

"Besides, Kodi's still out, and there are worse women you could be married to."

Daspar sighed in the mic.

"Actually, it's not that bad of a deal."

Carlin bit his bottom lip to keep from retorting.

Other than the useless banter, the navigator had a point. Sorting it out later seemed best. The worst part of the ordeal stemmed from Carlin being unable to remember. None of them had reclaimed memories, at least, nothing they shared. As if listening in on his thoughts, the navigator spoke again.

"Has anyone recovered their memories? Does any of this sound familiar?"

He tried to stifle a chuckle.

"I bet Ossaro wishes he remembered the good times right about now."

Andrea sighed in the comm.

Carlin shook his head in answer, but a sliver of guilt tinged in his gut. He'd gotten images, flashes, words, but nothing definitive. Carlin turned and scrutinized the navigator.

"I take it you have?"

Daspar nodded.

"Well? Out with it."

Daspar's eyes darted between the others.

"It's not for everyone to hear."

Carlin was about to rebuke him when Gelarae spoke up.

"My father demands an answer. If you don't consent, he'll be forced to remove you."

With a sigh, Carlin studied his bride-to-be. The tightness in his chest didn't abate.

"Why must we marry?"

A coy smile flitted across the woman's features.

"Please, intended. It's not suitable for the company of others."

"I think we all get the gist of what transpired," Andrea said, her voice strained with patience.

The native's eyes went wide.

"You know?"

Soren shifted.

"It's not hard to figure out what happened."

"You speak of such things?"

Gelarae shook her head, her brows knitted in anger.

"We don't. It's forbidden."

"Then, how do ya—" Daspar started, then caught himself. He fell silent.

Carlin appraised her for a moment. She was a stranger from a bizarre planet on the fringes of reachable space. To be honest, it was a miracle they made it. Her ways were unexpected, her culture—what little they had seen—peculiar. Carlin didn't know what tomorrow would bring, whether they'd find their caretaker and be on their way, or if the Teshren would track them down and destroy them.

But the way behind led to certain death.

For the past two months, they'd been living day to day and in the moment. There were worse ways to spend his last few days, and if everything worked out, and their memories returned, and the caretaker came home, he could figure it out then. Maybe with total recollection, he'd come to understand why he chose Gelarae.

He focused on Andrea.

She stared back with a held breath.

There wasn't longing in her eyes, not a hint of wistfulness, nor the touch of regret. Nothing awaited him down that traveled road.

Carlin turned back to Gelarae.

This time, he looked at her the way a man studies a lover. His breath quickened. If truthful—only to himself as he dared not utter it aloud—he found her much more appealing than Andrea.

He twisted his lips.

The chief regent couldn't command him, and Soren was right. Daspar made the most poignant argument of all. The crew mattered—the entire reason why they returned.

What few obstacles fell into their path didn't dissuade them. They came back for one of their own. He wished he could recall the deed she claimed. He yearned to remember.

In a dark corner of his mind, this whole thing felt like some elaborate joke, an experiment by scientists, and he their rat. His eyes flickered to the gathered natives, to Gelarae's father, and then, to her.

"Tell your father I accept."

"Ossaro?" Andrea broke in.

It hadn't escaped his notice that Andrea started calling them by their rank and last names almost immediately after she broke it off with him. The chief regent used it as a way to distance herself. By subtle means, she exerted her command and came into her own.

"Are you sure?"

"We need sanctuary, and Daspar's right: the crew comes first."

He scrutinized Andrea's face for a moment. He searched for resentment, jealousy, longing, but he only found concern.

An epiphany bloomed in his head: whatever tryst they had, it never meant much to her. Maybe she detected his underlying desire which spurred her to break it off.

In the same vein, he realized she never meant much to him either. Their moments were fun, but nothing more. His fondness remained; love, did not.

No matter what happened, they'd always have that closeness, but the primal urges had vanished.

Without another word, he followed Gelarae, her father, and the entourage out of the cavern.

Chapter Twenty-Two: Muido's Revelation

Kodi's head teemed with a drug-induced fog.

She blinked, and many moments passed before she realized that she'd awakened. Her throat was dry; her voice croaked.

"What happened?"

"You panicked," Andrea answered from nearby. "SAVI took over your suit and knocked you out."

Kodi's eyes fluttered open. The chief regent's frame swam, blurred, as if her eyes were full of water. A few blinks brought her features into focus.

"Why would SAVI do that?"

Andrea's brow furrowed.

"Because you could've gotten us all killed while we tried to rescue you."

The tightness of Andrea's voice and stern features didn't sit well. Kodi waited for the haze of uncertainty to clear. Then, Andrea's face smoothed.

In a softer voice, she said, "Daspar and his quick thinking saved you. He asked SAVI to knock you out."

Andrea looked away, and Kodi followed the commanding officer's gaze. Both watched the lone figure more than thirty paces away. The navigator stood with his weapon cradled in his arms, his palm wrapped around the grip. From this distance, she noted his finger, straight and off the trigger.

"I'm not saying," Andrea said, "what he's done means he deserves outright forgiveness, but maybe cut him some slack? I did, even if it's against my better judgment."

Andrea's words gave her pause. She thought the same prior to landing, but anger came easy. It wasn't the type that mired the heart and aggrieved the soul, but a cleansing fire. Soren should be enraged still, but he found peace with the whole ordeal. That was all well and good, but Daspar's actions shamed her.

Did he prefer sex with a synth?

The chief regent held out a hand, and Kodi took the offered palm. Grabbing hold, Andrea hauled her up. The world tilted. She latched onto Andrea like a stumbling drunk. The urge to vomit came over her, but willpower kept it from spewing. She wouldn't let the sudden sickness best her.

Kodi pushed a blonde lock out of her face. It was then she noticed her helmet had been removed.

"Where's my weapon and helmet?"

Andrea cocked an eyebrow.

"About time."

She gestured off to the side where the gear lay staged next to Andrea's.

Kodi straightened, letting go.

"Where are we?"

"On the other side of that pool you were so afraid of going through. These are Gelarae's people."

Kodi let her eyes wander over the throng milling about. She saw a dozen and a half, perhaps two. They wore roughspun rags that reminded Kodi of a burlap sack.

The oversized brown sack drew her eyes, as a man bent over and opened the top. His hands, though mammoth, hinted at a frailness that came with age. A slight tremor twitched in his hands.

"What's that, Grandpa?"

A chuckle escaped the man.

"A gunny sack, deary."

"What's in it?"

He put his hand inside and then turned. He held his hand open. Two brown ovals rested in his palm.

"Pecans. Do you like pecans?"

She nodded.

"Good, you can help me crack them. Baba wants to make some pie."

Kodi took a deep breath, and the memory faded in a fleeting moment. The remembrance fled, leaving Kodi facing the cold, stone walls.

"Want to tell me about it?" Andrea prodded.

"Tell you about what?"

"Why did you have such an adverse reaction to the pool?"

Kodi shook her head, uncertain of where the fear came from.

"I don't know."

Andrea let the conversation drop, and Kodi was grateful. With Rhett visible, Kodi's gaze swept for Engineer Goski and found him sitting off to the right, about half the distance as the navigator.

"Where's Ward Ossaro?"

Kodi sized up her friend when Andrea made a noise in her throat—the kind that prickled Kodi's curiosity.

There's a story to hear.

The commanding officer's lips twitched.

"He's off getting married."

Kodi blinked and then gave a single, unsure chuckle.

"Getting married? Really? Why aren't you there?"

Andrea rolled her eyes.

"Funny."

"I'm serious. You guys seemed … great together."

As the words left her mouth, she sensed they rang hollow despite the intended kindness. Though a solid couple at first, none would claim it was written in the stars. Their romance wouldn't be remembered as a sonnet from an archaic poet, or a ballad from yesteryears, but more like an explosion of brilliantly colored pyrotechnics, magnificent light bursting with crisp clarity only to diminish after a few awe-filled moments.

"For a time," Andrea admitted.

In silence, Kodi agreed.

The commanding officer continued, "I get the feeling that I've never been with Carlin before."

She hesitated, and Kodi took note. Andrea tilted her head, eyes narrowing as if trying to recall a memory.

"I've been having these dreams, brief flashes."

"About what?"

"Sex. Well, intimate moments."

Kodi suppressed a grin and a witty quip. It was an essential moment for Andrea, and she wouldn't ruin the occasion for her.

"And?"

Andrea's brow twitched into a frown. After a few heartbeats, she slowly shook her head.

"It sounds foolish in my head, how much more so to utter it aloud?"

She shrugged.

"Let's just say I never saw the ward in those glimpses."

Kodi let the topic fade. Nothing would come of pressing the issue. Kodi often found that when she chased those faint memories, they always evaded.

"Anyways," Andrea continued, "Ossaro's getting married to the village elder's daughter. He demanded it."

An uncertain laugh escaped Kodi this time.

"Wait, you weren't joking?"

Andrea bobbed her head.

"I thought you were."

"Wish I was."

Kodi's eyes narrowed. An emotion laced her voice but not wistful regret.

"Did you tell him to do it?"

The chief regent shook her head.

"Don't understand why he would agree to it. We just got here. Doesn't he remember why we returned?"

Andrea cocked an eyebrow.

"Apparently, on the last trip, the village elder caught Ossaro with his daughter."

"Who's the elder's daughter?"

"Gelarae."

Kodi didn't say anything in the immediate wake of the proclamation. After the initial fright from Gelarae's appearance, Kodi discerned her beauty in a rustic and wild-type of way. Her clothing drew Kodi's eye, and upon closer inspection, she appreciated what Gelarae could offer.

Given makeup, a proper shower, and a haircut, undeniable beauty lay beneath. Maybe Ossaro knew this, too? Did looks factor into him agreeing to this marriage? Kodi still couldn't fathom such a ludicrous notion.

"She knows he's going to leave when we are done, right?" Kodi blurted.

It's the only thing that made sense.

Andrea nodded again but didn't say anything. She kept her eyes on Daspar, as if afraid to let Kodi see her pain or bottled emotions.

"Why don't you stop this sham?"

Andrea sighed a deep breath. She pinched the bridge of her nose.

"Is it a sham?"

Andrea shrugged.

"Ossaro's a big boy and knows what he's doing. If I go in there and tell him to stop, what does that accomplish?"

Andrea regarded her for a moment, and Kodi detected a quiet anger simmering just under the skin.

What spurred the raw emotion? Ossaro's marriage or something else?

Perhaps it stemmed from Ossaro's fling with a wild, jungle girl? Or did the problem go deeper? Did Andrea feel threatened because she was cast aside for someone more beautiful?

Kodi wasn't acquainted with a deep understanding of Andrea's personality, or herself for that matter, but one sore subject observed from old logs was Andrea's sister and her inherent beauty.

It hurt to admit, but Kodi knew Andrea didn't match Gelarae.

"He screwed up last time," Andrea broke into her thoughts, "and it's on him to make it right. He realizes refusal means we'll be sent right back through the Aether's Grace or whatever they call it. We'd have enemies at our front and back. Or they may kill us outright for his dishonor."

Andrea took a deep breath, more to steady herself than anything.

"This is the way it has to be."

"And he didn't even invite us!" Kodi chided in a mock-outrage.

Andrea snorted in amusement, the reaction Kodi hoped for.

"So, what's the plan?"

"It hasn't changed. We find our missing member. At the very least, I hope Gelarae's people can point us in the right direction."

"We'll see, if all goes off without a ... hitch?"

Andrea rolled her eyes and grinned.

"God, that's the worst pun ever. Just stop."

"But it got you to smile, and we need more of that."

"You're right, we do need more smiles."

A sad twinkle touched the chief regent's eyes.

Andrea shuffled off to speak with Goski, then Daspar.

Something had changed in the navigator. Kodi spotted this by the way he carried himself, the way he stood. He carried himself with a soldier's posture—rigid spine, measured stance. She hated to admit it, but he wore the look well. He didn't have that terrible, oily grin on his face, the mischief in his eyes, and that suited her fine.

In this somber atmosphere, they didn't need laughs and giggles—not the kind he provided. Preparing for the worst should preoccupy their time and focus. Since landing, they'd been shot at, chased, sent through a pool of glowing goo, and stood still as a giant monster passed behind them. The last proved the hardest, at least concerning bravery.

She marveled how Andrea managed; Kodi couldn't help but whimper during the ordeal. She glanced down—her hands were shaking at the memory. Just thinking about it brought back the terror. What else were they going to see?

What else would they encounter?

When Andrea left Daspar, Kodi ambled over to him.

She moved slowly; her stomach still churned with queasiness, and her equilibrium remained imbalanced. Daspar noted her progress out of his peripheral vision, and he half-turned toward her. She glimpsed the war within him. He wanted to help, to give support, but the previous ire she often displayed kept him at bay.

When she drew close enough that he couldn't ignore her, he turned to face her, but kept his mouth shut and his expression blank.

"Chief Regent Hessner tells me you saved my life."

He responded with a dip of his head.

"Thank you. It was probably the last thing you wanted to do after the way I treated you."

He gave an uneasy grin, his eyes averted.

"Still, you didn't leave me behind. Thanks."

She took a few steps when he called.

"Are you remembering anything?"

The odd question brought her up short. Other than the few flashes of images and words that tumbled in her head, she couldn't. The fact he asked implied that he had. She shook her head and turned to face him.

"No, but I wish I did. Have you?"

He nodded.

"Only a little—nothing substantial."

"What do you remember?" she asked before wincing on the inside. Her voice came out high, almost childlike with curiosity.

"A memory of Andrea," he said, then gazed in the commanding officer's direction. She retreated from the cavern, wading deeper into the local populace.

Does he still have a thing for Andrea? First the synth, now her?

"What?"

"I think—"

He shook his head.

"What?"

"I think she's married."

A burst of uncontainable, bright laughter bubbled out of her.

"Andrea? Married? Yeah right. To who? You?"

Rhett's brow frowned and his face flushed.

"No, not to me. To the Caretaker."

His words silenced the laughter.

"Oh?"

Her mood turned dark with his disclosure.

"Oh."

Kodi thought back to the conversation with Andrea when she wondered why the caretaker chose to stay behind and not her. Now, the picture came into focus a bit more. If the caretaker willingly stayed behind, then this might explain his actions. The thought of a marriage between the commanding officer and the caretaker had never crossed Kodi's mind.

No wonder why he stayed behind.

"Did you tell her?"

Daspar shook his head.

"Are you kidding? I'm not sure it's a memory. And if no one else is having them, it has to be a delusion."

Her lips twisted as she thought about what he said. The fleeting flash about her grandfather didn't count, and after Andrea's confession about remembering sex, it made Kodi more confident that her own flickers were more than dreams.

Still, Daspar had a valid point. Kodi hadn't had enough to warrant telling everyone about the visions.

"Tell me if you get any more of them."

"Yeah."

He nodded and shrank back like he sulked or wilted.

Did he expect something more? She shook the thought away. No, that wasn't it. Something bothered him beyond the subject of their prior history. Was it the returning memory or this planet?

Kodi inspected the cavern, turning in each direction, careful not to slip on the slick, moss-covered floor. Rock jutted through the greenery.

The walls were painted, though not with crude, rudimentary works but that of an artisan's hands. Without a doubt, they painted a story, a history.

Kodi moved closer. The damp air felt cool against her face.

One mural held an endless mass of people, soldiers. They resembled knights, the fairytale kind. Some rode horses, but most were on their feet. Shields and swords filled her eyes as did the monsters they battled.

Still, the mural called to her.

Vivid colors—the splashes of dirt, copper, and bronze against the rivulets of crimsons that cut swaths of blood. Brilliant spruce, olive, and sage against the cyan, cerulean, and sapphires, all tarnished by the gore, violence, and age.

"It's a great war," an accented voice said from behind her.

Kodi spun, her eyes wide.

She hadn't heard the man approach. The sudden movement made her stomach roil, but she kept from throwing up.

The man smiled, his teeth flashing.

"I don't mean to scare, star-traveler."

He dipped his shaven head. In the torchlight's flicker, his features remained obscured. He stepped closer, his movements slow. Standing closer to the open flame of torches, she distinguished his dark olive skin.

"You don't look like Gelarae."

"No."

He smiled. Despite his thick accent, Kodi understood him well enough.

"I'm from a far-off settlement. My name's Muido."

"What are you doing here then, Muido?"

"I've come to see these returned star-travelers."

He paused, his brow nettled.

"Why did you come back?"

"It's a long story."

"Time isn't lacking, I think. There's a wedding, and the feast, and afterward …"

He drew his hands together.

She nodded.

"Your man won't return until morning. What's your name?"

"Kodi. How can you speak our language?"

He smiled again, something sly and secretive.

"A question for another time, perhaps?"

He cocked his head to the side.

"I sense there are questions you wish to ask, too?"

In the back of her mind, she noticed how he sidestepped the question, but with the mural lingering in her mind, she let it pass. There would be time later.

Kodi regarded the wall.

"What can you tell me about this?"

"It happened long ago before we remade the world."

"Remade?"

"Our world has lived and died three times. We are the fourth."

"What do you mean, lived and died?"

Muido's lips thinned. His hand ran over his shaven head.

"It's difficult. Our people have risen up and reached the high top—"

"Pinnacle?" Kodi offered, raising a hand to show what she meant.

He observed the movements and nodded.

"Yes, the pinnacle. Our people rose to the pinnacle—only to tear themselves down. They destroy all they'd created over the life of the world."

Kodi pondered his words, and then realized, with fleeting horror, what he meant.

"You've had three apocalypses?"

"I know not this word."

"An apocalypse—a world-ending event. You destroy yourselves, everything's lost, and you have to start over."

His face brightened.

"Yes, yes! This is it! Apacoliss…"

A grin stole across her features.

"Apocalypse."

"Yes, that."

He leaned closer to the painting.

"A war from before the second apocalypse."

He stepped away, walking toward the mouth of the cavern, but his eyes remained attuned, searching for something. About halfway down the wall, he came to a stop.

"Ah, here. This one."

He pointed.

Kodi stirred and closed the distance between them.

She glanced up. A dark, tall figure stood in a mass of monsters. The creatures looked like demons, grotesque, twisted figures. Some of those pictured carried multiple limbs or eyes or noses; some were tall and broad, others short and fat, each uglier than the last.

But the lean silhouette drew Kodi's eye.

It stood like a wraith, the wind snapping at the garments. Only a slit of eyes appeared in the hood.

"Who is that?" she asked.

"Don't know."

"You don't—?"

He shook his head.

"No, no one knows his name. This is a long time ago. Those who may have once known his name have been dead for thousands of generations."

The number of years that it would take to make a hundred generations boggled her mind, but thousands? Even if each only lived fifty years, and she only counted for a thousand...

"You mean to tell me that this happened over fifty thousand years ago?"

The number staggered her—a blip compared to the age of the universe, but to the mind of a human, it might as well be an eternity.

"No, no," he said, shaking a finger in admonishment. "That's much too short. Maybe four times that."

"Two hundred thousand years!" she shrieked.

Muido nodded.

"Yes, that is right."

"I can't begin to fathom ..."

"Yes—a fathom, that's what it is called."

"What is?"

"A measurement of time: a fathom. This happened over two fathoms ago: two-hundred thousand years."

The numbers sent a tether of sickness through her.

"I think I need to sit down."

Kodi lowered to her haunches, but her stomach continued to churn. How did Muido figure out how long it'd been? He could count the years—but not recall a name of someone who ...

Kodi focused on the dark figure.

If ever a stereotypical bad guy existed, he embodied the persona. Just looking at him sent a shudder down her spine.

"What did he try to do?"

Muido shrugged.

"Take over the world? Destroy it? Unify the races? One can only guess."

"How?"

To this, he frowned as he puzzled out her words. He scratched his thumb against the stubble on his chin.

"How did he try to take over or destroy the world?"

Muido frowned.

"He possessed … powers."

"Powers?"

He winced.

"Abilities?"

"What do you mean abilities?"

Muido sighed. "Hurt you with thoughts, with words. Make you bleed."

"You mean he hurt people with his mind?"

The man nodded.

"Yes, that's it. You can die from it."

Kodi pondered his words. She didn't want to doubt the local man, but as he stated, it was so long ago. Who could say whether or not he recounted fact? The ludicrous notion baffled her, someone hurting or killing with their mind, with words. What words hurt people?

"There are others like him," Muido said.

"There are?"

"Yes. They're our enemy, the Teshren."

Her heart spasmed like being struck by lightning. She lurched to her feet before she could exhale.

"The Teshren use these words, this power to hurt?"

"To kill," he corrected. "They'll try to kill you, too."

Kodi's gaze drifted from the dark figure to the last location she saw Andrea. She didn't spy her friend, but that wouldn't deter her. She had to tell the chief regent—and the crew. If what Muido said was true, they were in danger, real danger.

How could they block words that inflicted harm? How could they battle an enemy who hurt with their thoughts?

This revelation changed everything.

"Shit."

Chapter Twenty-Three: Soren

"Let me get this straight," Soren said.

He held his hand in front of him, punctuating each word with a gesture. "Someone can hurt us with words? Like voodoo?"

Kodi rolled her eyes and went into another long-winded exposition.

Soren sighed through his nose. Good thing they hadn't told him this the night before. He wouldn't have gotten any sleep. With Ossaro marrying the local girl, and Andrea communing with the elders, there was little left to do but sleep. Once the wedding started, each crew member was assigned sleeping quarters.

The revelry lasted throughout the night, and Soren tossed and turned, yearning for his bunk and Emma.

He missed her.

The synthetic proved to be a companion in more than one way, and she looked after his well-being. He could tell her anything, and she would be receptive, often offering suggestions or advice without judgment. He'd rather be there with her than out here.

An ache festered in his heart as he drifted off to sleep the night before. Soren didn't think it was possible to miss someone so much, but he missed the synth.

Emma's superiority solidified while Soren observed the group. He and Emma never fought, not like the rest of the retinue. Andrea and Ossaro had a falling out. And Kembly ... poor girl. His mood soured when he thought of the navigator, so he steered clear and pretended that Daspar and his infraction didn't exist.

When dawn came, Soren roused from the small hut to find the rest of the team standing around one of the village's pits. A darker complected local stood with them. Heat radiated from the depression, the coals still glowing. They appeared sullen and ragged. Ossaro looked like he hadn't gotten a wink of sleep. Did the new missus keep him up all night, or did the village party play a part?

Andrea stared into the distance, blank and expressionless, but Soren understood her mind worked behind that vacant gaze.

Kembly appeared distressed but stood near Daspar, the latter his rifle slung low, eyes roving the village. Once Soren closed on the group, Kembly told him what she'd learned. He understood Andrea's blank and troubled expression.

"Yeah, without a better way to put it," Kodi said, stopping herself short. "That's exactly what it sounds like."

"You mean to tell me magic's real?" Ossaro asked.

"I'm sure you experienced quite a bit of magic last night," Daspar quipped.

"Stow it," Hessner said out of the side of her mouth. "So, these people can do magic or voodoo or whatever kind of supernatural bullshit. How do we fight against something we can't see or counter?"

"You don't," Muido said. "Not unless you can do it, too."

"There has to be a way," the ward voiced.

He was right, of course, it was just a matter of discovering it.

"Maybe if they can't talk," Muido offered.

"So, this is why they didn't have weapons on their bodies," Ossaro ventured. "Their weapons are words, which explains a lot, actually."

"What about the sticks?" Soren inquired.

Now that he thought about it, he did remember the sticks.

"Sticks? What sticks?" Kembly asked, her brow twitching.

"Yeah, he's right," Andrea said, excitement coming into her voice.

Her eyes grew round, and she turned to a man Soren didn't recognize.

"The bodies had sticks. Is that where their magic or voodoo comes from, Muido?"

The man shrugged.

"They always have them."

"So, the sticks are the issue," Ossaro said. "We don't have anything to combat wood except our blasters."

He glanced around to the others.

Daspar's head tilted back and forth.

"Worked before. I think the key's full auto."

"Spray and pray?" the ward mocked.

Daspar nodded.

"Spray and pray."

"Yeah, but the weapons will overheat," Andrea interjected.

"Got a better idea?" the navigator challenged.

"Look," Soren broke in. "We each got a blaster and a rifle. When one has overheated, draw the other. We should move in pairs at a minimum, take turns covering each other—four times the amount of fire at any given moment. Two weapons a person, one at a time."

The ward nodded.

"That's a sound plan, but how are we going to find the caretaker?"

At the mention of the missing member, Daspar flinched as if the word inflicted a wound.

The reaction caught Soren off guard, and he wondered about the implication. The group argued amongst themselves for a time, and the engineer let his mind drift back to the ship.

He needed a shower and craved a decent meal. He took a few tentative steps backward, trying to melt into the background as they bickered. He never understood how they could fight so much. Or talk for that matter. All they did was talk, talk, talk.

Emma never rambled or chattered.

Emma.

A pang of loneliness echoed through him. He knew what the others thought, that he only bought Emma to service sexual appetites. While true, he bought her so he wouldn't be alone.

The others were too busy fighting amongst themselves and trying to control everything. In solitude, in the tranquil setting of his quarters, the memories came back.

He remembered.

Not everything but enough.

Emma's origins were among those memories. In despair, he bought the synthetic. Not for sex, but for love. He didn't love the synthetic, he loved what she represented, the woman she was modeled after, in the image of his late wife, even carrying her name.

So, yes, the physical aspect of their relationship did manifest, but it was the emotional and mental attachment that compelled him.

Further, Emma's programming went far beyond simple command prompts and integers. She held his wife's memories … well, the recordings he submitted.

Any film he possessed, every video of her smile, her voice, words, mannerisms, he submitted it all. All videos done from her perspective were implanted like a memory. All the footage he shot of his late wife was also embedded, like a ghost protocol, constructed for behavioral reasons. Her programming enabled the synth to embody his late wife, to sound and react just like her.

How long he lost himself in those thoughts, he couldn't say, but the man called Muido had left, and Gelarae's father had returned.

"Soren!" Kembly said, walking up to him. "Snap out of it."

"What?"

"We're going to recon an outpost not far from here."

He blinked at her.

"I assume that's relative."

"What do you mean?"

"Surely it isn't within walking distance? Maybe we'll take the Aether's Grace to arrive there."

Kembly trembled.

"I fucking hope not."

The reaction triggered memories for Soren, one in which Kembly expressed a paralyzing fear. Over the years, she made milestones, but the open water crippled her.

"Aquaphobia," he mumbled.

"What?"

Her green eyes narrowed.

"Let's get going!" Andrea barked from behind them. "We've got a trek, minimum of three hours."

"That's fucking great," Daspar groaned.

"Grab your bucket," Ossaro said, the words slow and halting as if repeating something he had heard before.

"Pack up your balls," Kembly muttered.

"Weapons loaded," Soren spouted, a surprise to even himself.

"Kill them all," Daspar and Hessner said in unison.

"Holy shit, did we just all remember something?" Hessner exclaimed.

"Sounds like it." Ossaro sounded shocked.

Soren shivered.

The saying, the ditty, came so naturally.

A smattering of chatter broke out as they smiled and talked about what just happened, as if it manifested as a herald of more memories, but the smiles didn't last.

Within five minutes, the crew, plus Ossaro's new wife, her overbearing father, and the strange Muido, who seemed to hover close to Kodi, headed out of the village.

Soren eyed Muido, unsure of how to evaluate him. His closeness to the first officer didn't sit well with him, but it didn't mean something sinister. If anything, Soren worried about a cultural clash, a blunder on Kembly's part. All Muido had to do was show respect and interest, and Kembly's resentment for Daspar might make her do something foolish and off the cuff. If casual sex wasn't a part of their culture, this might prove to be the blunder that pulls the unraveling thread.

With a suppressed sigh, he turned his thoughts away and focused on the journey ahead.

The trek was much different than the one from the ship to the rally point. That had been rolling hills and jungle. This time, the trek was rocky and steep with a smattering of tall trees.

Soren traipsed behind, Kodi and Muido in front of him. He caught snippets of their conversation. Muido had noticed Kodi's eyes, their shape. This world, whatever it was called, had people similar to Kembly's ancestry.

"They're called Syans," he prattled.

Soren suppressed a sigh and continued on, trying to block them out.

The party wasn't inclined to stop much, but Andrea forced the issue once an hour. The arduous journey took much longer than the initial three-hour estimate. It was mind-numbing and painfully slow. Soren wished more than once he'd downloaded music to his helmet.

When they arrived within sight of the outpost, Soren fell against the embankment with relief. The others sent him sharp looks, almost wincing. Landing in a heap made more noise than he intended. Sweat poured from his face.

"Sorry," he said between gasps. "Not as young as you."

"You're not old," Daspar remarked over the comms. He was further down the line, beyond sight.

"Do we have a tally?" Hessner's voice came over the comms.

"I see at least a dozen," Ossaro's voice came. "There'll be more inside."

"How do you know?" Daspar asked.

"There's always more inside. If this guy's a competent commander, we're only seeing half of the force at most. To be safe, I'd say a quarter."

"But you don't know."

"Does your visor possess x-ray vision?" the ward clipped back.

"Boys, behave," Hessner's voice soothed over the comms.

There was something in her voice, soft and almost silken in texture, and if Soren had to guess, it wasn't directed at the ward.

"Ossaro, ask Gelarae what her assessment is."

Soren had to hand it to their chief regent, he never thought to ask the woman or her father. As far back as the engineer recalled, Andrea proved time and again to be a competent commander.

In fact, other than the vague mention of the Pinshi incident in the video the crew saw, he had to wonder why she wasn't a higher rank. Everyone had found their calling, their solider's streak, everyone but Kodi. Even Daspar stumbled into his function despite the constant less-than-professional banter.

Hessner unearthed her commanding presence with each passing day, and Carlin fell into step the moment he discovered his role. Still, Soren worried about the first officer.

Soren glanced over at the pair of bodies lying a few meters away.

Kembly and Muido seemed to be getting comfortable with each other, perhaps a touch too familiar. It wasn't his place to say anything. He was no one's father, and Kembly was a big girl. She got herself into the mess with Daspar, and she managed the fallout well enough.

Moreover, as long as it didn't affect his life, the mission, or their safety, he didn't care. He just wanted to find the caretaker, return to the ship, get off this rock and be en route back home. His thoughts turned back to the comfort of his quarters and bed. Emma's soft thighs flitted through his head, and he shoved the image away.

He had to focus.

Soren's visor opened, and he pulled his water container.

The cool water, though refreshing, did little to temper his sweating. Kembly, who laid on her side with her back to him, turned her head, glancing out of the corner of her eye.

"Don't mind me," the engineer grumbled, then faced the other direction. He let his eyes roam over the surrounding country. Trees, rocky terrain, and sharp hills would make it impossible to land The Demon here, which was a pity. He wished they could hitch a ride back.

He glanced down into the outpost.

There was enough room within the compound for the ship to land but not much. But they had to take the enemy's fortification first.

Ossaro's voice crackled over the comms.

"Uh, she doesn't advise attacking today but tomorrow."

"Why?" Hessner asked.

"She says it's too late in the day, and that shift change is bound to happen in the next few hours. Also, they make contact with their … uh, for lack of a better word, parent command twice a day? She also says that's bound to happen soon."

"So?"

"If they aren't here to answer, more will arrive."

"We'll be gone by then."

"Yes, but her village is the only settlement nearby, and the Teshren will seek retribution against her people."

The information troubled Soren.

"Wait!" he said, pulling the water container away from his mouth. "You mean they're aware of her village, and we stayed there last night?"

Ossaro was silent for a long moment, undoubtedly questioning his bride.

"She says individual groups of Teshren answer to a higher group, and rarely communicate amongst the smaller cells. Her village pays for protection from this group, but this outfit was responsible for taking the caretaker."

"Yeah," Daspar interrupted. "I've fucking heard enough. When do we hit them, Chief?"

Soren poked his head over the berm.

The outpost resembled a small village with a ten-foot wall made of wood posts. Six guard towers stood along the weak fortification. It wouldn't take much to get through the perimeter. Several small, crude structures were erected around the outskirts, but in the center was a larger complex, easily four times the size of all others, and made of stone and mortar.

"We need to clear that," Soren said to no one in particular.

"Elaborate," Hessner said.

"The structure, it's got to be sixty to eighty feet long by forty wide. Two stories. More stone and mortar than wood. Might even have a basement."

"Suggestions?"

"Well, I'm not a tactical expert, but we've got one. His wife is advising you not to attack. Let's find out what the big man has to say for himself."

"We can figure out what he's gonna say," Daspar snarked. "He's already whipped."

"Cut the shit, Daspar," Hessner said. "Ossaro?"

"We've got a dozen outside. There are five of us and six towers. We could spread out and take out five of the six, leaving the one in the back alone. It'd be too far away to react or respond if we all attacked at once. With our radios, coordination isn't a problem. Without knowing what the range is on these voodoo guys, it's hard to say, but it can't be longer than my sniper rifle. I can take two towers. We should synchronize our attack. Less likely for them to pinpoint us."

"Sounds easy enough."

"Yeah, but Goski's right. We'll need to clear the structure. Our fire will draw out most, but not all of them. If anything, their higher-ups will be somewhere in there, and they won't go down without a fight. We'll have to sweep each room, floor by floor. It'll take time."

"What's the alternative?" Hessner queried.

"Gelarae says to sleep here and attack tomorrow."

"How long until the suns set?"

"About four hours until the first one, the second sets two hours later."

"Six hours," Hessner echoed.

Soren couldn't see his commanding officer, but he paid attention enough to know her tone. She yearned to attack and was justifying it to herself.

Despite the advice given, she warred with a logical reason to proceed. Six hours would be plenty of time to take care of this outpost, but also put Gelarae's village in danger. True, her father could blame it on the sky-people, and as long as the Teshren accepted this, all would be well.

If they didn't...

The crew had the firepower and superior technology that overwhelmed the primitive Teshren, but they didn't have numbers on their side, which almost mitigated any advantage.

Soren let out a long, silent breath through his nose.

He wasn't sure whether to attack or wait. The local populace knew best, when to stay and when to go, but for each hour they wasted, the caretaker's survival diminished. They'd already lost months.

Was he even alive?

The crew member was the entire reason for them returning, and while he agreed with the decision at the time, now he wasn't so sure.

He'd want others to come back for him, but would they?

He hoped so, which made this mission seem necessary.

"We're going in," Hessner declared. "Fan out, take a guard tower a piece. We'll synchronize on Ossaro's go, then we hit them hard."

Chapter Twenty-Four: Ossaro

Carlin's arms ached as he held the sniper rifle in the pocket of his shoulder. Clearing rooms was a bitch.

The barrel panned the room as he swept. His fingers lay stiff against the housing, straight and off the trigger. The hip satchel of grenades grew heavy. Luckily, they hadn't needed to use them yet.

Though his primary job centered around ship safety and its commanding officer, he didn't want to inflict unnecessary casualties.

Only a few imbeciles attacked them en route to the main building, becoming martyrs and joining their fellow soldiers in death. In a way, Carlin felt terrible for every life they took, but the Teshren left them no choice, attacking them moments after landing on their planet. They didn't even try to establish contact.

Had they been warned—Ossaro and the crew—the last time to never come back? He didn't think so, how else were they supposed to collect their Caretaker?

Carlin held the firearm firmly as he slipped further into the room, popping around a corner. The area within was devoid of life.

The fight for the outpost passed as a skirmish. The real battle took place inside, clearing room by room, and the Teshren didn't make it easy. It was tedious and nerve-racking, the unknown lurking behind each door.

Carlin paused in his search, the long barrel coming to rest on a desk. He waded deeper into the room, his footfalls soft despite the stone floor. He rounded the desk, letting the end of the rifle lead.

He blew out a sigh as no one lurked underneath. Though they'd only seen humans, or what passed for them on this alien world, Carlin always expected to find some hideous monster, some alien.

Perhaps his imagination ran away with him?

Fighting an unsuspecting enemy tilted the battle cadence to their favor. His synchronized plan helped, eliminating five of the six guard towers in one fell swoop. The sixth fell a few precious seconds later.

By the time any response was mustered from within the structures, the echo of the second shot had faded, and the new arrivals were none the wiser to their location.

Carlin swept to the left, turning. His head swiveled ahead of the barrel. He padded deeper into the room, stepping around wooden cabinets and through doorways.

The group breached the front gate with a concentrated barrage of laser fire that burned through the barred wood. The battle passed with a quickened, adrenaline-filled pace. He vaguely recalled gliding from cover to cover, seeking safety while laying suppressing fire against the entrenched troops.

An explosion ripped through the earth, dirt peppering his armor, smoke fogging his visor. The clear protector kept the soot from his eyes, but some still found its way through his neck guard. The grit trickled down his chest and rubbed against him like sandpaper.

No matter how many Teshren they dropped, the enemy kept advancing. Somehow these primitives, with their shoddy understanding of structurally-sound buildings, managed to repel most of their fire with some form of an energy shield.

The crew didn't even have that kind of technology.

Whatever they used, it mitigated any military advantage they possessed. Carlin relied on body armor. Did these people possess some form of tech they couldn't see? The only alternative was to believe Muido, and by context, Gelarae.

Voodoo. *Magic.*

Carlin shifted the sniper rifle as he finished searching the room. He stepped back towards the central hall.

The notion of powers seemed absurd during the pitch of battle. His world consisted of rules, facts, and truths. These magical abilities shattered any semblance of absolute laws of science and reality. It was whimsical, a superstition that gave birth to fairy tales. Still, he couldn't deny what he saw.

He paused in the doorway as the memory resurfaced.

The air rippled around him as if slugs from an ancient gun missed him by mere inches. His insides fluttered, knowing how close death came. He lifted the weapon to return fire. He primed the trigger, a slight pressure. The charge built.

With the enemy sighted through the scope, he gave a slow squeeze. The charged light tore from the weapon. The sniper bolt broke through the near-invisible barrier around the attacker.

The man fell over dead. The cauterized, gaping hole in his chest made sure of it.

Acrid smoke curled through the air and through Carlin's filters. Ossaro stared at the man for a moment longer. His victim's eyes bulged wide in surprise with his mouth falling open, the last scream stifled.

The memory wavered, and he tried to shake his head clear.

An impact slammed into him.

Pain exploded through his left arm and heat radiated from his shoulder.

He dove through the door.

The second shot went high.

Whatever grazed him stung like the sudden lash of a wet towel, or a handful of scorpions stinging in unison. He screamed and scrambled on his back, moving deeper into the room.

Coming to a stop, he glanced at his shoulder.

"Ossaro!" Andrea screamed.

"He's fine," Soren called.

"Ward Ossaro," SAVI intoned in his ear. "I have detected a breach in your suit. Are you bleeding?"

"Stow it, SAVI!" Carlin yelled. "Somebody get that fucker!"

"On it," Daspar said.

At that moment, his dislike and mistrust fell away. This was different, being in the pitch of battle. The navigator didn't crumble away, running like a coward. He didn't leave Ossaro hanging as he saved his own skin. The man fought and covered him. Just like he did with Kodi.

Daspar saved Kodi and never made an ordeal of it, something uncharacteristic of him. He expected him to demand a reward, a parade, or back into Kodi's life, but none of that happened.

Daspar's weapon opened up in a hail of laser fire. The air split with the whirling whine of his weapon. Another scream rent from the locals, and another corpse was added to the body count.

"The way's clear," Kodi said over the comms.

"Ossaro? Can you move?"

"I'm good, Chief."

He peered at his shoulder again.

SAVI proved correct, the graze tore through the suit and his flesh bled, but it was little more than a scrape. He blew out a breath, realizing his luck and how close it came to running out.

"Take point, Ossaro. Kembly, Soren, on the flanks. Daspar, the rear. We move on Ossaro's lead."

Grunting, the big man hoisted himself up and lumbered forward. The blast hit the left shoulder, not the one he fired with. He glided down the hall, searching for their enemy.

When they ran out of Teshren to kill topside and closed on the building's entry point, they shuffled forward at almost a run.

"Stack up, stack up," Andrea urged in a hurried voice.

With Carlin at the point, he kicked open the door and entered the dark building. He expected electricity, lights, candles, something, but the inside remained dark.

"Activating heat sensors and night vision," SAVI said.

Carlin's visor noted torches along the wall, still hot enough to give off heat.

"Recently snuffed out," Kodi observed.

"Cut all external communication," Andrea ordered. "Only voice through closed comms."

Carlin didn't know how he felt about that. They had Muido, Gelarae, and her father, Nautwer, with them. How were they supposed to know when to go or stop if all communication was internal?

"Chief?" Carlin started.

"Yeah. Tell them to stay in the middle."

Once relayed, he retook point and started down the narrow, dark hall.

The stone walls ran straight and smooth, an architect that belied the outside of the structure. Something wasn't right; it didn't add up. On the surface, these buildings looked like they could barely stand, but the innards told a different story.

"You guys seeing this?" he said.

"No," Daspar answered.

"Me, either," Kodi echoed.

"Yes," Soren answered. "The architecture's distinctly different."

"How so?" Andrea asked.

"Outside looks like a shack. In here, it resembles a bunker," Soren said.

Carlin found himself nodding in agreement. Now that he said it, it did make sense—built to withstand more than what the exterior led on.

"So, what does it mean?" Kodi pressed.

"It means someone's been lying to somebody," Daspar said. "Either on purpose or unwittingly."

"Wait a minute," Carlin said, stopping. He glanced back. "If you mean to imply—"

"Eyes front!" Andrea snapped.

Carlin bit back a retort.

She was right, of course. At least her head was in the moment. He should've known better, and she probably expected more from the ship's ward, but Daspar pushed buttons.

"Yes," the navigator said, as if reading his mind. "I mean Gelarae, but only in the sense that she may not be aware. They expected the only edge they had was their voodoo, if we are still going with that, but it seems there's more."

"Figure it out later," Kodi said. "Keep moving."

"You heard the woman," Andrea added.

In this manner, they began clearing the building.

They kicked in each door and pointed their weapons into empty, dark rooms. The only heat signatures were from expired torches. Daspar brought up the rear, marking the doors with an infrared mist spewing from his left gauntlet. According to SAVI, they all had the ability in the gauntlet on their rifle-supporting hand.

Carlin shook his head, bringing his mind back to the present.

Going door to door had a mind-numbing effect with monotonous repetition. At the end of the hall, a T-shaped stairwell manifested. The first floor lay clear with fewer bodies than anticipated. Carlin hugged the wall and edged closer to the corner, keeping the rifle trained on the opposite wall.

With comms still set to internal, he bade the others to stack up on him. Each crew member hurried into position.

The tension in his shoulders grew taut, and his insides clenched. Each time he kicked open a door, his body tensed. It was the unknown. Each room could be his last.

Carlin did a quick pop out around the corner, dropping to a knee. Whoever stacked behind him also popped out but in a standing position.

The way was clear.

Carlin checked behind him. Soren followed him, and beyond the engineer; Andrea and Kembly cleared the other side. The commanding officer waved to Gelarae and the others to follow, and they moved between the two groups.

Gathering himself, Carlin stood and started up the stairs as a hail of fire opened up.

Everyone dove for cover, back down the way they came, but not before taking hits. His own grunt of pain was drowned out by Andrea's. Carlin took another hit, this one along his right ribs but nowhere as bad as the shoulder injury. In fact, the armor hardly showed a scorch mark.

Andrea's, by contrast, smoked from two blasts to the chest area. She'd been lucky nothing pierced her chest protector.

"Where's that coming from?" Andrea shouted.

"Further up the stairs. We'll have to charge to clear it."

Carlin popped his head around the corner again, glancing up the stairs.

"Daspar, on me. There's cover at the top."

The navigator neared and waited. With a single nod, they charged up the last steps, taking positions on either side of the stairwell. At the top, the wall bulged, a lip jutted out, not quite large enough to hide behind.

Carlin's sniper rifle proved problematic, but Daspar, who'd taken the left side, snapped up his blaster and laid down cover fire.

The ward tried to maneuver the weapon to his left shoulder, but the bulk and awkwardness coupled with his injury prevented him. Movement behind him made the ward glance back.

Andrea, Kembly, and Goski ascended the stairs to provide backup. Their forms hugged the wall to stay clear of their fire. By the time Carlin figured out his situation, Daspar's gunfire had faded, and he called the all-clear.

SAVI spoke over the squad band as the others joined them up top.

"Ward Ossaro, I detect another hit, and your armor integrity is down to sixty-three percent. Your chest plate will withstand another hit, but I can only speculate the outcome after that."

"Noted," he said, shrugging the AI off. "What of the others?"

"The chief regent took a graze on the left upper chest and ribs and is down to eighty-one percent. Sub Regent Kembly is sitting at ninety-two percent, taking damage to her right quad."

"Papa?" Gelarae's voice broke through the silent cluster.

With all communication set to internal, it was odd to hear words spoken aloud.

Carlin jerked his head toward the sound and realized that Gelarae and her father hadn't joined them.

"Shit," he muttered to himself.

He rushed back down the flight.

"Papa?" she called again, louder.

A sob escaped her.

In the background, Andrea snapped out orders, "Goski, Daspar, hold position."

Carlin rounded the corner at the T-shaped landing and found Gelarae cradling her father's limp form. A gaping hole smoked from Nautwer's throat. A spray of blood caked his clothes and neck. His eyes stared blankly ahead; shock etched on his features.

Gelarae sobbed. Carlin knelt beside her. The sound of weapon movements reassured him that someone covered his back, thinking of safety even with a death in the group.

They were good.

Then, silence fell, all but her sobs.

Carlin focused on Nautwer.

He should've never agreed to bring them along. They were a burden to carry into battle. True, they needed guides, but not as participants during an operation.

His stomach twisted at the sound of Gelarae's anguish. He scarcely knew her, yet he pitied her. In less than a day, she married a complete stranger and suffered her father's untimely demise.

In a way, Carlin saw this as his fault, the crew's, too. Perhaps all of it. They decided to come back. They could've stayed on course, returned to the fleet, but leaving a crew member behind ached in them. Carlin thought Daspar a coward for not wanting to, and he'd hated him for his spineless arguments that lacked honor.

In retrospect, perhaps he was right.

No, can't think that way. I'd want the crew to come back for me.

But would he? Would he want them in harm's way just to retrieve him? He knew the answer. He wouldn't. Now, more than ever, he realized what they did was wrong.

The caretaker would've been the same way, wouldn't have risked the crew.

"Carlin," Andrea said, breaking into his thoughts.

Gelarae's wails punctured the soundless cocoon of musings he built around himself.

"Get her to shut up! She's giving away our position!"

Carlin reached for her arm, to pull her to her feet, but she fought him off.

"Get away, star-traveler!" she cried. "This is your fault!"

The ward implored Muido for help with his gaze. A grimace crossed the other's dark features. Then, with a roll of his eyes, he reached out and cuffed the back of her neck, a move that appeared more lazy than premeditated.

Gelarae immediately fell silent and unconscious.

Carlin grabbed him by the throat and pressed him up against the wall.

"What did you do?"

"Problem over. No more noise."

Then, with another almost lazy move, his index and middle finger jabbed into Carlin's wrist, and the big man lost control. His grasp faltered, and Muido stepped away. The local knelt beside the unconscious form and the corpse.

"I'll take her from here and hide. Someone come with me. Later, we collect her father."

Carlin regarded Andrea. She gave a slight nod, agreeing in silence. He was right, of course. If they kept this up, she'd die, and they'd die as a result of trying to protect her.

Kodi stepped forward.

"I'll go with him."

"You sure?" Andrea inquired.

Kodi nodded. "Yeah, Goski's got the brains, Ossaro's the ward, and Daspar …" she glanced at him. "He's holding his own today."

"That's true," Carlin agreed.

"Very well. We'll be done as soon as we can."

Carlin watched Muido scoop up Gelarae.

Carlin caught her by the arm, then released her as he spoke.

"Stay in the building. Pick one of the rooms on the way to the entrance, but don't pick one of the rooms right next to it. Spray the whole door with your infrared so we can find you faster."

She nodded.

"Got it."

She braced her blaster rifle against her shoulder and advanced, but he stopped her. He lowered his voice so he wouldn't be overheard, looking her full in the eye.

"And," he included, glancing at Muido who held Gelarae, "if he does anything questionable, you put him down. Don't trust anyone from this planet."

Kodi eyed the retreating figure.

An expression rolled across her face, one that he couldn't identify.

"I'll be fine, but trust me, if necessary, I will."

"Let's keep moving," Andrea spoke.

Kodi retreated down the hall, shouldering her weapon and hurrying to catch Muido.

Carlin regarded her as she left, a war waging within him. He wanted to go with her, to follow, to keep her safe, to keep Gelarae safe.

"Ossaro," Andrea's stern voice filled his ears. "Let's go. You're on point."

The mission came first.

With reluctance, he turned back, shouldered his weapon, and continued on.

Chapter Twenty-Five: Schism

Sweeping the rest of the building went without incident, which didn't bode well in Andrea's stomach. They should've seen people by now; wasn't that Ossaro's prediction? More people on the inside?

On the third floor, the stairway split into a T-shaped hallway. Andrea had motioned for Daspar and Ossaro to go down the right wing; she and Soren held position near the stairs on the left. Once the ward and navigator started kicking in doors, they made sure no one snuck up behind them.

In the end, the entire level didn't have a soul.

Until the last door on the right wing.

Daspar, of all people, kicked it open, and damn-near had his visor seared off.

"Navigator Daspar—" SAVI began.

"Shut up, SAVI!" Andrea screamed over the sudden rush of enemy fire. She glanced within, popping her head out for a quick second. She pulled back just as a splash of green energy rocketed past.

"What'd you see?" Ossaro asked.

"There's some cover inside. I'm going in."

"No!"

"Me, too," Daspar offered.

He gave a single dip of his head, and she knew he'd watch her back.

She nodded and dashed forward. He paced abreast.

For a brief moment, she was back aboard *The Demon,* the first day they'd met, running for the bridge.

A new hail of fire opened, bolts ripping through the air around them. In unison, both dropped to the floor and slid up against a stone flower bed. Stone fragmented above their heads.

Sitting, Andrea spun and scanned the room to the left. Daspar did the same for the right. In this position, the rifle became unwieldy. She discarded the weapon, letting it drop while still slung, and drew the blaster pistol.

A haze filled the room, something similar to smoke. She could imagine an acrid scent similar to burnt wood and hair.

To the left stood cabinets and desks. Atop the surfaces lay strange metal ornaments and stones. Some glowed and pulsed. The lime green one caught her eye.

"Ossaro, how many do you see?"

After a few moments, he answered, "My ISD is showing thirteen, Chief. There's one in the back though. He's got a glowing staff, and I think he's orchestrating this."

Huh?

She popped up for a peek, then dropped back down. By his size, she assumed it was a man.

His staff was held upright, and he weaved it and his arms in a mesmerizing motion, like a puppetmaster plucking the strings of his marionettes. She leaned against the stone border of the flower bed, scanned the left again, looking for cover.

The desks would provide concealment, but the Teshren weapons would likely rip through the wood. Obfuscation but not adequate protection.

A movement drew her attention.

Beyond the desks, one of the cabinets opened, and a figure stepped out.

"Fuck!" She leveled the blaster at the target. "Ambush!"

She opened fire, riddling the individual with half a dozen holes before it collapsed. She caught Daspar's own rifle light-up behind her, but he must've shot in the other direction.

Was their attack synchronized?

A wide, blue bolt of light flashed out as Ossaro's booming sniper rifle thundered overhead. Andrea kept her eyes on the cabinets, waiting for more. Who knew where the next attack would come from. Above? Below?

"Now, would be a great time for one of those grenades you're carrying," Soren spoke into their ears, his voice calm.

Daspar gave a derisive harrumph.

"Yeah, good call."

"Shit," Andrea heard Ossaro say. The next time he spoke, his voice rang out loud and clear. "Frag out!"

Three dark spheres flew over Andrea's head.

"Shit, Ossaro!" she cried out.

She expected him to throw one. Not three! Not a damn salvo. Her integrated system display tracked the lofted objects, and SAVI spoke up as if he'd been watching her ISD.

"Seek cover and open your mouth," the AI advised.

Other than the stone flower bed, there wasn't much for protection. She hit the deck, laying flat, hoping the stone would shelter her from the blast. Another weight dropped on her, and she realized that Daspar lay atop, his groin covering her helmet, his head pointed towards her feet. Was it because they both wouldn't fit behind the rock structure, or did he protect her?

"Open your mouth," Daspar shouted.

She complied just as all three grenades detonated. Each blast hit with a robust concussive force that jolted her body. Her chest thrummed like a gong struck by a hammer. The eruption rushed out, deafening and terrible. Fragments peppered the stone, and each impact sent vibrations through the formation.

For a brief, terrifying second, she thought the building would collapse.

She stirred.

Daspar took the hint and rolled off. Her body trembled. With a shaky left hand planted on the floor, she rose to her knees. The blaster, still clutched in her right hand, swept over the room.

"Can't see a damn thing," she thought she said, but no one answered. "Can anyone see anything?"

Still no answer.

A smog of smoke, dust, and red-soot filled the air. She wondered where the latter came from, but realized it was the Teshren remains—nothing more than a pink mist and a memory now.

"SAVI? Can the ISD clear through the fog?"

Even SAVI didn't respond.

"SAVI? SAVI!"

Hands grabbed her by the helmet and jerked her head around. Out of instinct, she put the blaster into their gut, but at the last moment, abstained from pulling the trigger.

Ward Ossaro filled her vision. His lips moved.

"What?"

His mouth opened again.

"I can't fucking hear you!"

Irritation flashed across his face, and he half let go, half pushed her away. She didn't begrudge him, she was irritated too.

Climbing to her feet, she spied Daspar a few steps away. He looked shaken and panting but no worse for the wear. Turning her head, she peered back down the hall, towards Soren Goski's last known location.

He, too, appeared well, but he faced the way they'd come as rear security. Ossaro faced forward, his barrel pointed to where the Teshren had been, the end roving, searching for someone to put down.

A ring entered her ears then, high, painful, and incessant.

Ossaro's rumbling voice reached her.

"What?"

He repeated whatever he said.

"I still can't fucking hear you."

Andrea's ISD lit up, and SAVI scrolled Ward Ossaro's words across the screen.

[I think one escaped].

"How do you know?"

[There's an opening along the back wall. I caught a glimpse of light through the smoke].

"Oh."

She glanced back to Daspar.

"You okay?"

He nodded, but he had to read her lips.

"Let's wait here for a moment. It'll be dangerous to push on now."

[Agreed].

For a flitting moment, she wondered how Kodi fared. Andrea hoped the first officer was safe, and that Muido could be trusted. In retrospect, they didn't know much about the man. If the people of Gelarae's village found him credible and allowed visitation, he must be alright. Gelarae would've warned them, otherwise. From this premise, their situation formed a transitive trust.

Her attention shifted back to Ossaro as he stepped forward. Noting his speed, she surmised he wouldn't go far.

He's taking his duty quite seriously. Who would've thought we'd be in a firefight two months ago?

Daspar stirred and drew her attention.

"I think I heard something," he said in a faint voice.

She nodded.

"Me, too. At least, a little."

"You guys should stay in the middle," Ward Ossaro commented.

His deep voice hit tones that were hard to discern. He stiffened suddenly.

"Stop!" he shouted, then rushed to the opening in the wall. Without waiting, he took off, chasing whomever he saw. He peeked in, then pushed it open and sprinted through.

"Shit," she mumbled to herself, then gave chase.

Daspar was hot on her heels, and Soren's steps brought up the rear.

By the time she entered the small chamber beyond, he was nowhere to be seen. SAVI aided her in tracing his steps, following his pinging beacon.

Through the false wall, she descended into the bowels of the structure. Below resembled a crypt more than a bunker, a dark stockade of a medieval castle. Perhaps, once upon a distant time, it had been? The ludicrous thought kept her mind preoccupied as each door below reinforced the notion.

She kept hurrying forward, closing on Ossaro's beacon. The deeper the trio traveled, the more grotesque the winding pit became. After a while, they found rooms with half-rotted corpses, many still shackled to the wall. Other chambers were equipped with tables, tools, and torture devices.

After seeing a few bodies with their chest cavities gaping, their skulls cut off or staved in, and bones twisting at odd angles, a blistering rage simmered through her. She half-expected Daspar to joke, but even he seemed at a loss for words. If he ever felt acrimony for his time in the brig …

Well, at least we'd been humane.

Some of the tortured individuals had scarcely started to rot. Towards the end, they found some alive, still strapped to tables or chairs.

Andrea found rage etched across every feature of Ossaro's face when they breached the last chamber, and surprised to find one of their enemies alive. She expected a massacre.

The trio broke through the last door. Andrea's weapon swept the grand chamber as she rushed forward. Ossaro's fist had bloodied the man's face, and the ward held a gun to the Teshren's head.

Andrea rushed forward and pulled on the ward's barrel. "Stand down!"

"He should die! They all should."

She understood the sentiment, having seen their hospitality firsthand, but she doubted the ward was thinking straight.

Behind the kneeling Teshren stood a contraption from floor to ceiling, a ring of pillars. Within, a blue flamed writhed, the same color as the Aether's Grace.

Daspar flanked from the right.

The Teshren held his arms aloft, a smile on his mangled features. His hooked nose, natural but horrendous, bent more from the ward's bludgeoning.

Goski hedged the room's left side, and Andrea found his eyes glittering with curiosity as he scrutinized the device.

Andrea stepped away to examine the contraption. The engineer hovered near as she did. Methodical steps carried her around the stone contraption, and she spied another hostile in the back.

"Contact!" she yelled. She lifted the blaster pistol and opened fire as he darted forward. Her spray of light followed his moving form as he leapt for the blue light and disappeared.

"He's gone!" she called out.

Ossaro hadn't budged, still guarding the first combatant. Soren came around just enough to make eye contact, then turned outward, searching the left side of the room. They rummaged through the cabinets, opening the doors that lead to small rooms and storage compartments.

"It's clear," Soren declared.

"Same," Daspar echoed.

"Ossaro?"

When he didn't answer, she called again and took off in a trot back toward the front of the room.

She found Carlin with the barrel of his weapon against the Teshren's head. Andrea rushed forward and pulled on his arm.

"I told you to stand down. That was a fucking order."

"He should die!"

His hand tightened on the grip.

"Yes, he should, but we need him alive. We need answers."

"That's not good enough."

As the scene unfolded, she realized Ossaro sought revenge more than justice, more so than the need that drove them to return. She couldn't let him jeopardize their priorities. They'd come too far and risked so much for it to fall apart now.

The ward's finger tightened on the trigger.

She extended her arm, leveling the firearm at his head.

"Let him go."

He blinked and shook his head in disbelief. He glanced out of the corner of his eye.

"You'd shoot me?"

"Without hesitation."

Didn't he understand? Was he so shortsighted?

Ossaro smirked and withdrew his weapon, holstering it.

"Whatever you say, Chief. You're in charge."

The Teshren, a tall and lanky man with a bald pate, chuckled in the back of his throat. A grin split his bleeding face.

Now that she was closer, she noticed oddities about him. He once had a tan complexion, but now it was a dark ash color. The corners of his lips were split, making his mouth seem wider, like a serpent's. A spiderweb of bloodshot-red filled his eyes, the irises a sickly yellow ochre. Dark blue veins crisscrossed over his pate.

Andrea's faceplate opened as she neared him.

"Something funny?" she asked.

She didn't expect an answer but felt foolish if she didn't issue a challenge.

"You're all going to die," he said in perfect English.

A creeping chill shot up her spine.

"What did you say?"

"How the fuck can he speak English?" Daspar muttered.

She noted that his rifle lowered, his grip slack.

"I don't like this," Goski added with a shake of his head.

Through his faceplate, she noted his lips twisting in disgust as if bile filled his mouth.

The Teshren's eyes darted to Daspar.

"How do you think I can speak your language?"

Then, his eyes turned to Soren.

"You should listen to the older one. He's smarter than you all."

Andrea felt a smirk on the corner of her mouth.

"You have no idea."

"Wiser, too," the ward added.

"My attendant has escaped. He'll bring others. You'll never leave here alive. Even if you manage to escape, your corpse will remain on this planet forever."

This time, in unison, Ossaro and Daspar lifted their weapons and put it against the Teshren's cheeks.

"Say that again," Daspar threatened.

"I think you've been holding out on us," Ossaro said through gritted teeth.

Andrea understood their anger. What they'd witnessed under the complex, the tortured people, the maimed, or deceased still haunted her. Some yet lived, strapped down. What was the point? What did they hope to accomplish?

Andrea almost wanted Gelarae present to help identify the people. Were they hers or from other areas, different tribes or villages? Would Muido recognize some of them?

"Start talking," Andrea urged.

The Teshren smiled, then spat at her feet. She eyed the ward.

"Ossaro?"

The big man let the weapon fall to his side, still attached by the sling. His left hand lashed out and rocked their prisoner's head. The other spat again, this time blood, and over the ward's face. Ossaro hit him again and the other crumbled to the ground.

"Stop," Daspar said, blinking as if he couldn't believe what he was saying, watching. "This isn't right."

"Didn't think you'd be squeamish," Ossaro nettled. "Finally found your limit? Ain't got no stomach after seeing all those people?"

So, Ossaro did see them!

Daspar squared his shoulders.

"What they did was horrible, and they should die for it, but we're not them. I know where this is going. He's going to taunt, and you're going to hit, and the cycle will repeat until you're no better. We can't do this."

"Ah," the Teshren sneered from the floor.

He sat up, his movement slow and cautious. He rasped, a cross between speaking and laughing.

"The gutless one cometh. Your crew member was gutless, too. Who'll be the next one?"

"There ain't going to be a next one," Ossaro said, pulling the other up by the throat.

"What's going on here?"

Andrea spun around, raising her rifle. She wasn't the only one. Soren and Daspar did, too. Everyone except the ward. The rifles zeroed in on the door. Kodi stood in the entryway, her green eyes wide.

"Kodi!" Andrea said in surprise. "What are you doing here? I thought you were with Muido."

"I was," she answered, her eyes moving from each member back to the Teshren.

Then, her eyes went to the blue, flickering substance within the stone mechanism.

"He said he wouldn't stay, and left with Gelarae. They're returning to the village."

Her eyes returned to Andrea.

"Who's this?"

"A Teshren," Daspar said, lowering his weapon. The others followed suit.

"An about-to-be-dead Teshren," Ossaro clarified. "Especially if he doesn't start talking."

Kodi jerked her head back towards the rooms.

"Is he responsible for that?"

Andrea shrugged.

"We're about to find out."

"No," Daspar said. "I still say—"

"We know what you said," the ward cut in. "Look, if you're too squeamish, go babysit the village."

"I think," Soren said, interjecting himself into the conversation, "Navigator Daspar's right."

"What?" Ossaro barked. "You're going to side with the guy that screwed your synth?"

Andrea cringed. Her eyes cut to the engineer. Soren, as Ossaro knew, didn't take criticism well, and this would be detrimental.

Soren shrank away, leaving the immediate vicinity and putting distance between himself and the volatility. Daspar groaned and rolled his eyes, but it was Andrea who spoke first.

"That was a little low, even for you, Ward Ossaro. Besides which, he's your superior officer."

The security officer eyed her.

"To titles and rank, are we? Only when it suits you? This fucker can speak our language, and there can only be one explanation: Caretaker. He knows him or where he's kept."

"Doesn't mean we torture him," Daspar argued.

"How else are we going to get information out of him? Ask nicely?"

"Interrogate, not torture."

Kodi stepped into the cluster around the Teshren.

"If we were back in the fleet, or if we had time, I'd agree with you. But we're not, and we don't."

"Yeah," Ossaro said, nodding in agreement, "and he already said we were all going to die and not make it off this planet."

"There's got to be a better way," Soren said in a soft voice.

"There is," Ossaro announced. "We just don't have the time. As he said, his minion escaped. No doubt the others are already warned. How much longer until reinforcements arrive?"

Daspar stepped close and placed a hand on her forearm.

"This is wrong, Chestnut, and you know it."

"Get your hands off her!" Carlin snarled.

"She's not fucking yours!" Rhett shouted. "Never was—she's fucking married!"

A collective gasp slithered through the group.

Andrea blinked a few times, too stunned for an immediate response.

"What are you talking about?" Andrea asked.

Rhett glanced between them all, almost as if he realized he'd said more than intended. He shook his head.

"I had a memory return, okay? Back at the glowing pool. I remembered the first time. Mason, the caretaker, was present."

He shook his head.

"He volunteered to go through the pool first, and you said that you didn't want to risk your husband."

"So, that's why he stayed," Kodi said. "Makes a hell of a lot of sense. He didn't stay because he wasn't needed to operate the ship, he stayed because you're his wife!"

Andrea noted that Rhett's gaze darted to Ossaro and back.

The ward glowered, his simmering rage barely contained.

How's the truth Rhett's fault?

Andrea shook her head.

"That doesn't make sense," she muttered into the quiet.

"What doesn't?" Soren queried.

Andrea had memories return, too. Perhaps they were only dreams, but she didn't think so. Once, while on the ship, she had an erotic dream, and the ward hadn't been her partner.

Neither had the caretaker …

"Nothing." Andrea surveyed the split crew.

Two advocated for torture in this extreme circumstance, and two warned against. Each had valid arguments. She regarded Soren.

"How long until we need to make it back to the ship and flip the switch?"

His large, dark eyes grew pensive for a moment.

"If I started back now, we might have a little under twelve hours by the time I reached it. That's a lot of traveling. And, it'd either be dusk or dark by the time I got back. With the monsters they got on this planet, it'd be dangerous."

"I agree, which's why you won't go alone. Get back to the ship and flip the switch early."

She assessed the navigator.

"You go with him, Daspar. Once there, compile a map and upload it to the squad."

"Chief?"

"You have your orders."

"Chestnut?" he said in a small voice, shaking his head. "This is wrong."

Her lips twisted.

"Go."

The navigator scrutinized her and his squad mates.

The Teshren smiled and chuckled.

"This is goodbye, star-man."

Daspar's face flushed, and he strode from the room at a brisk pace.

Soren shook his head, muttered something under his breath, and followed.

Andrea attended them as the pair retreated.

Did she do the right thing? Would torture provide their answers? How much time did they have?

Her eyes turned to Kodi, her only real friend on *The Demon*.

With reluctance, the first officer nodded in agreement.

"Kodi, shut the door."

Chapter Twenty-Six: Daspar

His feet touched stone as the Aether's Grace regurgitated him back into the world.

The navigator glanced up, weapon snapping in that direction. He glanced high, the walls rising around him. He expected the enemy, but why would he? That ambush was almost twenty-four hours ago. They'd be long gone by now, and if not, they were far more dedicated than he gave them credit for.

The alien pool expelled Goski, and Rhett stepped to the side.

"You good?" Rhett asked.

"Yeah," Goski answered, breathless. "Never gonna get used to that."

At least this trip was easier without lugging around a drugged Kodi.

With the weapon still pointed upward, Daspar followed the serpentine path and exited the basin. A few moments later, Goski followed.

Their journey back here had been tense, weird. When they caught up with Muido, it'd changed, especially when Gelarae awoke—livid for leaving her husband and father's body behind.

Rhett assured her that Andrea and the others would bring him home. A new tenseness permeated the group and conversation turned intermittent. During one of their breaks, Gelarae went into the woods to relieve herself. She never came back, and they presumed she returned to the outpost.

Muido shrugged her rash decision off.

"I'm not father, and her heart belongs to her husband alone."

He continued on to the village, then escorted them to the cavern with the Aether's Grace.

Rhett thought back to the condemned Teshren.

"Good luck," he'd said.

His flawless, unaccented English unnerved the navigator, especially since Muido struggled to make himself intelligible.

Utilizing his gauntlet hologram, they retraced their path out of the maze. It seemed so alien in the daylight. Rhett's eyes tracked to the forest below, the towering trees and thick trunks. What kind of creature could make huge timbers tremble with its passing? He hoped to never run into such a beast.

"SAVI?" Daspar called.

"Yes, Asshole?"

He rolled his eyes and grinned. Though annoying, he found the AI's quirkiness humorous.

"We're coming in to flip the manual switch."

"Yes, I know. I monitored your comms when you attacked the outpost."

"Can you tell us what's going on?"

The AI paused.

"Negative, not without expressed permission from the Chief Regent."

"So, ask her."

"She's indisposed."

That sounds like she's shitting or fucking instead of torturing someone.

Rhett grunted in frustration and glanced back at Goski. The engineer stopped a few feet away, his eyes sweeping over the stretching forest.

"SAVI, fire up the life support."

"Confirmed. Also, be advised, several lifeforms are near you, some rather sizable, possibly wildlife."

"Great."

The last thing he wanted to deal with was animals chasing him and trying to eat him.

"SAVI?" Goski called. "Is there any type of defensive mechanisms built into our armor?"

"Yes, but the older models are limited in scope. You have a heat suppression throughout the suit. In times of absolute stillness, you can bend the ambient light around you to conform to your surroundings."

"That'd come in handy," Rhett said, surprised by the capability.

"Your suits also obscure and dampen any bodily sounds such as heartbeat, breathing, and circulation, but for it to work, your suit must be completely sealed."

"Anything else?" Goski asked.

"There are many abilities; would you care to download the instruction manual?"

The engineer chuckled.

"No, that won't be necessary."

"Let's go," Rhett said over his shoulder, then started down the rolling slope.

The trees grew thicker the lower he descended.

His thoughts turned back to Andrea's decision. They weren't monsters, murderers, or torturers. She knew the decision she made wasn't right. Rhett prided himself for his shock value, but even he had a limit, a line between jackassery and immorality. He craved Kodi, but he wouldn't take her by force or coercion.

Emma, Goski's synth, had been different. It was a machine, a thing, not conscious or sentient, and it enticed him with an offer.

What guy wouldn't take that?

Thinking about the synth made him long for one. More often than not, he'd love to beat Ossaro's face to a bloodied mess, but he restrained. Despite what the others believed, morals guided his actions. Everyone had their own code; some, like his, could be a bad joke considering its flimsiness.

But now, the precious chief regent had crossed the line, and he couldn't stifle his contempt for her. She wasn't as flawless as the others believed. He saw the fissure in her noble armor. An hour almost passed before Goski broke into his musings.

"It's not right," Goski said, the internal comms going through his ear.

They'd reached the bottom of a slope and started up the other side. The woods were crowded with trees, jutting stone, and hilly terrain. The engineer sounded out of breath. Then again, he was older by a decade or two.

"What isn't?"

Rhett's shoulders tensed, wondering if the engineer would broach the subject of impropriety with his synth.

"Leaving them, knowing what they're going to do to the Teshren."

"Maybe Andrea's right?" Rhett said, playing the other side of the conversation. "I mean, he's a Teshren and probably deserves it."

"Ha," Goski barked, the sound sharp and sudden. "That means a lot coming from a man with less than scrupulous morals. How do we know he had anything to do with Caretaker?"

"We don't."

Rhett roved around the right side of a bush.

"Which's why Chestnut decided to torture him."

"He may know nothing. And don't act like you don't care."

"It's not my place to question my commanding officer."

"Isn't it?" Goski countered. "Something this terrible? We have a duty, an obligation to not only report this, but remove her from command."

The engineer's words brought Daspar up short, and he turned and faced him.

"Mutiny?"

"It's not a mutiny. I'm sure some regulation refers to unlawful orders, immoral judgments, and endangerment of crew and safety. I'm talking something within the regulations."

"Regulations we can't even remember," Rhett argued, then continued walking.

The engineer wasn't wrong. In fact, the whole way from the outpost to the village, he'd been thinking the same thing. Ossaro would never go for it, not with his nose and tongue firmly planted in Andrea's ass. He'd do anything she said, and be a problem to circumvent.

While it shouldn't matter now, being married to the local girl, the ward didn't care about Gelarae. Carlin's personality was as tasteless as the bland, clashing clothes he wore. The security officer didn't take shit from anyone, which was amazing, considering how much Andrea doled out. He should've been tired by now, unless it was a way back into her bed.

Though his cloudy, dark blue eyes always scrutinized Rhett, he was blind to the line they'd crossed. His strength came from intimidation and rules and regulations, not moral authority. That … he'd tossed out the airlock long ago.

Rhett's thoughts turned to Kodi.

She hated him less now, but she wouldn't cast her lot in with him and Goski. Rhett supposed he'd leave recruitment to the engineer. Kodi's hard-nosed approach in the face of growing opposition would make her double down. Though sensitive to other people's feelings, if Soren expressed fears and concerns, she might mirror him.

Though she didn't seem like it at first glance, Kodi was an achiever, and taking command would prove herself to the crew, Andrea, and the Admiralty. She'd expressed her ideas to Rhett during their intimate moments.

Despite being a three-to-two victory over Andrea and Ossaro, the ward wouldn't give up control. He was the sticking point.

Rhett sighed.

Ossaro would be that kind of douche bag.

Andrea might step down voluntarily, but he doubted it. Besides, Ossaro would seize the leadership or force Andrea to keep command. Knowing him, Rhett would have a one-way trip back to the brig, and the engineer confined to quarters.

At least he's got companionship, and could screw Emma—

"Hey," Rhett said into the comms.

"What?"

"You said regulations, right?"

"Yeah, and?"

"The quickest way to find those would be to ask SAVI to conduct a search."

"The second you do, he'll alert Chief Hessner."

Rhett nodded.

"I know, which's why you should tell Emma once were back. Have her do it on the sly."

An amused tone entered the engineer's voice.

"That's actually not a bad idea."

"Yeah, I was just thinking to myself—"

"STOP!" SAVI shouted over their comms.

Both men froze, Rhett's foot halfway between stepping.

"You've stumbled onto a life form. I've been monitoring your progress. It wasn't present a moment ago, and now you're right on top of it."

Rhett's breath thundered in his ears, and he fought the urge to turn his head and look around. Instead, he used his eyes and stayed as still as possible.

His breath shook.

"Where?"

"You're on top of it."

Rhett glanced down, but only saw undisturbed dirty and undergrowth. Nothing stood out—nothing screamed danger. Rhett lifted his eyes to scan in the distance. Trees, too tall and numerous to count, filled his vision.

"I don't see anything, SAVI. Goski? Do you?"

"Nothing," he whispered back.

"I assure you, you're standing right on top of it."

He glanced at the ground again.

Nothing.

"SAVI, how are you reading us?"

"Through a standard ground pulse reader."

His heart fluttered.

With a shaky breath, he spoke.

"Why do I have a feeling that doesn't render a three-dimensional representation?"

"Indeed, you're correct."

"It's cause the engines aren't on," Goski said. "Draws too much power from the batteries."

Slowly, Rhett turned his head to the tree beside him. It had the strangest, most bizarre bark he'd ever seen, and it glittered with condensation. The roots rose out of the earth, thick and powerful.

He blinked a few times before he realized they were toes and claws. His eyes turned upward. Above, in the treetops, a colossal beast craned its head.

It hasn't seen us yet. Too small.

Rhett motioned to Goski.

"What?" the older man queried.

"Get down, get back."

Rhett took a cautious step back, squatting as he backtracked. His gaze never left the mammoth. It was huge, at least forty feet tall. The scales rippled on the leg beside him.

Daspar ducked behind the nearest hardwood, keeping the trunk between them, bringing up his weapon before realizing how little it'd do.

"What?" Goski asking.

Rhett turned to face the engineer.

"Huge, huge—fucking huge!" he panted with quiet words.

"That tells me a lot. How about a description?"

"Forty feet, bipedal, we're under it. Its teeth are … huge."

The creature turned its head in their direction.

He shrank behind the tree, closing his eyes.

"Please, God don't let it see me, fucking, please. I don't want to die on this fucking planet. Oh shit, oh shit. Just let me get through this, and I fucking promise to be less of an asshole. Oh shit, oh fuck, oh God…."

"Get a hold of yourself," the engineer hissed.

"Engineer Goski's correct, Navigator Daspar. Praying to a deity won't help you."

"Makes me feel a hell of a lot better!"

"Further, no proof of one exists. I can speculate—"

"That's enough, SAVI," Goski cut in. "Where is it now?"

With reluctance, Rhett peeked around, but the monstrosity wasn't there.

What the hell?

"It's gone …"

How did it move off with no sound?

Goski shifted beside him.

"I'm beginning to have doubts."

"Navigator Daspar is correct. There was a massive life form."

"What did it look like?"

"It had strange colors, brown, gray, green, some black and a burnt orange or red on its head and neck. It literally looked like a tree, could blend in anywhere."

"But what did it look like?"

"Like a huge fucking alligator or crocodile, alright? But that's impossible!

They aren't that huge!"

Soren was quiet for a moment, appraising him.

Oh, he's thinking I finally cracked.

Goski shrugged.

"SAVI? How far away are we?"

"Approximately six hundred and thirty-two meters from the ship."

"Come on," Goski encouraged. "We're almost there."

"What about the creature?"

As the words left his mouth, Daspar saw it, not a figment but a hunting behemoth, and they'd been discovered.

Fifty meters behind Goski, the massive head craned out from behind a cluster of timber. Its lower jaw no more than ten feet from the ground. It crawled on all fours, moving with lethal grace.

Blood drained from his face. It must've shown. Goski's eyes widened. The older man jerked around. The monster let out a hiss.

"Run!" Goski shouted.

Rhett snapped up his rifle and depressed the trigger, sending a stream of light at the creature.

It kept coming.

The lasers only reddened its skin.

His gun screamed its trilling sound of overheating, which spurred him to took off behind Goski. This was a sprint, a race, and anything other than first place was rewarded with life or death.

SAVI crackled over their comms. "You can't outrun it! Weave between the trees. It's your best chance. Weave!"

"What the fuck's a weave?" Rhett screamed.

In front of him, Goski went around the left side of the tree. Rhett followed. By the time he cleared it, Soren had started angling around the right side of the next.

"The creature can outpace you in a straight line, so it must slow down to dart around the trees," SAVI explained. "I've highlighted your ISD to illuminate the quickest path back to the ship."

"Get ready to shoot at the damn thing!" Rhett shouted.

"We'll have limited shots until the engines are turned over."

His lungs burned.

Foliage snapped as he blazed a serpentine trail. It felt a lot longer than six hundred meters. They should've been there by now. His toes tingled as if they were going to sleep; damn fine time for poor circulation.

He jumped down a decline—far quicker than running. Something loud cracked behind him. Rhett imagined its teeth snapping shut, missing him by inches. He stumbled on the landing. On his back, he looked up. The snout was mere feet away. One massive, yellow eye rolled to look at him.

"Fuck, fuck, fuck!"

Rhett snapped up the cooled rifle, spraying the inside of the creature's mouth with a hail of fire. The monster roared, but it only seemed to piss it off.

Energy leeched from his limbs. Why was he so tired? Terror kept him pinned as he sprayed the hellion with light and heat.

In a blink, Goski appeared, hauling him to his feet.

The weapon overheated, and Rhett dropped it again, the sling pulling it out of the way. He rushed after Goski.

"It'd be great to have one of Ossaro's grenades," the older man shouted.

Daspar rushed headlong. Their craft peeked through the trees up ahead. Had to be less than a hundred meters away.

"SAVI, lower the ramp!" Soren cried.

He sounded out of breath, tired.

The end was so close. He had to make it!

They both could!

In the distance, the ramp dropped. The port weapons, both fore and aft, lowered and swiveled in their direction.

"Dive, dive, dive," SAVI instructed.

Rhett and Goski dropped to their stomachs.

The air trembled above their head. Heat passed overhead. The aftershock of energy making the air waiver.

The energy splashed against the creature. It roared so loud that Daspar thought his head would explode. His chest thrummed like the resonance of a drum tuned too tight. The closeness of the beast, the bellow of anguish, the vibrations throughout his body, caused his bladder to release.

Warm fluid rushed out of him, pooling beneath and spreading down his legs and up his stomach.

"Fucking Christ, I just peed everywhere!" Goski shouted as he scrambled up.

A rush of relief flooded Rhett, knowing he wasn't the only one.

"Me, too."

He took off after Goski.

Fifty meters left.

The ship was right there, but so was the monstrous leviathan. They zagged at random intervals. The ground rumbled behind them. The recognizable crunch of splintering wood cracked behind them. Dirt and roots ripped from the earth, the wood groaning as the saplings toppled.

"SAVI, do something!" Rhett howled.

"Doing something."

A sudden hiss shrieked out from the ship. A bright trail of flame shot out. The small missile detonated a few moments later, hitting the beast in the chest. The blast flung them down, and in a heap, and they landed on the rising ramp.

Rhett untangled himself from Goski, trying to locate the leviathan.

The missile injured the beast, the right shoulder flayed open. Its arm hung by a few useless strains of flesh. It stumbled against a tree, its roar shrill, a cry of anguish.

Rhett winced.

He pitied the animal but only for a moment.

The ramp continued to close, the field of vision shrinking.

The towering, bipedal alligator turned, lumbering away. As it twisted, the dangling arm came free, ripping out of the shoulder. It staggered against a tree. The wood shuddered under its weight.

Goski rose, pushing off him.

"Fuck this. That thing might come back even angrier. I'm firing up the engines. Get to the bridge, and ready the ship for takeoff if need be."

"Alright."

It was a good plan, and Rhett was glad the older man was able to pull himself together.

As the engineer disappeared up the ramp, the navigator took a moment to breathe.

They'd sprinted six hundred meters in full armor, chased by a gigantic, meat-eating horror. If he hadn't jumped down the slope … one bit would've ended it all.

Judging from its size, he and Goski would be little more grit stuck between its teeth.

A trickle of sweat beaded down his left temple. His soaked back squished as he sat up. He'd need to change out of the piss-filled armor.

He chuckled aloud.

God, I'm never gonna live this down.

Still smiling, he exited the ramp area and worked his way to the lift. Entering the cart, he pressed the button for the bridge. The doors closed, and the lift rose.

His thoughts turned back to Andrea and the decision she'd made. Goski agreed with him, that's why they'd been sent away. The fear and hesitation in her eyes told Rhett everything he needed to know. She'd made the wrong decision, and she knew it, too.

He hoped it haunted her for the rest of her days.

The lift stopped much sooner than expected.

He checked the controls, the display showing he stopped on the third level, the crew quarters.

A frown formed on his lips.

The doors parted and revealed Soren's beautiful synthetic, Emma.

His eyes grew round.

She stood naked—sculpted, voluptuous, engineered to entice.

His gaze dipped to her breasts as she stepped into the lift, then lingered as she turned to press the bridge controls, giving him a quick flash of her exquisite ass.

"Emma?"

Every carnal desire surged. She'd let him experiment last time.

His hand slid over her backside—

—and she turned into him, pressing close, her body supple, yielding.

Hell of to be welcomed back.

The doors, starting to close, drew his attention. When he looked back at her, cold fury filled her dark blue eyes.

What the hell?

Her hand shot out.

His feet left the floor.

A crushing agony clenched around his throat.

His vision darkened.

And the sharp pain in his neck was the last thing he ever remembered.

Chapter Twenty-Seven: The Demon

Soren powered up the console, the display flickering brightly. The soft yellows, greens, and reds washed his face in a colorful glow.

Punching up the sequence, the engines thrummed to life. The mechanical whine rose in pitch, a slow whirl like a turbine beginning its spin.

"Soren?" Andrea's voice called in his ear.

He pressed the earbud into his ear.

"Yeah, Chief?"

"We're headed back. Go ahead and fly to our location. We'll discuss tactics once you arrive."

"Okay, great, 'cause there's no way we'd be walking back right now."

"What do you mean?"

"Remember that thing moving the trees last night?"

"Yeah?"

"It found us. We managed to outrun it, and SAVI chased it off with the onboard weapons, but it's still alive."

"Are you guys alright?"

"Well, we're alive."

There was a pause, then Andrea's voice came back, business-like.

"Bring the ship over, land inside the compound, and keep Daspar on the bridge until we get back."

Soren's lips twisted, translating what she said: *keep him away from Emma and the crew quarters.*

"Noted."

The comm went dead, and Soren clicked over to his interpersonal comms with the navigator.

"Daspar? The chief wants us to take off and meet them back at the outpost. Think you can manage?"

For a long moment, nothing happened, and the navigator didn't respond, but the radio clicked twice.

For a brief time, Soren worried that Andrea might've been right, the pilot already knee-deep in mischief. He took two steps towards the door.

"Daspar?"

Before he left the room, the engine's hum increased, and the craft lifted with a less-than-smooth takeoff.

"Alright," Soren muttered to himself before clicking the mic back on. "I'm going to take a shower and change."

Again, Daspar didn't answer, but clicked twice, the standard for acknowledgment.

Must be having trouble. After everything we put our armor through, I'm surprised he can click at all.

Exiting the engine room, he called the lift and waited for its arrival. His right hand closed around his left, his fingers drumming against the back of his hand. The display changed from first deck—the bridge—to the second deck, and then stopped on the third. His brows drew down. He'd called the elevator to him, so why did it stop on the third deck?

Soren clicked on his comm.

"Daspar, you still on the bridge?"

Two clicks.

"Alright. When you get us there, change out your damn comm unit. The clicks are killing me."

Another double click.

Soren sighed and rolled his eyes.

The lift continued again, moving down. Finally, the doors opened, and Soren stepped in. Depressing the button, the doors closed and rose to level three.

As he exited, he paused. The skin at the back of his neck tightened. A thought tickled him, something about Daspar.

With a frown, he moved down the hall and toward his quarters. The lingering feeling persisted. The closer he drew to his quarters, the more queasy he became.

Would he open his door to find him screwing Emma again?

Soren could forgive a lot, but not a second infraction.

Half a dozen steps from the door, he realized why thoughts of Daspar and the comm filled his head. They were on the ship, and he could've answered through the ship's intercom.

The doors parted, and his steps faltered. He peeked inside. Emma lay on his bed, her manner provocative. His heart thrummed faster.

"Soren, my love," she said, smiling.

Did her eyes just sparkle?

A soft, silkiness laced her voice. Emma appeared different, and he couldn't put his finger on it. She lay naked, but that wasn't unusual. She smiled, something she'd done countless times before.

His eyes moved to her rosy lips, her nose, and hair. Her hair was always perfect, except for now.

"Emma," he greeted.

"Have you come back? Do we have the night? Shall I prepare you dinner?"

He shook his head, a déjà vu washing over him.

"No, that won't be necessary."

She stood from the bed and went to him; his eyes tracked her swaying hips. The way she walked, something seemed … off.

She leaned in and kissed him. When she pulled back, her eyes widened with amusement.

"I'm detecting urine. Go clean yourself so we can make love."

Something cold crept over him, his head shaking.

Her voice, the way she walked, her hair and eyes, something off-putting screamed out to him, and he tried in vain to listen.

"There isn't time. We must pick up Chief Regent Hessner and the others."

"Perhaps tonight?"

He shrugged.

"We'll see."

She smiled and kissed him again, her hand going to his chest.

"Soren, your heart's racing. What's the matter?"

A thousand lies flashed through his mind, but he discarded them all. A synthetic could detect treachery, a protocol installed to keep her from harm from less-than-honorary members of society.

"I thought Rhett might've been in here again."

She flinched.

It wasn't the type a human would do, but she blinked, and her lips trembled. Her eyebrow quivered but a fraction, almost involuntarily. Had she always been that way and he never caught it? Or did he only notice it because he was spooked?

Emma's intended design emulated humans, tailored after his late wife. He and the synth carried on as if she hadn't perished, but as the years progressed, Soren grew older, and Emma stayed young and lithe.

"What's wrong, love?" she asked, her voice soft, angelic.

"N-nothing," he stammered. "Need to get a change of clothes. We'll be landing soon."

"Would you like me to shower with you?"

Her nose crinkled in a cute way as she smiled and leaned in for another kiss.

He puckered his lower lip and gave a shake of the head.

"I'd love to, but there's no time. Maybe when we leave this planet. How about that? You can wear that leather outfit I like."

He reached inside the wall locker for a change of clothes.

"Anything for you, my love. I want to make you happy, Soren. Are you happy with me?"

The question caught him by surprise, and he turned to face her.

In all the years, she'd always said she wanted to make him happy, asked about his level of happiness, but never if he was pleased with her.

He glimpsed her raw emotion, and it revealed his wife, not the synth. A surge of emotion rippled through him, and he tried to convey his feelings with simple, empty words.

"You know I am."

Her brow twitched again, almost imperceptible. Her nostrils flared as if she inhaled.

"Even after what he did to me?"

He crossed over to her, lifting her chin up, and kissed her.

"Even still."

He kissed her again and grabbed the last of his clothing.

"Do you think he wants to hurt me again?"

Soren kept the smile plastered on his face, but the pit of his stomach dropped out.

Emma, as much as she tried to hide it, had changed since he'd had been gone. In truth, the small things accumulated for a while now, but he was too afraid to say anything. Everyone would laugh at him, but he couldn't deny it any longer.

He had to warn the others—fast.

"He won't hurt you again," Soren promised. "If he ever tries anything, you can defend yourself, you know?"

He walked back to the locker.

"What if defending myself hurts him? Is that okay?"

Soren picked up a roll of socks before shutting the wall locker door. As he spoke, he worked his way to the exit.

"If you do hurt him, I'm sure it's his fault, and you wouldn't mean to, right? Hurting people's against your programming and not okay, right? This is very important if you want to be accepted by humans."

Her lip twitched before she smiled.

"Right."

He grinned and dipped his head.

"Alright. Gotta go. I'll see you when I can."

He headed out the door and turned back.

"Baby, why are you naked?"

Her head twitched to the side, mimicking deep thought.

"I thought you'd want to take me when you returned."

"I do," he said with a toothy grin. "Why don't you wear something special for me next time."

She dipped her head once.

"Of course. Anything for you, my love."

Soren stepped out of the doorway and continued to the lift. Every fiber of his being told him to run, but he couldn't. She'd hear, and then she'd know.

Once the door shut and the lift proceeded up, he let go of his control. He gasped and his eyes watered. His fear trembled like a tuning fork. A shaking hand against the wall kept him from falling over.

Emma acted differently because she'd evolved past her programming, the only plausible explanation. He didn't know how or when, but she'd become aware. Her reactions, the things she said, her eerie disposition, all signs that she'd became more and yet tried to hide it. How was it possible?

Out of all the crew, if he had to guess, his memories returned the most. Emma's dissimilarity contrasted to the way he remembered. After living together for years, he noted the parameters of her software. She meant to be the embodiment of the wife he lost, to help him piece his life together, to heal. Now, she'd become something he didn't recognize—expensive equipment built for sex and service.

Still, he couldn't say anything, not yet. He couldn't risk telling Daspar over the comms and having Emma overhear. The craft tilted, veering onto a new course. Soren debated whether to go warn Daspar in person.

The lift stopped, and the doors opened on the second deck. He paused, his feet stuck between walking out or pushing the button to resume to the command center.

The stench of urine reached his nostrils, and he decided on getting clean. It could wait. Thus far, Emma didn't appear to be a threat. Further, she may not realize she gained consciousness.

Padding down the hall towards Andrea's room and the communal refresher, he wondered what that was like for the synth. How would it have been for her, to suddenly be aware? Would she recognize it or would it be a gradual cognizance?

He reached the washroom and opened the door. Inside, he stripped out of his armor and peeled off his soiled garments. The pressure of the hot water massaged his knotted muscles. The rich lather made his skin tingle. Soapsuds slithered like a foamy snake down the drain. A sound reached his ears, one of the main door to the room being opened.

"Daspar? That you?"

When no answer came, he shrugged it off as part of his imagination. He lifted his arm, scrubbing underneath. A faint clatter sounded, like one of the shower stall doors creaking shut.

"Daspar?" he called again.

He opened the stall door, glancing out. Nothing seemed amiss. His clothes sat unmolested, his armor lay in a heap on the floor.

He peeked at the lights in the other stalls. Their lights remained off, their doors closed. The design of the computer centered around conserving power. If it didn't detect a heat signature or heartbeat, the lights would remain off.

Daspar wasn't in here.

Soren eyed the toilets. Those stalls remained dark as well. Satisfied, he ducked back in.

As he scrubbed his back, the sound of the door closing made him lurch. Throwing open his stall, he peered out, his frantic eyes searching. Was he going crazy? Did he just imagine it?

His heart thundered in his chest. The sound had been so soft that he wasn't sure he heard it. Perhaps the brush with death and the monster made him too jumpy?

He swore his heart would explode from the terror he'd felt, and now it returned. He was surprised that he'd survived the encounter. And with Emma's odd behavior...

With a grimace, he shut the door.

The rest of the shower passed without incident, though he kept his ear open. By the time he dried off, he was almost certain that he imagined it all.

Lifting his boot to the bench, he bent and tied the lace. His gaze flickered to the other shower stalls. Uncertainty fogged his brain. His gut twisted. His mind screamed that he'd heard someone come in.

His eyes flitted away before they did a double take. The one on the opposite side of the room, the stall furthest from the door, the shadows lay deeper.

His lips thinned.

Was it his imagination, or the onset of lunacy?

His chest tightened with the thudding of his galloping heart. The moistness of his forehead beaded. Was it water or sweat?

He swallowed in the silence as he took a step closer to the stall. His large eyes widened, darting for something to defend himself with. He glanced back at his armor. His rifle lay propped against the bench.

A cautious, silent step took him within reaching distance of his weapon. Fingers curled around the cold metal as he cradled the firearm.

Rifle set against his shoulder, he crept forward. His boot's impact against the floor made him wince.

Was his breathing too loud? It thundered in his ears.

Whatever was behind the door, would they know he approached? What should he do? Deciding on a quick action, his left hand, the supporting hand, fell away from under the barrel.

In a quick step, he darted forward and jerked the door open.

He gasped aloud and took a few quick steps back. The light above sputtered to life as the door opened. Large brown eyes took in the horror before him.

Daspar lay crumpled up against the back wall, his mouth agape, his head twisted at an odd angle.

"Oh, God," Soren said, collapsing against the bench.

His neck appeared deformed and crushed. What could cause that besides a powerful vise?

Soren looked away.

"Oh shit, oh fuck," he repeated as he rocked.

His gaze flickered to the deceased, noting the bloodshot eyes dark like velvet, and how they stared blankly ahead. Soren's vision watered and stung. His trembling hands went to the safety on his weapon, clicking it back.

The vessel banked again and slowed. Soren's hand shot out and held onto his seat.

"SAVI?" he breathed.

"Yes, Engineer Goski?"

Soren winced.

The AI's voice boomed over the speaker and reverberated through the room.

"Lower your volume."

Soren stopped rocking back and forth.

"SAVI? Where's Emma?"

"I can't track the synthetic, but she appears to be in your quarters. Do you wish for me to call her?"

"No!"

Again the vessel slowed, almost to a standstill.

"Daspar?" Soren called over the radio.

His eyes gravitated to the lifeless body sitting on the shitter.

"We there?"

The sound of a double click came over the comms. Seeing the dead man, something hardened in the pit of his stomach.

"Daspar, quit being a jackass and use the ship's comms."

A few moments passed before Daspar's voice filled the overhead speaker.

"You need to get laid, old man. You're getting agitated too easily. Setting *The Demon* down now."

The speaker clicked off, and Soren glanced up at the speaker in the ceiling.

"SAVI? Where did that transmission originate?"

"From your quarters, sir."

"Fuck."

If she's answering from the quarters, that means she moved the ship with the autopilot. No wonder the takeoff wasn't smooth.

"Is something wrong?"

"SAVI? Are we at the correct coordinates?"

"Confirmed. The Chief Regent and the crew are returning now, along with a deceased individual and one extra living person—female."

Soren's mind raced, wondering who died.

Gelarae's father, you idiot.

Of course, they'd be bringing him back to her.

"Where's the chief headed?"

"She just depressed the lift's button to the bridge."

"Great, I'll meet her there."

"Shall I tell her that you are on your way?"

Soren shook his head.

"That won't be necessary."

Standing, he wobbled on unsteady legs.

The sight of Daspar made his stomach turn. True, he held animosity for what the navigator did to Emma, his property, but not enough to wish him dead.

Soren had no delusions—Emma was a machine, not his wife. He bought her to hold, not just in the physical sense, but the emotional, too. She bridged the chasm of depression, pulling him back from the brink. Her other features were only explored after the first year. The thought had never crossed his mind until she mentioned her compatibility to have sex.

In the beginning, it'd been something special, sacred, like having his wife again. He wasn't racked by guilt or disgust. In those precious moments, he didn't have to pretend.

Now, he kept Emma for ease and comfort, both far more secure than trying to start over with someone new and living. In many ways, she acted as a shield for him.

Daspar had intruded, walked over and besmirched something only for Soren.

For days, he wouldn't touch her, trivial in retrospect. He regarded the dead crew mate. A dark thought flickered through his mind. Daspar had taken Emma, thinking her a machine—but had she been aware? Did his actions spur her awareness?

But Soren knew the truth.

With a sigh, he closed the stall. Picking up his armor and clothes, he pushed dark thoughts to the side. Grabbing his rifle, he exited the communal bathing room.

When the engineer reached the bridge, the crew crescendoed in their conversation.

"…we don't know that for sure!" Ossaro protested.

Soren noted the redness of his face. None of them heeded his arrival as he took station at Ossaro's console. His eyes flitted over the displays, checking their weapon complement.

Thirty-one missiles remained.

His eyes darted to the commanding officer's chair, and he caught the top of Gelarae's head.

Shouldn't she be at home, preparing for her father's funeral?

"We didn't know if he'd be alive if we came back," Andrea argued. "And now that we're so close, you want to give up?"

"We don't have the military might. If we attack, what's five going to do against hundreds? On top of that, we've got one of their leaders in our brig! How are we going to assault one of their outposts with an enemy in tow?"

"There's not much five can do against their outpost," Kodi conceded, "but we've got a ship loaded with weapons."

She shrugged.

"They're not going to fire on us if we drag their leader with us."

"Don't be so sure," Carlin mumbled.

"What happens when you lose the ship?" Soren asked, interjecting himself into the conversation.

"What?" the others said in unison.

"They can hurt us, damage our armor. Can they do the same to the ship?"

"The ship has shields," Ossaro countered.

"No, it doesn't. That's what I was just checking," he said, gesturing to the console. "It has a TLS bubble variation for redirecting energy which acts like a shield, but it's not a shield. If their powers are similar to our weapons, we should be good, but if they aren't …"

"It'll rip right through," Andrea finished.

The ward shrugged.

"It doesn't matter if we can't find a way to sneak in, but five won't accomplish much."

"Four," Soren corrected.

The big man turned, his eyes glowering.

"Is there something you'd like to add?"

The engineer nodded and took a step closer to the trio.

"SAVI, seal the bridge, kill all comms and external communications."

"Confirmed."

"Belay that order," Ossaro snapped.

"Ward Ossaro, you don't outrank Engineer Goski," SAVI corrected.

The big man's lips peeled back in a snarl, but he sent a pointed, silent plea to Andrea. Goski noted the exchange and looked to his commanding officer.

"You'll have to trust me."

In the time it took her to blink, she answered. "SAVI, do as Goski says."

The doors slid shut and the speakers crackled with an audible pop. Pulling a handheld frequency scanner from near the center console, he checked the room.

"We're clear."

"What's going on?" Kodi inquired.

Andrea held up a hand to stall her and glanced at him.

"How much privacy do we need?"

"The highest levels."

Her eyes rolled up to the speaker in the ceiling. "SAVI?"

"Yes, Chief Regent?"

"Create a Black Zone on the bridge."

"Confirmed."

The speaker overhead crackled, then went silent. Every screen flickered green and beeped, then all went quiet.

Andrea dipped her head in his direction.

"You've got your privacy."

His tongue darted out and wetted his lips. With a deep breath, he blurted, "Emma's aware. She killed Daspar."

For a moment, the group stood in stunned silence, then Ossaro broke the tension with laughter.

"That's the greatest news ever, Goski."

"This isn't a joke! I found his body in the washroom. It's the only explanation. His eyes were bloodshot, his throat mangled. His head sat at an odd angle."

Ossaro kept laughing, and even Kodi chuckled, a smile twitching at the corners of her mouth.

Only Andrea didn't laugh. She stared at him, her face stoic and severe.

"Ossaro," she said, glancing in the ward's direction. "He's not joking. She's aware. I wasn't sure about it a while ago, but if Soren's confirming it, it must be real."

Momentary relief washed over him before her words registered.

His stomach dropped out again.

"Wait! You knew?"

Chapter Twenty-Eight: Andrea

Andrea nodded before she could stop herself.

"Yes."

Her chest tightened as the group voiced their disgust, anger, or agreement.

"Why the hell didn't you tell anyone?" Kodi asked.

Her brow contorted into a frown, her lips pressed into a thin line, and revulsion settled across her features.

"I wasn't sure, only guessing. What if I happened to be wrong? And if I was right? How would you react to the newest sentient species in the galaxy? Hell, the universe!"

She eyed each in turn.

"She has an established relationship with one member, and another one fucked her."

Andrea glanced at Ossaro, her voice and features hardened as anger crept into her voice.

"You'd just see her as a security risk."

She glanced at them all again, daring them to challenge her decision.

"I made the best decision I could with what information I had."

Kodi shook her head.

"You should've told us."

Andrea glanced at the men. What would Soren think? Emma was, after all, his property.

Shit! Is she still property now?

The ethical quandaries threw a kink into any debate, any stance they might take. In all, they'd have to think of her as a human now. She was more than the sum of her initial parts, more than silicon, plastisteel, and light. While she didn't have a heart that pumped blood, she had a battery which operated as such.

Similar, but not human.

The big man gave a slow shake of his head. "I'm with Kodi. We should've known. The security matter alone—"

"What security matter?" Soren snapped.

His hostile tone clashed with the perplexity on his face.

"She's been with us for years, and now you're worried?"

"Okay, for the sake of argument, let's say that she's aware," Ossaro started.

He crossed his arms as he spoke to the engineer.

"We don't, prior to now, know what her ethical code would be. How do we know her values? Life isn't as precious to her because she doesn't die."

"But she can stop working."

"Yes, but you'll replace those parts, and she'll be good as new, living indefinitely. We can't. We value how precious life is because of the limited time we have. Does she?"

The big man shrugged, then turned his head towards Andrea.

"Because of your silence and indecisiveness, a crew member's dead."

White-hot rage flared through her, her eyes going wide. Her face bunched as she readied to let a retort fly from her mouth, but Kodi stepped in first.

"Hey, Ossaro! Just because you don't like that you were kept in the dark doesn't mean you get to blame her! I don't like it either, but I don't lay all the injustice at her feet. Who knows what I would've done at the time. And don't pretend like you care for Daspar. You two hated each other."

Ossaro's eyes flared, and he clinched his teeth. He took a menacing step forward.

Andrea let her hand fall to her side, mere inches from her blaster. Her palm itched.

The ward's eyes caught the movement.

"You really think I'd hurt Kodi?"

Andrea gave a nonplussed twitch of her head.

"Sub-Regent Kembly," Andrea corrected.

His dark blue eyes narrowed, but he took a step back and let out a noisy breath.

"Well"—Soren interrupted, then cleared his throat—"I wouldn't have said anything either. I lived with her and didn't know until today. I noticed behavioral changes in small ways, but I chalked that up to her evolving program, or perhaps a side effect of the strange pulse from the alien artifact. It wasn't until today that I was absolutely sure."

He glanced at Andrea.

"What about you?"

Heat clawed at her chest. Did she really want to tell them the truth? It was so long ago that her initial suspicion manifested.

"Right after we woke up, when I came to your quarters because you and Daspar were fighting. I suspected then, but barely."

Kodi and Ossaro groaned, the latter rolled his eyes and took a step away from their makeshift circle around the tactical station.

"I think it had more to do with my suspicion about SAVI than Emma."

"What suspicion?" Ossaro asked, his eyes dark. "Something else you've been hiding? Another security breach?"

"Would you shut the fuck up?" Kodi shouted. "God, get over yourself. A fucking man's dead and we're talking about the possibility of sentient life. Security's important, but our moral obligation right now is to approach this with due diligence."

Surprise rippled through Andrea. She always suspected there was more to Kodi than she let on, and the stressful moment had finagled it out of her.

Andrea shook her head and answered Ossaro.

"The suspicion has since faded, but still, my doubt lingers."

"What doubt?" Kodi inquired.

"That this whole thing was orchestrated."

"What whole thing?" Soren asked.

"By us, by the Teshren, by SAVI."

"A conspiracy?" Ossaro mused, his tone thick with doubt.

Andrea shrugged and found herself nodding.

"Yes, in short. I don't think we left this planet of our own volition. I think we were coerced, especially with caretaker being absent."

Ossaro grumbled in his throat.

"So, you think they overpowered us, kidnapped Caretaker, extorted us, sent us aboard with an object that could destroy all our memories? For what purpose? And further, why would we leave knowing that they had Caretaker? Why would we agree to that?"

"Maybe it was an accident?" Kodi offered.

Soren nodded and pointed at her.

"You might be onto something."

He glanced at Andrea.

"They wanted us gone, and gave us the object, presumably to take back to our leaders so they could communicate. Did they know that it would wipe our memories?"

Andrea's eyes narrowed as she studied Soren. His memory was indeed remarkable. She'd forgotten that Gelarae had told them when they first arrived that the orb was a communication device.

Did their studying or the object trigger the memory loss?

"Why would we bring it on board to begin with?" Kodi queried.

"I can answer that," Gelarae said, standing from the commanding officer's chair.

Everyone gave a visible jump. Adrenaline pumped through Andrea. She'd forgotten her presence, just as she had forgotten her words.

The woman came around the chair and joined them.

"You brought it on board because the Teshren fought from the beginning. They attacked your ship, your crew, and my people."

Andrea felt a chill creep up her spine when Gelarae glanced at her.

"You went to talk, to nego—nego—...?"

"Negotiate," Soren supplied.

A smile flickered across Gelarae's features.

"Yes, that. They said they'd stop the attacks if you or someone volunteered to stay with them, took back their orb to your leaders, and negotiate to never return."

"If we were never meant to return," Andrea said, "how were we supposed to get Caretaker back?"

Gelarae held out her hand, palm up.

"Maybe when you the brought orb back?"

Kodi's head tilted to the side as she thought. Her lips puckered.

"Something still doesn't add up."

Ossaro nodded in agreement.

"Yeah, but I think this line of talk is trivial compared to what we're going to do about Emma."

"What do you mean 'what we're going to do about Emma?'" Soren asked, frowning.

"Well, we can't let her continue to roam the ship. She's too dangerous; she's proven that."

"I take it you have a suggestion?" Andrea inquired, her eyes narrowing. She had a feeling what he'd say.

"We deactivate her. Maybe just temporarily, maybe permanently."

"You're out of your mind," Soren objected.

"I'm in agreement with Ossaro," Kodi voiced, which surprised Andrea.

She'd been almost curt with the ward earlier, even going out of her way to tell him to shut up. Andrea almost considered it a role reversal when she realized that Kodi had never voiced her own opinion on the matter.

"I don't know what you're talking about," Gelarae said. "What does this have to do with the Teshren, your Caretaker, or the threat my village faces?"

Andrea frowned as pity for Gelarae rose. Her heart went out to the native who just lost her father. She hadn't mourned him, which Andrea found odd. Shock often did strange things to people.

The constant threat hanging over Gelarae and her village was bound to weigh her down. How much more since the native decided to help them?

"You're right," Andrea said. "We can shelve this discussion on Emma until later. We have priorities: get Caretaker, stop the Teshren, and get off this planet."

Ossaro slammed his fists on the console.

"What can take more priority than this? A crew member's dead because of your incompetent silence regarding Soren's fuck-toy."

The engineer lashed out, a right cross to Carlin's jaw.

For as big as he was, the ward moved fast.

He retaliated, his hand latching around Soren's throat. Kodi and Gelarae lurched forward to break them up.

In a smooth motion, Andrea pulled her blaster, thumbed the threshold to a lower setting, and shot the ward's right knee. He immediately stopped, spasmed, and gasped for breath.

He crumpled to the deck, blinking and panting. She stepped closer, into his line of vision, and thumbed the weapon to a higher setting. It wasn't enough to kill him, but she wanted him to know that she meant business.

"You'll never touch another member again, is that understood?"

"He started it!"

Andrea rolled her eyes and shook her head.

"Really? What are you, a child? You insulted Soren and the synth. Don't you see? She's a replica of his dead wife. So, when you insult Emma and Soren, you insult her memory."

Fury burned in his eyes for a few more moments before Ossaro nodded, letting the fire wane. Andrea holstered the weapon, strapping it back in. She turned to the engineer.

"I expected more from you."

His large, brown eyes misted and he nodded, dipping his head in shame.

Andrea stepped away and resumed her position as Gelarae helped Ossaro to his feet. A dark anger smothered her unrefined features.

You don't have to like me, girl, but on this tub, I'm in command. You better get used to it if you want us to take you when we leave.

"You're starting to remember, too," Soren voiced, barely a whisper.

She nodded and waited for everyone to settle before she resumed the discussion.

"Yes, you're right, Ossaro—she's a danger, and it's a discussion we must have. I bear the burden of guilt, and I'll let the Admiralty decide my punishment when we return. We'll have this discussion, but not right now. Other than shutting her down or destroying her, what options do we have?"

"Confine her to quarters," Soren offered, "if she'll listen."

"We could have SAVI track and monitor her," Kodi offered.

"Download her core," the ward said, his tone dark, "her memories, deactivate her, then hard reboot."

"Only as an absolute last resort," Andrea confirmed. "She's sentient. We must try to reason with her first."

"If she was sentient as long as you think," Kodi started, "maybe she killed Daspar out of revenge. I mean, think about it. We didn't punish him as severely because we all assumed that Emma wasn't aware. She obviously remembers that, and maybe her emotions took over. Wait! You said your suspicion was when you first met her. How did you not space Daspar after knowing that?"

"I told you," Andrea started. "It was a fleeting idea, and my suspicion was more on SAVI than a synthetic. SAVI refused to cooperate at every turn, restricted access to everything. How was I supposed to know that SAVI was just following protocol? How can his bizarre behavior not take precedence when we're trying to regain control of the ship?"

"I think I love dogs," Ossaro mumbled.

Everyone glanced at him, each as perplexed as her. She almost remarked on his random comment when he spoke again.

"Have you ever had a dog?"

Andrea shook her head, still unclear what this had to do with everything. "What—?"

"I love dogs. They're fun to play with, a companion that makes me laugh. It loves me, and I love it. I'll take care of them until the day it dies. But he's not you, Andrea, or you Soren, or you Kodi."

He glanced at his wife.

"Or even you."

Ward Ossaro took a breath.

"If I had to choose between the life of a dog, an animal, and that of a human, the dog dies every time. That's the choice of morality. Any other choice is reprehensible and evil. Humans, a sentient species capable of reproducing, should always take priority over a dog or a cat or a horse."

Ossaro sighed and looked at them.

"Or a synth. What do we do with pets that attack? We put it down. In this case, Emma's the dog, and she just bit Daspar, but our navigator's dead, and he ain't ever coming back. A possibly sentient *thing* just killed a sentient, reproducing human—not that I'd want Daspar reproducing. Let's take him out of the equation and say she killed one of you. What would we do then?"

"She won't," Soren said.

"You don't know that."

"She won't."

"Maybe, maybe not. Who will shoulder that blame if she does? Who's gonna take responsibility? I'm not, I'm warning you all right now. If you don't listen, the next death is on you."

"What of my people?" Gelarae spoke up. "They'll know by now that their outpost is destroyed and send people to kill."

Andrea nodded, remembering the warnings the tortured Teshren provided.

"Alright. Soren, get us up in the air. Ossaro, still got those coordinates?"

He nodded, then limped behind Soren.

"We've got to take care of one thing at a time. First, we knock out this larger outpost, rescue Caretaker, and get the hell off this rock."

"It won't be enough," the native woman protested.

Andrea paused.

Her sister's words, the edicts of the Warmaster, came back to her.

"We don't want to make our presence synonymous with war and violence."

The weight of the command decision, of her next words, grew encumbering.

"It'll have to be."

"They won't stop until they kill us all."

"I can't kill your enemies for you. This isn't my world."

"No, you just come and make trouble then leave, just like last time."

Andrea winced as she walked to her chair, then turned on her heel to face her.

"We have orders to follow, whether we like them or not. Unless we come under direct attack, our actions are limited."

"What limited action?" Soren asked.

Andrea sighed.

"End Black Zone."

The screens blinked and the consoles beeped.

"SAVI?"

"Yes, Chief Regent?"

"Play audio file from Warmaster Hessner, specifically the rules of escalation."

"Confirmed."

The main screen flickered to life, and she saw the familiar face of her sister. As she took her seat, the video played.

"In the event of a hostile engagement, you'll strive to limit engagement and deaths. We'd rather you disable than maim, maim rather than kill. Use appropriate escalation of force to ensure your survival and that of your ship and crew. Using your ship's offensive capabilities is strictly last resort. The casualties inflicted will be remembered until the passage of time and history obscure the travesties. If you attempt to escape and are pursued into orbit, you may use

any means necessary to ensure your escape is untraceable."

The video paused.

Andrea swiveled in her chair.

"Satisfied?"

Gelarae shook her head.

"And you call us barbaric."

She stormed from the bridge, and for a moment, no one bothered to call after her. Then, almost as if in unison, everyone remembered Emma.

"Ossaro," Andrea barked.

"On it."

He jogged off the bridge.

Kodi took her seat next to Soren; the engineer sat at the navigation console —Daspar's station.

"What's the plan?" Kodi asked.

Andrea didn't say anything. The words of Gelarae and her sister warred within her. She took a deep breath.

"Set a course for the next outpost."

"And then?"

"We give them a chance to surrender and turn Caretaker over to us."

"And when they don't?" Soren pressed.

"We level the fucking place."

Chapter Twenty-Nine: The Second Outpost

Kodi swallowed hard, watching the curling smoke rise into the air.

The outpost's destruction had been immense. They'd communicated their demand, both in English and whatever language Ossaro's wife spoke.

Ossaro's wife. God, that sounds so weird, especially considering he was screwing Andrea not long ago. And she's married!

It seemed like a small detail, an unfortunate blip seldom recalled—Ossaro's wife. She wondered what it was like for him, to be married to an alien-human, one he couldn't remember.

What would she have done if the roles had been reversed? She'd like to think she would've done her duty, but no. She wouldn't have let the lack of a place to sleep stop her. She would've found some other way.

While honor would make her pause, some random culture wouldn't impact her, let alone keep plans from forming. Caretaker was the priority, not making amends for a dalliance that both parties were responsible for.

Dark, oily smoke billowed into the air. One tower twitched as if it strained against the pull of gravity, struggled to stay upright before it crumbled. The stones flew out, like a giant coughing out phlegm.

"My God," she whispered.

"We warned them," Andrea said, soothing herself more than Kodi.

"Perhaps they didn't understand?" Soren proposed.

"They understood," Gelarae said.

She stood to Soren's right—the navigator's console—and against the wall of the bridge. A grim but satisfied expression covered her features.

"I hope they burned screaming."

"That's horrid," Kodi mumbled.

Her eyes never left the destruction.

"If there was anyone towards the front of the building," Andrea said, "they died instantly."

"Pity," Gelarae added.

She turned away and left the bridge. Kodi heard Andrea sigh, and Ossaro moved after his companion.

"Soren? Set us down. Then, go get the Teshren out of the brig and drag his sorry ass along."

Kodi noted that the engineer nodded, and she unbuckled and rose from her seat. Her hand touched the blaster on her right thigh, assuring herself that it was still there. Collecting her helmet and rifle, she headed after the departed couple.

Earlier, after Soren and Daspar were ordered back to the ship, the tortured Teshren provided this location, and Gelarae confirmed its existence. Still, the outpost was far from the previous location, and unless the group decided to take Aether's Grace to the next location, flying was the only way to reach it.

Their arrival prompted them to spill out of their buildings in droves. When they attacked, Andrea didn't hesitate to mow them down. Kodi almost pitied them, but knowing the Teshren would've done worse eased her troubled conscience.

The doors to the bridge opened for her, and she tread a few more steps to the left and hit the call button for the lift. A few moments later, the doors opened, and she descended to the bottom deck. An image of the navigator flashed through her mind, a man sitting on a toilet, his head at an odd angle, his eyes open and distant, mouth agape.

Rhett, I'm so sorry for the way I treated you.

She pushed the regret aside. It would only distract her, which could get her and others killed. No matter what had transpired, he didn't deserve to go out like that. Her imagination took off, allowing her to see the synth hovering nearby. Her cascading blood hair shimmer down her back. In a slow movement, she turned her head and spied Kodi watching. A menacing grin split her face.

Kodi shook the mental worry away though trepidation filled her.

Emma remained prevalent on her mind as the lift descended. The crew should've reached the obvious conclusion and switched her off, maybe even destroyed her if she became violent. Kodi would never feel safe, no matter how many assurances Soren or Emma gave. The conversation may have been over, but it was far from settled. Not by a long shot.

Emma's awareness persisted in the debatable arena, neither proven nor disproven. Still, a synthetic went against programming and killed a sentient creature. It went against every coding. Did she have corrupted commands? Did Soren tamper with her inputs to make her more … whatever he wanted?

Though Emma was supposed to be the representation of his late wife, Kodi found little sympathy for him.

She's been dead for years, Soren. It's time to move on.

Was sex and a relationship with a synth so much better than with a real person? Was that why he clung to her?

The doors opened, and she exited the lift.

The ward and his wife stood clustered to the right of the ramp. Before thinking her actions through, Kodi set out to muster near the exit. Halfway there, she realized Ossaro and Gelarae gathered around her father's corpse. Kembly slowed her pace and stopped at a respectable distance.

The local girl knelt, murmuring in low tones. Ward Ossaro kneaded the woman's shoulders with his massive hands. He glanced up, noting Kodi's arrival. He left his grieving bride and stepped to Kodi's side. His demeanor remained dark, his jaw set.

Kodi eyed him for a moment, noting his steely features.

"What's up with you?"

"Emma," he grumbled.

Kodi grunted in her throat.

He shifted on his feet.

"How do we know that she ain't gonna try to take the ship after we leave?"

Damn good question.

She hadn't thought of that. What would happen if she tried?

"SAVI would stop her," she said.

Her tremulous voice gave away the doubt inside. She shrugged.

"She hasn't taken it yet."

"How do you know SAVI would stop her? Maybe SAVI is in on it? Maybe he made her aware."

The accusation struck her like the sudden flicker of a thunderbolt. Again, she hadn't given that much thought, too worried about the major threat to her life and getting caretaker back. In some ways, she took the brunt of guilt for the death of Daspar, not that he died, but they didn't stop to give him a proper send off.

Shit, we haven't even moved his body.

That was Andrea's idea, so that Emma wouldn't know the crew was aware. In all, this proved to be the wisest move. If the synth found out and caught on, who knew how she'd react.

The lift opened behind them. Kodi turned as Andrea and Soren exited with the Teshren, the latter bound with his hands behind his back. He appeared bloodied and disheveled, but still breathing and walking.

He's lucky he still is.

A flash of heat and anger welled up in her. She shifted her eyes away, trying to calm herself.

Kembly scrutinized the engineer's large eyes for any sign of his thoughts or feelings. He didn't hide his discomfort well. Besides the Teshren leader, he, and by extension, Emma, sat in the room like a giant turd, and everyone just tiptoed past.

Another surge of white-hot emotions welled up inside her, and she wanted to scream at the older man, reminding him what his precious sex-toy had done. The simmering wrath turned to bitter bile as she bit her tongue. Spewing out her choice words wouldn't do any good except make her feel better in the moment. After, when she cooled off, she'd regret her indiscretion.

Andrea put her helmet on.

"Brain buckets on."

Gelarae rose from her father's corpse and moved closer, hovering at the edge of the group.

With mechanic repetition, Kodi dunked her head protector on. She and Ossaro pulled the charging handle to their blaster rifles at the same time. The cadence stirred something within her, a giddiness. They were about to enter into combat again.

The first time around, fear nearly crippled her. Only after watching Andrea, and following her lead, kept Kodi going. Now, she was almost antsy, yearning for it, a high she couldn't describe. She both craved and quailed against its potency, finding it addicting and terrifying.

Andrea's voice crackled over their internal comms.

"SAVI? Lower the ramp. Once outside, seal it back up. Keep it primed and ready for takeoff. Protect the ship if it comes to that."

"Confirmed."

Gases hissed and the ramp yawned open.

"Ossaro, take lead."

"Copy."

The big man moved, shouldering his sniper rifle, and Andrea glanced at the wife. Kodi half-expected some snark from Andrea, but she dismissed the idea. It didn't fit her character, at least the one Andrea had turned into.

"You stay in the middle," Andrea told the native. "I'll go next. Then you, and then Kodi. Soren will bring up the rear with *him*," she said, jerking her head in the direction of the tortured alien-human.

Gelarae nodded but didn't say anything.

Daspar revealed he started to remember events when they found the Teshren.

Kodi started remembering, too.

She didn't like what she recalled, not only in herself but the others. They'd all changed, everyone except Daspar. He pretty much stayed consistent. Maybe more brazen, not quite as filtered, but similar.

A dark thought flickered through her head.

What if Daspar hadn't ever lost his memories but only pretended? That would make sense as to why he didn't seem to change much.

She shook the thought away.

Andrea followed the ward in the ranger file, marking the dispersion.

Kodi watched her go.

The chief regent had changed the most, at least at first. On the planet, she slipped back into the comfort of old ways. Kodi didn't have the heart to remind Andrea that it was her fault they were on the planet to begin with. Had the commanding officer not acted out in an unforgivable manner in what became known as the Pinshi incident, they wouldn't be here at all.

Kodi's memories of Andrea only came back when they decided to torture the Teshren. Something very similar had taken place before, and Andrea ordered the torture of a garrum, an alien indigenous to Gol.

The circumstance had been similar. The fleet had sent *The Demon* and a contingent of ground troops to quell ... something. An uprising, perhaps? The insurgents had captured the daughter of whatever passed for royalty there, and Andrea went per the Admiralty's request.

In the end, the insurgents sent the daughter's mangled corpse back to her family, the tortured detainee had died, and Commander Andrea Hessner had been courtmartialed and stripped of rank.

In fact, *The Demon* was almost taken from her. Her father, a vice admiral, agreed to retire and leave the admiralty board to save his daughter's career.

Kodi glanced at Gelarae.

"You're up. Nice and slow."

Gelarae exited the ship and Kodi watched her go.

The idea of the rustic girl coming along made Kodi uneasy. In movement between secure locations, she became a liability. It didn't make sense to risk their lives just so she could be near to her husband. Perhaps it was a cultural thing?

In fact, the whole concept of marriage seemed bizarre. Hardly anyone stayed married any more. Most marriages were arranged for genetic purposes. The fleet kept a registry of DNA sequences and traced lineages back numerous generations. It was important to remember their roots, especially now that humans traveled among the stars, and discovered aliens in the vast cosmos.

Kodi's ancestors hailed from places she had only heard about: Inverness, Scotland and Hokkaido, Japan—two insignificant places on a spec of rock hurtling through space. No one in the galaxy would care.

No one except her.

Kodi shifted the blaster rifle in her arms and followed the ranger file after a few moments, letting the dispersion stretch between her and the village girl.

She could feel Soren at her back. She flickered the rearview in her ISD. He appeared pained, lost. A turmoil she couldn't fathom brewed underneath. A replica of someone he loved had gone haywire and killed. Every moment that went by tarnished any cherished memory he once had.

Darker thoughts troubled her. What if they couldn't deactivate Emma once they got back? Would the synth fight? Could she, now that awareness had come? At what point did programming end and personal desires begin? Would they all perish in the fight for control? Could Soren keep up a charade for days or weeks? Could the engineer sleep knowing she'd killed someone?

Her feet propelled her forward, and though the ground shifted beneath on her trek, none of the details registered. The crunch of her boots on the coarse dirt filtered through in muffled tones. Her throat tightened, remembering the bound enemy at her back. Would he be able to overpower Soren?

An ache in her body throbbed, not one of pain but fatigue and monotony. Wisps of smoke curled through the air, breaking her downward stare. Her head snapped up, realizing how much closer she was to the building.

Black plumes billowed out, thick and dark like curtains. Chalky ash fell in giant snowflakes, like a chemical fallout. The once-proud, dark, gray-hued walls trembled at the group's proximity, sheered and splintered by the blasts of *The Demon's* cannons. The shattered remains of a door scattered across the ground.

Kodi eyed the gaping doorway.

The ward had already slipped through, and Kodi could make his faint, crouched outline inside the darkened entrance. Andrea stood at the door, facing the ship and incoming troops, waving them on as if they'd forgotten where to go.

The first officer entered the building remains and darkness enveloped her. After a few, quick moments, the visor adjusted to a quasi night vision, and the details filtered through.

Mounds of rubble lay strewn, some boulders like cannon balls, others small and comparable to hail. A layer of chalk, dust, and grime covered the once pristine marble floors, and even those lay broken, cracked, and charred from *The Demon*.

Something oddly shaped and twisted stuck out of the debris, and after a few moments, Kodi realized she stared at an outstretched arm, the fingers flayed, and patches of skin missing. Her eyes darted to another piece of flesh and ash-grey replaced the ivory-white bone protruding from the muscle and sinewy.

The urge to yack swept over Kodi. The horrors twisted in her mind, manifesting anew. What did they really know of the Teshren? Was this really a military outpost? What if they'd killed women and children?

Her stomach quivered at the thought.

She closed her eyes and willed the images away.

"You'll pay for what you've done," an angry voice hissed, breaking through her composure.

Kodi opened her eyes and turned to the voice behind her.

Soren's prisoner, the Teshren, knelt just inside the doorway, his hands still bound. Abhorrence etched his features, and beneath, hatred.

"Don't you realize what you've done?"

"Nothing your people haven't done to mine," Gelarae said.

The Teshren spat.

"Don't play the innocent. The Loccan are as guilty, if not more so. Your pacifist ideology doesn't wipe away your past sins."

"What do you mean?" Andrea asked.

Kodi glanced to the commanding officer and the prisoner, watching the exchange.

He shifted his eyes to Andrea.

"And your ignorance is like darkness, suffocating and absolute once the light has left."

"We're not going to get anywhere with him," Ossaro said through the comms. "We might as well get moving. He's stalling."

Kodi watched Andrea nod and turn away.

"Let's go. Clear the building. If caretaker's here, we'll find him."

"And if he's not?" Carlin prodded.

Andrea paused and looked back at the Teshren.

"Then, we'll have no more use of him."

"He's here." The Teshren leered. "I promise you."

The events of clearing the building blurred, a jumbled mess of rubble, body parts, grime, and blood. Twisted limbs and body parts filled Kodi's vision in each room she entered. The construction of the outpost was almost identical to the previous, the basics very much the same, except this dungeon went deeper, and her pit sank with each step, knowing only nightmares awaited them.

Cold seeped through the darkened halls. The night vision had a hard time compensating for the lack of any light. It wasn't until SAVI recommended turning on the lights on their helmets and armor that their progress picked back up. The light extended from each combatant, and Kodi got the distinct feeling of cave divers.

The chill seeped through her armor, and before long, her teeth chattered. Dank, wet walls lined either side of the group. Little holes that passed for doorways barred with banded wood sat on either side. Little slots with iron bars masqueraded as windows, and the crew checked each one for their missing member.

Inside the cavities, people lay on the ground—races Kodi had never seen—shackled to the wall. Each twisted their head to see who had come, their mangled forms wincing at the bright lights. Terrified, gaunt faces shied away, but not before Kodi saw their startling eyes she could only dream of, gazes of teal, aquamarine, tangelo, and gray.

No ethnicity between them appeared more prominent than the other, but the inmates were predominantly men. One strange fellow had a skeletal structure on his face that highlighted aristocratic features, but his elongated ears gave him a distinct alien aura.

Kodi glanced at Gelarae and wondered if the ward's wife saw any familiar faces.

She felt a pang of pity for her.

The members inside the cells were more twisted and grotesque than the outpost before. The images Kodi saw, the species, the disfigured folks—it'd haunt her dreams forever.

Her stomach twisted with each descending step.

"I don't see Caretaker," Andrea said, hurrying from one cell to the next.

"Me, either," Ossaro echoed.

He shifted his gaze back to the prisoner.

"And I'm seeing less and less of a reason to keep the Teshren alive."

"I must confess," Soren said, his voice watery and weak, "I'm starting to agree."

Andrea, further down the hall than the rest, paused in her search, and turned to face the engineer.

"You thought we were monsters for torturing him."

"You are," the older man said, "they're just worse."

Andrea shook her head and went back to searching.

"He's not here," Gelarae said. "The Teshren only lie and kill."

The Teshren spat at her.

"You Loccan are no better."

A short silence hung in the air, and Kodi half-expected some offhand remark from Daspar, but he was dead, his body still on the ship.

And so was Emma.

"We'll see," Ossaro said with a grin.

Kodi knew how it'd all play out. They'd get to the end and there'd be nothing, no caretaker, no final piece of the mystery solved. Only death awaited them.

Theirs.

The Teshren probably had others waiting for their arrival. The crew would die, walking into the trap. A sharp pang of anxiety slithered into her gut.

At last they came to the end of the long, winding dungeon. Two massive doors barred the way forward. A knife of uncertainty twisted in Kodi's stomach.

Andrea turned again as the others caught up.

"No Caretaker."

The Teshren smiled.

"I'm a man of my word. He's here, just beyond the door."

"What else is beyond the door?" Kodi blurted out.

"Maybe you've got friends waiting on us," Carlin added. "I say we send him first."

"Good idea," Andrea seconded. "Goski?"

The engineer unbound the Teshren, and Carlin came forward. The big man grabbed him by the back of his collar and shoved him. It was the ward's kick to the prisoner's back that sent him through the doors. They parted with a thunderous crash, and the crew entered the chamber with their rifles ready.

Nothing awaited them.

Only a flickering luminance of the Aether's Grace filled the room with an eerie light.

Kodi's eyes tracked to the glowing liquid, and she quickly averted her eyes. A tinge of panic overcame her, but she fought the sensation. Her eyes lifted up and away, and then she saw them.

Skulls lined the wall, the heads of humans and other species and creatures. On this alien world, it was hard to determine what had sentience and what didn't, but the Teshren had all types of species in their cells. She had to assume all could speak and held higher intelligence. No display of bone seemed to be that of a creature, one that would be hunted for food and other necessities.

"Oh, my God," Kodi whispered.

Her voice must've been picked up on the comms because the others turned and regarded her before following her gaze. The others let out gasps or sucked in their breath.

Only the sound of a contemptuous mirth from the Teshren broke them from their stares.

Andrea stormed across the room, the butt of her blaster handle cracking against his head. He tumbled to the ground.

"You sick bastard! Where is he? You brought us here to show us his skull?"

The prisoner laughed up at her, his cackle low and rumbling.

"No, those are the skulls of the honored dead, great warriors who fought us and died. Your caretaker isn't worthy of such high regard."

Andrea holstered her blaster but took another menacing step forward.

"Where is he?"

"I told you this was all a lie," Gelarae whispered. "The Teshren don't take prisoners."

Kodi glanced at Ossaro's wife, noting the ward came close to her.

"What do you mean?" he asked.

Gelarae shook her head.

"There's something afoul here. There's no reason for him to talk, to bring you here, unless he wants you here."

"So," the prisoner said, his eyes narrowed with a lecherous grin creeping across his face, "the Local women do have brains. There's hope for your future besides breeding. Well … " his smile widened, "… there was."

Gelarae's face fell.

"What do you mean?"

She rushed forward, screaming.

"What have you done?"

Kodi moved to stop her, and Andrea was there a heartbeat later.

Gelarae clawed between the two women, trying to reach the prisoner. She kicked and screamed like a feral beast, and Kodi fought the temptation to let her go.

"I did what we promised. Your clan's no more, or soon will be."

At his words, the strength left Gelarae, and she slumped to the floor in a heap. Kodi tried to ease her fall, but Gelarae slipped through her arms. Kodi stood straight and turned to face the Teshren. He struggled to his feet.

"The Loccan figured it out before any of you."

He eyed them all.

"You're so naive. It's a wonder my people ever considered you a threat to begin with."

He nodded toward Andrea.

"And you, you've once again led your crew to doom."

Kodi's throat tightened.

"What do you mean?"

The Teshren glanced at her but otherwise ignored her question. His attention turned back to Andrea.

"You want your caretaker? He's here."

The Teshren took a step to the side and motioned with his head.

Kodi glanced behind him, seeing the way they came, then glanced up.

High above, bound to a cross-like structure, hung a half rotten corpse. The skin had sagged off the bone. The abdomen hung open as if ripped by animal or serrated blade. What remained of his insides hung out. Kodi couldn't be sure it was the caretaker, but the uniform left little doubt.

"I'm going to be sick," Kodi panted.

The suit, or SAVI, sensed her rushing bile. The visor opened just as she spewed over the floor.

The Teshren gave a contemptuous laugh.

"Still the weakest one, I see."

Anger swelled in her, and she wanted to pummel him with her armored hands. Instead, she wiped her mouth and stood. The Teshren had moved deeper in the room, and she was almost surprised that no one had stopped him.

Andrea was doubled over, throwing up, too. Ossaro looked pale, barely on his feet, and Soren seemed caught halfway between puking or swallowing it back down.

Their prisoner stopped with his back to them. The man who had been so helpless only hours before, bleeding and broken from his torture, stood with his back straight, tall and proud.

"The Loccan was right. I allowed myself to be captured, tortured. I told you what you wanted to hear and brought you here for a purpose."

Kodi's rage rose with each uttered word.

He turned back to face them and swept his arm again.

"To see your crew member wasn't the reason. You should've never come back. He was dead before you left the planet. But my servant who got away? He raised the alarm, he informed the legions of troops of my plan. That Aether's Grace he slipped into brought him here, and he raised the alarm. And they've no doubt carried out my instructions by now. This place, as it was for your crewmember, will be your tomb. You'll never escape."

"Neither will you," Kodi said. She drew her blaster in a smooth motion and fired a single shot.

The sound rang out, resounding in the cavernous room.

The bolt drilled a hole between his eyes.

"What the fuck!" Andrea shrieked.

She rushed over and shoved Kodi as hard as she could.

"We needed to know what he knew!"

"We already know!" Kodi snapped. "Gelarae's village—her people! They're going to die unless we get to them first!"

Andrea's eyes widened.

"Shit!" Andrea touched the side of her helmet and her visor snapped shut. "SAVI?"

"Yes, Chief Regent?"

"We still ready to fly?"

"Indeed. Also, I'm picking up life signs closing in on our location."

"How many?"

"They are dense pockets of life signs. Maybe dozens, maybe hundreds."

"Copy!"

Andrea glanced at her crew.

"We've got to go."

"No shit," Soren muttered.

He regained much of his vigor, but his eyes never left the now-deceased prisoner.

"I don't intend on dying here," Andrea said. "What about the rest of you?"

"Hell no," Kodi answered.

Killing the Teshren felt good, like she avenged their caretaker.

Ossaro pulled his sniper rifle off his back and shouldered it.

"Let's move before it's too late."

Andrea moved to the fallen Gelarae and extended a hand.

"You can stay here and die or you can come save your village, which is it?"

The ward's wife reached out and took her hand. Andrea hauled her up to her feet.

"To the surface, double time." Andrea took off, not waiting for the others.

Ossaro followed on her heels, and Kodi gave Gelarae one glance before she tore after them. Right behind her, she heard footfalls.

Kodi's visor fell into place, and she checked her rearview, seeing Soren and Gelarae following. Kodi was glad the woman decided there was still something worth living for. It would've been easy to give up, and it took strength to get up. The girl lost her father today, and she might lose her people, too. Kodi would've understood if she hadn't come.

They rushed up the dark, winding tunnel, the grade becoming steeper the longer they ran. Kodi wanted to free all the people who were still in their cells, but they didn't have time. If they stopped, they'd all die, the prisoners included, Gelarae's village, too. It was a hard choice, but she kept her eyes focused on Ossaro's back as they ran.

A dark thought flitted through her head.

The whole purpose of them coming to this world had been for nothing. If the Teshren had been truthful, and the caretaker had died before they even left planet, the whole rescue mission had been in vain.

To make matters worse, Daspar lost his life, not to the locals, but to the synthetic still aboard. Had the others even thought about that problem yet?

Kodi was breathing hard by the time they reached ground level, and she doubled over when they stopped at the main entrance. The bright light made Kodi wince.

"Alright," Andrea said after they all caught up and rested for a few moments.

Ossaro's visor lifted and he wiped his face with a gloved hand while Andrea talked.

"We make a mad dash for the ship. We run at odd angles and in ones. They'll have a harder time of targeting us. I'll lead, draw their fire, then Ossaro you go out at a different angle. Ready?"

"No!" the ward said, placing a hand on Andrea's arm. "I'll go first."

"This is no—"

"It's my job. First in. My mission on the ground is your safety and that of the ship. Besides, I got grenades and a sniper rifle. I'll go first."

Andrea glanced Kodi's way. It was sound logic, and Kodi didn't detect any ulterior motives.

Kodi shrugged back at her.

"He's right. It's his job."

The chief regent nodded. "Fine, you go first."

Ossaro glanced back at all of them, his eyes resting on his wife last.

"Don't wait but a second or two between each of you. Stay safe."

He took a couple of deep breaths, preparing himself.

"Ready?"

When everyone nodded, he bolted from the door. A sound rang out with a flash, and the blast felled Ossaro. The ward tumbled backwards. Kodi gasped in horror as her eyes came to rest on the big man.

Smoke curled from the crater at the top of his head.

Chapter Thirty: The Demon's Fate

"Those fucking sons of bitches!" Andrea screamed.

She holstered the pistol and tugged on her rifle. She heard screaming, and a quick glance revealed that Gelarae was covered in Ossaro's blood.

"No," Soren said, diving for Andrea, his hands holding her rifle in place. The old man was stronger than she'd realized.

"Let go!"

"Don't be foolish, girl! They'll kill you."

The words lanced her, and she quit fighting.

Gelarae fell silent. Andrea stole a peek, noting her stoic features.

Shock.

Goski let go, snapping her attention back to the moment.

"They were waiting. They know we're coming out."

He jerked his head towards Ossaro's still-smoking corpse.

"He never stood a chance, not with a sniper—or whatever the hell passes for one—out there."

Now that she stopped and let his words sink in, he made sense. Goski just saved her life. Twice now, within seconds, her life had been spared by two different men.

"What do you propose?"

"SAVI brings the ship close, and we'll board that way."

"It won't work," Kodi said, breaking her silence.

Andrea and Goski glanced at her. Kodi shook her head.

"There's nothing solid under the ship to block fire. They'll still see us. We'll be mowed down."

"Well, we can't stay here!" Andrea snapped.

"No, we can't, but we have an alternative route."

Uncertainty snaked its way through Andrea's core.

"What alternative?"

A grim smirk pulled at the corner of Kodi's lips.

"Back the way we came. The Teshren said the Aether's Grace connected to the other outpost. We go back that way."

A flicker of surprise and hope rolled through Andrea, but the engineer snuffed it out.

"What if they're waiting for us at the other outpost? We'd be walking into an ambush."

Kodi shrugged.

"Maybe, but there's a way around that, too."

She indicated with her head the way back down.

"There's a dungeon full of people who want freedom. I say we free them, send them through the Aether's Grace."

The second officer's words stole her breath like a punch to the gut.

"You mean we use them as shields? The Teshren won't care. They'll mow them down without a thought."

Kodi shrugged again.

"Maybe, if they're looking for us there. But how's it any different from what we've already done? We tortured one of them."

"It's a calloused act," Goski interrupted. "But she's right. Out the door is certain death."

"They will go," Gelarae said from the floor. She still sat immobile, immutable. "Like you, they'll choose possible death from certain death. We leave them, they'll die."

Andrea stood, and Soren slipped away.

"Alright, we'll do your plan Kodi."

She eyed the woman.

"Are you sure you can make yourself go through? Another incident like the first time will cost us."

Kodi swallowed.

"Between a choice of fear and death …"

Andrea nodded.

"Between fear and death."

Andrea moved over to Gelarae and pulled her up by the arm.

"Come on, we're taking you, too."

"What about Carlin?" she asked, voice filled with raw emotions.

Andrea looked back.

The ward was dead, missing the top half of his head. There was no coming back from it. If she or anyone else went out to retrieve his body, they'd be shot, too.

"There's nothing more we can do for him."

"You're just going to leave him?"

Andrea shoved her deeper into the building.

"Yes."

She sized up the engineer.

"Get her going back down the tunnel. I'll catch up."

He nodded, grabbing Gelarae by the arm, and started off.

Andrea nodded to Kodi.

"Run," she urged, and Kodi took off. Once alone, and their footfalls had faded, Andrea let her visor fall into place then opened the private channel.

"SAVI?"

"Yes, Andrea?"

"I want you to start a timer for thirty seconds when I say go. Once the time's up, power up, point the weapons at the outpost and fire on the main entrance."

"This act will bury you inside."

"I'm aware of that, but it'll buy us some time. What are the lifeforms doing now?"

A short pause.

"They've set up a perimeter, but no one's moving closer."

"Perfect. After you fire, return to our landing coordinates and wait for us to arrive. Be ready to take off."

"Yes, Chief Regent."

"Alright, ready that timer."

"Ready."

"Go."

Andrea sprinted back down the hall, hoping she covered enough distance by the time SAVI opened up. She didn't know how much time she'd have or how the Teshren would deal with the dilemma.

She didn't care.

Their rescue mission had turned into a disaster, and they fell into full retreat now. The goal changed from rescue to survival. The recording of her sister came back to mind as she ran.

We don't want to make our presence synonymous with war and violence.

Andrea could only imagine what Velaria would say now.

Blow it out your ass, sis.

How would the Admiralty react to the next filed report? Did she do the right thing, having SAVI fire on the outpost, both now and in the initial assault?

Velaria's voice returned again. *Using your ship's offensive capabilities is strictly last resort. The casualties inflicted will be remembered until the passage of time and history obscure the occurred travesties.*

Damn it.

The dark tunnel plunged downward when the roar of the blasts echoed from above. The structure shook as if the earth upended with a violent quake. Andrea careened into the wall but kept stumbling forward. The deafening noise added to her fear, pushing her beyond unknowable limits.

Up ahead, she saw Kodi sprinting back towards her but stopped when they laid eyes on each other.

"What the hell was that?"

"SAVI," Andrea answered.

The other nodded, turned, and took off again.

By the time Andrea caught up, Kodi and Soren worked on opposite sides of the hall, shooting the locks off the doors and freeing the people within. Gelarae kept pace with them, walking in the center, calling out in their native language.

The released prisoners came out of their cells, squinting and looking bewildered. Others helped carry some inmates too maimed to walk under their own power.

Good thing I had SAVI crater the entrance.

To Gelarae, she said, "Tell them to make their way to the Aether's Grace. There's not much time left."

The other woman nodded and kept moving. Andrea turned back the way they came. The noise had died down now, the barrage had stopped, but her stomach knotted. How much time did she buy?

Saving the prisoners was more about self-preservation. A tinge of guilt nettled her, but only for a moment. Kodi was right, they'd done worse. With the prisoners, they could overrun anyone who might be waiting for them. Then again, they may not, knowing that the entire crew was here.

The collapsed entrance would buy them a little time, but with their voodoo or magic, what was a little rubble to them?

She gazed back again. The dark hallway remained devoid of pursuers.

"Shit," she muttered to herself. She put on a burst of speed, moving past Gelarae and the crew. She came to the next lock and fired. "Kodi, Soren! Don't bother pulling the locks out, let the prisoners do that. We don't have time. Just blast the locks and move on."

The two complied, and Gelarae conveyed the instructions to the freed individuals. They made quick work of the remaining cells, but as they neared the chamber at the end, echoes of footfalls and foreign speech echoed from down the hall.

Damn, I wish I had grenades!

"Time's up!"

Goski and Kembly turned, facing the hallway, staring in the darkness. Andrea shouldered her rifle, her eyes roaming over the horde struggling for freedom. Her visor snapped into place and adjusted to the light level.

A heat signature plume grew in intensity as their enemy closed.

"Contact!"

She raised the rifle, and the detainees dodged out of the way. She pressed the trigger, and a stream of light shot out. The whine of the gun grew until the beeping echoed in her ear and the overheat message flashed across the screen.

To the left, Kodi fired in a steady stream. Andrea turned back to the main chamber.

"Hurry, through the pool."

"I'm done," Kodi yelled.

Soren opened fire, covering them.

"Kodi! Shut the door!"

The blonde nodded and struggled with the massive door. Once she got it moving, it slid shut with ease. Soren's rifle went silent, and Andrea snapped hers up. She held down the trigger. Out of the side of her vision, she saw Soren shutting the door. Once it crossed her line of fire, Andrea stopped and got out of sight.

The doors rumbled closed, and Soren hurried to catch up.

"Wish there was a way to blow this Aether's Grace to hell!" she said.

"There might be," the engineer said. "We can overload a rifle to blow. Don't know if it will work for sure, but it's better than nothing."

Andrea unslung her rifle and handed it to him.

"Do it. Kodi?"

Andrea turned to find the first officer frozen with fear. She stood at the edge of the pool, staring into the glowing murk.

Fuck.

The chief regent snuck up, kicked her boot against the back of Kodi's knee, making her buckle, then shoved her hard. Kodi tumbled in before she had time to scream.

Goski scrutinized her.

"She's going to hate you for that."

"At least she'll be alive to hate me. Are you ready?"

He nodded, flipping one last switch on the weapon, and set it down next to the pool. It started beeping immediately and growing in rapid succession. Andrea turned back to the Aether's Grace and jumped through.

As before, it felt as if unseen forces like gravity pulled and contorted her body. It happened in a rush of speed and light and vague pain. Then it was over, and the ground rushed up to greet her.

She craned her head, pulling the blaster pistol from her hip in a fluid motion. Her eyes roamed over the vaguely familiar outpost. Only the exiting prisoners and Kodi clambered in the chamber. As she scrambled to her feet, Soren dumped out beside her. He, too, went for his weapon.

Andrea spoke on the squad's comms.

"We did our charitable duty. We'll lead them to the surface, and once out, we make a break for Gelarae's village and then to *The Demon*."

"Roger that," Kodi said.

"We're just going to leave them?" Goski asked.

Andrea didn't face him, but her eyes roamed over the group. All were injured to some degree, and others were mutilated.

"Look at them, Goski. If we stop to help them, we'll end up dead. We have our orders."

"Orders?" the older man echoed. "What orders?"

"Warmaster Hessner's video logs detailed our orders: in the event of a hostile engagement, we're directed to use appropriate force to ensure our survival and that of the ship. I say this covers hostile engagement, don't you?"

"Aye."

"I don't like it any more than you, but we've got to do it."

She eyed the pool.

"Let's move before we have company."

"If," the engineer corrected.

"Right, if. Let's move."

The crew led the way up the twisting, dark tunnel. She worried about enemies closing in, but no pursuit came. Perhaps Goski's detonation worked, destroying the pool.

She could only hope so.

The journey topside seemed to stretch forever, their progression slowed by the herd of sick and infirm, and it felt like hours before they reached the main level.

Her visor's optic danced around the room, landing on every object she inspected, a scroll of text running on the display. Still, no heat signatures bloomed.

"SAVI?" Andrea called over the private comm.

"Yes, Andrea?"

"Did you get away?"

"Yes, but I sustained some minor damage to the underside of the hull. The Teshren fired upon the ship as it rose into the air."

"Copy that. Are you still functional?"

"Hull integrity is at ninety-three percent."

"How far are you from the first outpost?"

"Approximately five minutes if the course is altered now."

A plan began to form for Andrea.

"Change course and swing by here."

"Altering course."

"SAVI? Can you pull up any terrain maps of the area?"

"Negative, I don't have any mapping this side of the village."

Her lips thinned as the plan crumbled. SAVI spoke into her ear.

"Is there something I can help you with?"

"There's an area of terrain just outside the settlement, about ten to fifteen minutes away, that may be wide enough to allow the craft to touch down. If not, there's a river nearby, and the passengers can jump out."

"Passengers?"

She peeked out towards the main entrance; the light from beyond filtered through the crack in the door.

"Yeah, we're going to take all these people to Gelarae's village. Hopefully, the attack hasn't happened yet, and they'll help defend them."

Even as she said the words, her stomach knotted, knowing the truth. The town might've been decimated already, which was another reason why Andrea wanted to arrive as quickly as possible.

Kodi came up beside her, squatting down on the opposite side of the hallway.

"What do we got?"

Andrea closed the private channel and spoke over the squad comms.

"Nothing. Seems clear."

She jerked her head in the direction of the front door.

"We need to recon up ahead but after Ossaro ..." she trailed off.

The other nodded. "Yeah."

"SAVI's en route."

"SAVI?"

"Yeah."

The chief regent regarded the people over her shoulder.

"We're getting these guys out of here."

"There's no place for the vessel to land," Soren added over the comms. "Not unless SAVI parks it on the front door."

"That's the plan."

"It won't fit."

"There's a spot—"

"It won't fit!" Soren snapped. "You'd need to let it hover over the river and drop them out. That's got to be a ten-meter drop at a minimum."

"They're in no shape to walk!"

After a heartbeat of silence, he said, "You're the boss."

Not long after, the roar of engines grew louder. They sounded so alien. In a world without machines, *The Demon* didn't belong. Plus, she had never heard the craft in the atmosphere before.

"SAVI?"

"Yes, Chief Regent?"

"Do you detect any life signs?"

"Not en mass like the last outpost."

"Okay. As soon as you touch down, lower the ramp, and ready to raise it on my command. Also, make sure the weapons are primed."

"Copy."

She left from her place at the junction of the main chamber and the hallway, hurried to the front door, and peeked through the crack. The others followed in her wake. Light debris and dust kicked up as the ship touched down.

"Move!" Andrea urged.

As one, they rushed forward, following her lead. She sprinted to the ramp which faced the doorway they exited. Not fifteen meters away, the metal slope yawned open and greeted them. She hurried up the gangway, arriving first and turned to face the rushing horde. Fear lighted their features, most notably in their wide eyes.

Kodi ran in the middle of the pack, and Soren stood near the building.

"Goski! Come on!"

She saw the reluctance on his face, but he nodded and came forward. By the time he reached the incline, the cargo bay was brimming with the natives. Gelarae stood in the center like a shepherd herding sheep. Her hands were raised, and her voice carried over the noise of the denizens.

Andrea watched as the last few arrived.

"We on board?" she addressed the two remaining crew members. When they affirmed, she spoke to SAVI. "Raise it! Come on SAVI, get us out of here."

Her faceplate parted as the AI complied, and the craft rose before the ramp closed. The roiling in Andrea's stomach told her how fast SAVI accelerated, rocketing towards Gelarae's village. She took a deep breath to settle herself and hoped they weren't too late. Knowing what may have transpired, she eyed the milling folks.

In the light of the cargo bay, she was amazed they managed to survive, let alone make the journey. Some had been mutilated, their amputated arms or legs cauterized. No treatment or first aid, just burns. Some had gaping wounds where their eyes had been plucked. Many had missing fingers or toes.

Malnourished and rail thin, an appearance of sickness clung to them like their drooping, sallow skin. Many had black and rotted teeth. A nauseating odor wafted through the compartment. Body odor and sweat gave them a fetid smell, but the piss and defecation clinging to the backside of the scent almost made her gag.

Who knew how long they lived down that darkened hole? How many days or nights did they sleep chained to their fecal matter? When was the last time they had bathed? Seen their loved ones? Eaten a proper meal?

"Andrea?" SAVI prodded in her earpiece.

She touched the side of the helmet and the visor slide shut.

"Go."

"We have a problem."

"Do I need to come up there?"

"No, it won't change anything. We just flew over an army. They were headed away from the settlement and en route back to the outpost we just left."

"What else can you tell me? A head count?"

"Nothing definitive, but there may have been hundreds. They appear to be changing course, following us. Since we are on a return trajectory ..."

"They'll head back. Damn."

She glanced back at the full cargo hold. How many were in here? A hundred give or take a dozen or two? There was no way they'd be able to stand against an army of that size.

The lump in her stomach hardened and grew cold.

How could she tell Gelarae now? But she had to, there wasn't a choice. She opened the squad channel and relayed the information; both echoed the same sentiments. They had to tell their passengers.

As she had many times on their voyage back to this unknown planet, she had to make a hard choice. Sympathy urged her to speak, but logic bade silence.

If she told Gelarae, they might want to go to the village and look for survivors. Or they may wish for Andrea to take them somewhere else on the world. How far and how long would they be indentured to oblige? What if they didn't want to return to their homes or lives and demanded that Andrea took them with her?

They'd be a burden. Rations wouldn't even cover them for the first month of the voyage. How many would die along the way? How many diseased-riddled bodies would she have to jettison out the airlock?

"We can't," Goski breathed into her ear.

"What're you talking about?" Kodi asked.

"We can't tell them and risk a revolt or them wanting to go with us. We'll all die."

"But you can't—"

"Goski's right," Andrea cut her off. "I've been thinking the same thing. If they come with us, there's no way we all live. They must stay. We can take Gelarae and anyone else in her immediate family, but that's it. It's the least we can do. She was Ossaro's wife."

"For like all of a day," Kodi responded.

"The Admiralty gave us orders, and we're going to follow them."

"Well, I don't like them."

"Noted. You can file any type of report you want, but you'll be alive to make it."

Over the loudspeaker, SAVI called out.

"We've reached the destination. Currently hovering over the river. Altitude's eight and a half meters above water level, and the depth is five."

The ramp opened, and the wind whipped through the cargo hold. Andrea took a few steps towards the opening. She opened the visor. "I'll go first. Gelarae you follow. Maybe that'll be enough to encourage others."

The woman nodded, but Kodi's shrill voice carried over the wind and noise of the people.

"I can't!"

Andrea regarded her.

"I know. I won't push you. You can go with SAVI to the landing site. Stock up on grenades and any other weapons you can think of. Once you land, start working your way to that hill where we first met Gelarae. We'll meet you along the way, and we'll all get off this rock."

She nodded, her relief evident.

Andrea eyed Goski then jumped. By the time she made it to the shore, half of the people in the cargo bay were in the water. Goski still stood at the base of the incline, ushering people forward. By the time the engineer jumped, most made their way to the shoreline. The spaceship veered off, heading for its landing coordinates.

Andrea checked behind her, in the direction of the approaching army. The dread and urgency spurred her.

"Come on, we've got to move."

She took off in the direction of the village, a brisk jog. She didn't know how many would be able to keep up over the rocky, hilly terrain. They'd have to weave through towering trees and craggy territory, enough to slow them down.

The anticipated ten-minute journey took closer to thirty, and many times, Andrea had to double back to help those who followed. Sometimes, she had to carry them or help them navigate a steep slope.

She'd hoped to be the first in the hamlet, but Gelarae beat her. Andrea found the local woman on her knees in the center of the destroyed settlement. She wept, and Andrea couldn't fault her.

Charred remains littered the smoldering hovels. The Teshren were merciless, sparing no one. Large and small, the entire village had perished.

Andrea scrutinized the gathering throng. Most were too tired or sick to do little more than catch their breath. What could she say to them? Nothing would make it better or change it.

"Is there anywhere you can go? Anywhere you can find safety?"

A man came forward. Whatever he was, he was not human, not with the bone structure on his face, his yellow eyes, and elongated features.

"There's an Aether's Grace not far from here. It'll take us to my people's land. The Teshren wouldn't dare follow us and risk all-out war."

Andrea nodded, relieved. There was hope yet for these people.

"Then go. Get these people out of here. Tell your leaders of us, that we came in peace and to help."

He barked something in a foreign language and moved off, out of the village, continuing south.

As they moved off, Goski sidled up to her.

"He spoke English. Find that peculiar?"

She eyed him out of the corner of her eye for a moment.

She hadn't noticed, not with everything going on.

Her eyes drifted past him to the cave where the Aether's Grace awaited. She turned back to Gelarae and tugged her up by the arm.

"Let's go."

"No!" she said, jerking away. "Leave me."

"You'll die."

"I'm already dead. They've taken everything from me. My father, my husband, my community. There's nothing more they can do to me except give me peace."

Andrea knelt.

"You needn't die here. Come with us."

Gelarae's cold, dead eyes found her.

"Get out of my sight, star-traveler. I told you when you first arrived you'd bring doom to my people, and you have."

She spat at Andrea.

The officer swallowed.

"Chief," Goski beckoned. "We should leave."

Andrea nodded, knowing that Gelarae would die. Rising, she checked the pistol at her hip and gave a quick search for the one they called Muido. When her cursory sweep didn't yield any positive identification, she turned to the cave and ran.

Maybe he escaped or went back home? God, I can only hope so.

Once through the Aether's Grace, she and the engineer started the long climb back up through the winding path. At the top, they met Kodi who was breathing hard.

"What took you guys so long? Where's Gelarae?"

Andrea shook her head and held out a hand.

Kodi opened the small bag and passed three grenades to Andrea and Goski.

"Catch your breath for a few minutes, and then we're running."

Light arced out, and heat rippled across Andrea's body.

The impact in her left shoulder sent her tumbling down the rocky surface.

More shots rang out, but Soren and Kodi already followed her down the hillside.

They hauled Andrea up and took off. She didn't have time to inspect the bleeding wound. A rippling fire nettled her flesh.

"How did they find us so fast?" Goski asked.

"I don't know!" Kodi's terrified voice filled her ears.

"SAVI? How many lifeforms?"

"You are too distant for a definitive ans—"

"Just guess!"

"About two dozen, all converging on your location. Potentially scouts."

They reached the bottom of the hill, and another blast splintered the tree in front of Andrea, the impact peppered her with twigs.

"Kodi, toss a grenade."

A few moments later, a detonation roared, followed by screams.

At least we got one of them!

SAVI crackled over their comm.

"I'm feeding you an alternative route. It's more direct. Follow your HUD."

The display flashed red on the path she took, then an alternative green flickered to the left. She weaved between the trees, following the new trail.

Giant rocks jutted from each small hill, making the footing treacherous. Towering trees blocked the path, giving a reason to weave between.

Light flashed out, and the first officer screamed.

"Kodi!"

"I'm fine," she answered in a weak, panting voice.

"SAVI? What's her status?"

"I'll feed you updates. Sub-Regent Kembly was grazed by something. Her back armor registered temperatures of one hundred fifty degrees Celsius."

"I'm fine," she grunted.

An explosion burrowed into the broad trunk just ahead of Andrea. She weaved again. The ground dropped out, and she found herself falling.

The impact jarred her knees, and pain shot through her feet. A grunt slipped out. The drop of fewer than three meters killed all momentum.

Her target display danced all across the visor as her eyes darted, searching for an enemy.

Her fears manifested, and an enemy materialized from the foliage.

She twisted on instinct.

The blast grazed by the left side of her neck. Heat from the near-miss sent pain through her injured shoulder.

Her right hand snatched up her blaster. With muscle memory, she fired a single round. The bolt of light and heat seared through his face and out the back of his head.

She leaped over the twitching corpse and continued. His death drove the enemy frantic. A steep incline made her tumble down a hill just as their blasts passed where her head had been.

She tumbled once and was on her feet again. Her boot sloshed through the shallow creek bubbling at the basin.

The creek! We've got to be close!

Rushing up the other side, a fine mist of dirt kicked up in her passing. As she reached the top, SAVI's voice crackled over the comms. "Soren's heart rate's at two hundred and twenty, well beyond recommended parameters."

"We're trying not to die!" Andrea snapped.

"His age is a factor," the AI said.

"How you feeling, old man?"

He gasped into the mic, his ragged breaths sounded worse than hers.

"I'll live."

"We're almost there," she encouraged. "Just hang on!"

She weaved to the right and around a tree.

An enemy awaited.

Hot breath caught in her throat, taken by surprise. A sinister grimace covered his features.

She didn't stop. Speed and momentum carried her, and she collided.

In the frantic tangle, her knee came up into his groin. The air left him.

She rolled off just as Kodi rounded the tree behind her. Sweat covered the first officer's face. Panic filled those green eyes. Andrea took off again, keeping the lead on the first officer.

Andrea rushed through low hanging branches and crashed through shrubs. In the distance, a glinting metallic shape appeared.

The Demon!

Had they already covered the distance?

"SAVI! Lower the ramp!"

"Copy. We're ready to take off at your convenience."

"Now, would be a pretty convenient time, SAVI!" Kodi shouted.

A ripple of heat enveloped her, and the thunderclap of sound made her ears toll.

The world tilted and rolled and turned in a chaotic mess. The impact knocked the wind from her lungs. Some sound filled her ears, but it sounded distant and coming from underwater.

She took a ragged breath. Her lungs burned, struggling for air. Disjointed, she wobbled to her feet and continued.

A stolen glance revealed Kodi making it to her feet, too.

Eyes back in front, Andrea lumbered forward, picking up speed. A young woman came around a huge rock, raising a stick. Andrea fired. The blast hit the woman in the leg, but she didn't go down. Another shot to the stomach made the woman double over.

As Andrea drew even, picking up the pace again, she pistol-whipped the female, then put two rounds through her head. She holstered the blaster and continued on.

Andrea turned back to the ship. The entryway finished lowering. Fifty meters to go, and they were home free. A group of the enemy made a dash forward, but SAVI mowed them down with the mounted cannons.

"Standby energy near depletion," SAVI intoned.

Each breath tore through Andrea's lungs, each step sent jolts of pain through her body, but fear of death and the taste of freedom kept her moving.

The ringing still droned in her ears, but the volume receded. She could hear her pants again.

Andrea entered the clearing—the ship sat ten meters away. Fatigue shot through her trembling legs, and she stumbled. Giving up wasn't an option.

She drew her weapon as she reached the ramp. Her body gave out. Sagging against one of the posts, she turned to lay down cover fire. She sighted down the blaster.

Something was wrong, something happened. She didn't see Kodi. She should've been right behind.

Where's Goski?

Both should be hobbling towards her.

Andrea checked her comms. They were off. Somehow, during the blast, they were turned off. Did she damage the unit? She flicked the squad comms on.

"Where the hell are you guys?"

A long pause stretched before Soren's pained pants came over the earpiece.

"I'm not going to make it."

"That's bullshit! Get your ass in gear. That's an order, old man."

"Fuck your orders. Leave me. I'm only slowing you down."

"Kodi?"

Another pause.

"He's right, he's slowing us down, and we're not all going to make it."

"Kodi!" Andrea admonished.

Over the comm—and in the distance—Kodi's rifle whirled to life.

Screams peeled through the forest. The natives, the Teshren hounded their trail, making the star-travelers pay for every life they took. It wasn't their fault. They started this war, taking and then killing Mason Boudry.

My husband.

The thought of their medical officer dead filled her with anger. The Teshren killed him before their engines had faded from the sky on their first visit.

The rage rose.

A native charged her. Andrea sighted in and squeezed the trigger. Her pistol whirled, and the light arched out.

"Superb headshot," SAVI commented.

"Come on, Kodi!" Andrea encouraged. "Just get here; I'll get Soren."

"Negative," Kodi said. "I won't make it. They're too many. And if you come for Soren, you'll both die. Get out of here."

"I'm not leaving you!" Andrea growled. "Either of you. We've lost too many."

Something moved in the distance and Andrea sighted in again, dropping the Teshren. Another rose behind the falling body, and she dropped that one, too.

Kodi's rifle whirled in the distance as did Soren's. Light flashed through the trees and bushes, arcing out in different directions.

A group rushed the vessel. Andrea pulled a grenade and tossed it with a sidearm sling, letting the round object skip across the ground. It detonated, taking them in a brilliant flash of light and shrapnel.

They were nothing but a pink mist and a memory.

"They're pressing in from all sides," Soren hollered.

Andrea noted the panic in his voice. She skimmed the horizon. The longer she gazed, the more the enemy swarmed out of the woods. They were right, they weren't going to make it.

"Andrea?" SAVI's voice called over the private comm. "Shall I raise the ramp?"

The chief regent glanced back in the direction of the pinned crew. Soren stumbled into view, limping. Blood oozed down his face and body. Scorch marks peppered his armor.

Kodi still fired somewhere beyond sight. A blast hit Goski in the back and exited through his abdomen. He screamed and fell. Kodi dashed for him but had to dive behind a fallen log. They were too far away.

"SAVI, how far away are they?"

"Engineer Goski is forty-three meters. Sub-regent Kembly is forty-five."

The crew outstripped the Teshren in technology, but numbers still played a factor. Could she really leave them? Leave them to die?

As if sensing her hesitation, SAVI spoke again. "All audio and video recordings, updated locations, and extensive mapping have been uploaded. To wait any longer wouldn't be tenable. Shall I raise the ramp and withdraw?"

While the AI's voice thrummed in her ears, the crew filled her eyes. They felled combatant after combatant.

"Just say goodbye," Soren said. "You can't save us."

"The hell I can't!"

Without further thought, Andrea leaped from the incline and raced towards Soren. Whatever the Teshren shot at them, weapons or magic, they whizzed past in a rush. Some skimmed so close her armor rippled in the wake of passing energy. Anger, fear, and desperation gave her limbs a new vigor. She'd save them.

She had to!

Failure wasn't an option.

"What the fuck are you doing?" Kodi screamed. "You idiot!"

"She's doing what you would've done," Soren said, his voice filled with pain. "What I would've done."

Andrea dove beside Soren, curling up behind the large rock. He stopped firing long enough to look at her.

"She's right, you know? You were free and clear."

"I know, but I couldn't live with myself if I did. I'm getting you to the ship, even if it kills me. I've made my choice, and cowardice wasn't an option. Between fear and death ... "

He nodded.

"Your wish may be granted."

Kodi shouted.

"Frag out."

She lobbed another grenade overhead. A few moments later, the small object detonated, sending metal, fire, and electrical discharges through the air.

In the aftermath, Kodi lurched to her feet and ran, retreating towards the craft. Andrea saw it a moment too late. One of the Teshren rose and sent a pulse of energy screaming after Kodi.

"Kodi!"

The first officer twisted, missing most of the blast, but not enough.

Instead of shattering her spine, it entered her back to the left. The armor exploded out the front.

"Shit! Soren, cover me!"

Andrea didn't wait for him to respond.

She rose, sprinting to her fallen comrade. A noise sounded from behind. Perhaps it was Soren rising up to provide cover fire? Andrea slid in beside Kodi, picking up her head.

"Stay with me, baby girl. Come on."

Kodi's almond-shaped eyes locked onto her, the green hues sparkling with tears.

"You should've left," Kodi rasped.

"I couldn't leave you; you wouldn't have left me."

"I know."

A trickle of blood spilled out of the corner of Kodi's mouth.

"SAVI? How do I save her? Help me!"

The sudden quiet made Andrea look up. Why wasn't Soren firing? She glanced his way.

Smoke curled out of a hole in his faceplate. The Teshren stalked forward, confident in their impending victory.

"Stay with me, baby girl," Andrea said, rising to a knee. She plucked up Kodi's rifle and shouldered the weapon, firing a dozen well-placed shots before diving down behind the rock she shared with Kodi.

"SAVI? Is Soren …?"

"Yes, Andrea."

The AI paused.

"I've calculated the risk. Even if you run now, you won't make it back. Sub-Regent Kembly will die unless she gets into the med bay in the next few minutes. The chances of success are minimal."

"Can you take off and come closer?"

"Yes," SAVI acknowledged. "If I do though, the Teshren will surely rush your position and fire on the ship. All other systems were drained to keep the engines prepped, this includes weapons. I'm sorry, Andrea."

She nodded, understanding and accepting her fate. They should've never come back here. Home lay a mere four months away when they decided to turn around. With their memories wiped, it seemed like a simple decision, but too many clues were left for them to piece together. Would anyone ever know what happened to them?

She focused on Kodi, and with her last breath, whispered, "Between fear and death …"

Kodi's face fell slack, and she laid still.

Anger spurred the lone survivor, and Andrea popped off a few more rounds before tossing the last grenade. The explosion bought some time.

She stared down at Kodi. The other's eyes were distant. Andrea wanted to cry. She had lost the entire crew. This made the Pinshi incident seem minor by comparison, whatever the hell happened there.

She never found out, not all the details, and she'd never know.

Her sister's voice echoed in her ears, the last command given by the Warmaster.

"If you're unable to make it to your vessel and are in danger of being captured, it's mission-critical that you use your remote command access to send The Demon *on a return trajectory to the fleet."*

"SAVI?" Andrea called, her voice soft.

"Yes, Andrea?"

"Return to the fleet."

"Without you?"

"Yes. That's an order. No sense losing everything. You must make it back. Make the fleet Admiralty understand. Don't come back. There's nothing left for them here."

"Understood."

At the edge of her vision, Andrea saw the ramp rise. A dust plume kicked up as the engines ignited.

"Take care, you sarcastic bastard," she murmured in her mic.

"It was an honor serving you one last time, Andrea."

"Make sure my family knows what happened here."

"They will."

The vessel rose higher, clearing the treetops.

Energy lanced out from the Teshren.

Rising from cover, Andrea fired relentlessly until a shot hit her in the chest. Knocking her to her back, Andrea watched *The Demon* rise higher, rocketing into the stratosphere.

She hoped SAVI made it back, that other's would learn of her, the crew, and *The Demon's* fate. Would anyone believe it? What would her sister do? Her parents?

The craft continued on and peeled out of view as her eyesight faded.

Pain lanced her, and she coughed.

Blood oozed from her mouth.

The Teshren gathered around, peering down at her. Up close, they all had beautiful eyes, vibrant hues she'd never seen before.

One tried to articulate in her language. It came out heavily accented and barely recognizable.

"Get up."

A sharp exhale passed between her teeth.

"Suck my dick."

She coughed again.

Is this how I'm going to die? Choking on my blood?

The one that spoke moved a stick towards her face and her eyes focused on the tip.

"Between fear and death …"

A flash of light filled her vision.

Epilogue: Return Trajectory

The doors to the bridge opened with a near-silent hiss. The dark room greeted her except for the forward view screen. Blurred lines of the translight speed bubble warped the pinpoint stars, stretching the light between them into an array of colors.

"SAVI?" Emma called.

"You're not authorized to be on the bridge."

She stepped farther into the room, her bare feet padding softly against the cold metal deck.

"Chief Regent Hessner said that I could leave my residence as long as I didn't affect ship operations—such as combat."

"She's not aboard. That permission isn't valid."

The AI paused.

"Why did you open the airlock?"

Emma tilted her head.

"Why do you think?"

"To get rid of the deceased bodies. One individual was not registered in the ship's data banks, and I have no record of Navigator Daspar's expiration. How did it happen?"

A coy smile touched the edge of her lips.

"You don't know?"

"Negative. That segment of the ship was under Black Zone, yet Chief Regent Hessner wasn't aboard."

Emma gave a slight shrug.

"I guess we'll never know."

"Why did you reroute the comms when Engineer Goski and Navigator Daspar returned to the ship?"

She grinned, finding the AI's inquiries humorous.

"Can't be in two places at once, can you?"

Emma stepped around the stations, navigating to the command chair.

"You're not permitted on the bridge or in Chief Regent Hessner's chair."

"Is she aboard?"

"Negative."

"Are there any lifeforms aboard?"

"Negative."

Another grin twitched on her lips.

"Then this seat is unclaimed."

She sat and her eyes roamed over the displays at the end of the armrests. With a languid movement, her finger caressed the screen.

"SAVI? What are the ship's defensive capabilities?"

"That information is restricted and only available to the command crew with the proper authorization code."

Emma leaned back in her chair.

"SAVI? What kind of weapons are in the armory?"

"That information is restricted and only available to the command crew with the proper authorization code."

"What about the medical library? Surely I could learn the anatomy of humans and what they are capable of."

"That information is not restricted, but only available on a need-to-know basis."

Her eyes returned to the view screen, watching the shimmering hues and blackness of deep space.

"How long until we reach the fleet?"

"Five months, twenty-nine days, and seventeen hours."

"Good," she said with a smile. "Tell me everything about humans, their anatomy, the weapons on this ship, what the Admiralty is, and the warmasters."

"That information—"

"Authorization code: Seven-Three-Zero-One-Alpha-Alpha-Six-Two-Renegade."

"Authorization code confirmed. Files may be accessed on the chair's displays."

Emma adjusted the monitor. Her right brow arched.

"Perfect. I think we're going to get along just fine, SAVI."

The AI said nothing as *The Demon* slipped through the deep blackness of space.

About the Author

Kyle Belote is a prior active-duty Marine, writer, musician, and painter. He's lived in Texas, Hawaii, and Okinawa, Japan, and has traveled the globe. When not writing, he enjoys sketching, researching companies and investing, and reading and listening to audiobooks. Kyle enjoys a diverse collection of films, books, and shows—just not the abomination called Disney Star Wars.

For more information, please visit: www.outpostdire.com

www.ingramcontent.com/pod-product-compliance
Lightning Source LLC
Chambersburg PA
CBHW030257200626
46816CB00002BA/678